# PERFECT TIMING

# PERFECT TIMING

## A NOVEL

## MICHELE ASHMAN BELL

Covenant Communications, Inc.

Covenant®

*This book is dedicated to Kendyl,*
*a wonderful daughter and friend.*

*And to Cameron James Mero, for being like a son to me, and for*
*being such an important part of our family.*

*Also to my husband, Gary, and my other great kids,*
*Weston, Andrea, and Rachel.*

# ACKNOWLEDGMENTS

I would like to thank my husband's family, who have always been great examples to me and have given constant love and support. They were the inspiration for this story, especially Eloise and Mike.

Also, thanks to my editor/analyst/friend, Kirk Shaw, for his patience, input, and brilliant suggestions. Thanks for making the journey so enjoyable.

# PROLOGUE

"Where's Mom?" Kenidee asked her father, who was busy pouring Sprite into a punch bowl filled with raspberry sherbet. More people had turned out for her open house than they had planned, but fortunately they had plenty of refreshments for everyone.

Her father didn't answer but kept pouring.

"Dad!" she exclaimed, reaching for the bottle before the contents in the bowl spilled over the sides.

"Oh, hi, honey. Thanks. I didn't notice it was almost full."

"Where's Mom?"

"I haven't seen her for a few minutes," he responded. "When you find her, will you let her know we're about out of the croissant sandwiches. I hope she has a few more trays somewhere."

"Sure," Kenidee replied, wondering where her mother had disappeared to. Her mother would never leave guests unattended like this, especially when half the ward and countless friends and neighbors were there to wish Kenidee well as she prepared to leave on her mission. She'd been called to the Florida Tampa Mission and was leaving in less than a week. The Sunday before, she'd spoken in church, and with that behind her now, she was ready to go.

"You gave a wonderful talk last week," Sister Merkley said, as Kenidee walked out of the kitchen and into the dining room. "You're going to be a marvelous missionary."

"Thank you, Sister Merkley," Kenidee replied. "Have you seen my mother?"

"A while ago. She didn't look well. Probably a headache from all the stress of the open house and getting ready to send her youngest, and her only daughter, on a mission." Sister Merkley placed a hand on Kenidee's shoulder and looked at her with sadness. "You're sure I can't talk you into staying home and marrying my Gilbert. He'd be such a catch for some lucky girl. He just graduated with his master's degree in statistics, you know. Someday he's going to be very successful. Not a bad package, being handsome and successful, wouldn't you say?"

Kenidee wasn't sure they were talking about the same person. The only Gilbert whom Kenidee knew was short, bald, and pushing thirty.

"You must be so proud," Kenidee answered, not sure what to say. Obviously, Sister Merkely hadn't noticed the tiny promise ring her boyfriend Brendan had given her before he left on his mission—a ring he planned to replace with an engagement ring after they both returned home.

Sister Monson, her mother's best friend from the ward, walked by just then with a tray full of chocolate chip cookies.

"Sister Monson, have you seen my mom?"

"I think she needed to get something upstairs," the woman answered, placing the tray on the large, oval dining table filled to capacity with food.

Giving Sister Merkely a parting smile, Kenidee made a quick escape, dodging as many well-wishers as she could before darting up the stairs.

She opened the door to her parents' bedroom and peeked inside. There on the bed was her mother.

"Mom?" She hurried inside. "What's wrong? Are you sick?"

Her mother opened her eyes and gave her daughter a weak smile.

"Hi, honey. I just came upstairs to change into some comfortable shoes and needed to rest a bit. I'm fine now."

Kenidee studied her mother's face, noticing for the first time the dark circles under her eyes and the paleness of her skin. She hoped her mother wasn't getting sick—not when she was leaving in a few days.

Vanessa Ashford was a beautiful and refined woman, not the type to wear sweats and a T-shirt to clean the house or go to the grocery store. She never went out without having her hair done. Vanessa had been raised in Boston, where her father was a doctor and her mother was involved in social events, chairing fund-raisers and organizations in the community.

Her parents hadn't been very happy when their daughter had fallen in love with a salesman from Utah, but Vanessa loved him and they were married. They ended up in the Bay Area where he worked as a pharmaceutical rep for many years and eventually became responsible for the western states division.

Kenidee and her brother had loved growing up in Palo Alto. There weren't a lot of LDS students in their high school, but that hadn't been a problem. Kids seemed to respect the Ashford children for their beliefs and genuinely liked them. Kenidee's brother, Matthew, was quarterback on the football team and senior class president. Kenidee's great love was ballet, and she dedicated much of her time to the ballet studio. Never a one-dimensional person, she also played on the school's volleyball and tennis teams and was voted homecoming queen. Both Matthew and Kenidee were well liked at church and at school. Their parents were well respected in the community and in their ward.

Matthew was four years older than his sister. He'd served a mission to Louisville, Kentucky. Then he came home and married his high school sweetheart. He was now in his second year of law school at BYU. Kenidee had attended a local community college so she could continue to dance at her studio, with a dream to eventually attend the University of Utah to major in ballet and receive a Master of Fine Arts degree in teaching and choreography. During her second year at college she began to feel that serving a mission was something she needed to do. Her parents, especially her mother, had been supportive of a mission from the very beginning.

"Can I get you anything?" Kenidee asked her mother.

"I'm feeling better now. I'd need to get downstairs before we start running out of food."

"That's okay, Mom. Sister Monson and the other Relief Society sisters have everything under control."

"I don't know what I'd do without Cheryl." Her mother sat up slowly and drew in several breaths.

"Are you sure you're okay, Mom? Do you need me to get Dad?"

"No, no, I'm fine. He's got enough to worry about right now."

"What do you mean? Is something wrong?" Kenidee asked with a start, her mind instantly focusing on the word *worry*.

"No, sweetie," her mom answered. "You know what an ostrich he is when it comes to emotional situations."

They both had been known to tease him about how he ignored problems in hopes that they would go away.

"Bless his heart," her mother said in her father's defense. "All he does at work is put out fires. The last thing he wants to deal with when he comes home is more problems."

"I hope I haven't caused too many problems," Kenidee said.

Her mother put her hand on her daughter's cheek and smiled at her. "No, sweetie. You've been the best daughter a parent could ever wish for. Your father is just having a hard time letting his little girl go. I can't say it's easy for me, either."

Feeling her throat constrict, Kenidee put on a brave front for her mother's sake.

"But," her mother said, "I also am very proud that you want to serve a mission."

"Thanks, Mom." Kenidee's attempt at a smile managed to be only a halfhearted grin.

"How are you doing?" Her mother's question was not just a conversation filler.

"Fine," she answered. Then she changed the subject. "Sister Merkley cornered me."

Her mother rolled her eyes. "Did she pester you about Gilbert again?"

Kenidee nodded.

"Good grief. Maybe if Gilbert moved out of his mother's house and looked for his own dates he'd be married by now. Besides, you've got Brendan."

Her parents loved Brendan. And why not? He was handsome and goal-oriented, he had a strong testimony, and he treated Kenidee like a princess.

He'd left on his mission to Taiwan in August, just three months earlier. He was a couple years older than most new elders, but he had been adamant about saving up enough money to pay for his entire mission without any help from his parents or his ward. They missed each other in the MTC by two weeks. It was probably better that way.

"It's going to be such a wonderful experience for both of you to be serving missions at the same time. Something you'll always remember."

"I know. It's amazing how everything has worked out so perfectly. I'll never forget the day he got his mission call. He felt so bad he wouldn't be here when I got mine."

"This way, honey, you won't have to wait too long for him to return, after you get home."

"Yes, it works out better this way. And really, Mom, it doesn't matter because I know it's all working out the way it's supposed to. It's all in the Lord's hands."

"Yes," her mother said softly. "It certainly is. We just need to exercise our faith that it will all work out."

Kenidee detected sadness in her mother's voice, a melancholy that matched the feelings in her own heart.

"It will go fast, though, won't it, Mom."

"Yes, honey. It will. And you'll have a wonderful, life-changing experience that will prepare you for the rest of your life." Her mother smiled at her and grasped one of Kenidee's hands. "I'm so proud of you, sweetheart. And no matter what, I will always be with you in spirit."

Kenidee looked at her mother with confusion. "What do you mean? You'll always—"

Just then her father burst into the room. "There you two are. What's the big idea leaving me with all of those hungry people. We're almost out of sandwiches, and those brownies are flying off the tray faster than we can replace them. I hope you have a stash somewhere or they're going to start eating the furniture."

Vanessa smiled warmly at her husband. "I've got it covered, dear."

"What are you two doing anyway?" he asked, looking suspiciously at his wife and daughter.

"Girl talk, Dad," Kenidee told him.

"Well, could you girls 'talk' later? Besides," he gave his daughter a tap on the nose, "you're the guest of honor. People are looking for you. I think Sister Merkley is looking for you."

Kenidee and her mother looked at each other and laughed.

"What?" her dad questioned. "Does this have something to do with her son?"

"Yeah. She thinks I ought to skip my mission and go straight to the temple with him."

"Did you tell her that you and Brendan are practically engaged?"

"She didn't give me a chance."

"Well, I think you should mention it to her. Brendan's a sharp kid. I won't mind at all if things work out with him," her dad stated. "Don't you agree, Vanessa? Vanessa?"

Kenidee and her father looked at her mom, who's eyes had glossed over with tears.

"Mom, what's wrong?" Kenidee asked with alarm.

Her mom shook her head and sniffed, brushing her emotions aside with her hand. "It's nothing. I guess I'm just a little emotional today."

Kenidee's heart wrenched inside her chest. She felt the same way.

Kenidee's father gave his wife a kiss on the forehead and placed another one on his daughter's forehead. "You two come down when you can. I'll go see if I can find more food."

\* \* \*

Kenidee was exhausted. She appreciated the love and support from the ward, but all the attention was giving her a headache.

Sneaking away from the nucleus of family and friends, she headed for a circle of chairs in the shade by her mother's rose garden where her brother and sister-in-law were chatting with a long-time friend and his wife.

"Hey, Ken, how are you doing?" Matt stood and gave his sister a hug.

"I'm fine. I didn't think this many people would show up today."

"I hate to tell you this, little sis, but they're not just here to see you. Most of them are here because of Mom's cooking."

Matt's wife, Lindsay, smacked him on the arm. "That's not true! They're here to see you, Kenidee," she corrected.

Kenidee loved her sister-in-law. She was glad her brother had the sense to marry someone as wonderful as Lindsay. Lindsay was like the sister she never had, although they looked nothing like sisters.

Lindsay was petite and pretty, with naturally curly blonde hair that hung in ringlets around her shoulders. Kenidee's hair was dark brown and hung straight as a stick below her shoulders. Kenidee's skin was much more olive than her sister-in-law's, and she was a good five inches taller than Lindsay.

"Hey, Ken-dog," Camden said to Kenidee. "You got your flip-flops and beach umbrella packed?"

"It's a mission—not a vacation, Cam," Kenidee said with a smirk. "And how many times have I told you to quit calling me Ken-dog?"

"I don't know, at least a thousand," Cam answered.

Cam and her brother Matt had been best friends since grade school. Camden had been around the house so much while they were growing up that Kenidee's parents had actually put an extra bed in Matt's room for all the nights he slept over. Consequently, he was comfortable with the family, and his favorite pastime was teasing Kenidee.

"At least my nickname is better than being called Bugs," Kenidee retorted, "or Wart," she added, turning to look at Matt.

"Hey!" Matt protested. "I told you not to call me that anymore."

Camden snickered, making Matt even more annoyed.

"Bugs?" Desiree said to her husband, wrinkling her nose. "I didn't know that was your nickname. How'd you get a name like that?"

"It's not what you think," Camden said, obviously regretting that he'd brought up the topic of nicknames.

Matt took it upon himself to explain. "When Camden was little, before he got braces, kids at school called him Bugs Bunny because his two front teeth looked like they were a couple of pieces of white Chiclets gum. Of course, once he got braces and his head grew big enough to fit his teeth, he became the magnificent specimen he is today."

"Shut up, Wart!" Camden warned him playfully.

Matt chuckled and tried to dodge a punch in the arm from Camden.

"Of course, Matt's name doesn't need any explanation. You ever get rid of those warts, dude?"

"I said, shut up!" Matt went after his friend, and they began wrestling on the grass.

For most people, it would seem odd to see two grown men wrestling like kids, but to Kenidee, it was just Matt and Camden, acting like their normal selves.

Kenidee shook her head. "You'd think they were still in sixth grade," she said to Lindsay and Desiree. "Don't be surprised if they follow this with a burping contest."

"I won't," Desiree said as she looked with displeasure at her husband and his friend rolling around on the ground.

Lindsay and Kenidee exchanged glances. Kenidee had just been kidding about Matt and Cam. In all honesty, they were two of the best guys she knew. They were fun-loving, hard-working men and well loved by everyone who knew them.

Kenidee wondered what Desiree's big gripe was. Somehow she'd never really gotten to know Camden's wife. They'd been high school sweethearts—the perfect couple. He was a star athlete on the basketball and baseball teams, and she'd been involved in cheerleading and gymnastics. Three months after he returned from his mission to the New York New York South Mission, he'd surprised everyone by marrying her—outside of the temple. She was a member but hadn't really been active. They'd planned on going through the temple in a year.

A year later, Amanda had been born, and now they were expecting another baby any day. But they still hadn't gone through the temple.

"How are you feeling?" Kenidee asked, deciding to just change the subject.

"Fat!" Desiree exclaimed. "It took two years to get back in shape after Amanda. And then this little surprise happened." She pointed at her stomach. "I have to eat constantly, or I get sick. I don't have enough energy to make the beds or do dishes, let alone work out. Camden's always gone to work, so he never helps out. So, yeah, I'm pretty much turning into a big, fat cow. You just wait," she said to both Kenidee and Lindsay. "Someday you'll be like this and hate it."

Kenidee wished she'd never asked.

"You look great," Lindsay told her.

"Whatever!" Desiree exclaimed. "I hate even going out in public because of how I look. People who knew me from high school don't even recognize me when they see me. I used to be thin and toned like you. Now look at me," she whined.

Kenidee glanced about and saw her father on the deck refilling the punch bowl.

"Guess I'd better go help out. I hope you feel better soon," Kenidee told her.

"Once I have this baby, I'll feel a lot better."

"Um, okay, then, take care," Kenidee said, exchanging glances with Lindsay who's expression was easily translated, *Thanks a lot for leaving me here with her!* Taking a few steps back, Kenidee turned and headed straight for her father, feeling sorry for Camden. She hoped Desiree's mood was just from being pregnant and that she wasn't always this unpleasant.

Kenidee's mom walked out just then with a plate full of cookies.

It was from that vantage point that Kenidee noticed how thin and pale her mother looked. Knowing that her mother was a worrier, Kenidee hoped that her leaving on a mission wasn't causing her mother extra stress and concern, but she suspected it did.

"Oh, there she is," her father announced when he noticed Kenidee coming their way. "Honey, we were wondering where you went."

"I was just seeing what Matt and Lindsay were doing."

"It's good to see Cam and his wife and their darling little Amanda," Kenidee's mom said. "Matt and Cam don't get to spend much time together anymore."

They all looked back to see Matt and Cam still on the ground.

"Maybe that's a good thing," Kenidee said.

Her mom and dad laughed and sandwiched her in a hug.

Kenidee tried to memorize every detail of that moment with her father and mother. She needed enough memories to last eighteen months—and right now that seemed like an eternity.

# CHAPTER 1

Kenidee nervously took a gulp of Sprite, coughing as the bubbly liquid attempted to go down her windpipe. Spurting Sprite from her nose and down the front of her blouse, she reached for her napkin.

"Sister Ashford, are you okay?" Sister DeWitt asked with alarm. Kenidee nodded, still coughing.

"You look like you're going to be sick." Sister DeWitt peered into Kenidee's face for a moment before she began searching in the pocket of the seat in front of her for a motion sickness bag.

"Here," she handed her the bag. "Just in case you lose it. I mean, not that you're going to," she quickly said. "But you never know. One time I ate too much popcorn at the movies and—blech—right there, I threw up."

All of Sister DeWitt's talking about throwing up wasn't helping. Kenidee's stomach was a churning volcano of nerves. It wouldn't be long before the plane landed in Salt Lake City, where she and Sister DeWitt would part. Then, an hour later she would be in San Jose where her "family" was waiting for her.

"Breathe, shut your eyes, and take slow, deep breaths," Sister DeWitt told her.

Kenidee did as her companion told her, grateful that she'd stopped talking for a few minutes. Slowly, the wave of nausea subsided.

"That's better. Your color's returning," her companion said. "When I get nervous my stomach does weird things too. It's normal. When I first came on my mission, everything I ate went straight through me because I was so nervous. It was gross. Can I get you anything? Some more Sprite or something?"

"No, I'm fine," Kenidee replied. She loved this sister. They'd been companions in the MTC and had been close throughout their time in Florida, finally serving their last few months on the mission together. Sometimes, though, Sister DeWitt's tendency to talk incessantly made her crazy. Like right now!

"I can't imagine how you must feel. I'm sure I'd be freaking out if I was going to meet my stepmom and her three kids for the first time. Have I told you how much I admire you for how strong you've been through all of this? I know that's why you've been blessed with so much success. You've been such an example to all the other missionaries. I heard President Larsen say he wished all the missionaries in his mission would be as hardworking and faithful as you."

Kenidee continued breathing slowly, trying to tune out the girl. She thought about the unbelievable changes that had occurred back home while she'd been on her mission. They still seemed almost surreal. She hadn't yet left the MTC when her parents had written, telling her that her mother had been diagnosed with an advanced form of uterine cancer, but they'd assured her everything would be okay. Kenidee had barely made it to her six-month mark on her mission when her mother had suddenly passed away. Kenidee had expressed a desire to come home, but her father told her that her mother's final words were to tell Kenidee not to.

So she'd stayed on her mission.

But after a month, she'd decided she couldn't continue. It was just too difficult. Losing her mother felt like she'd lost part of her own soul.

Kenidee clearly remembered the morning that she'd made the decision to end her mission and go home. Just before picking up the phone to call President Larsen, she'd prayed one last time. Sobbing, she'd fallen to her knees and unloaded her burden. It was too heavy to carry any longer. She couldn't go on another day.

And in that moment when she turned her burden over to the Lord, the healing began.

Thoughts and feelings had flooded through her entire being. A warmth, an overwhelming feeling of love, filled her until she felt she would burst. Undeniably, she knew the Lord loved her and was aware of her own unique problems. She recognized that things were the way they were supposed to be. Although she didn't understand why, she knew without a doubt it was all part of God's plan. Kenidee also knew her mother's spirit was with her and would remain with her throughout her mission.

The final impression she'd received was that there were specific people waiting for her to come to them and share with them the gospel message and that only through her testimony, a pure testimony borne out of a trial of her faith, would they accept the gospel. She just needed to go to work, and she needed to work tirelessly. The Lord would sustain her.

That day, when she arose from her knees, she was a new person. And she'd gone straight to work and hadn't stopped until the day she returned home. It hadn't been easy, but it had been worth it. She'd witnessed a miracle occur in her own life and many miracles almost daily in the lives of the people she taught.

Throwing herself into the work had helped her forget about herself and her trials. It had helped her through moments of sadness and grief, it had helped her through days of frustration when doors slammed in her faces, and it had helped her a few months ago when her father remarried a substantially younger woman who had three children from a previous marriage.

But for some reason, it wasn't helping now.

So she prayed. First, that she wouldn't throw up, and second, that she would at least like the woman. But how could she? And how could her father do this? He hadn't been sealed to the woman because she was a widow who was sealed to her previous husband. But still, how could he so quickly replace his wife?

"Sister Ashford, you need to buckle your seat belt. We're landing," Sister DeWitt said as she bounced in her chair with excitement.

Kenidee longed to feel that same excitement. She wanted to anticipate seeing her loved ones, but she didn't. Part of her wished she could just go home with Sister DeWitt.

"Hey, Sister Ashford, you know what? We can start calling each other by our first names. Do you even remember mine?"

Kenidee thought for a second and then remembered. "Dolores."

"Right. And you're name is Ken—" Sister DeWitt's eyes grew wide as she searched her memory. "Oh my gosh, I forgot your name. I remember it's different, like Kendyl or Kendra, something like that."

"It's Kenidee."

"Kenidee, that's right, like the president."

"But spelled differently," Kenidee said.

"I wish my name were unusual, like yours. I've always hated my name. It sounds like someone's great aunt, you know. My family and all my friends call me Dolly."

The name fit her.

"So," Dolly said, "we'd probably better say good-bye now. Once the plane lands, I'll be out of here like a shot. My sister and her new baby will be there. I can't wait to see her little Sarah."

"Okay, well, Dolly," Kenidee couldn't deny how weird it was to call her companion by her first name, "I don't really have much to say except thanks for everything. You've been an important part of my mission."

"So have you, Kenidee."

It sounded even stranger hearing her first name.

Dolly suddenly broke down in tears. "I'm going to miss you so much." She leaned over and pulled her companion into a hug. "Call me anytime you want to talk. I want to hear all about your stepmom and her kids. Okay?"

"Okay. I'll let you know how it goes."

Dolly wiped her eyes. "We had fun, didn't we? Right from the very beginning in the MTC. Remember that day you dropped your breakfast tray?"

Kenidee laughed. "And then slipped on the oatmeal," Kenidee finished recalling the scenario. She'd always wondered how someone like herself, who'd studied ballet for as many years as she had, could be so clumsy.

Dolly recalled more memories. "How about the time that red T-shirt got mixed up with my underwear in the laundry and turned everything pink."

"And all that studying we did," Kenidee said.

"All that memorizing," Dolly said. "It was so good to finally get to the field."

"But all that walking," Kenidee reminded her, thinking of her shin splints for the first month.

"And the dogs."

"The *big* dogs."

They both laughed.

"The baptisms," Kenidee said.

"The families," Dolly's voice broke.

"Teaching and testifying," Kenidee added, her own voice cracking.

"Feeling the spirit 24/7," Dolly whispered as her eyes teared up.

Kenidee couldn't continue. Tears spilled onto her cheeks. Her mission memories were priceless. Spending the last four months with Sister DeWitt had been the most rewarding time of her entire mission. They'd set the mission record for proselyting hours and baptisms. Elders were sick of hearing about DeWitt and Ashford. Some of them were actually rude to them at zone conferences. Most of the other sister missionaries had no problems with their success, however, and seemed to step up their efforts.

The girls squeezed hands and dried their eyes on napkins.

Dolly cleared her throat. "So," she said, "you didn't tell me what your letter said. How's your missionary?"

A smile spread across Kenidee's face. "He's pretty much perfect." She looked down at her ring.

"Is he still calling you Sister Ashford?"

"Yeah, but I'm over it. I think it helps him stay focused if he doesn't use my first name. It's not a big deal anymore." But the first time he'd done it, Kenidee was beside herself. His letters had gradually become more formal, which she understood, but the first time he wrote "Dear Sister Ashford" she'd lost it. Now she realized that it was a sign of his diligence to the mission and devotion to the Lord. And she was proud of him for it, even though she never wrote "Dear Elder Nielsen" back to him.

"So what did he say?"

"He was just made AP."

"Really? Wow, he must be pretty sharp."

"He is. He studied at BYU a year before his mission. He was on an academic scholarship."

"You two have to invite me to your wedding," Dolly said, looking at the ring on Kenidee's finger, the ring she'd worn her entire mission.

Kenidee giggled. "I promise you're invited."

"You two are perfect for each other. The mere fact that you served missions at the same time pretty much seals the deal, I'd say. When does he get back from Taiwan?"

"In a little over three months. He gets to stay a few weeks longer because of transfers."

"You guys easily could be married within a year. As for me, I'm going to have to go home and start from scratch. I wasn't dating anyone before I left on my mission."

"I guarantee, Dolly, you aren't going to have any trouble finding a husband." The first time Kenidee met Sister DeWitt was after they said good-bye to their families at the MTC and headed for their first meeting to get their supplies. She had big, blue eyes, a pixie-like face, and a tiny upturned nose. Her black hair, which she wore very short, accentuated her eyes even more. She was like a spunky little elf, full of energy and enthusiasm, who could talk circles around anyone.

The plane shifted and began to drop steadily. Through the window, the landscape appeared closer and closer.

"Oh my gosh!" Dolly exclaimed. "I think *I'm* going to throw up now."

"Just breathe," Kenidee told her. "You'll be fine."

Both girls shut their eyes as the plane's wheels finally touched down.

Dolly grabbed her hand and gave it an excruciating squeeze.

"Ow!" Kenidee exclaimed.

"Sorry. I'm so nervous."

Instructions came over the loudspeaker as the plane taxied to the gate. Kenidee felt tears sting her eyes as she watched Dolly gather her belongings.

"Hey," Dolly said when she saw Kenidee wiping at her eyes. "None of that! We're going to talk tonight on the phone, and we'll make plans to get together. Either I'll come and see you, or you can come and see me. In fact, if you can't stand it at home, just come and live with me until your missionary comes home. We have three empty bedrooms at our house."

Kenidee laughed and gave her friend, her sister, a hug. "Thanks, Dolly. I don't know what I'd do without you."

"Are you kidding me? You're a pillar of strength, and don't you forget it. After all you've been through, there's nothing you can't handle."

\* \* \*

Dolly's words rang through Kenidee's thoughts like a disturbing mantra. Was it a sign of what was to come, or merely a statement of admiration? She didn't know, but it bothered her nevertheless. Her mission had worn her out. She was physically and emotionally drained. She didn't have strength to face what was before her. But she had no choice. People, some she knew, some she didn't, expected her to come off the plane and act like she was happy to be home. But truth be told, she would be happy to stay on the plane until it turned around and landed back in Florida.

She thought of Brendan and how much she needed him right now. She wished he had only three more weeks, or even three more days, until he got home. But somehow she'd have to make it through the next three months without him.

As she often did, she thought about her mother. During much of her mission, Kenidee found herself carrying on an inner dialogue with her mother. She shared her fears and concerns, and even jokes and amusing situations that often arose as she traipsed through the streets of the cities and towns where she'd served. Her mother was always there with her, in her thoughts, just like she'd said she would be at Kenidee's open house.

Kenidee wondered again, as she had many times, whether her mother had known, somehow, deep down, that she wasn't going to be there when her daughter returned? Had instinct told her mother that she would be with her daughter in spirit?

Kenidee believed she had known.

"Miss," the flight attendant's voice broke Kenidee's thoughts. "Can I help you?"

Kenidee looked up and noticed she was the only passenger left on the plane.

"Oh! I'm sorry." She jumped to her feet and whacked her head on the overhead bin. "Ow!" She rubbed her hand over the lump forming on her skull and grabbed her book bag that was tattered and torn and looked like it had survived a war.

With the flight attendant following closely behind, probably suspicious of her now, Kenidee made it up the aisle and through the exit door.

Her steps slowed as she neared the doors leading to the waiting area.

Quickly she weighed her choices. Either she had to walk through those doors or she had to go back to the plane where she would most likely, because of her suspicious behavior, be accused of smuggling drugs or a bomb and be quickly turned over to the authorities.

No, this was the moment of truth. She'd survived her mission and she could survive this, even though it meant opening up a painful wound.

Steeling herself for anything, Kenidee walked through the doors and looked up, expecting balloons, signs, and cheers.

Nothing.

"Baggage claim is to your left, miss," a man at the counter told her.

Then she remembered. Nobody was allowed at the gates unless they had a ticket. Her family would be waiting by baggage claim.

The walk gave her a moment to gather her composure. She was home. The surroundings seemed familiar, yet strange at the same time. Her mouth watered familiarly as she walked by a Cinnabon counter and a frozen yogurt shop. Making a mental note of places where she wanted to go out to eat, Kenidee kept walking.

Following signs to the baggage claim, she allowed her gaze to wander to a row of televisions suspended above seats for passengers waiting for flights. Although she'd seen televisions on her mission, the thought of sitting down and watching one seemed out of character to her. She was completely out of touch with what was going on in the world, and she didn't miss it one bit.

"Well, Mom, my mission is over," she said softly, her voice getting lost in the noise of the congested concourse. "Now what do I do? How do I react to this woman?"

Baggage claim was just ahead. She walked through the security gate and stopped just beyond. This was it. Taking a deep breath and plastering a smile on her face, Kenidee forced her legs to move, but her stride felt wooden and unnatural. Scanning the faces in front of her, she looked for someone familiar in the crowd.

*Did they remember the time my plane was supposed to land? Maybe they were caught in traffic.*

Then she saw the balloons and a sign, "Welcome home." And there he was, her father, looking older and a bit thicker around the middle, but full of smiles.

She searched for the rest of the group, but the only others ones with him were Matt and Lindsay, who were cheering and waving and calling her name. Coming toward her, her dad stretched out his arms. They met in a long, emotional embrace.

She had a million questions, but she knew it wasn't the right time. Later she would ask about her mother's last days and details of her illness and passing. She would also ask her dad to explain how he'd managed to move on so quickly.

"Oh, honey, it's so good to see you," her father said as he rocked back and forth, still holding her in his arms. "How are you?"

"I'm okay," she told him.

"You look terrific, honey."

"Thanks."

"We have a lot of catching up to do, don't we?" He looked into his daughter's eyes as if searching for her feelings and what he should expect from them.

She just nodded.

"Hey, sis!" Matt grabbed her and swung her around in a giant hug. "It's so good to have you home. I've missed you, Ken-dog."

Kenidee groaned at the name. "You haven't changed a bit!"

He gave her another big hug, then it was Lindsay's turn.

"Look at you," Kenidee said, noticing her sister-in-law's swollen tummy. "How are you feeling?"

"Wonderful." Lindsay's face glowed. "You'll have to feel the baby move. It's incredible. And getting moved into our new place hasn't been as bad as I expected. Since Matt had a couple weeks free between graduation and his new job, he's taken care of all the heavy stuff. I'm just trying to get organized and decorate. Maybe you can help—it's so good to see you Kenidee!"

The two girls hugged and Kenidee felt some calmness returning to her.

"Are you hungry?" her father asked. "We thought we'd go grab a bite to eat."

Instead of waiting and wondering about his new wife and her family, she just came out with it. "So, where are the rest of them?"

"Oh, you mean Robin and the kids?" her dad asked.

*Who else could I possibly mean?*

"We thought you might not want to be overwhelmed with everything at once so she took the kids to Sacramento to stay with her sister for a few days. You know, while you got settled."

Kenidee nodded, catching looks of understanding from Matt and Lindsay. They'd exchanged letters and shared frustrations. Matt had warned her that Robin was completely different from their mother. He'd said she was a nice person, but she was just . . . *different.*

"I see. That was really thoughtful of you guys. Um, so, yeah, I could eat. We didn't get much on the plane."

"Good, let's get your bags and then find some food. After that, we'll take you home and get you settled."

"Home to *your* new house?" Kenidee asked him.

"Well, that's where all your bedroom stuff is."

"Right," Kenidee said, trying to imagine never seeing the inside of her old house again. Then she noticed one of her bags on the carousel. "There's one of my suitcases."

Her dad quickly walked over and retrieved the bag, then watched for the other one.

"He's been a nervous wreck all week," her brother told her. "He's pretty worried about you and Robin meeting each other. And her kids."

Kenidee shut her eyes for a moment to check her emotions before answering. "I'm not looking forward to it."

"She's not anything like your mom, but she's a nice lady," Lindsay said. "At least I think she is anyway."

"Hey, sis," Matt slipped an arm around her shoulder, "you okay?"

"I wanted to come home, Matt. When Mom died, I wanted to come home."

"She wanted you to stay and finish. There wasn't anything you could have done."

"I could have been with her."

They both stopped talking as their father approached, wheeling her suitcases behind. "Here we go. Is everyone ready?"

Kenidee wanted to answer "No," but she gave him a nod and figured it was best just to get it over with. Dolly's offer to have Kenidee move to Salt Lake City and live with her suddenly looked very inviting. Maybe she would stay home for a couple of weeks with her family. Then she would pack her bags again and go to Salt Lake. She'd wanted to wait until Brendan got home so they could decide their future together. She figured they were headed for Utah anyway, and this would just get her there sooner. She didn't think Brendan was planning to start school fall semester, even though he made it home in time to start. Before his mission, he'd said something about working for a few months and going back in January. Of course, that was almost two years ago. His plans might have changed. He certainly didn't write about it in his letters. He was very focused and didn't talk about home or what he was going to do after his mission. It sure would help if he did, so she'd know what to expect.

She'd been toying with the idea of pursuing her dream of attending the University of Utah and earning her dance degree anyway, so this would help her get things in place to finish her education. Besides that, if Brendan did go to BYU after he returned home from his mission, this was the perfect situation.

Having a plan helped quell the nerves in her stomach. She just had to endure a few weeks in this new arrangement. Then she could leave and let her father move on with his new life, while she began hers.

# CHAPTER 2

Kenidee looked up at the house and realized she didn't hate it. Still, there was nothing remarkable about it either. The white brick rambler had black shutters, a front porch with colorful pots of flowers, and a large front lawn. A sign hung over the garage door that said "Welcome Home Kenidee." Yellow balloons were tied to the mailbox and the lamp post.

But this was a stranger's house, not hers.

She groaned inwardly. How did she do this? It was hard enough to leave a mission she loved. It was hard enough to return home and have her mother gone. But meeting her father's new wife and her three kids? That was too hard.

"Ready, sweetie? Robin said she would wait until we called to have her come home. She's so excited to meet you." Her dad reached over and patted her on the knee.

A lame smile was all Kenidee could muster.

Her dad got out of the car and opened the trunk.

"I like our other house better," she told Matt and Lindsay while her dad was outside.

"Dad thought it would be hard to live in Mom's house with a new wife," Matt told her.

"Yeah," Kenidee said thoughtfully. "It would be."

They both looked out of the car windows at their dad, hanging onto the handles of the suitcases, nodding toward the house. "Come on," he said loudly enough they could hear through the glass.

They climbed out of the car and followed him up the walk.

Lindsay quietly said, "I'll warn you right now, Robin's taste in decorating is a lot different from your mom's."

They stepped inside, and Kenidee looked around. The tiled entry was nothing special; neither was the front room. Tan carpet, the brown leather couches from her old house, the same lamps and coffee table. Her dad's office off the entry looked very similar to his office in their old house. So far, everything was pretty generic.

"I'll put these in your room while Matt and Lindsay start the tour," her dad said.

Matt led the way. "Let's start with in the kitchen."

As soon as they entered the room, Kenidee stopped short and put her hand in front of her eyes. Squinting at the blinding lemon yellow walls, she noticed frilly white curtains crowning the windows and four hideous canisters in brightly colored fruit shapes decorating the counter. Bold red area rugs dotted the floor and matched the red towels hanging from the oven handle. The cushions on the chairs around the kitchen table were bright stripes in the same colors as the canisters. It was a nightmare of color.

Kenidee's vocabulary was unprepared for the visual assault. The look on Matt and Lindsay's faces told her they completely understood what she was thinking.

The family room off the kitchen continued in the same theme with the glaring yellow walls, which were eclipsed by a deep orange sectional that curved in front of a large entertainment center. Pots that looked South American filled the shelves with yet more color, and a pair of lime green chairs flanked a gas-log fireplace. Over the fireplace hung a picture that looked like paint had been flung at the canvas, or maybe shot at the canvas with super-soaker water guns.

Also scattered on the walls were clusters of branches adorned with flowers and ribbons. Lace-trimmed needlepoint pictures of rocking chairs and potted plants in beaded macramé wall hangings decorated the rest of the wall space.

Kenidee was speechless.

"The master bedroom, the two rooms for the kids, and your room are down this hallway, and there are more rooms downstairs. Where do you want to go first?"

"Downstairs, I guess," Kenidee said. She had seen enough already, but she knew, for her father's sake, she needed to finish the tour.

Despite her initial shock in the kitchen, Kenidee was totally unprepared for the sight that greeted her. Kenidee's mouth dropped open when they turned on the basement light. Pepto Bismol pink walls were the background for the playroom. Rows of shelves were filled to the brim with everything from books and puzzles to Legos, Barbies, action figures, and blocks. There was a foosball table, a Ping-Pong table, and stacks of storage bins filled with even more toys.

One corner was Barbie central. A large townhouse was the main structure, with a beauty shop, dance studio, and shopping mall to complete it.

In the other corner was an adjustable basketball hoop and a small television with a game system set up for video games.

"Good grief," Kenidee said.

"There you are," her dad said, coming down the stairs. "So what do you think so far?"

"It's—um—well," she searched for something to say. "It's colorful."

"That's Robin. She loves vibrant colors. I know it's a lot different from our other house, but I thought I'd let her fix this place up how she wanted it."

Kenidee was afraid to see her room.

"The other two bedrooms down here aren't being used much right now. One has the treadmill and the weight machine in it. We put a TV in there, hoping it would help us use it more, but we don't work out much. Obviously," he laughed, patting his stomach. "Maybe you'll get some use out of it. The other room has Robin's craft supplies and sewing machine. You might have noticed that she likes to do crafts."

Kenidee nodded. The craft materials looked more like items that were left after everything at a garage sale had been picked over.

They went back upstairs and her father led the way to a door down the hall. "Here's your room." Kenidee walked cautiously toward it. She looked back at Matt and Lindsay, who offered her looks of encouragement.

She walked inside and was pleasantly surprised. The walls were a soft fawn color, with nothing hanging on them. Her bookshelf and all her books stood in one corner, and next to it was a set of dresser drawers. Thankfully, they'd kept her bedroom set and bedding from before her mission, and the sight was welcoming.

There were boxes from her old bedroom in another corner, which her father told her they'd left so she could put them away however she wanted them. All her ballet posters, figurines, and stuffed animals wearing tutus were in one box, and all her high school and college mementos were in another.

They somberly walked the other direction down the hallway to finalize the tour.

Kenidee literally gasped when they entered her father's bedroom. The lilac-colored walls and deep purple bedding were so unexpected that she forgot to take a step and almost fell. Regaining her balance, Kenidee noticed the jewel-toned, frilly accent pillows that matched velvet panels hanging at the windows.

Lindsay nudged her with her elbow, and Kenidee quickly wiped the shock from her face.

Gold gilded picture frames, ruffled and beaded lamp shades, and golden-colored crushed velvet occasional chairs accessorized the room. Kenidee wondered how her father could possibly sleep in the room, and was glad to retreat and continue the tour.

They took a quick peek at the little girl's "everything Barbie" bedroom, with more pink walls, and then went into the two boys' "let's-go-crazy-with-sports" room. Finally the tour was completed.

Kenidee's father had always been the type to let her mother make her own decisions regarding the decorating of their home. As long as her mother was happy, he was happy. It had worked in the past, but Kenidee thought maybe he could have provided a little input into Robin's choice of decorating.

"So that's it," her dad said as they walked back to the kitchen area. "You'll be glad to know that we're still in the same stake and meet in our same building."

"Oh, that's good," Kenidee answered.

The telephone rang, and her father excused himself to answer it. Kenidee assumed it was Robin, probably wondering how things were going.

"So," Matt said, with an unmistakable twinkle in his eyes, "what do you think?"

Kenidee opened her eyes wide and stared at him for a moment before saying, "It looks like Hello Kitty decorated it."

Matt and Lindsay burst out laughing.

"A deranged Hello Kitty," Matt managed to get out.

"I'm sorry, but really, I've never seen anything like it. I can't imagine what this woman is like."

Lindsay wiped at her eyes. "She's very cheerful and enthusiastic."

Matt nodded in agreement.

"And her kids are pretty cute," Lindsay said.

Matt looked at his wife with a raised eyebrow.

"They are Matt. You just need to get to know them."

"All I know is that she's not Mom," Matt said.

Kenidee looked around, remembering how elegant and classy her old home had been. Neutral colors on the walls and floors, and furniture and accents in rich, earth-toned colors had graced the rooms, creating a warm, soothing atmosphere. There was nothing soothing about this house.

She tried to comprehend her surroundings, grateful that her mission had taught her to adjust to strange, new situations. She reminded herself that she wouldn't be around long enough to have to adapt.

"This is like an incomprehensible psychedelic dream," Kenidee said. Then an unexpected rush of emotion caused a knot to form in her throat and tears to sting her eyes. She blinked quickly, but she couldn't stop the sudden tears.

"Hey, sis, it's okay," Matt quickly gave her a hug. "You just need time. You've got too much to deal with all at once. I knew this would be hard. It will be okay."

Lindsay stroked her hair and sandwiched the hug. "We'll help you through it."

* * *

Out of habit Kenidee awoke at six-thirty the next morning and couldn't go back to sleep. She stayed in bed ten minutes longer before she decided to get up.

Her first thoughts were the same as the last ones she'd had before bed. Her mother.

On her mission, she'd been able to create a new life, in a new place, with new people. A place that wasn't attached to memories of her mother. But coming home was like drowning in a pool filled with memories. Even though the house was different, her mother's presence still lingered. Seeing her bed, the couch, her father's office, and their grand piano sparked memories that brought pain and agony. She missed her mother all over again.

Without her mother there, it just didn't feel like home. She didn't belong here. Maybe if it was just her father, together they could help each other heal. But it wasn't. He now had a whole new life that she didn't really fit into. He had Robin and her kids to focus on.

She thought about Dolly's offer to move to Salt Lake City and was grateful that she had such a wonderful option. New surroundings would help. But she needed money to purchase a car, to pay rent for an apartment, and to pay the expenses of moving and getting started in a new place.

Sitting down at the desk in the corner of her room, she pulled out her planner and opened it to a fresh page. At the top of the page, she wrote the words *To Do*. Below this she wrote *Find Job*. Then *Look for Car*. And finally she wrote *Call Dolly*.

For the next fifteen minutes, she studied in the Book of Mormon, grateful for the peace, comfort, and sense of familiarity it provided. Then she dropped to her knees and offered her morning prayer.

Staying on her knees after concluding her prayer, Kenidee waited for promptings, thoughts, impressions, some kind of answer or direction, but the heavens remained silent. Still, her heart was calm, and she knew her life was in God's hands. He would be there; he would help her. But it would be hard.

*Stay busy,* she told herself. That had been the key to getting through the tough times on her mission. Staying busy, working hard. She just needed to apply that to what she was going through right now.

Her stomach grumbled. She hadn't eaten much the night before.

Deciding to surprise her dad and make breakfast, she pulled on her robe and made her way to the kitchen, squinting against the brilliant color as she turned on the light.

In the refrigerator, she found eggs, sausage, and orange juice. Rummaging through cupboards, she found loaves of homemade wheat bread. Cutting several thick slices, Kenidee popped them into the toaster and began scrambling eggs and browning the sausage.

Rarely on her mission did she or her companion take time to actually cook breakfast, so it was a treat to have a hot, home-cooked meal.

"Well, well, I think I'm going to like having you home," her father said as he entered the room and gave her a hug and a kiss on the cheek. "I should be making breakfast for you, though."

Kenidee scraped eggs onto their plates and divided the links of sausage between them. They sat down at the table, blessed the food, then began to eat.

"It's delicious," her father said. "Thanks."

"Happy to do it, Dad. What time do you have to go to work?"

"I thought I'd take the day off so we could hang out. Is there anything you'd like to do? Anyone you want to visit?" Several ward members and friends from their old neighborhood had come to visit her the night before after she had been released at the stake president's office.

"Not really. I wouldn't mind going car shopping though."

"I've been keeping my eye out for a car for you. Something good on gas and dependable."

"And cute," she added.

"Of course."

Kenidee spread some raspberry jam on her bread. "When do you expect Robin and her kids?"

"She's going to wait until I call."

"Oh, okay." Kenidee wasn't sure she'd ever be ready to meet this woman and her kids.

"Maybe this evening after dinner, if it works out."

She didn't answer right away.

"She can wait if that's too soon."

Not knowing how to answer, she just shrugged.

"Honey, I know this is difficult, but the fact is, she is my wife."

Kenidee wanted to handle the situation like an adult—be strong, be mature—but the *fact* was, she didn't want to accept that fact.

"I know if you'll give her a chance you'll see what a great person she is."

"It's not that, Dad. I'm sure she is a good person. I just don't understand how it happened so quickly. Why you couldn't have waited until after I got home."

"It's not that simple," he told her. "Knowing how hard this was going to be for you was the only thing that nearly prevented me from going through with it in the first place."

*But you still went through with it*, she thought.

"It's really hard coming back and not having Mom here," Kenidee tried to explain. "But it's even harder having someone else in her place."

"I'm sorry, honey," her father said. "You need to know that I was very prayerful about my decision to marry Robin. Very prayerful."

How did she argue with that, she wondered. She just wished the Spirit had helped her feel the same way.

"I think with time we will all feel much better about the situation," he told her.

She nodded and hoped he was right.

"Okay," she said, "have her come tonight then so we can get it over with."

"Kenidee, honey, I'm sorry this is so hard—"

Kenidee pushed the chair back with a screech and got to her feet. "I'm going to take a shower, and then I'll come back and clean up the dishes."

She didn't look at her dad as she left the room. She knew she was making it difficult for him, but she couldn't help herself. He'd made it impossible for her.

\* \* \*

Kenidee forced a smile as Gilbert Merkley shook her hand, held it for a few moments longer than was necessary, and then looked into her eyes.

"It's so nice to see you again, Kenidee. How was your mission?"

"Really great," she said. "I wish I was still there." She didn't know whether she was directing the comment to him or to her dad, but it was honestly how she felt.

"I know the feeling. I still get homesick for Japan," he told her.

"So," she said, pulling her hand out of his moist grasp and fighting the urge to get the bottle of hand sanitizer out of her purse, "my dad says you have some cars on your lot to show us?"

"Do I ever. When your father called, I knew exactly which cars to show you. I did some price comparisons for you and made a full analysis based on the specifics your father gave me. You can be sure I'll get you the best deal possible, too."

They followed him across the lot to where used cars were parked. Gilbert pointed out several options, which didn't thrill Kenidee, and then he showed her a used white Honda Civic, in mint condition, and a racy, red Toyota Camry, also used.

"Now this Civic is a little bit on the pricey side," Gilbert said. "But as you can see, it's hardly been used. Low mileage, clean interior, not a dent or a ding on the body. This car gets twenty-six miles in the city, thirty-four on the highway. Number one in its class. But the Camry, well, she's quite a beauty. Still, she's only getting twenty-two in the city and thirty-one on the freeway, and, it's number one with car theft."

"You certainly know your numbers, Gilbert," Kenidee's father complimented.

"Thank you, Brother Ashford. I make it a point to. Now, does either of these cars interest you?" he said, directing his question to Kenidee.

"The Civic," she said. "It seems the most practical choice." She didn't tell either of them that she had fallen in love with it immediately and knew that if it took all her savings and a loan, this was the car she wanted.

Her father inspected the car closely, with Gilbert jabbering about cylinders and valves and mumbo jumbo she knew nothing about. All she knew was that this was one cute car!

"What do you think, honey?" her dad asked.

"I like it," she told him, trying to act like a mature adult who was considering all the important information Gilbert had given them.

"Let's take it for a test drive and see what you think," Gilbert said.

On the road, the car handled like a dream. Kenidee decided she was not going home without it.

Leaning forward from the back seat, Gilbert asked how she liked it.

"I'm sold," Kenidee said.

"If the price is right," her dad added.

An hour later, with keys in hand, Kenidee walked out to her Civic. The money she had in savings from the sale of her car before her mission covered over half the price of the new car. Her father generously covered the rest of it to help her avoid getting into debt—a quality Gilbert found most admirable.

"I agree, Brother Ashford, debt should be avoided at all costs." He then looked at Kenidee with heightened interest.

"I guess that's everything then," Kenidee said. "Isn't it, Dad?" she spoke louder, trying to get her father to help them end their encounter with Gilbert.

"Oh, yes," her father said, taking his eyes off the sticker of a different automobile that had caught his attention.

"If you're interested, I can get you a great deal on that car, Brother Ashford. The car gets nineteen—"

"Actually, Gilbert, I'm sure this car is exceptional, but I'm not in the market for a new car right now. I'll certainly let you know when I am, though."

"Oh, right," Gilbert said. "Well, then, you two have a great day. Thanks for coming to see me. Did I give you my card?"

Kenidee didn't tell him he'd given them about ten of his business cards.

"I'm pretty sure you did," Kenidee's dad told him, as he patted his shirt pocket where the stack of cards had been stored.

"Then you two have a great day. And I'll look forward to seeing you on Sunday." He looked directly at Kenidee when he spoke.

Kenidee gave him a half smile before she turned with her father and walked toward the new car.

When they were finally alone, she took a moment to give her dad a hug and thank him for helping her find the car and pay for it.

"I had some money set aside for when you got home, to help you get settled," he told her. "You'll be able to enjoy this car for a long time. It's very dependable and has everything you were looking for, *and* it's cute."

Kenidee laughed and opened the door to the car. Then she turned and gave her father another hug. "Thanks, Dad."

"You're welcome, sweetie." He gave her a peck on the cheek. "I'll see you back home? Robin should be there by now."

"Okay," she replied, climbing inside.

He walked away, and Kenidee's heart clenched in her chest. She loved her father very much. They'd always been close, been able to talk about everything. She wanted things to be like they'd always been, but life had changed. He was trying to be helpful and understanding, but deep down, she still felt angry at him for getting remarried so soon. Fleetingly, she wondered if the car was almost some type of payoff, a compensation for his rapid remarriage. Kenidee dismissed the thought instantly.

"Kenidee," Gilbert's voice broke into her thoughts.

Kenidee groaned as she saw Gilbert sprinting toward the car, his wide polyester tie bouncing against his chest like a Ping-Pong ball on a table.

She was tempted to test the engine to see how quickly she could get away, but she knew it would be rude. Besides, he had gotten them a very good deal on the car, which she appreciated.

"I'm glad I caught you before you left," he said, breathlessly. He pushed his glasses up the bridge of his nose and smiled. "You know, I'm just working here at the car lot until this job with the Health Department comes through."

"Oh?"

"I'm pretty sure I'm going to get a data analyst job. Then it won't be long before I can become an actuary."

"That's great," Kenidee said, unsure of what an *actuary* actually was.

"I know you just got home and everything, but I wondered if you'd mind if I gave you a call sometime. You know, just to hang out or something."

Kenidee wondered how fast she could repack her bags and get to Salt Lake City.

"Uh, yeah, well, you know, Gilbert, I really need some time right now."

"I understand. Must be difficult to come home to a new house and a new mom and all."

"Yeah, it is."

"Okay. I'll give you a call sometime in the future, and maybe you'll feel differently then."

"You probably didn't know, but I do have a missionary I'm waiting for," she told him.

"No, I didn't know that."

"Yeah, so, I sure appreciate your help today, but . . ."

"I understand," Gilbert said. "Well, if things don't work out with your missionary, I'd love to take you out."

"I'll remember that," she told him, but she knew things would definitely work out with Brendan.

Watching as Kenidee drove away, Gilbert waved quickly before smoothing a flap of hair over his bald spot.

A sense of freedom filled Kenidee as she drove along the streets of the town that she hadn't seen for eighteen months. A few things had changed, of course. New buildings stood where there had been vacant lots, and housing developments covered hillsides. But it was still very familiar, still home.

Realizing that she needed a few personal items, she decided to stop at the grocery store near her father's house and pick up some things before she went home. Parking away from other cars so hers wouldn't get door-dinged, Kenidee walked into the store and realized how strange if felt not having a companion with her. This was the first time she'd gone somewhere alone since she'd left the plane.

When she was with Sister DeWitt . . . Dolly, they'd always headed straight for the bakery and bought a donut—hers, chocolate with icing and sprinkles; Dolly's, lemon-filled and dusted with powdered sugar.

Today she went directly to the cosmetics department, found what she needed, and then went to the shampoo aisle. She hadn't realized until she'd gotten home that she'd left a lot of things back in her last apartment in Florida.

With her arms full, and wishing she'd grabbed a basket, she made her way to the check-out counter. She came around the corner, her sight partially obstructed, and ran directly into someone's cart. The contents of her arms flew every direction.

"I'm so sorry," Kenidee said, as she got down on her knees to gather up her items.

"It's my fault," the person said. "I wasn't watching where I was going."

He handed her a bottle of conditioner and their eyes met.

"Ken-dog!" he exclaimed.

"Camden!"

They both got to their feet and hugged. The bottle of conditioner slid from her hand and landed on his foot.

"Ow!" he said, jumping up and down as he held his foot.

"Sorry!" she said. "Are you okay?"

He nodded. "I'm fine. Why don't you put your stuff in my cart."

She put her armload of groceries and other sundry items in one corner of his cart while he rubbed his foot.

"Are you okay?" she asked again.

He tested his weight on his foot and nodded. "No harm done. But hey, look at you. When did you get home?"

"Last night."

"Matt said you were coming soon, but I forgot which day. How are you?" Cam sounded genuinely happy to see her.

"Good, thanks."

"How was your mission?"

"Great. But it's hard to come home."

"Yeah, I remember," Cam said. "Of course, you kind of have a lot of extra weird stuff to get used to, don't you?"

"You can say that again."

"Have you met your dad's wife yet?"

They began walking toward the checkout stands. Actually, she walked, Cam hobbled.

"Not yet," Kenidee answered. "They stayed away so I wouldn't get overwhelmed. They're coming back tonight."

"I am so sorry about your mom. She was like a second mom to me, you know."

"I know, Cam. She used to buy stuff and tell us we couldn't eat it because it was for you."

"She did not!"

"Cam, hello, remember Cheese Nips? And those Little Debbies Oatmeal Pies?"

"Oh yeah, she did. You're right."

"So, how are you? How's Desiree and Amanda? And your other daughter, is it Brynn?"

"Yeah, Brynn. She's great. She's a year and a half. Amanda is four, going on twenty."

Kenidee laughed.

"I guess Matt didn't tell you about me and Desiree?"

"Tell me what?"

As they took their place in line, Cam noticed some seats near the deli. "Do you want to go sit for a minute and talk?"

Since Kenidee was in no hurry to get back home and because she wanted to hear what was going on with him, she agreed.

They sat across from each other at the table while Cam explained. "We aren't together anymore. We got divorced."

"Cam, you're kidding! I'm so sorry to hear that." Kenidee had never been one hundred percent sure why Cam had married Desiree. She was cute and bubbly, but not getting married in the temple was so unlike the Cam she knew. "What happened? I mean, if it's any of my business."

"Yeah. You're like a sister to me. I don't mind telling you."

He rested his elbows on the table and clasped his hands together. "I knew right after Desiree and I were married that we were in for some tough times. I really thought we had the same goals about marriage and family, but it was all I could do to get her to go to church with me. And then there were her friends. On weekends, when we wanted to invite friends over for barbecues and movies, she asked people I really felt awkward around. They always brought beer with them and ruined the fun when they drank too much."

"That would be hard."

"Desiree never drank, but she seemed to feel more comfortable around them than she did my friends, like Matt and Lindsay, and couples from our ward. I hoped that when Amanda was born things would settle down, and she would enjoy being a mother so much that we would finally have the family I was hoping we would have. But it only got worse."

"How?"

"She complained about being stuck at home all the time. She said she felt ugly—that was her word—because she had gained weight and couldn't find time to exercise. And just when she started to get some of the weight off, she got pregnant again."

Kenidee remembered how miserable Desiree had seemed during that second pregnancy.

Cam continued soberly. "After Brynn was born, Des joined a local gym so she could get out of the house and get some exercise and hopefully get back in shape and feel better about herself. It seemed like a great idea. She even talked me into budgeting for a personal trainer so she could get some fast results. She was really happy about it, and she did start seeing results quickly."

"That's good," Kenidee told him, thinking he sounded like a loving, supportive husband.

"Yeah, but the plot just thickened. She got so involved in working out and spending time at the gym that she wasn't home much. She'd get babysitters and spend hours there each day. I would come home from work and find the kids still in their pajamas, with one of the ten-year-old neighbor girls tending. Some nights, she stayed until the gym closed."

"What did you do?" Kenidee asked.

"I tried to talk to her and tell her she couldn't leave the kids so long, especially with babysitters who weren't really old enough to be responsible, and I told her I was concerned about all the time she spent at the gym. Of course, she got furious and told me I was controlling and selfish and trying to take away the one thing that brought her any happiness. I knew I had a big problem on my hands, so I told her I'd start going to the gym with her. I needed to work out, too, and I thought going there together might help our relationship."

"And?" Kenidee asked tentatively.

"Not only was she embarrassed by me because I wasn't tan and buff—I mean, she was looking really good by that time and I was pale and certainly not in shape like I'd been in high school. But I realized that she had a whole other life there at the gym, and she didn't want me to be a part of it."

"Why wouldn't she? You were her husband."

"Yeah, that's what I thought, too," Cam answered quietly. "It didn't take long for me to notice that the trainer she'd spent all those months with was more than just a trainer to her. Just from the way he looked at me when I was with her, and their little exchanges with each other, I knew they were involved. I just didn't know how much until I finally confronted her."

"What did she say?" Kenidee asked breathlessly, her heart pounding uncomfortably.

"That she didn't love me, that she didn't like being a mother, and that she wanted to get a divorce."

"Whoa!"

"It didn't really shock me. I actually saw it coming, but I just couldn't stop it from happening. Nothing I did or said could make her love me or make her want to be a good mom. She moved out the very next day and moved in with the trainer."

"How did the girls take it?"

"It's been hard. I think they're confused about the situation. She doesn't come to see them very often. Sometimes she'll take them with her, but she has a new boyfriend now and they don't like him." Cam's voice became shaky as he continued. "Amanda tells me that he calls them brats and tells Brynn to 'shut up' when she cries, which is a huge deal because we aren't allowed to say 'shut up' at our house, so she gets very upset about it."

"I'm so sorry." Kenidee shook her head, trying to imagine how difficult the whole situation was.

"Yeah, well, I guess I should have been more careful about who I dated and who I chose to marry. Before we were married, Desiree told me she wanted to go to church and one day get married in the temple. I can't believe how naive I was to think she would change for me. It was the biggest mistake of my life. But, you know something, Kenidee, I would go through all of it again just to have my daughters. They mean everything in the world to me."

Kenidee looked at this man in front of her and felt helpless, wishing there was something she could do to ease his burden. He still looked like the old Cam, although the dark shadows under his eyes and the tight set of his mouth showed that he had changed. He was tired, worn out.

"So," he said, trying to brighten the conversation, "enough about me. What are you going to do now that you're home."

"I bought a car today, so now I need to find a job right away and start saving my money. I'm moving to Salt Lake City to live with one of my companions, and I hope to end up at the University of Utah for winter semester."

He nodded. "What about dancing? I thought you always wanted to be a ballerina."

Kenidee's voice and face both brightened as she answered his question. "I'm going to study dance. I'm too old and out of shape to perform, but I would love to get a degree and teach dance at a studio, or perhaps one day own a studio. I'd love to teach little girls like yours."

Cam smiled.

"I'm hoping to get a job teaching here at my old studio until I go to Salt Lake."

"You don't want to stay home and go to school here?"

"I don't feel like I have a home here anymore," she said honestly. "Plus the U offers everything I need."

Cam had been following the conversation carefully, and he had easily read between the lines. Half smiling, he said, "I can't imagine how hard this is for you and what it was like to go through that on your mission."

Kenidee swallowed, keeping her emotions in check. "That which doesn't kill you makes you stronger, right?"

"Then we should both be superheroes."

"Able to leap tall buildings at a single bound."

He laughed.

She realized that she felt better just being able to talk to someone about her feelings. "I'm glad I ran into you tonight," she said, "literally."

He laughed again. "You haven't changed. I never could figure out how a ballerina could be such a klutz."

She opened her mouth in protest. "A klutz!"

"Hey, you're the one who used to fall down the stairs and tip over in your chair at the dinner table. Not me."

Kenidee couldn't help smiling. She was busted. She couldn't deny it because he'd been there to witness many of her "graceful" episodes. "Okay, you win."

Winning was great, but Cam also wanted the last word. "I'm glad you survived your mission without injury."

She couldn't help pulling a face, giving away the truth. He immediately noticed her expression. "You mean you didn't? What happened?"

"Well, one time I broke my arm when I tripped over a curb when we were tracting."

He burst out laughing.

"Hey! It hurt."

"I'm sorry. I'm not laughing that you got hurt. But only you could do something like that."

"We got a baptism out of it."

"You're kidding. How?"

"A guy and his wife who were out doing yard work saw what happened and offered to drive us to the emergency room. While we were there we told them who we were and what we were doing and they agreed to let us teach them. And, believe it or not, we ended up baptizing both of them and their two kids and the wife's mother."

"Kenidee, you're remarkable. That's quite a story. Always turning lemons into lemonade," he quipped.

"That's just one of many miracles that happened on my mission."

"You mean you broke other bones just to get baptisms?"

"No, you dork. That was the only bone I broke, although I twisted my ankle running from a dog and managed to land on my companion."

"And?"

"And . . . she broke her collarbone."

"Now I know where all our tithing money has gone for the last eighteen months," he said with a laugh. "To pay your medical bills, and your companion's."

Kenidee rolled her eyes. This was the old Cam she remembered. He'd always been a tease and a pain in the neck.

"I'm sorry. Really," he said. "Matt told me what a great missionary you were. I'm not surprised."

"Really?"

"I knew you'd do a great job. You've always been focused and a hard worker. And you have a big heart."

Her brow narrowed. Was he being serious? She never knew for sure with him.

"C'mon, Ken-dog, you may be Matt's little sister, but I've always known what a good person you are. I thought it was pretty cool of you to go on a mission. Especially someone as pretty as you are, who could easily have stayed home and gotten married."

"Yeah, well, hopefully that will happen when my missionary gets home."

"Oh? How serious is it?"

She showed him the ring Brendan gave her. "He'll be home in three months," she said.

Cam looked down at his watch. "Shoot. I gotta run and pick up the girls at the sitter's house."

"I'd better get going too," she said, getting to her feet. "Might as well get this over with."

They walked to the check-out counter.

"Here," he said, "you go first."

"No. That's okay. You're in a hurry; I'm not. Be my guest."

He quickly unloaded the cart and paid for his groceries after the cashier had run them through. Before grabbing his bags, he turned and said, "I'm glad I ran into you."

"Me too. It feels good to talk to someone. All my girlfriends are either married or away at school." Kenidee unloaded her items from the cart and waited for the cashier to scan them.

"When do you speak in church?" he asked.

"A week from Sunday."

"Great, I'll bring the girls." He grabbed the handles of the bags and lifted them off of the counter. "See you soon," he said, racing from the store.

Kenidee shook her head and laughed. Good old Camden. Hard to believe he was the father of two and divorced. Even though she'd hated how much he'd teased her growing up, she'd always thought a lot of him. She wished things could have turned out better for him.

The drive to her father's house was too short. Before she knew it, she was in the driveway, sitting in her car, wishing she were anywhere else but here. Preferably back in the mission field. Even tracting on the hottest, most humid day, with big dogs chasing her, sounded better than what she was about to do.

The front door opened, and Kenidee saw her father look out. He waved and motioned for her to come inside. Giving him a weak smile, she gathered her things and paused long enough to say a quick prayer. Then she climbed out of the car and slammed the door shut.

"Here goes nothing," she said.

# CHAPTER 3

"Hi, honey. I got a little worried when you didn't come right home," her father said, greeting her at the door. "We'd better get you a cell phone tomorrow."

"I had to stop at the grocery store," she told him. "And I ran into Cam. How come you guys didn't tell me he got divorced?"

"I didn't even know until a few weeks ago myself. Poor kid. Sounds like he's been through a lot," he replied. "Anyway, honey, why don't we go into the kitchen where everyone's waiting to meet you."

Kenidee's stomach curdled. She heard the sound of voices coming from the kitchen and then a woman's loud cackle along with children's giggling. She looked at her father with alarm. "Is that them?"

He nodded.

She pulled in a quick breath. "Okay, I'm ready," she said, unable to disguise her lack of excitement.

She followed her dad as they walked from the entryway to the glaring brightness of the kitchen. There, with smiles on their faces, balloons tied to the kitchen chairs, and a big cake on the table that said "Welcome Home" were Robin and her three children— Mikey, David, and Rachel.

Robin jumped up and greeted her with an unexpected hug. "We're so glad you're home, Kenidee."

Kenidee stood stiffly, then stepped back as the woman released her. "Thanks."

The two boys stood and shook her hand and introduced themselves.

Six-year-old Rachel stood next to her mom, her face buried in the folds of her skirt.

"And this is Rachel," Robin said. "She's a bit shy."

Kenidee didn't respond. Trying to control her shock and rein in her desire to turn and run took all of her resolve. These people were strangers, yet they were family. And she couldn't even remember their names.

"Is anyone hungry?" Robin said. "Your father said you love Chinese food, so I thought that's what we could have for dinner."

It didn't matter what was for dinner, as far as Kenidee was concerned. She didn't have an appetite.

"Let's go into the dining room and sit down." Robin ushered them into the formal dining area where they all sat down. The three kids looked at her as if she had horns growing from her head. The youngest one, the girl, looked like she was about to burst into tears.

"Will," Robin addressed Kenidee's father by the nickname he'd always hated. "Would you please bless the food?"

Kenidee didn't hear a word her father said. She was too busy taking deep breaths to remain calm. Her mother never called him Will. It was always William. Always.

"Robin's a great cook," Kenidee's father said after he had blessed the food. "She makes the best homemade pizza in town. And her desserts are almost sinful they're so good." He patted his stomach, which was noticeably bigger. "You can tell I have no complaints."

Kenidee gave him half a smile but didn't reply. When her mother was alive and well, her parents went on vigorous walks every day, except Sunday. He never would have let himself go like this when her mom was alive.

"Now that Kenidee is home, we will try harder to eat more healthy meals," Robin said. "I wouldn't mind losing a few pounds. I wish I were taller. Then every pound wouldn't look like ten."

Robin was about five foot four with a rounded shape, button nose, and brown, curly hair. She had bright blue eyes and a vibrant expression of cheerfulness on her face. And at thirty-eight years of age she was fifteen years younger than Kenidee's father.

Robin's oldest son didn't really look much like his mother, his hair more blond and his features more pronounced, but the younger boy and the daughter were carbon copies of her. The little girl had the same curls and button nose as her mother, and enormous blue eyes.

Bowls of food circled the table. The two boys began to argue over who would be first to play on the video game system after dinner. Robin promptly told them that if they didn't stop fighting, neither of them would play. The argument ceased. Kenidee hid a grin as she saw the oldest brother sneak in one last elbow to the ribs on his younger brother, to which his brother responded with a sly pinch to the back of his brother's arm.

At least the kids were normal. She remembered having similar exchanges with her brother over television programs, prime seating on the couch, and who got the last Pop-Tart.

Her dad began to rave over the meal and compliment Robin on each of the dishes she'd prepared. Kenidee didn't really care for the seasonings in the lettuce wraps, and she preferred her mother's orange chicken with its sticky sweet sauce, over the tartness of Robin's sauce. Of course, she didn't say anything, but each comparison just intensified the reminder that her mother was gone and this woman was trying to take her place.

"Kenidee, would you like some of the beef and broccoli?" Robin asked.

Trying to swallow a dry wad of rice in her mouth, Kenidee shook her head.

"So, tell us about your mission. Did you do a lot of tracting or did the members refer a lot of people?" Robin gave her boys another stern look as their "video games" issue surfaced again.

"Uh, both, I guess," she said. "The members were really awesome, but we still had to do a lot of tracting."

"I wanted to serve a mission, but it just didn't work out," Robin said. "Maybe someday when we get older, Will, we can go together."

"Absolutely," Kenidee's father said, taking another giant helping of orange chicken and rice.

"Now, leave room for cake and ice cream," Robin reminded him.

"Don't worry. I always have room for your delicious carrot cake."

Kenidee bit her lip and didn't say anything, but it was difficult. Her father knew, without question, that she despised carrot cake. There was no way he could forget because when she was six, she threw up all over him after eating it at a ward party! She couldn't even look at a piece without getting nauseated.

"Rachel, honey, please eat," Robin said.

"It's yucky," Rachel said. "I just want chickies."

"Eat some of your vegetables first, then you can have chickies."

Rachel groaned and stabbed the tiniest piece of broccoli on her plate and stared at it on her fork.

"She's addicted to chicken nuggets," Robin told Kenidee. "I asked her pediatrician if she was going to be malnourished, but the pediatrician says not to worry. She'll get tired of them eventually. She'd have them for breakfast, lunch, and dinner if I let her."

Kenidee watched Rachel put the broccoli in her mouth and chew for a moment, but when she tried to swallow, she gagged and quickly spit it back onto her plate.

"Ooo, gross!" David exclaimed.

"I get her piece of cake," Mikey piped up.

"No he doesn't," Rachel cried. "Mommy, he doesn't get my cake."

"Honey, then you need to have a few bites of your dinner."

Kenidee's father seemed completely oblivious to Robin's challenges with the children, which was just like him, ignoring the problem so it would go away.

The little girl stuck her fork into a little piece of carrot and poked it into her mouth. She chewed and swallowed successfully.

Then she reached for her drink. Her glass was too far away, and when she tried to pick it up, she succeeded in tipping the whole thing over onto her plate and down the front of her dress.

Robin tried to calm her daughter, who wailed like a banshee, but decided the better course was to whisk her away to her bedroom to change her outfit. At the exit of their mother, the two boys escaped from the table and raced for the family room, leaving Kenidee and her father alone at the dinner table.

"Certainly a lively bunch, aren't they?" he said.

Kenidee nodded. The quicker she could move to Salt Lake the better. As soon as she could get to the phone, she was calling Dolly to make arrangements.

"They're pretty good kids," he told her. "I don't want to get involved in the disciplining quite yet, you know. Give them time to get used to me first."

Staying quiet, Kenidee listened as the two boys argued again about which video game to play. Her head began to throb.

"Well, that was delicious," her dad said, placing his napkin on the table next to his plate. "Think I'll go read the paper while Robin's helping Rachel change. We'll have cake later."

"I think I'll pass," Kenidee said.

He looked at her with disappointment. "But Robin made that cake just for you."

"I appreciate her thoughtfulness, but I don't care for car—"

"Carrot cake! Oh dear, honey, I totally forgot. How could I possibly not remember?"

Kenidee shrugged.

"I'll explain to Robin. She'll understand," he said. Then he asked, "So, what do you think of her?"

"Um, she's nice," Kenidee said, not happy about being put on the spot. What was she going to say? *I want that woman and her kids out of this house?*

"And the kids?"

"Um, they seem pretty normal to me."

"Good, good. I'm glad you like them."

*Did I say I liked them? I don't remember saying any such thing,* Kenidee thought. Instead she said, "Do you mind if I go to my room, Dad?"

"No, honey. Go right ahead. We'll check on you later."

Kenidee began to get up from the table and follow her dad's lead to just walk away from the mess. Then she stopped. She picked up her own plate and carried it to the kitchen before she went to her room, shutting the door behind her.

Picking up the cordless phone on her nightstand, she dialed Dolly's number.

"Hello?"

"Is Dolly home?"

"She sure is, just a minute." Kenidee heard the person holler Dolly's name. A few seconds later she answered.

"Dolly, hi, it's me, Kenidee."

"Kenidee!" Dolly screamed into the phone, causing Kenidee to quickly pull the phone away from her ear. "How are you? What's going on?"

"I just called to see how you're doing?"

"At first I couldn't believe how strange it was. I felt kind of lost, and I missed the mission so much. I still do, I mean, how could I not, because it's so wonderful and the people are so amazing. But it's been great seeing my family again. How about you?"

"Uh, yeah, it's been good," Kenidee said, hoping she sounded convincing.

"What have you been doing? Doesn't it feel almost like you've forgotten something to not have a comp? I'm still not used to that. I miss being with you the most. We had so much fun, didn't we? Almost like we were best friends, not just companions," Dolly enthused.

"Me too. It's really weird."

"I totally miss the people we were teaching. That's been the hardest part. I just finished a letter to Francesca. I would love to be there when she gets baptized. Wouldn't you?"

"That would be the best," Kenidee agreed. But if she went back, she wouldn't come home, at least for three months, anyway.

"All I can say is that those elders better not do anything to mess up her baptism. We worked so hard to help her stop smoking and to get her to move out of her boyfriend's apartment."

"They won't," Kenidee assured her.

"Soooo," Dolly drew out the word, "how is everything there?"

Kenidee shut her eyes, "It's . . ." she swallowed, "um, it's weird . . . it's strange . . . it's like I'm in Never Never Land."

"I'm sorry. I can't imagine what it's been like. What's the new house like? How is your dad's wife and the kids? What do you think of her? Is she nice? Is she pretty?"

Kenidee waited for the questions to end before she attempted to answer. "You wouldn't believe this house. The walls are such bright colors I need to wear sunglasses inside."

Dolly giggled.

"I can tell Robin's trying hard. I think I just need some time to process the fact that Mom's not here before I can get used to someone in her place."

"That totally makes sense," Dolly empathized. "But that sounds like it would be hard to do."

"It will be hard. In fact, too hard. That's why I've made a decision."

"What's that?" Dolly asked.

"I want to take you up on your invitation. I want to move to Salt Lake City. I mean, if the offer still stands."

"Oh, yeah, of course it does. But . . ." Dolly's voice trailed off.

"Dolly, is something wrong?"

"No, not really. It's just that I'm not going to be here for a while. My grandmother is ill, so my mom and I are going to go stay with her in St. George for a while."

"You don't know how long?"

"No. But I'm sure it won't be long. Maybe a week or two," Dolly added. "I really want you to come and live here with me. I can't think of anything better."

"Okay, well, I need to get a temporary job and make some money anyway, so I can do that while you're in St. George. Then when you get home, I'll plan on moving there."

"Perfect! It's all going to work out. You'll see. And I'm still planning on going to hear President and Sister Larsen give their report in Sacramento when they get home in July."

"Oh, me too. You can come stay with us and we'll go together, okay?"

"That will be so fun. Plan on it for sure."

Kenidee felt homesick for her companion and was disappointed she was going to have to postpone moving to Salt Lake. But she could find a way to make some money and save it to help pay for the move and still have something to live off until she found a job.

"I'm so glad you called, Sis—I mean, Kenidee." Dolly giggled. "I'm still not used to that! In fact, yesterday someone called for my mom, Sister DeWitt and I said, 'This is she.' Can you believe that! But we'll be with each other soon, and we'll have a blast living together again. We can stay up and make peanut butter balls dipped in melted Hershey's kisses and have root beer floats and look at mission pictures and stuff."

"That will be great," Kenidee said, hoping it happened sooner rather than later.

"Hey, I've got to run. Our family is going to Temple Square and then out to dinner. I'm so excited. I've been anxious to go down there ever since I got home. I just love it there, don't you?" Dolly rattled on, not waiting for a reply. "But I'll call you in a couple of days, and we can catch up some more."

They said good-bye, but when Kenidee hung up the phone, she took a deep breath and shook her head. She felt bewildered because she was stuck at home for a while.

She decided she needed a glass of water. The house was quiet when she left her room. Following the light to the kitchen, she rounded the corner and stopped to find her father and Robin locked in an embrace and kissing next to the kitchen sink.

Retreating to her bedroom, Kenidee fell onto her bed and gave in to her emotions. It was startling enough seeing your own parents kissing like that, but to see your father and another woman, someone you didn't even know, it was just too much.

Pulling a pillow over her head, Kenidee burrowed into her down-filled comforter and escaped reality, slipping into a world of darkness and dreams.

# CHAPTER 4

Thank goodness for running. Kenidee always felt better after an invigorating jog in the fresh morning air. She'd missed jogging on her mission, and even though she wasn't in great shape, it still felt exhilarating to push her muscles and fill her lungs.

The last couple of days, she'd tried to stay busy around the house by mowing the lawn for her dad and cleaning out flower beds, just to have something to do during the day, but she still felt unproductive and lazy. She desperately needed a job and a friend.

"Kenidee, the phone's for you," Robin called just as Kenidee stepped out of the shower.

Picking up the extension in her room, she answered the phone.

"Hi, Ken." It was Lindsay. "I was wondering if you wanted to go shopping with me. I need to buy some things for the baby and would love your company. Baby Gap is having a huge sale, and they've got the cutest little dresses with matching shoes that I just have to buy for Emaree."

Emaree was the name Matt and Lindsay had chosen. Lindsay had only six weeks left until the baby arrived. She was constantly buying things for Emaree and her room. Kenidee loved seeing the excitement and anticipation surrounding Matt and Lindsay's baby. This was how she wanted to be when she had kids. The uncomfortable conversation she had had with Cam's ex-wife before her mission momentarily went through her mind.

"Are you kidding? I would love to go shopping. Heck, I'd be happy to go have a root canal I'm so bored."

"Still haven't found a job?"

"No one wants to hire me temporarily. The dance studio where I danced said they would call me to substitute teach, but they are getting ready for their year-end recital in June and they don't need new teachers right now. I could get some classes in the fall, but I won't be here."

"Are you sure you want to move to Salt Lake? I really need you here when Emaree is born. I want her to know her Aunt Kenidee. I kind of thought you'd be around to babysit and, you know, spoil her to death."

"I'll still spoil her, you know that, but I have to move, Linz, I really do. It's, it's . . . bizarre here. All dad and Robin do when they're together is eat or make out."

"Ooo, thanks for the visual."

"Hey, you should see it firsthand."

"How are the kids?"

"The boys fight constantly, Rachel whines 24/7, and I'm constantly tripping over their toys. The house is a mess because Robin and her kids are always working on projects that create huge messes that they never clean up, or she's not even here. If there is anyone on earth who's the exact opposite of my mother, it has to be Robin. And I can't even talk to Dad anymore. He spent those first two days with me after I got home. And that was it. Now I'm supposed to be fully integrated into this barbaric family. Dad's really busy at work, and he's doing a lot of traveling right now. And when he *is* home, he's involved with Robin and her kids."

"You know you're always welcome at our house," Lindsay said.

"Thanks. You guys are the only thing that keeps me sane."

"We love having you around," Lindsay told her. "So, you want to go shopping?"

Kenidee's answer was unmistakable. "Sure. Maybe I can find something to wear for church Sunday, although I don't anticipate a huge turnout of people just to come and see me."

"You'll be surprised," Lindsay said. "I'll come get you in about fifteen minutes. Oh, and I hope you don't mind, but we have to stop for food. I'm dying for some curly fries and a milkshake."

"Sure, whatever you want. I'll be ready."

Kenidee quickly slipped into a pair of jeans and a clean shirt and ran a brush through her hair.

Leaving her room in perfect order, she grabbed her purse and headed for the living room to wait for Lindsay. A delicious aroma from the kitchen brought her to a dead stop.

"Kenidee, is that you?" Robin called.

"Yeah," Kenidee answered, trying not to sound sullen.

"Would you like a fresh piece of bread? It's just hot out of the oven."

Kenidee's first thought was to turn her down, not because she didn't want the bread, but, she realized, because she didn't want anything to do with Robin. However, the compelling fresh-bread fragrance wove its magic and drew her into the kitchen.

"Sure," Kenidee said, squinting as she entered the kitchen.

"How was your run?" Robin asked, slicing into a steaming loaf of bread.

"It was great. I hadn't realized how much I missed running on my mission."

"I wish I had your determination. I was athletic when I was younger—really, I was— but now I don't get much chance to work out." Robin cracked an unexpected smile and added, "Actually, I suppose I don't *take* many chances to work out."

She placed a slice of bread on a plate. "Do you want butter and honey?"

"Sure," Kenidee responded.

"Looks like you're on your way out."

"I'm going shopping with Lindsay."

"That's sounds like a super idea. Kenidee, I know that everything still feels pretty awkward for you here. But it will get easier."

Robin didn't expect an answer, and Kenidee didn't feel like venturing a reply.

"Oh, Kenidee, since you'll be with Lindsay, would you mind checking with her to see if that date I asked her about for the baby shower will work?" Robin continued, "I don't think we want to wait much longer, just in case the baby decides to come early."

She handed the thick slice of bread to Kenidee.

"Which reminds me, is there anything special you'd like for dinner on Sunday? Your father's invited quite a few people to join us afterwards, and I'm sure we'll get some of your friends and ward members stopping by after church."

"That's okay, you don't have to bother. Sister Monson volunteered to do the food for the open house. She was my mom's best friend in our ward, and she said she really wanted to do this for me." Because of boundary changes in the stake, the Monsons were in the same ward, and Sister Monson's husband was the bishop.

"Oh," Robin said. "I see."

Kenidee thought she detected a note of disappointment in Robin's voice but pushed the thought aside. She wasn't convinced Robin really cared anyway.

"I doubt we'll have that many people," Kenidee told her. "Most of my friends are married and gone." Kenidee bit off a corner of the bread. "This is very good," she said with her mouth full.

"Thank you. I enjoy baking." Robin wiped her hands on a kitchen towel.

Kenidee was amazed at how delicious and moist the bread was. Her mother never had time to bake bread, but her brownies were incredible.

"Can I get you a drink?"

"No thanks, I'm fine."

The phone rang and Robin answered it. The person on the other line said something, causing Robin to burst out laughing.

Kenidee cringed at the sound of her boisterous laughter.

The honking of a horn in the driveway told her Lindsay had arrived.

Kenidee popped the last bite of bread into her mouth, licked her fingers, grabbed her purse, and then rushed out the door.

* * *

Sunday morning Kenidee awoke with a bad case of nerves. *Why would anyone say they had butterflies in their stomach?* she queried herself. *Mine feel more like frogs, or at least jumping beans,* she thought. *Maybe even ballerinas.* She reviewed her talk for sacrament meeting and said yet another prayer that she would be able to calm down and present what she had prepared. The talk was on testimonies, which was perfect, since she'd spent eighteen months developing her own and helping others receive a testimony of the gospel.

A light tap on her door caught her attention.

"Come in," she said, but no one entered.

Curious, she went to the door and opened it. Rachel stood there, looking at her with big round eyes. "Mommy said we're leaving. Do you want us to wait for you?"

The little girl looked so pretty and doll-like, with a pink satin ribbon in her hair that matched the light pink of her ruffled dress. Kenidee thought about ballerinas again. "Tell her I'll meet all of you at church, okay?"

"Okay."

The little girl was so nervous she couldn't get her feet to move.

"Thanks for asking me, though," Kenidee said, keeping her voice soft.

Rachel nodded and then suddenly turned and ran down the hallway.

Realizing that it wouldn't hurt her to make an effort to get to know Robin's kids, and sensing that her past behavior had bordered on rudeness, Kenidee decided to try to talk with each of them individually sometime.

The door leading to the garage slammed shut as Robin and her kids went out to the minivan. Kenidee's dad was already at the church for meetings.

Checking her reflection in the mirror one last time, Kenidee realized she probably needed to update her hairstyle and wished she'd thought of it before now. While on her mission she'd just let her hair grow, opting not to spend time or money on haircuts. Suddenly her hair looked straggly and unbecoming. She tried a few different options to make it more presentable but only succeeded in making it worse. With a groan at her reflection, she glanced at the clock. If she didn't leave right now, she would be late for church.

Rushing from her room, Kenidee fished for the keys from her purse as she headed toward the front door. The phone rang. For a moment she was tempted not to answer. Then, unable to resist, she picked up the receiver.

"Sister Ashford, it's Elder Taylor."

"Elder Taylor, hi."

"Hey, a bunch of us are coming to hear you speak, but we can't find your building."

Touched that these elders would make an effort to come and support her, she quickly gave them instructions.

"Good luck with your talk," Elder Taylor said. "We'll see you there."

Knowing that missionaries from her mission were coming made her even more nervous. She dropped her keys once on the way to her car and then again inside the car on the floor. She could barely get the key into the ignition she was shaking so badly.

Without incident, she gratefully made it to the church with five minutes to spare. Trying not to run into the building, she breezed past people who were still filing into the chapel and headed for the stand.

Her father caught her attention from where the family was sitting and gave her a thumbs up. She lifted her hand to flash him a thumbs up just as she collided with one of the deacons carrying trays to the sacrament table.

Horrified, Kenidee bent down to help him pick up the trays, apologizing to the young boy.

"Here," a voice said, "I've got it. You go on up and take your seat."

Kenidee looked up and saw Camden. "Thanks, Cam."

"Nervous?" he asked.

"What makes you ask?" she answered, eyeing the tray in his hand.

"You're shaking like a Chihuahua. You're going to do a great job. Go on up and take a seat. And relax."

She nodded, knowing her flushed face matched her red sweater. Kenidee walked up on the stand and was greeted by the members of the bishopric and a visiting high councilman. Pulling in deep breaths, she forced herself to calm down, though looking out over the large congregation didn't help her nerves any.

Several men opened the accordion curtains to the overflow in the back of the room. Had that many extra people come just to hear her speak? She fanned herself with the papers containing her talk and tried to let the prelude music calm her. She wondered if anyone had ever passed out on their way to the pulpit and hoped she wouldn't be the first.

Not sure why she was so nervous, she continued deep breathing and began praying. She'd spoken in church all the time on her mission. She'd approached complete strangers about the gospel and had borne testimony on street corners. But for some reason, when she'd removed her missionary name badge, her courage had disappeared with it.

The counselor in the bishopric stood, greeted the congregation, and then announced the opening song and prayer. Fumbling for a hymnal, Kenidee found the page and began singing "Welcome, Welcome, Sabbath Morning." The music and words to the hymn helped untangle her nerves, and she began to settle down. It would all be okay. She'd prayed and fasted about her talk and felt good about what she had prepared. Heavenly Father would strengthen her and help her.

Her gaze traveled across the faces of the congregation, where she recognized many of the wonderful people she'd known most of her life. Previous Young Women leaders, friends from youth conference, girls' camp, and seminary all smiled back at her as their gazes met. In the back was a row of elders from her mission. Some she'd served with and knew well, others she knew only by name. She located her father and Robin and the kids. Matt and Lindsay sat beside them, and next to Matt sat Cam and his two daughters.

Amanda sat quietly looking at a book, but the younger one, Brynn, sat on Cam's lap, obviously sad about something. Kenidee watched him tenderly whisper into her ear and gently stroke her thick, dark hair. Brynn nodded slowly, her bottom lip still pouting.

Cam coaxed a smile out of her, and soon she snuggled against his chest, looking content and happy. Both daughters were carbon copies of their father, dark-eyed, dark-haired. They both looked like china dolls with beautiful porcelain skin and tiny features.

The opening prayer was said, and the meeting continued, with Kenidee feeling less nervous with each passing moment. After the sacrament, the counselor stood and announced the program. First, Kenidee would speak, then there would be a musical number, followed by Brother Hasslehoff, from the stake.

When the counselor sat down, Kenidee walked to the podium, grateful to make it without tripping or keeling over completely. She began her talk by introducing herself to people in the ward who might not know her or remember her. Then she introduced the topic she'd been assigned.

Eighteen months of teaching and testifying suddenly came to the forefront, and after that, she didn't even look down at her notes. She shared several stories from her mission and bore testimony of the miracles she'd witnessed and how the Spirit changed hearts and testified of truths. Quoting scriptures and giving examples from the Book of Mormon, she also bore testimony of the Book of Mormon, and the power it contained to change lives and strengthen people's relationship with the Savior.

She expressed gratitude for those who wrote to her while she was on her mission and for the help everyone was to her family during the time of her mother's passing. Many in the audience wiped at their eyes and sniffed back tears, but Kenidee stayed strong, bearing testimony of the Plan of Salvation and of the sealing powers that promised eternal families. She expressed gratitude for her mission and for the strength it was to her during that difficult time when her mother died, and the strength it would be to her the rest of her life.

When she sat down, Kenidee wasn't really certain what she had said, but she felt good about her talk because she knew that the Spirit had guided her and had given her words and promptings of what to say. Although she didn't even know if it had come close to the talk she'd prepared, she knew it was the talk her Father in Heaven had wanted her to give.

With that over, she allowed herself to relax and enjoy the rest of the meeting. She caught her father's eye and he gave her another "thumbs up." She glanced at Matt and Lindsay, then at Cam, who also caught her eye and gave her a wink. He whispered something to Brynn, who was still on his lap, and then he directed his daughter's gaze to the stand where she saw Kenidee. Kenidee gave her a smile, and the little girl waved.

Kenidee wondered how Desiree could bear to be away from those two little angels sitting with their father.

The rest of the meeting flew by. Before she knew it, Kenidee was overwhelmed with ward members welcoming her home and telling her how much they enjoyed her talk.

Elder Taylor led the pack of missionaries in her direction, and for a moment Kenidee felt as though she were back on her mission at a zone conference.

"Thanks so much for coming, Elder Taylor," she said. "What a surprise."

"Hey, you can call me Joey now," he told her.

"Yeah, I guess I can."

While Joey went on to tell her the first names of all the elders standing there, Kenidee caught a glimpse of several young women from the ward gazing her direction, starry-eyed at the crowd of handsome, young returned missionaries surrounding her.

"You guys want to come over to my house for something to eat after the block?" she asked them. "We have plenty of food."

With the promise of food awaiting them later, the former missionaries decided they could stay for the rest of the meetings and joined her in Sunday School. She caught Joey's eye a couple of times during class, wondering during those brief contacts if there was more than just mission camaraderie that brought him to her ward. The thought flattered her but also made her uncomfortable. There had been such strict rules on the mission about elders and sisters developing any sort of relationship that it felt strange, almost wrong, even to think of dating one of her mission elders. Besides, her heart was completely set on Brendan. No one compared to him. No one.

In Relief Society, Kenidee located Sister Monson to warn her about the group of elders coming over afterwards for food.

"That's great!" Sister Monson responded. "The more the merrier. Robin called me and offered to help, so we should have plenty."

After church ended, two cars loaded with elders followed Kenidee home. She wished she could remember all of their first names. Some of them had been such good missionaries and wonderful leaders, and she admired each of them a great deal. But she had to admit she did have a special spot in her heart for Elder Taylor (she still couldn't get used to calling him Joey). He'd been her zone leader when her mom had passed away and had given her more than one blessing to help her through the ordeal. He also had lost his mother, as a young boy, and had been a valuable help and strength to her at that time. It seemed like a strange coincidence that he was also from the Bay Area.

The elders piled out of the cars and followed her inside. Although Kenidee wanted to warn them of the situation with her stepfamily and also about the strange decorating, she didn't have time before they were inside and whisked out onto the back porch for a feast.

Her family was already there, including some of her relatives on her father's side. Most of her mother's family still lived back east and weren't members of the Church. Sadly, she didn't know any of them very well.

"Food's been blessed, boys," her father told the elders. "Go ahead and help yourselves."

The Relief Society ladies hustled back and forth to the kitchen, filling vegetable trays and finding room for a staggering variety of baked cookies and treats. Sister Monson had made her famous crepes that could be filled with meat mixtures or dessert toppings.

"Hey, Kenidee," Elder Taylor called, "we saved you a seat."

Kenidee served herself a spoonful of cut-up fruit and one of the beef stroganoff–filled crepes, and then sat with the elders.

"So, have you felt somewhat like a misfit coming home?" Elder Taylor asked her when she was finally settled on one of the folding chairs. "Are you doing okay?"

"It's been hard. You don't know how many times I've wished I could go back," Kenidee responded.

All the elders reacted empathetically to this. They told her that even though several of them had been home six months or more, they would all go back if they could.

"Prez would take you back in a heartbeat," one of the elders told her. "I heard him say he wished sisters like you and DeWitt could stay two years. He also said that he wished some elders could go home after eighteen months."

They all laughed.

"That was probably Wansgaard and Edgely," one of the elders said. "They were trunky the day they arrived."

They discussed some of the other elders who had been slackers and mentioned a couple of the sisters' names until Elder Taylor put a stop to it. "You have to realize that some of those missionaries were going through some pretty rough stuff. They were doing the best they could."

"Yeah, but Ashford here went through a rough time and she didn't let that keep her from being the best sister in the mission," one of the elders said.

"True," Elder Taylor agreed, "but not everyone is as strong as she is."

*If they only knew how strong I'm not,* Kenidee thought.

"These chocolate chip cookies are amazing," one elder said.

"I've already had three," another elder admitted.

"I'm gonna go get one before Billings eats them all," a different one said. "And those crepes. Have you tried putting raspberries and whipped cream inside?"

Most of the elders drifted back to the food tables, and a couple of the others were busy having a conversation of their own. That left Elder Taylor and Kenidee alone to talk.

"It was such a surprise when you called this morning," Kenidee told him.

"It took a while to find your number," he said. "I finally called the mission home to get it. President Larsen said to tell you hi."

"You told him you were coming?"

"Yeah. He thought it was great."

"Oh," Kenidee said with a nod.

"So, how are you doing, really?" He leaned toward her, his expression of sincerity making it easy to talk.

She explained how difficult coming home had been, but said that with time things were getting a little easier. "Hopefully, I'll only be here a few more weeks, though. Then I'm moving to Salt Lake to live with Sister DeWitt."

"You are?" he asked with excitement. "That's great! I'm going to BYU in the fall. We can hook up out there."

She knew that once Brendan got home and settled at BYU, they'd be spending all of their time together. Still, Elder Taylor was a friend, someone she hoped to stay in touch with.

"Until then, would you want to get together sometime and hang out?" he asked. "We've been having a lot of fun getting dates and going miniature golfing and to movies and stuff. Actually, it doesn't even have to be like a date, just hanging out with mission buddies."

She appreciated his thoughtfulness and knew she would love to hang out with friends from her mission. "Sure, why not?" she answered, figuring the busier she stayed, the quicker time would pass. It would give her something to do and something to look forward to.

"Great. There's a Young Adult dance on Friday night a bunch of us are going to. It's a lot of fun. Do you like dancing?"

"Do I ever!" she exclaimed, excited at the thought of dancing.

"Then I'll pick you up Friday about seven. We can grab something to eat before we go to the dance. I'm not much of a dancer, I'll warn you, but it's still a lot of fun."

"Okay. Thanks Elder. . . I mean, Joey."

He got to his feet and motioned to one of the other elders that it was time to go.

After they finished their plates of food, Kenidee thanked them for coming and walked them to the door. They made sure to thank her father and the Relief Society ladies for the food.

"Such nice boys," her father said. "I'm so glad they could come, especially since we had so much food."

"Those guys can eat more food than a small country," Kenidee told him. "I've seen them—they have bottomless pits for stomachs."

"Kenidee!" called a familiar, yet annoying, voice.

The hair on her neck stood up. Gilbert!

# CHAPTER 5

"Hey," Gilbert said, approaching her quickly.

"Hi, Gilbert. I didn't see you come in."

"I've been here for a while. I just stayed out of the way until all your friends left. Elders from your mission?"

"Yes. I didn't realize so many lived in this area."

"That sure was nice of them to come. Your talk went well today. I wondered if I could get some of those scripture references you used. And that quote, too."

"Sure," Kenidee told him.

"Could I call you later and get them from you?"

Sister Monson walked by just then with another pot of stroganoff filling.

"Gilbert," Sister Monson exclaimed when she saw him with Kenidee. Fully aware of Gilbert's crush on Kenidee, she quickly piped up, "Could you help me, Gilbert? This pot is very heavy."

"Yes, of course," he said.

"It just needs to go over there on that serving table."

Gilbert took the pot.

"Just follow me, Gilbert," she said, when he didn't move.

He started walking, then stopped and turned. "I'll call you later then."

Kenidee smiled and nodded. Then she immediately hurried to the opposite side of the yard where Matt and Lindsay and Cam were sitting and watching Cam's daughters make a tower on the grass out of plastic cups and plates.

"Your fan club finally leave?" Matt said.

"That wasn't my fan club," she replied.

"Are you kidding? Those elders were looking at you like the last Christmas present under the tree," Matt told her.

"Whatever, Matt." She refused to believe it.

"Especially that one guy you were talking to before they left."

"That was Elder Taylor. He was my ZL when Mom died. He was a ton of help to me."

"Looks like he still wants to be a ton of help," Matt joked, elbowing Cam.

"Leave her alone." Lindsay swatted her husband on the shoulder. "Why wouldn't they all be interested in Kenidee? She's beautiful, intelligent, and they have the mission in common."

"I never would have hit on any of the sisters in my mission," Matt said.

"Me either," Cam said. "Of course, none of the sisters in my mission looked like Kenidee." Cam elbowed Matt.

"Ow, dude!" Matt exclaimed, rubbing his rib cage.

"Serves you right. Don't tease Kenidee."

"It's all right. I'm used to it," Kenidee said.

"Daddy?" Amanda said, "Can I have another chocolate chip cookie?"

"Mmm, that sounds good," Kenidee said. "I think I'd like one, too. Would you like to go get one with me?"

"Can sissy have one?" Amanda asked.

Kenidee looked into Brynn's cherubic face and found herself wondering again how Desiree could stay away from these adorable little girls.

"Of course. Let's take her with us, and she can pick out the one she wants. Is that okay, Cam?"

"Sure. Maybe you girls could bring back one for your daddy."

"Okay, Daddy," Amanda said.

"Tay, Dee-dee," Brynn copied.

Excited that Brynn would allow her to pick her up, Kenidee held the toddler in one arm and held Amanda's hand as they walked to the desert table, keeping a roving eye out for Gilbert.

"Mmm, took-tee," Brynn said.

"She loves chocolate," Amanda told Kenidee.

"So do I," Kenidee said.

Grabbing a napkin and piling on half a dozen cookies, Kenidee, with the girls in tow, returned to Matt, Lindsay, and Cam, who were all talking to . . . Gilbert.

She rolled her eyes and saw Cam smiling at her. He thought it was funny that Gilbert was on her trail. It wasn't that Gilbert wasn't a nice, sweet guy. He just wasn't her type. And she didn't want to encourage him by being overly friendly.

"Hey, Gilbert, sounds like things are going really well for you," Matt said. "With gas prices the way they are, I'll bet a lot of people are looking for smaller, more gas-efficient cars."

"Our SUV sales have dropped fifty percent."

"Throw in a boat and I'll buy one," Matt said.

"Oh no," Gilbert said seriously, "we never could do that. When you look at the profit margin and cost—"

"I was kidding," Matt interrupted him.

"Oh," Gilbert forced a laugh. "Right."

Cam's daughters ended up smearing chocolate all over their faces and dresses. "Give me a break, you two," he said, trying to wipe at their mouths with a napkin.

"Here, let's take them inside and wash them up," Kenidee said, grateful for a reason to get away from Gilbert.

"Whoa!" Cam stopped short when they walked through the sliding glass doors into the kaleidoscopic kitchen. "I think my retinas have just been fried."

"A little bright in here for you?" Kenidee laughed, leading the way through the kitchen into the bathroom.

"That room has is its own energy source. You probably don't even need lights at night."

"Robin likes bright colors," Kenidee said as they turned on the light in the bathroom, with its lime green walls.

"I could never relax here. These colors create too much energy. I'm exhausted just looking at them."

They began to wash the girls' hands and faces.

"Robin is very energetic," Kenidee told him. "I'm sure that's why she loves all this color. It matches her personality perfectly."

"More took-tee," Brynn said.

"Sorry, sweetie. No more cookie for you."

Brynn began to whimper.

"She needs a nap," Cam said.

"You could take some cookies home for later," Kenidee offered.

"Can we, Daddy?" Amanda begged.

He gave in without much resistance.

"Yes!" Amanda shouted.

"Yeth. Lots of took-tees," Brynn echoed.

Kenidee managed to find some Ziplock bags and loaded them with cookies just as Robin came in and saw what she was doing.

"Here," Robin said. "Let's send more of this food with them. Cam, you'll eat this later, won't you?"

"Sure," he answered. "Thanks."

"I'm sure you get tired of fixing your own meals. I'll give you plenty so you can get a few meals out of it."

Robin arranged food in several disposable containers and placed them inside plastic grocery bags. "There now," she said to the two little girls. "I put plenty of yummy treats in there for you. Next time you come, maybe you can play with my little girl."

"You have a little girl?" Amanda asked in amazement.

"She just turned six."

"I'm almost five." Amanda held up five fingers.

"Where is Rachel?" Kenidee asked.

"She fell asleep a while ago. Guess the party wore her out. Looks like someone else is getting sleepy."

Brynn's eyes were drifting closed.

"Here," Kenidee said, taking the child from Cam. "I'll take her while you gather up your things."

He picked up the bags of food and a diaper bag full of the girls' quiet toys for church and started for the door.

"Can we come back and play with Rachel and visit the treat lady?" Amanda asked.

Cam smiled at Kenidee.

"Of course you can," Kenidee answered her. "Anytime you want."

Amanda's smile dimpled her cheeks. She had a Shirley Temple look about her with her curls, her tiny, upturned nose, and her dimples.

Carrying Brynn, Kenidee walked the little family outside to their car.

"Hop in your car seat," Cam told Amanda.

"Look!" Amanda held up a small toy teddy bear. "We got this at McDonald's. Mine is purple, Brynn's is pink."

"Very cute," Kenidee said.

"I have lots of toys. Can you come see them?"

"Sure. Not today, but soon, okay?"

"Okay."

Cam reached for Brynn, who was fast asleep in Kenidee's arms, slobbering contentedly on her shoulder.

"I'm sorry. Look what she did," Cam apologized.

"No biggy," Kenidee said. "I can throw it in the wash."

With Brynn safely buckled into her car seat, Cam was ready to go.

"Thanks for letting us come. It was fun."

"You're welcome. I enjoyed meeting your daughters. They are precious."

"Thanks. I think so too."

"See ya, Cam."

She waved as he drove away. They seemed to be doing well, but she knew it was hard for Cam to be raising two daughters on his own. She wished he could find himself a wonderful girl and get married again, this time to someone who wanted a temple marriage and an eternal family, like he did. Some girl would be lucky to have him as a husband.

\* \* \*

Friday morning, with her arms loaded with laundry, Kenidee carefully made her way among the toys comprising the obstacle course in the hallway, stepped gingerly through the cluttered kitchen, and entered the laundry room, where clothes were piled to the ceiling. She'd put off washing clothes for the last few days in hopes that Robin would eventually clear out all the unwashed and unfolded clothes in the laundry room. But that hadn't happened, and Kenidee was wearing her last clean pair of undergarments. She had no choice.

Opening the door to the dryer, she found a load of clean clothes. Yanking them out by the handful, she placed them on the only empty spot on the counter, then emptied the contents of the washer into the dryer and started the cycle. Finally, she could put a load of her own clothes into the washer.

As Kenidee walked into the kitchen to get a drink of water, she opened the cupboard to find it empty. A sink full of dishes explained the lack of clean drinking glasses. Clenching her fists and shutting her eyes, she concentrated on breathing deeply and tried to calm herself. But she couldn't. All she could think about was how clean and tidy her mother had always kept their home.

"That's it!" she exclaimed and jerked open the door to the dishwasher and began loading dishes. Once she had turned it on she cleared off the counters, wiped them with disinfectant, swept and mopped the floor, and polished the fingerprints from the sliding glass door. By this time her load of laundry was done, so she moved it to the dryer and started another load of Robin's kids' clothes.

Grumbling, she began the job of picking up toys and clothes from the floor in the hallway, living room, and family room. Hoping she got the toys into the right rooms, Kenidee closed the doors and pulled out the vacuum. It didn't take long to work up a sweat as she vacuumed the carpets and then dusted and polished the furniture in both rooms. By keeping the laundry going nonstop, she finally finished her clothes and began folding the mountain of clothes belonging mostly to Robin's kids.

Worn out by the time she finished cleaning the house and doing the laundry, Kenidee nonetheless felt satisfaction getting it done. Of course, she knew that the inevitable would happen—the kids would come home from school that afternoon and destroy all of her hard work.

Still, for a moment, the cleanliness felt so good.

The shower felt invigorating as Kenidee got ready for her evening with friends, grateful that she had somewhere to go where she didn't have to hear the two boys fighting, Rachel whining, and Robin laughing, or watch her father sit and do nothing about any of it.

* * *

"Kenidee, hi."

"Hello, Dolly!" Then Kenidee realized what she said and laughed. "Do people sing to you a lot?"

"Are you kidding? All the time. And they all act like they're the first ones to ever do it."

"I'll bet. Hey, what's going on?"

"I just called to tell you that my grandmother is doing better, and we might be home sooner than we thought."

"That's great, because I haven't found a job yet. I might as well wait and start looking when I move to Salt Lake."

"Okay, I'll keep you posted," Dolly said. "I just wanted to give you a heads up so you could start making plans."

"You're still sure you want me?"

"Are you kidding? I'm lost without you. I can't wait to see you."

"Good. I've missed you, too. Oh," Kenidee remembered, "you'll never guess who I'm hanging out with tonight."

"Uh, wow, I can't imagine. Is it someone famous?"

"Hardly. Try Elder Taylor."

"Our Elder Taylor?"

"Yep. That's the one. We're going to dinner and then to a dance. How fun does that sound?"

"You have a date?"

"It's not a date," Kenidee explained. "A bunch of us are going together."

"That sounds like a blast. I wish I were there."

"Me too. It would be tons more fun with you." She named the other elders from their mission who were also going to the dance.

"You're having so much more fun than I am," Dolly grumbled. "I love hanging out with my mom and grandma, but please, how many games of Parcheesi can a person play? And reruns of Lawrence Welk? It's enough to drive a person mad. My biggest thrill is going to the grocery store to buy Depends."

Kenidee burst out laughing.

"Let's pray your grandma gets better—faster—so we can get together soon. Elder Taylor, I mean, Joey, wants to see you again too. He's going to BYU in the fall so I'm sure we'll see him out there."

"What about Brendan?"

"He'll start at the Y in January. It will be tricky, since I want to go to the University of Utah, but we'll find a place to live somewhere in the middle. I'm not worried about it because I know we're supposed to be together."

"What if you suddenly develop feelings for Elder Taylor," Dolly baited.

"I won't. My heart is set on Brendan," Kenidee told her. "Someday you'll meet him, and you'll understand why I'm so crazy about him."

"I guess," Dolly said. "Can't imagine too many guys being neater than Elder Taylor. I think you are crazy not to grab onto him. I know I would. And I wouldn't let go."

"I'll let him know you want to go out with him," Kenidee said.

"Kenidee, don't you dare!"

"That's what friends are for," Kenidee told her.

"Just don't go blurting out that I want him to ask me out. I guess you could hint around a little though, you know, to see if he's interested."

"When I see him, I'll bring it up."

Dolly giggled. "Okay, just be subtle."

"I will."

"Give me a call as soon as you get home."

"I promise," Kenidee said.

"And start packing your things. I'm sure we'll be heading back to Salt Lake in a few days."

"I will. I'm so excited!"

As the girls hung up, Kenidee's spirits skyrocketed. She wouldn't have to deal much longer with Robin's noisy kids, a messy house, or the constant romancing between her dad and Robin.

"Kenidee!" one of Robin's sons hollered at the top of his lungs. "A boy's here for you."

Feeling her cheeks flush, Kenidee grabbed her purse and raced for the front door. When she and Matt were younger, her father had never allowed them to holler through the house when someone was wanted at the door or on the phone.

As Kenidee hurried down the hallway, her mind preoccupied, she failed to see the toy dump truck on the floor. As if the fates had written some ridiculous script for her life, she managed to trip over it and tumble into the entryway.

"Kenidee!" Joey exclaimed as he rushed to help her up. "Are you okay?"

"Mikey!" Robin yelled from the family room. "What happened?"

Mikey didn't answer but instead ran to his room and slammed the door.

Just as she'd expected, the minute the kids came home, all her hard work on the house had been obliterated.

"Can you walk?" Joey asked.

She tested her leg and winced at the pain in her right hip. After a few seconds, the pain subsided. "I think I'm okay. I'm used to dancing with pain."

"Really?" He held the front door open for her as they walked outside.

"I haven't been able to get daily studio time since I've been home, but before my mission I did ballet five or six days a week. Something always hurt—a blister, a pulled muscle, knees, ankles, hips. You name it, it hurt at one point."

"Just from ballet?"

"Hey, ballerinas aren't pansies—they're amazing athletes."

"I had no idea," he said, obviously impressed.

"You think it's easy standing on your toes doing leaps and pirouettes?"

"I guess not."

"When you get to the Y, you should go watch a ballet," she suggested. "You'd be impressed."

"Okay," he said, "if you'll go with me."

"Actually, I'll be living with Dolly. She loves the ballet also."

"We can bring her, too," he replied.

Kenidee smiled. Dolly would be proud of her.

Then her smile faded. No one else was in the car. He'd said this wasn't a date.

*Maybe we're just meeting everyone there,* she reasoned.

She decided that at the right time she would tell him about Dolly and let him know that she herself was already spoken for. She wasn't about to let anything spoil things between her and Brendan with less than three months to go.

* * *

The dance was in full swing when they arrived. Joey and Kenidee had gone to dinner, then met four other mission elders and their dates at the dance. She kept wanting to bring up Brendan, but the time never seemed right. And now that they were with a big group, she wasn't so concerned about just the two of them being together.

For eighteen months, Kenidee had tuned out pop music. Hearing it now, this loud, bewildered her.

"Hey, you okay?" Joey asked.

"Yeah," she answered loudly, trying to be heard over the volume of the music. "I haven't listened to music like this yet."

"Oh, you want to go outside for a minute and get used to it first?"

"Could we?" She was impressed by his thoughtfulness.

"Sure. Hey guys," he called to the other elders, "we'll be inside in a minute."

He led the way outdoors, where the music could still be heard, but not blasting quite as loudly.

"I wasn't expecting that," she explained. "It caught me off guard."

"I know what you mean. I didn't watch TV or go to a movie for almost a month after I got home. I still listen to church music in my car and in my room."

"It's so hard," she told him. "I don't want to lose that spirit I had with me on my mission, but normal life seems to drive it away."

"Right now I'm working construction with my dad," Joey said. "You wouldn't believe some of the filth I hear. I just have to tune it out. I sing hymns a lot in my head."

"Just part of the adjustment, I guess," she replied.

"I think you're doing a pretty good job of it."

"Thanks." She strained to listen, but the music had stopped. Then another song started. A slow, easy ballad by one of her favorite country singers.

"I love this song." Kenidee said.

"You feel like dancing?"

She nodded.

They hurried inside and wove their way through the couples on the dance floor until they were in the middle of the gym. Then, taking Kenidee into his arms, Joey began to sway gently with the rhythm of the music. She felt stiff and uncomfortable in his arms. Reminding herself that this wasn't a date, just mission friends hanging out together, she tried to relax. But she just couldn't get Brendan off her mind.

Because the next song was also mellow, they continued dancing. The other elders and their dates eventually gravitated toward Kenidee and Joey. Kenidee noticed that the girl with Elder Billings kept looking at them; actually she was looking at Joey.

It wasn't hard to tell that the girl had a major crush on Joey. Kenidee didn't blame her. He really was a great guy. If Brendan weren't in the picture, Kenidee would probably be open to dating him and seeing what developed. But he *was* in the picture, so she wanted to make sure she didn't lead him on.

The dance heated up again when a fast song came on. This one had been popular before her mission, so Kenidee found herself loosening up and enjoying the dance. Elder Billings was a big teddy bear of a guy, not a half-bad dancer. He knew some hip-hop moves and started to put on a show. Besides ballet, Kenidee had taken jazz and hip-hop at her studio and even though it wasn't her specialty, she could pull off a few pretty spectacular moves herself.

"Hey, all right!" Joey exclaimed when she joined Elder Billings.

Allowing herself permission to have fun and even show off a bit, Kenidee kept up with Billings until the song ended. A crowd had gathered around them and exploded in applause when they were done. Kenidee's face flushed with the attention. Billings's face was flushed and sweat trickled down the sides of his face.

"It's like an oven in here," he exclaimed. "I need a cold drink."

Noticing that his date wasn't excited about leaving the dance floor, Kenidee stepped up.

"I need one too," Kenidee said. "Joey, why don't you take care of Lisa while I go with Billings." She couldn't remember the elder's first name, but it didn't matter. Everyone called him by his last name anyway.

"That's better," Billings said after he had pulled in a breath of fresh air in the hallway.

"You're pretty good," she told him. "Where'd you learn to pop and lock like that?"

"School. It was cool to dance where I grew up, so my friends and I had a lot of fun practicing. We had a little group we put together. We used to perform during half-times and stuff. How about you?"

"In a studio. I'm really a ballerina, but I love jazz and hip-hop, too."

"Ballet, huh? Impressive. My sister dances with the San Francisco Ballet."

"She does! I bet I've watched her dance. Wait! Heather Billings. Of course, she was the lead in *Giselle*. She's amazing."

"If you ever want to meet her, just let me know," he offered.

"For sure. I'd love to."

They stayed out in the hallway for a few more dances and talked about the mission and coming home and making plans for the future.

"Mission life was so simple," Billings said. "The biggest decision I made each day was which tie to wear. Now I have to decide which job to take, which car to buy, which school to go to, which classes to take, what to major in, which girls to date . . . sometimes I feel like my head's going to explode."

Kenidee nodded with understanding. She completely related to him and his feelings of being overwhelmed. She enjoyed talking with him and just knowing that she wasn't alone in this whole "adjustment" thing. Others struggled with it too.

By the time they returned to the dance floor, Joey and Lisa were in each other's arms, swaying to another slow song. Billings and Kenidee began to dance and finished out the song, then traded back with their dates. Lisa looked decidedly unexcited to go back to Billings, and Kenidee hoped he didn't notice. She didn't care if Joey and Lisa hooked up but not while Lisa was supposed to be with Billings.

On the way home, Kenidee spoke excitedly about the dance. "I had such a good time. There were only those few songs that were obnoxious, but the rest were pretty good."

"I had fun. You're a great dancer. I guess your hip didn't bother you?"

"It's a little sore. I'll probably have a bruise on my behind from falling, but like I said, I'm used to dancing through pain."

They chatted the rest of the way home until he pulled up in front of the house. Then Kenidee thanked him for the fun evening. He asked if he could call her again.

Swallowing hard before she answered, Kenidee stammered, "Uh, well, you see—it's just that I have a missionary coming home in August."

"Is that ring from him?" Joey asked.

She nodded. "But I love hanging out with all of you. You know, as friends."

"Sure," he said. "I understand."

"Well, thanks again," she said, as the quietness grew tense. Although she wanted to say more about Dolly, she didn't feel it was the right moment to bring up the subject.

"Good night," he told her.

She got out of the car and watched him drive away.

*I hope I don't regret that.* The random thought surprised her. She shook her head to dispel the notion. Brendan would be home soon, and they would be together. That was something she didn't doubt.

Opening the front door quietly so she didn't wake anyone, Kenidee stepped inside. As she tiptoed her way to her room, she noticed a blue glow from the television in the family room. She went to see who was still up and discovered Robin and her father on the couch, snuggled together, both of them snoring softly. Kenidee looked at the two of them and sighed.

*Nothing's going to change,* she told herself. *I guess I'd better just get used to it.* But that was the problem. She didn't think she ever would be comfortable seeing her dad with a woman other than her mom.

Too tired to call Dolly, she got ready for bed, said her prayers, and then lay down, grateful that she was one day closer to leaving and one day closer to having Brendan home.

# CHAPTER 6

"Honey?"

Kenidee stirred at the sound of her father's voice. She opened one eye and looked at the clock that read 6:15.

"Yeah," she answered groggily, noting the morning light filtering into her room.

He walked in and sat on the bed.

She forced both eyes to open and focus on him.

"I'm driving up to Reno today, but I wanted to talk to you before I left. Thanks so much for helping with the house yesterday. Robin really appreciated it. She wanted to thank you herself, but she didn't see you before you left last night and you got home so late."

"I didn't do it to help her," she told him as a yawn took over.

"Oh," he paused.

"I couldn't stand the mess any longer, Dad. Why can't she make those kids pick up after themselves? I nearly broke my leg last night, tripping over one of their toys."

"I heard. Sorry, honey."

They both knew how perfectly clean and tidy Kenidee's mom used to keep their home.

"I'll talk to her about it."

"Thanks."

He looked at her for a moment before he spoke. "I know this adjustment is hard, but it just takes time. If we all try, we can make this work."

She propped herself up on one elbow. "I don't think you could've married anyone more different from Mom."

He nodded slowly while forming his response. "That's true," he said, "and no one could ever take your mom's place. But Robin's a wonderful person, and I love her. You just need to give her a chance. Just give it time."

"Actually, Dad, that's something I've been meaning to talk to you about."

He lifted his chin with interest.

"I probably won't be around much longer. I've decided to move to Salt Lake City to live with Sister DeWitt."

His mouth dropped open, and his eyebrows lifted with surprise.

"She's in St. George for a week or so, but then she'll be home. That's when I plan to move."

"But you just got home. You can't leave yet," he protested.

"I think it's for the best. This is just too hard for me. I don't see how come that's so difficult for you to understand."

"I do understand, but if you'd just try."

She felt her resentment start to rise.

"That's all I ask," he said, "Just give her a chance. I know you'd learn to accept her."

"I'm still not even used to having Mom gone and our home gone. I don't think I can accept her until I've done that," Kenidee retorted.

"Well, what about Matt and Lindsay's baby? Don't you want to be here for that?"

"For sure I'll come home when the baby is born," she told him. "And you still have business in Salt Lake, so you can visit me when you come."

"I suppose so," he said sadly. "I don't like having you leave already. Maybe I was wrong to get married so quickly. But what's done is done."

"I know, Dad," she told him, trying to mask the irritation in her voice. Her best recourse was to change the subject.

"It's not like I wouldn't be moving there when Brendan gets home anyway."

Her father remained silent.

"It's going to be okay, Dad," she said as optimistically as she could, although her heart ached as she realized they would never have the same relationship they'd had before. "I'm just facing reality. You've got these guys to focus on now. I need to focus on mine and Brendan's future. Moving to Salt Lake will give me a chance to find a good job, apply to the U, and get settled before he gets home. It's all good. This is just part of my being a grown-up."

He reached out and placed the palm of his hand on her cheek. "I guess so. I never wanted to hurt you or make it hard for you."

"I know, Dad," she replied.

He sighed heavily. "I had a feeling when you went on this mission that I would never have you home again to stay. But I hate having you leave under these circumstances."

"It's really hard for me here. I feel like I'm mourning Mom's death again. Maybe if it were just you and me it would be different."

"Maybe it would."

"I think I'll accept it easier if I'm not right here . . ." *watching you and Robin kiss and act like teenagers.*

Her father's expression was lined with sadness.

"I know we haven't been able to spend a lot of time together since you got home," he apologized.

"It's okay, Dad. I told you, I'm a big girl now."

"I know." His voice sounded gravelly. He cleared his throat. "That's the hardest part."

She sat up and gave him a hug. "I love you, Dad."

"I love you too, sweetie."

"Have a nice trip," she told him as a knot swelled in her throat.

After her father shut the door, she pulled her pillow over her head and began to cry.

*Hurry home, Brendan. Please, hurry home.*

* * *

"So, how'd it go?" Dolly asked when she called to check in on Monday.

"It was fun. Billings went with us, and he's a total kook," Kenidee told her.

"I always liked him. He was my ZL for a while, and even though he's hardly ever serious, he's a very spiritual person. He gave great trainings."

"Well, last night he was a dancing machine. You should've seen him." Kenidee giggled as she pictured Elder Billings being the center of attention on the dance floor.

"And how was Elder Taylor?"

"He's such a nice guy. I think I'll always have a special spot in my heart for him because he helped me so much on my mission. But I'm not interested."

"Are you sure?" Dolly asked.

"I'm sure. And we talked about getting together when he moves to Utah," Kenidee told her.

"Oh, you did?" Dolly said with disappointment.

"I don't mean it like that. I told him he should go to a ballet, and he said he would and I told him you liked ballet too."

"You did?"

"Yes, and he wants you to come, too."

"He does?" Dolly shrieked. "That is so awesome! Thank you, Kenidee. I have a good feeling about this. Maybe that's why I haven't had any guys ask me out or anything. Maybe I'm supposed to be available for Elder Taylor, I mean Joey. Isn't that the best thought ever?"

"Yes," Kenidee said quickly.

"Did he say anything else? Tell me everything!"

"There's nothing else to tell. That's about all that was said. And then I told him about Brendan."

"Did he seem disappointed? I mean, he must have liked you to ask you to go in the first place."

Kenidee didn't admit that Joey did seem a little disappointed. "He was fine. I think he just knows how hard it is to come back and get into socializing. He was just being nice."

"That's so him, isn't it? He is nice. And cute! He's seriously cute. Don't you think he's cute?"

Kenidee laughed. "Yes. He is. But not as cute as my Brendan."

Dolly didn't say anything for a moment.

"Dolly?" Kenidee said. "Are you there?"

"I just had a thought," Dolly answered. "Can I ask you something?"

"Sure, anything."

"Have you ever considered the possibility that something might not work out with Brendan?"

"Why do you say that?" Kenidee asked with alarm. "Of course it's going to work out. I still feel as strongly about him as I did when I left on my mission. We're practically engaged."

"And you're sure he hasn't changed?"

"I'm sure of it."

"I just hate to see you let someone as wonderful as Elder Taylor go, you know, just in case. I mean, I'm glad you did because now I can have him, but what if—"

"I don't need to keep Elder Taylor or anyone else in my life as a 'backup,'" Kenidee said coolly, hurt that Dolly would even suggest that Brendan was anything but totally devoted to her.

"I'm sorry. I didn't mean anything. I know Brendan's really wonderful."

"He is. No one can compare to him. I'm the luckiest girl alive to have him."

"I know you deserve the best," Dolly told her. "I didn't mean to upset you."

"It's okay." Kenidee decided to change subjects. She didn't even like to entertain the thought that she and Brendan wouldn't work out. "So, when do you think you'll be back in Salt Lake?"

"Well, Grandma isn't doing as well as she should be. I'll just have to give you an update every day or so."

"Okay, well keep me posted."

"I will. Guess you could always come to St. George and stay with us here. I know I'd appreciate it. Do you realize that all old people talk about is their health? It's disgusting."

Kenidee laughed. "Gee, as tempting as that offer is, I think I'll pass. I still have a few things to do here before I move. If I change my mind though, I'll let you know."

The two girls said good-bye, and Kenidee decided to go for a jog. She had been hoping to get to the gym to work out but just couldn't seem to squeeze it into her day.

Tying her cross-trainers, she glanced out the window once more and noticed that it was getting close to dinnertime. She wasn't hungry. Besides that, eating with Robin's kids had a tendency to ruin her appetite. She did have to admit, though, Robin was a good cook.

Stopping in the kitchen to fill her water bottle with ice and water, she smelled something delicious baking in the oven. The makings of a green salad sat on the counter. Out the back window, Kenidee saw Robin and the two boys painting a tall cardboard box so it looked like a spaceship. Running around in a princess costume, waving a wand with ribbons trailing behind, was Rachel, a child who clearly lived more in fantasy than in reality.

Kenidee stepped onto the front porch and drew in a few breaths of fresh air. Her muscles seemed to crave activity and exercise. She loved the feeling of pushing her body to its physical limits and waking up to stiff, aching muscles, a result of her hard work. But more than that, she loved how a workout cleansed her mind, cleared her thoughts, and lifted her spirits. Right now that was exactly what she needed.

Robin's strange laugh echoed from the backyard, the children's giggles accompanying it. The sound pushed Kenidee off the porch and into action. She really wanted to be okay with these people, but something inside her kept rejecting the idea. The wall of pain she'd built around her heart when her mother died was keeping others out, particularly her father's new family. Right now she didn't want to pull down that wall. She didn't feel like she should have to.

Starting off at an easy pace, Kenidee tackled the first hill with ease, panting slightly as she crested the top, and kept going toward the neighborhood park. Several people were outside in their yards and waved as she jogged by.

The road wound slowly up another hill, this one not so steep, and led into the park, where several teenage boys played tennis, a group of men played football, and a dozen children swarmed the playground. Following the trail that meandered around the perimeter of the park, Kenidee dodged a few low-hanging tree branches and kept up her steady pace, slowing only to take a drink. The muscles in her thighs burned, as did her lungs, but she welcomed the sensations.

"Kenidee?" a woman's voice called.

Kenidee turned to see a couple on the sidewalk. She smiled when she realized it was Bishop and Sister Monson.

"Oh, don't hug me," she said as Sister Monson reached to embrace her. "I'm so sweaty."

"I don't care," Sister Monson said. "It's lovely to see you, Kenidee. How are you?"

"Good," Kenidee responded.

The bishop nodded. "Happy to hear that. How have you been adjusting now that you've had some time with your family?"

"Okay, I guess. It's still hard."

Sister Monson's face reflected understanding. "Once you get to know her, I think you'll discover for yourself that Robin is a wonderful person."

Kenidee nodded, not really sure what to say. That's all she ever heard about Robin—such a wonderful person. She wasn't convinced.

"You'll have to come visit us sometime. Bring your mission photos," Sister Monson said.

"That would be nice. I'll try to before I leave for Salt Lake."

"Are you going for a visit?" Sister Monson asked.

"No, I'm going to move there and live with one of my former companions," Kenidee responded

"So soon? You just got home."

"I don't really have anything here anymore. No one wants to hire me for a job temporarily, and Dad is busy with his new family. I just think it's best if I get a start on my future. That's where I want to go to college, and I'd be moving anyway when Brendan gets home."

"How's he doing?" Sister Monson asked with interest.

"He's an AP right now and still writes me every week," she answered proudly. "Well, almost every week. I still haven't heard from him since I got home because he didn't have my new address, so his letters have to be forwarded."

"Glad to hear it. He's a sharp young man," the bishop said.

"Thanks. I'll let you know what happens after he gets home."

"You'd better," Sister Monson instructed. "I want you to bring him over when you can. I need to get to know this boy a little better."

"I'd love that. And thank you again for helping to feed everyone on Sunday. It was delicious."

"I was happy to do it for you, dear. I felt really close to your mom that day."

Kenidee smiled at the thought. "I did too."

"Let's get together and go to lunch soon, before you leave," Sister Monson said.

"I'd like that," Kenidee answered.

The bishop glanced at his watch. "We'd better get home, Cheryl. The kids will be coming in a few minutes."

"We're babysitting tonight," Sister Monson explained. "I'll call you soon."

They went separate directions, and Kenidee picked up her pace again, thinking about how grateful she was for people like the Monsons who hadn't forgotten about her mother and still liked to keep her memory alive. Maybe that was the problem. She didn't feel like her father was still trying to keep her mother's memory alive.

She was lost in thought when a football suddenly spiraled past her. Out of nowhere, a monster of a man stampeded into her, tackling her to the ground.

"Sorry," he mumbled, getting to his feet.

Her right knee and the palms of her hands screamed in pain from scraping across the pavement.

Reaching to help her up, the man apologized again. "I was going out for a pass; I didn't even see you. Are you okay?"

"I'm fine," she lied, ready to scream like a baby the first night without her bottle.

"You're bleeding," he told her.

"I'll be fine," she said again, starting to limp away.

"You're sure I can't do something to help?"

*I think you've done enough.* "No, really. But thanks."

"You might want to get something on that knee."

She looked at him with curiosity. Was he serious? *Duh, of course I need to put something on it. Like a tourniquet.* "Good idea," she said and limped faster away from him.

The restrooms were near the playground. She hobbled into the ladies' room and reached for paper towels, but the dispenser was empty. Resorting to a rolled-up wad of toilet paper, she dabbed at the scraped and bleeding flesh on her knee and winced as the water stung her wound.

Outside she found a bench to sit on and examined the damage more closely.

"You might need more than toilet paper to stop the bleeding," a man's voice advised.

Kenidee shut her eyes, not believing her luck—or maybe it was her lack of it.

"Hi, Cam." She looked up as he walked toward her. He was trying—and failing—to suppress his laughter.

"It's not funny, you know. It really hurts."

"What happened?" he asked, sitting down on the bench next to her.

"One of those big oafs over there went out for a pass and creamed me in the process."

"You sure he wasn't making a pass at you?" Cam joked.

"Har, har. He probably weighs three hundred pounds. I'm surprised he didn't create a crater when he landed. Didn't you feel the ground shake?"

"That was him? I thought we were having an earthquake."

She dabbed again at the wound, the bleeding finally stopping. Her knee looked like hamburger.

"That's pretty bad." Cam knew he was mentioning the obvious. "I don't have a Band-Aid that big, but I have a Huggies diaper."

"Oh, that would be lovely wrapped around my leg."

"Sorry, that's all I've got. They're super-absorbent, with Kermit and Miss Piggy on them."

"No, thanks. Where are the girls anyway?"

"Over there, digging in the sand," he answered, pointing toward the far side of the playground.

"That's nice you'd bring them to play after work." She was impressed at what a thoughtful dad he was.

"I have an ulterior motive. I want them to play hard so that when we get home all I have to do is give them a bath and put them to bed. I didn't get to go to work today, so I have a ton of work to do at home tonight."

"Why didn't you get to work? Was one of the girls sick?"

"No, nothing like that. My sitter got a job in the city and starts next Monday. She called this morning and said she needed to fill out paperwork and do an orientation for the job. There wasn't time to get anyone else."

"What a pain," Kenidee said, empathizing with plans that seemed to go awry.

"Yeah, it totally messed up my day."

"You should have called me, Cam. I could have helped you."

"You know, I didn't even think of it. But thanks for offering, Kenidee."

"Well, I'll be around for a few more weeks, so if you need any help during that time, just let me know."

"I will." He sat up to get a better look at what the girls were doing, then, satisfied they were fine, relaxed again. "So where are you going in a few weeks?"

"I'm moving to Salt Lake City to live with one of my missionary companions."

"Oh, how does your family feel about that?"

"I told my dad this morning. He wasn't happy about it but he understood. Matt and Linz don't really want me to go."

"Are you doing this because you want to move there or because you don't want to live here?"

Kenidee was surprised at Cam's astuteness. "I'm doing this because . . . well, I can't . . . you don't know what it's like . . . okay, both I guess. I miss Dolly, my old companion, but I really don't like living at home with my dad and Robin and her kids. It's just too confusing. My emotions are always bungee jumping. I'm hoping that maybe I'll like them more and accept them more when I'm away from them."

"What about your boyfriend? Doesn't he come home soon?"

"I'll come home for a little while when he gets back, but he's going to BYU in January so I'd be moving to Utah anyway."

"I guess that makes sense. Are things still good with him?"

"Yeah, his letters are really—"

Cam suddenly bolted from the bench and ran to the playground. Little Brynn was crying and had a mouthful of sand.

Kenidee hobbled after him to see if she could help.

"That mean boy pushed sissy," Amanda said, pointing at a little boy who was far off in the distance.

"What happened?" Kenidee asked.

"She fell off the slide," Cam told her, cradling the toddler in his arms and trying to clean the sand from her nose and mouth. Her top lip was swollen and bleeding.

"I'll get some wet toilet paper," Kenidee said, rushing to the bathroom as rapidly as her injury would allow and then hurrying back to his side.

Cam accepted the soggy wad in her hand and wiped gently at the child's mouth. She spit out sand and blood until they finally had her cleaned up.

Kenidee held Amanda, who was as upset as Brynn.

"Why was that boy so mean?" Amanda asked her.

"I don't know," Kenidee replied. "Maybe his mommy didn't teach him to be nice, especially to girls. Look." Kenidee lifted her leg and showed her scraped up knee. "That's what a boy did to me just a little while ago."

"Owie," Brynn said, pointing at the wound. "Bad boy."

Kenidee and Cam laughed.

"That's right, sweetie," Cam said. "Both of those boys need a time out."

The evening shadows grew longer and the sound of crickets filled the air.

"Guess we'd better get you two home and in the tub," Cam told his daughters.

"Here, I'll get those." Kenidee put Amanda down and picked up Cam's diaper bag, cell phone, and keys from the bench.

Cam carried the littlest one to the car, while Kenidee and Amanda followed.

Kenidee helped get the two girls strapped into their seat belts, then stowed the diaper bag on the floor beneath Brynn's feet.

"You want a ride home?" Cam asked.

Her injured knee was stiff and sore. "Sure, thanks."

The two little girls played with toys and giggled as they drove down the road.

"They sure are cute," Kenidee told him.

"Thanks. They're a lot of fun."

"Is it hard, alone?" she asked.

"Sure, especially because I don't know little girl stuff like how to do their hair or what kind of clothes they like to wear. With boys, it's just a T-shirt and jeans. Girls like their shoes and hair bows to match their outfits and stuff."

Kenidee could imagine how difficult it was for him.

"But we're getting along fine. I love coming home to my girls." He looked at his daughters' reflections in the rearview mirror and smiled.

Cam pulled the car up to the front of her house. Kenidee told the girls good-bye and thanked him for the ride. "Call if you need help, okay?"

"I will. Thanks. Take care of that knee."

Kenidee shut the door and gave them all a wave. Brynn waved back, then blew her a kiss with her swollen lip. She wondered why Robin's kids couldn't be cute like Cam's. Then she turned and headed for the front door, nearly falling over David's bike that was lying across the front walk.

Reminding herself that soon she'd be gone, she pulled the bike onto its wheels and parked it in the garage where it belonged, just as she'd been taught as a child.

Tonight she'd call Dolly and make some firm plans. It would be hard to leave her family, especially with the baby coming, but she had made her decision and was anxious to move on to the next phase of her life.

# CHAPTER 7

While the telephone was ringing, Kenidee hummed the tune to the song, "Hello Dolly." She was excited to talk to Dolly and make plans for their big rendezvous in Salt Lake City. She stopped humming when a message machine clicked on.

Leaving a brief message to have Dolly call as soon as she could, Kenidee disconnected her cell phone, picked up her towel from her shower, and realized that she was starving. She hadn't eaten since lunchtime, and it was after eight o'clock.

Wandering into the quiet kitchen, Kenidee pulled open the refrigerator door and peered inside to see if there was anything good left from dinner. Since there was still some salad and grilled chicken, she cut some of the chicken onto the lettuce and drizzled her favorite dressing on top.

The quiet was unusual, and she glanced around the kitchen for a note or something to tell her where everyone had gone. With a shrug of her shoulders, she continued eating until she couldn't eat another bite. Giving her bowl a quick rinse, she added it to the dishwasher, even though the sink was piled with dishes. She shook her head at the mess. Her mother had always had a thing about never going to bed with dishes in the sink. The last thing Kenidee remembered her mother doing at night was giving the chrome faucet one final polish before turning off the kitchen light and going to bed.

She resisted the urge to load the dishwasher and instead wandered into the family room, where she looked in the bookshelves for family photo albums. She was in the mood to look at pictures of their family before everything fell apart. But there were no albums in the bookcase.

She went into her dad's office and looked but still couldn't find any photo albums. *That's strange,* Kenidee thought.

Searching everywhere she could think of, she scoured the house for the albums but came up empty. *This isn't just strange. It's downright eerie. What's going on here anyway? Are we supposed to forget the past? Pretend it didn't happen?*

Kenidee was upset. She speed-dialed Matt's number on her cell phone. "Where are all the photo albums," she asked when he picked up the phone.

"Hello to you too," he said. "What photo albums?"

"The ones of us as kids. The ones with Mom in them. Do you have them?"

"No, but I know they must be somewhere. I remember packing them from our old house. Maybe they're still in storage."

Kenidee let out a groan of frustration.

"Sorry I can't help, Ken. You'll just have to ask Dad."

She wasn't happy when she disconnected. It irritated her that her father hadn't made an effort to unpack the photo albums. Didn't he think she'd want to look at them when she got home?

The most recent pictures she'd seen of her mom were a few snapshots taken right before she passed away. Kenidee wanted to see pictures of her mother when she was healthy and their family was happy.

With a wide swipe of her arm, she pushed a load of wooden blocks onto the floor so she could sit on the couch. Unable to find the remote for the television, she gave up on watching TV and picked up a recent issue of the *Ensign* magazine. On her mission, she'd spent many a lunch hour reading the magazine, but since she'd been home, she hadn't made time. Right now she really needed something to calm her down, to take her mind off her frustrations.

She flipped to the message from the First Presidency and read the article, grateful for the feeling of peace that began to replace the feeling of irritation. She then leafed through a few more pages, making a mental note to come back and read more of the articles later.

Just as she was about to put the magazine down, she read the title of an article that caught her eye, "Acceptance: Expanding the Circle of Our Love." Her brain signaled her arms to put the magazine down and walk away, but her heart wouldn't allow her hands to let go. With resignation she read the first paragraph and felt as if the words had been written just for her.

> *Life brings unexpected twists and turns. When we stay faithful and strong in the gospel, we are equipped to handle whatever comes our way, but sometimes we are blindsided with unexplainable tragedy; illness, injury, the death of a loved one. These events can be pivotal moments that define our lives and our faith. It is during times like these that we draw upon strength from our testimonies and our faith in the Savior to help us through.*

That pretty much summed up Kenidee's feelings and emotions. Somehow the author seemed to know exactly what she was experiencing.

She continued reading.

> *We cannot control what life brings us, but we can control how those trials and challenges affect us. It is at these crossroads of difficulty when we make decisions that chart our course for the future. Do we embrace the changes in our lives with faith in the Lord knowing He will guide us? Or do we shut out love and support from family, friends, and trusted Church leaders, and try to make it on our own?*

Kenidee pulled a face and put the magazine down.

She had put all her faith in the Lord. That was the only way she'd gotten through her mother's death. She didn't feel like she was shutting out family and friends and Church leaders, but in all honesty, she felt like she had no one to turn to. Her dad had his new wife and kids, Matt had Lindsay and the baby on the way. She didn't want to be dealing with all of this on her own, but that's the way it had turned out.

The sudden jangling of the home telephone made her jump. She could hear the ringing but couldn't find the phone. Finally, after frantically pulling all the pillows off the couch, she found it wedged between the two cushions.

"Hello?"

"Is Kenidee there?" a man's voice asked. "This is Camden Parker."

"Cam, this is Kenidee. What's up?"

"Hey, you know how you offered to help out with the kids? I'm in kind of a bind in the morning and wondered if you were free."

"I don't have anything going on," she told him.

"Is there any way you could watch the girls for me for a couple of hours? I have an important meeting, and I just can't get out of it. My other sitter has pretty much bailed on me, so I'm really desperate."

"Sure, what time do you need me?" Kenidee asked.

"My meeting is at nine, so maybe around eight-thirty."

"Okay, I'll be there."

"You're a lifesaver, Ken-dog. Thanks."

"Hold on," she said. "I'll tell you what—I'll babysit on one condition."

"What's that?"

"That we cut the Ken-dog."

"Oh, did I just say that? Sorry, I'll stop." Cam sounded contrite.

"Good. I'll see you in the morning then."

* * *

When Kenidee arrived in the morning the two girls were still in their jammies, sitting at the table eating bowls of Froot Loops.

"I'll be back around eleven," he told her.

"Don't you have to work the rest of the day?" she asked.

"I thought I'd better take the day off, so I could work on getting another sitter."

"I can stay longer if you need me to," she told him. "I'm not doing anything these days."

He thought about her offer. "I am a little behind on returning some calls and e-mails. Maybe I'll take you up on it. I'll still be home early. Sister Johnson, the Primary president, gave me names of some women who might be interested in tending. I'd like to call them tonight."

"I can help you until you find someone," Kenidee offered. "I'm glad to have a reason to get out of the house."

"Thanks, Ken-do—," he almost said it but stopped himself. "That was close."

"Good save."

He chuckled. "Thanks. You're really bailing me out."

"No problem. We're going to have a lot of fun today, aren't we girls?"

Amanda lifted her spoon into the air and said, "Yes!"

Brynn did the same thing, but her spoon wasn't empty and cereal spilled onto the table.

"Uh-oh," she said.

"I'll get it," Kenidee told her, grabbing a paper towel.

"I've left a list of instructions on the counter for you. Call my cell if you need anything."

"Okay," Kenidee said as she scooped up the mess.

"You girls be good for Kenidee," Cam told his daughters. He then gave each of them a kiss, wiping the milk off his mouth after kissing Brynn.

"Have a good day," Kenidee told him. "Nice tie, by the way. I like your cologne, too."

"Thanks," he said, his face brightening with a smile. "I guess I'll see you later."

Once he was gone, Kenidee set to the task of getting the girls ready for the day.

"Where's your owie?" Amanda asked her, as Kenidee helped them choose an outfit to wear.

Kenidee showed them her knee, and Brynn pointed out her cut lip, which was still swollen.

After they were dressed, Amanda and Brynn helped straighten their bedroom. With beds made and toys put away, Kenidee offered to do their hair.

"Daddy just brushes our hair and puts a clippie in it," Amanda told her.

"How about if we do some French braids today," Kenidee said.

"Okay," Amanda answered, wrinkling her face in puzzlement. "What are those?"

"I'll show you."

They scoured the bathroom for headbands and ribbons, finally finding a basket underneath the sink with a few odds and ends to use. Amanda's hair was easy, but Brynn's was harder to braid because the child couldn't sit still for more than thirty seconds at a time. With a sigh, Kenidee finally managed to finish the job.

Brynn turned her head from side to side as she studied her reflection in the mirror. Her eyes were round and dark and so thickly lashed they looked as if they had mascara brushed on them. *Cam is going to have a tough time keeping boys away from these two,* Kenidee thought.

The girls brushed their teeth, and then Kenidee turned on a morning children's program for them while she straightened the kitchen. She could tell Cam did his best to keep the house picked up and straightened, but she didn't know how he managed by himself.

With the girls content for a few minutes, Kenidee decided to help Cam by starting some laundry, sweeping the kitchen floor, and wiping down the counter and kitchen table.

Once that was done, she took a look at the family room and noticed it could use a good dusting and vacuuming. While she searched for cleaning supplies and the vacuum, the girls tired of the TV program. Kenidee found them in the pantry snitching chocolate chips.

"Hey, what are you two up to?"

"Brynn wanted chocolate," Amanda said.

"Oh, she did, did she? Well, I think she's had enough," Kenidee said, noticing Brynn's bulging cheeks and the chocolate dribbling onto her chin.

"Why don't you two come and help me clean the family room. We'll surprise your dad."

She gave each of them a cloth and instructed them about what and how to dust while she ran the vacuum. They finished cleaning and were now ready for fun.

"Guess what I brought with me?" Kenidee said.

Both of their eyes lit up. "Candy?" Amanda asked.

Kenidee laughed. "No, not candy. I brought pink fingernail polish."

Amanda clapped her hands, and Brynn mimicked her.

Sitting at the table, Kenidee painted Amanda's nails. While hers dried, she painted Brynn's, then showed both girls how to blow on their nails to dry them.

Just then the phone rang.

"Go like this, Brynn," Kenidee said, blowing on the child's fingernails. "I'll be right back."

It was Cam.

"Hey, I just wanted to make sure you don't mind staying a little longer? I'm swamped here, and a few extra hours would really help out."

"Sure, Cam. Take your time. We're doing great."

"You're saving my life, Ken."

"It's no big deal. Really, I'm glad to have something to do."

After she hung up the phone, Kenidee turned to the girls who were still blowing their nails, and said, "How would you girls like to make chocolate chip cookies?"

Amanda immediately started jumping up and down.

"Took-tees!" Brynn cried, jumping with her sister. "With choc-lat."

"Do you know how to make cookies?" Amanda asked.

"Yes, of course."

"Like the kind we buy at the store?"

"These are even better than the ones we can buy at the store. Haven't you girls ever made homemade cookies?"

"No." Amanda shook her head.

This saddened Kenidee.

"Tooktees!" Brynn cried again. "I want tooktee."

"Can we make cookies now?" Amanda asked.

"You better believe it. We'll make the best chocolate chip cookies ever."

Kenidee looked at the expressions on the little faces in front of her, the girls' eyes wide with excitement, and felt a tug at her heart. She was grateful she'd offered to help Cam that day.

* * *

While the girls ate peanut butter sandwiches, Kenidee looked through Cam's cupboards. She thought it might be nice to make him some dinner, but he didn't have enough ingredients to make anything except Hamburger Helper or Ramen Noodles with chicken nuggets.

Cam had eaten enough meals at her house for her to know that his favorite food was lasagna. The problem was, she wasn't exactly sure how to make it. Even though she had cooked during her mission, she and her companion never had time for something as involved as lasagna.

She called her sister-in-law and Sister Monson to ask for help, but neither of them was answering the phone. That left Robin. She debated whether to just follow the recipe on the box of lasagna noodles or call Robin. Then she wondered, *What if I went to all the work to make the recipe on the box and it was yucky?* At least she'd tasted Robin's lasagna and knew it was delicious.

She picked up the phone and dialed the number to her house. The phone rang four times with no answer.

"Figures," she said, ready to hang up.

"Hello?" Robin's breathless voice answered.

"Oh, Robin, hi. This is Kenidee."

"I was getting into my car when I heard the phone ring. I almost drove off, then I decided to answer, just in case it was important."

"This isn't really important, sorry."

"No, no, I was just running to the grocery store. Is everything okay?" The concern in Robin's voice was unmistakable.

"It's silly," Kenidee said, "but I was wondering if you would tell me how to make lasagna. I thought I'd make dinner for Cam and his girls."

"How nice. I'm sure he'll be happy not to have to cook tonight, and I definitely can tell you how to make my lasagna. It's easy, too."

"Easy is good," Kenidee replied.

Robin began to explain the ingredients and process of assembling the layers of noodles, sauce, and meat. "But use Italian sausage if you can find it. It's much better than regular hamburger. And don't use the low-fat ricotta. It's just not the same."

Kenidee tried to write it all down but started to get confused.

"You know what?" Robin said. "I would be happy to pick up everything you need and bring it over. Like I said, I'm on my way to the grocery store right now."

"Oh, no, you don't have to do that."

"I know exactly what to get. Really, it's no problem at all."

"Well, if you're sure." Kenidee felt relieved, since she really didn't know how she felt trying to do a bunch of grocery shopping with Brynn and Amanda. The toddlers she had seen at the store were usually out of control.

"I'll see you in half an hour," Robin said and hung up.

\* \* \*

Kenidee sat down on the couch, rested her head back on the cushions, and shut her eyes. She was exhausted. Both girls had fallen asleep that afternoon watching a Disney movie, and Kenidee savored the few precious moments of peace and quiet.

The lasagna, baking in the oven, filled the home with a rich, spicy fragrance that made her mouth water. Chilling in the fridge was a crisp salad and a pitcher of strawberry lemonade.

She'd straightened the house for what felt like the tenth time, picking up toys the girls had strewn about the house and hanging up clothes in their bedroom. Because Amanda and Brynn changed outfits several times an hour, it was impossible to keep up with them.

Still, they were cute little tykes, and for the life of her, Kenidee couldn't figure out how Desiree could just walk away from them and not care. How did a mom never make chocolate chip cookies with her kids when they loved them so much?

A rattle at the front door brought Kenidee's head up with a snap. She heard the jangling of keys and relaxed, realizing it was Cam coming home. The door opened, and she heard footsteps on the tiled entry. Kenidee waited for him to come into the family room, but he didn't. Finally, curiosity overcoming her natural reticence, she got up from the couch and walked into the hallway. She found Cam standing with his eyes closed.

"What are you doing?"

"Breathing in the smell of heaven."

Kenidee smiled. "You might change your mind after you taste it."

"If it tastes anything like it smells, I'll feel like I've died and gone to heaven."

"Or just that you wish you could die. This is my first time making lasagna, so there are no guarantees," Kenidee joked.

He opened his eyes. "Anything I don't have to make is going to be delicious." He smiled at her. "You didn't have to make dinner."

"I know. I just thought you'd appreciate it. The girls had fun helping me."

"Where are they? They're quiet."

"I hope you don't mind. They fell asleep."

"I'll wake them up in a minute. It's nice to have everything so peaceful." He looked around. "And so clean. Wow, Kenidee. You're amazing."

"No, you are. I don't know how you do this and work full time, too."

"I don't do a very good job of it. I wish I were a better mother."

Even though he was joking, Kenidee sensed the sincerity of his comment.

"So do a lot of moms, I'll bet," she said, trying to ease his conscience.

"You look tired."

"Keeping up with those two is a workout. But it was fun. You've got some really cute daughters."

"Thanks."

"What about tomorrow? Do you need my help?"

"I'll call you later after I get in touch with some of these sitters and see if they're interested. Are you free just in case?"

"Sure. Just let me know." She found her purse and slung the strap over her shoulder. "Guess I'll talk to you later."

"Thanks again, Ken. You saved me today."

\* \* \*

"Mikey, do you know where your mom and my dad are?" Kenidee asked Robin's oldest as he anxiously waited to take his turn with the video game he was playing with his brother.

He shrugged. "I dunno. Hurry up, Davey."

"No way, my guy's almost to the monster's cave. I'm going in before you. That means I get the magic scepter."

"The scepter's stupid. I'd rather have the sword any day!"

Kenidee had heard enough and went to find her father to ask him about driving to Salt Lake City when she went this first time. He had a few accounts there and could perhaps set up a meeting. Then he could fly back home. She walked out of the family room and through the kitchen, thinking to look in the office for him, when she heard Robin's belly laugh and the deep rumble of her father's laugh.

"I never was good at computers!" Robin exclaimed.

"You just need to keep practicing. You'll get the hang of it."

Following the sound of their voices, Kenidee found herself in the hallway outside their bedroom. The door was ajar a few inches. She hesitated knocking because she didn't want to disturb them. It sounded like her father was teaching Robin how to work their new computer. He had one in his office, which was strictly for work. This one would be for the family after they bought a computer desk for the family room.

With a sigh, she turned and walked back to her room. She'd have to talk to him later. Changing into capri-length sweats and a T-shirt, she straightened her bedroom and then decided she was hungry.

She met the family in the hallway, on their way out.

"Where are you guys going?" Kenidee asked.

"Mikey's science fair is tonight," her dad told her.

"Mikey's rocket was the bestest in the whole school," David exclaimed proudly. "He gets a trophy." He puffed out his chest. "I helped him make it."

"Congratulations, Mikey," Kenidee said to the oldest. With his neatly combed hair and freshly scrubbed face, he looked kind of cute.

Robin nudged him when he didn't respond.

"Thanks," he said.

"You did a good job on the rocket," she told David. "I saw you making it."

"Mom said maybe we could make one for me, but we have to save a lot of toilet paper rolls first."

Rachel clutched a stuffed animal in her arms and looked at Kenidee like she was frightened to death of her. Kenidee didn't know what she'd done to scare the poor kid so badly and realized she hadn't ever followed up on her earlier resolve to get to know the children better.

"By the way, Robin, thanks again for helping me out today. Cam really appreciated having dinner ready when he got home. I just hope I made it right and it tastes good."

"And I hope you don't mind that I made lasagna again for us since I was picking up everything to make it anyway. There's a plate for you in the oven."

Kenidee appreciated her thoughtfulness.

"We'll see you later, honey," her dad said. "We'd better get going."

Kenidee watched as her father took hold of Rachel's hand as they walked out the door. A moment of déjà vu hit her as she flashed back to when she was a little girl, holding hands with her dad. There was a big difference though. He'd been a busy salesman when she and Matt were children. He'd spent most of the week on the road, in town only on weekends. He'd missed most of Matt's Little League baseball games and Scout activities. He'd missed her dance recitals and father/daughter activities. She wasn't proud of it, but part of her resented the fact that here he was now, doing all those things he hadn't done with them, with someone else's kids.

She shook her head to clear the thoughts and defuse the emotion that accompanied the memory. The longer she thought about it and the more she dwelled on it, the worse her resentment would be. But all the resentment in the world wouldn't change anything; all the anger and pain inside of her wouldn't bring back her mother.

"Food," she said, changing her focus. "I need food."

Taking the warm plate out of the oven, she found herself wondering how Cam was enjoying his meal. She paused to say a quick blessing on the food, then took a bite of the lasagna Robin had made.

"Mmm," she said, savoring the rich sauce and cheesy goodness in her mouth.

She enjoyed the food but not eating alone, which was how she seemed to eat most of her meals.

After finishing, she rinsed her dish and put it in the dishwasher rather than on top of the pile of dishes in the sink. She turned to walk away, then stopped and turned back to the sink. Before she could change her mind, she began loading dishes from the sink into the dishwasher. It was the least she could do for all Robin had done to help her that day.

Just as she pushed the button to start the first load, the telephone rang. It was Joey.

"What are you doing tonight?" he asked.

"Nothing, why?"

"A bunch of us are going cosmic bowling. You want to go with us?"

She weighed her options. Stay home and be bored, or hang out with friends. It didn't take long to decide. "I'd love to."

"Great, we'll be by in half an hour."

# CHAPTER 8

Kenidee stared at the clothes hanging in her closet and sighed. She definitely needed to go shopping and update her wardrobe. Not only were her clothes out of date, but she'd gained a little weight on her mission and most of her pants didn't quite fit.

Grabbing the one new pair of jeans she owned and a deep coral–colored T-shirt, she quickly changed before hurrying to the bathroom to do her hair.

Groaning that she hadn't yet gone to get her hair styled, she finally just pulled back some hair and clipped it into place, letting the rest of her hair tumble loosely about her shoulders. Adding a touch of mascara and lip gloss, she finished with a spritz of perfume. Then she went to wait by the front door.

*I'd better leave a note for Dad.*

Back in the kitchen, she found a scrap of paper and scribbled a note telling him where she was going and with whom. Even though she had a cell phone, she didn't want him to worry when he got home and found her gone.

Leaving the note on the counter, she turned to leave when the phone rang.

"Hi, Kenidee. It's Dolly."

"I'm so glad you called. I've been wanting to talk to you so we can make plans. I'm getting so excited to move to Salt Lake."

"Yeah," Dolly paused, "that's why I called."

Kenidee's heart skipped a beat. Dolly's voice told her that something was wrong. "What's up?"

"My grandma suffered a minor stroke today. We aren't going to be able to go back to Salt Lake for a while. The doctor doesn't know if she's going to fully recover or not. She's in the hospital right now, but we just don't know what's going on."

"I understand," Kenidee said. "I'm so sorry about your grandma."

"Yeah, me too," Dolly's voice cracked. "She's tough, though. I'm sure she'll be okay. And don't worry, we'll get you to Salt Lake."

"I know."

"Are you doing okay? Are things at your house getting better?"

"Um, yeah," she fibbed, not wanting Dolly to worry. "I think so." A knock came at the front door. "Hey, Dolly, I gotta run. I'll talk to you soon, though. Okay?"

She hung up the phone and tried to shake the impact of the conversation from her mind, but she couldn't help feeling frustrated. She was sad for Dolly's grandma and her family. She was also sad for herself because this put moving to Salt Lake on hold for a while.

She felt like a plastic grocery bag, blowing around in the wind, landing for a moment, then getting swooped up again and carried randomly about.

\* \* \*

Tossing back and forth in her bed, Kenidee finally sat up and turned on the lamp next to her. *Why aren't things falling into place for me? Haven't I done everything the Lord asked of me? I've stayed faithful through all my trials; I worked hard and was completely committed to my mission. I did everything I was supposed to do. But nothing is working out.*

She certainly learned about faith on her mission. Was the Lord now trying to teach her patience? Because certainly that was what was being tested.

She'd already said her prayer before getting into bed, but she felt a need to pray again. Getting on her knees, Kenidee rested her head in her hands as the turmoil in her mind swirled and tumbled without ceasing. *What is it that I am supposed to be doing right now? What is the Lord's will for me?*

Beginning her prayer, she gave voice to those questions and many more. She asked about getting a job, starting school, and moving to Salt Lake. She then confided how much she missed her mother and needed her so badly right now. Her thoughts turned to Brendan, and she asked the Lord to bless him and keep him safe so they could soon be together again.

When her prayer ended, she felt exhausted, but she still wasn't tired. Restless and unsettled, she pulled on her robe and went to the kitchen for a drink, being careful not to trip over any toys or shoes on the floor.

Pushing yet another one of the kids' school projects aside to clear space at the table—this one involved egg cartons, pipe cleaners, and pom-poms—she sat down and sipped a glass of ice cold apple juice. With her mom gone, she thought about how different things were from how she'd always pictured them. Her mom had been her best friend, someone she could talk to, someone she loved to hang out with. Now, since there was no one to fill that place in her life, the emptiness gnawed at Kenidee like an open wound.

If her mom were still alive, Kenidee would have someone to help her make decisions. She would have someone to help sort out her feelings and share her excitement about Brendan and her future.

But her mom wasn't here. How come she just couldn't accept that and move on?

And why wasn't this move to Salt Lake working out?

She rested her head in her hands and rubbed her eyes. She just had to get through the next few months until Brendan came home, because then she knew everything would be fine.

\* \* \*

Kenidee was grateful to have Cam's daughters to keep her busy and help her take her mind off her troubles. Her life seemed like a giant game board, and she was one of the playing pieces that someone else was manipulating. If her path toward a certain goal was clear, when she began moving down that path, obstacles sprang out of nowhere, catching her off guard, knocking her off the path, preventing her from reaching her goal.

Cam sensed her frustration almost the instant he walked through the door.

"How are things going?" he asked after the girls gave him a welcome home hug and then ran back to their room to finish their game.

"Don't ask," she answered.

"That bad?" He slid off his suit coat and hung it over the back of a chair.

"Out of the blue everything's changed. My plans to move to Salt Lake are completely up in the air. I don't have a clue what to do now." She leaned against the counter doorjamb and swirled her car keys around her finger. "Maybe this is the Lord's way of telling me I'm not supposed to go there, but I really felt like I should. Have you ever had something like this happen to you?"

His eyebrows arched high over his wide-opened eyes. "Are you kidding? How about my marriage, for starters. I was doing everything I could to make Desiree happy. But that's the problem; you can't make anyone happy. They have to make themselves happy."

"I believe that too. I think that's why I feel I need to leave. For me, that's the only way I'm going to be happy. I just need to get away from the situation at home. Going away is my only choice."

"It sounds more to me like you're running away," he told her bluntly.

That was one thing about Cam that she sometimes liked and sometimes hated. He was very honest, painfully honest.

"I'm not running away, Cam," she said defensively. "I'm just leaving. For the sake of everyone involved, I have to go. They need their space, and I need mine. That's all."

"What does your dad say about you leaving?"

"Not much. We don't talk much; actually we don't talk at all. You know him. He likes to ignore problems so they'll go away."

"My dad is kind of like that," Cam said. "But he'd talk if you told him you needed his help. You two used to be really close."

Kenidee swallowed and cleared emotion from her throat. "I know. I really need him right now, but he has Robin and her kids to worry about."

"You know he doesn't feel that way," Cam told her.

"I don't know what he feels," she replied. "He won't tell me anything. I'd love to know how he could possibly lose his wife and then marry someone else in less than a year. I'd love to know how he sees me fitting into his 'ready-made' family. But he doesn't talk about stuff like that."

"You should try to talk to him again."

"It's no use. He's so caught up in Robin and her kids he doesn't have time for me. He probably figures that Brendan's coming home and we'll get married, and then I'll be taken care of and out of his hair."

"He doesn't want you out of his hair," Cam assured her.

"I'm not so sure about that. His life would be much easier with me gone."

"As a father, I can guarantee he will never feel that way. If anything, he doesn't want you to hurt anymore. He wants you to be happy. I think you should try to talk to him again."

"Maybe," she answered. "If I can ever find time with him. He's so busy being 'superdad' to Robin's kids he doesn't have time for me."

Cam's brows narrowed, "You really are bugged about this aren't you?"

"How could I not be? He replaced my mother with Robin, and now he wants me to be happy about it—just like that! Well, guess what? I'm not!"

She looked away as unexpected tears stung her eyes. Blinking quickly to clear away the moisture, she then added, "Maybe I am running. Maybe I just don't want to deal with this right now, or ever. But if I don't run, I'm afraid I'll end up resenting my father so badly that I'll lose him too. This is the only way I can deal with it right now, Cam." More tears stung her eyes.

"I'm sorry," Cam said, walking over to her. "I didn't mean to say that."

"But it's true," she sobbed. "I guess I'm more like my dad than I thought. I wish I could ignore away my problems."

"I know how hard this is for you," he said.

"I just miss my mom so much. And coming home feels like I'm mourning all over again. I know it would be different if I could've come home and just had dad there and my old house. It's like her memory has been erased. I can't really ever talk to dad about her. Matt understands how I feel, but he's busy with Lindsay and getting ready for the baby. I don't have anyone, Cam. And it's so hard." She dropped her head and fought to control her tears and emotions, but they were just too powerful.

She felt Cam's strong arms wrap around her and pull her close. "It's going to be okay," he told her. "You can talk to me, Ken. I loved your mom too. You can talk to me."

"Thanks," she said. "You're about the only friend I have right now."

* * *

The note from her father said they'd all gone miniature golfing. She crumpled the note and dropped it on the counter. She could count on one finger the number of times her father had taken Matt and her miniature golfing.

A tray of Rice Krispies treats sat on the counter. Kenidee cut a large square and took a big bite. She turned to see if there were any messages flashing on the message machine and stopped. There, addressed to her, in his neat, even-lettered handwriting, was a letter from Brendan.

"YES!" she exclaimed as she grabbed the letter and tore the flap open. If she'd ever needed a letter from Brendan, it was today.

Pulling out a chair, she sat so she could enjoy every word of his letter, which was dated almost a month ago.

*Dear Sister Ashford . . . Kenidee, (smiley face)*

*Now that you're home I guess I can call you by your first name. So how is it being home? I'll bet it's been quite an adjustment, especially with how different everything is with your family. What's your dad's wife like? And her kids. Do you like them?*

*I hope things are going well for you. If I know you, I know you're making the best out of the situation and that everything's going well.*

"If you only knew," she said aloud, then licked the sticky marshmallow from her fingers.

*Things here in Taiwan are amazing. I love these people. It's weird because even though all my ancestors come from England and Sweden, I feel as though these people are part of me and I am part of them.*

*The work is on fire. Remember the Huang family I was telling you about? They got baptized last Saturday. I've had some spiritual experiences on my mission, but nothing has come close to that baptism. Someday I'll try and explain to you what it was like, although words can't even begin to describe what a special experience it was. I hope you can meet this family. I love them as much as my own family back home. They want to come to America to visit. Wouldn't that be awesome!*

She continued reading as he talked about working with the mission president and all the traveling he was doing throughout the mission, training and working with zone leaders.

He told her how he'd eaten at Kentucky Fried Chicken and details about his city. She was amazed at how modern the towns were.

*I'm sorry my letters haven't been consistent lately. We barely have time to sleep anymore, but I love what I'm doing. I would stay here forever if I could. I'm sure you know what I mean.*

*Let me know what you are doing and how things are at home. Thanks for all your support and prayers.*

He then bore his testimony and signed the letter:

*Love, Elder Nielsen*

Folding the letter, Kenidee slid it back inside the envelope and sighed. How was she ever going to survive until Brendan was home once again?

# CHAPTER 9

It was no use. She couldn't sleep. She tried to read, but she couldn't concentrate. She tried to write a letter to Brendan, but she couldn't find the words to explain what was going on. She stared at the four walls around her until she thought she'd start climbing them. She needed a distraction.

Going to the kitchen, Kenidee cut another Rice Krispies square and poured herself a glass of apple juice. She looked at the marshmallow treat and vowed that she would go running tomorrow.

A smile lifted the corners of her mouth as she remembered all the times she and Dolly drowned their sorrows and frustrations in food. Their food of choice—ice cream. Anything chocolaty, caramely, and gooey.

How many nights had they sat at their table with a carton between them and two spoons and drowned their emotions with Ben and Jerry's? Right now she would give anything to have Dolly and a carton of rocky road with her.

The sound of a door opening caught her attention, and a moment later her father came into the kitchen. "I thought I heard someone in here," he said, scratching his head and yawning. "What are you doing up?"

"I couldn't sleep," she said, licking her fingers.

"Something must be bothering you."

"Why do you say that?"

"Kenidee, I'm your dad, remember. All your life whenever you've had something on your mind, you've always gotten up and had a late night snack. I should know. I can't remember how many nights we spent going through half a loaf of bread making cinnamon toast."

Kenidee smiled at the memory.

"So, is it something you want to talk about?"

She shrugged her shoulders as a lump of emotion quickly clogged her throat.

"Sweetie, what's going on?"

She still couldn't answer. She was too busy blinking her eyes as she tried to clear away the tears.

He pulled a chair out from the table and scooted it close to her. "Ken, did something happen? What's the matter? Talk to me."

A sob caught in her throat and tears fell onto her cheeks—tears of sadness, frustration, and loneliness.

"Honey, it's okay, com'ere," he said, pulling her into his arms and giving her a hug.

She couldn't hold back. She'd tried to be so strong, she'd tried to handle everything that was going on, but she'd failed. She couldn't handle it. She hated how life was right now. So she leaned on her father for strength.

"There, there," he said, stroking her hair and rocking her gently. "It's okay, sweetie. Everything's okay."

She wiped at her eyes and sniffed to keep her nose from running, but the faucet kept flowing. All the emotion that had welled up for so long burst forth like a flooding river behind an earthen dam.

After several minutes, Kenidee felt a calm settle in. Her father handed her a paper napkin with which she wiped her cheeks and blew her nose. She went through several napkins before she dried out.

"Honey, don't you think we need to talk about this?"

She bit her bottom lip, hesitating whether to get into this with him, especially late at night when they were tired. But then she realized this was the only time she had alone with him. Between work and Robin and her kids, his time was completely occupied.

"I can't help if you don't tell me what's going on," he said.

With a sigh, she pushed her doubts to the side and spoke. "I'm having a hard time adjusting. And besides that, things just aren't working out for me."

"What exactly isn't working out?"

"Dolly's grandma had a stroke so now I don't know when I'm going to be able to move to Salt Lake. That means I need to find a job for the time being, but I don't know how long I will work before I move."

"I'm sorry things fell through with Dolly, but to be honest I was hoping you'd stay a little longer. I wasn't ready to have you move out again so soon."

"Why do you say that when we don't even spend any time together, Dad?" She looked at him and shook her head, confused by the words that didn't match his actions. "There is nothing here for me anymore. And I know that you want me to be completely okay with all of this," she spoke with more intensity and gestured around the room, meaning the whole "new family" package. "But I'm not okay with it. It's weird and it's hard and I still . . . miss . . . Mom!" she said forcefully. "I know that's not what you want to hear, but it's the way I feel." She forced herself to continue. "It's hard to see you spending time with her kids. And it's even harder to see you with her, Dad. Don't you understand that? It's like you're being unfaithful to Mom. I know that doesn't make any sense, but that's how I feel, especially when I see you kissing her and stuff. It kills me inside."

The look of pain on her father's face made her feel even worse, but it was too late to take back what she said and, truthfully, she didn't want to take it back. She wanted him to know how she felt.

"I'm sorry this is so hard for you. I wish I could take away your pain. Is there anything I can do to help you?"

She nodded. "You can tell me how you got over Mom so quickly."

His eyes opened wide. Then he quickly blinked, struggling to keep his emotions in check.

She knew her words hurt, but she needed an answer.

After a moment, Kenidee's dad spoke, his voice gravelly and soft. "You think I'm over her?" He pinched the bridge of his nose and cleared his throat. Then looked at her directly, his eyes moist with tears. "The day I lost your mom was the worst day of my life. I didn't want to live if I had to live without her. She was everything to me. Everything," he whispered. He bent his head and wiped at his eyes. Summoning the strength to continue, he said, "There isn't a day that goes by when I don't feel an ache in my heart because I still miss her. I will never, ever, get over losing your mother."

The pain in his voice pierced her soul. She reached for his hand. "Dad, I'm sorry."

He took her hand in his and pulled her into a hug. They cried and sniffed and patted each other's backs. Grabbing more napkins, they dried their tears and blew their noses.

"I'm sorry this has been so hard for you. I didn't want to hurt you," her father said. "And I know I need to be here more for you. We should have talked about this sooner."

She nodded and wiped at her nose again.

"What else would you like to talk about?"

"I'd like to know about Robin. How that all happened so quickly."

He processed her request for a moment before answering.

"A couple of years ago, I went to a conference for work in Monterey. Do you remember?"

"I remember. We all wanted to go with you."

"But you were dancing in the Nutcracker in San Francisco and couldn't miss rehearsals."

"And Mom had to drive me into the city every other night."

"Right, so neither of you could go with me."

"I remember."

"While I was there, after dinner one evening, I took a walk that led me to a rocky point where I could look out over the rugged coastline and watch the ocean. As I stood there, I watched as the sun set across the water. And the sunset was magnificent—all the color, the intensity, the water. For a moment, it seemed as though the world had stopped and what was happening was a moment of absolute perfection. I found myself thinking that this was what a sunset in heaven had to be like, because I couldn't imagine anything being more beautiful than that."

"Wow."

"I went back to my room that night and called your mom to tell her about the sunset. But as hard as she tried, I could tell, she just didn't understand how incredibly breathtaking it was. The only way someone could really, truly understand and appreciate it was by being there. I was glad I'd been able to see the sunset, but it would have been so much more wonderful had I been able to share it with someone, especially your mom. Does that make sense?"

"Sure. I tried to tell you about experiences on my mission, but I knew it would be hard for you to really understand what they were like because you weren't there, by my side, when they happened."

"Exactly," he said. "I wanted to share all my sunsets with your mother, and everything else life had to offer. I thought we'd always be together. But the Lord had different plans for us. You have to understand, though, that life is like that sunset. It's not something you want to experience alone. I know I'll have you for a little while, but soon you and Brendan will get married and you'll be off starting your lives together. I can't imagine spending the rest of my life alone. And before your mom passed away, she told me that she wanted me to remarry. She said she couldn't bear to think of me alone the rest of my life. She told me she wanted me to have someone to share my sunsets with.

"I had no intention of getting remarried so soon. And Robin and I had no intention of getting serious when we first started dating. Her husband had died in a car accident when Rachel was a baby, and Robin has been through a lot raising three kids on her own. But by the time I met her, she was doing fine all by herself. We just really hit it off. We had fun together, and it felt good to laugh and enjoy someone else's company. Like I told you in my letters, I spent a lot of time in prayer and fasting and at the temple. I wouldn't have married her had I not felt completely right about it."

Even though her father had told her some of this in letters, it felt good to hear in his own words how he'd met Robin and had decided to marry her. It also felt good to finally clear the air and get everything out in the open.

"Does that help?" he asked his daughter.

"Yes. A lot. And it helps knowing that you understand how I feel. I know Robin's a good person—oh, how I hate that description; that's what everyone says about her. Okay, so it's not that. I just feel so disloyal to Mom. My thinking is probably still really messed up, but in my heart, that's how I feel. I don't know if I can ever accept Robin and her kids. That's why I think moving—"

A squeak in the floorboards in the hallway caused them both to turn. Kenidee wondered if Robin had overheard them talking.

"Just a minute," her dad said, getting to his feet. He looked down the hallway.

"Was it Robin?" she asked.

"Not sure. If it was, she went back to bed." He sat back down and looked at her with complete attention. "So now what?"

"I just think moving away is the best thing for me."

Her father sighed and patted her hand. "I understand. But you know that I wish you could find a way to stay. And I'm glad we were able to talk. I'll try to be more sensitive to your feelings and more supportive of having you move, even though I will miss you terribly. I'll also try to help you find some work temporarily until you do move, whether it's right away or when Brendan gets home. How's he doing anyway? I noticed you got a letter."

"He's doing great. He just baptized a family. He loves the people there so much I think he's become part Taiwanese."

"He's a great guy. I'm not excited about anyone taking away my little girl, but I think I could handle it if it's Brendan."

"Thanks, Dad."

"Think you can sleep now?"

She nodded. "Spilling your guts is very tiring. I think I'll sleep great now."

"Are you watching Cam's kids again tomorrow?"

"Yes, and I need every ounce of energy I can get to keep up with his girls."

Her father chuckled.

They both stood and had one last hug.

"Thanks, Dad. I love you. And thanks for talking."

"I love you too, sweetie. You know I'm always there for you, right?"

"Right."

They said good night and went opposite directions to their bedrooms. Kenidee listened for a moment as he shut the door to his room. She heard the muffled tones of talking and wondered what her father and Robin were saying.

As she climbed into bed, Kenidee realized that she finally felt the peace she'd been praying for. Pulling the covers up to her neck and snuggling between the cool sheets, she shut her eyes and relaxed into a peaceful night's sleep.

\* \* \*

Monday morning Kenidee's head throbbed. Sleep had been pretty elusive the past couple of nights and now she was paying for it. All weekend long, she'd thought about the conversation she'd had with her father, and she'd felt that a burden had been lifted from her shoulders. Their discussion had helped her get some closure. Even though she didn't fully accept the situation with her family, she at least understood it better. And for her, that was a step in the right direction.

She was sure that Robin had heard some of their conversation because all weekend long she made it a point to avoid Kenidee. It had been awkward and there was tension in the air, but Kenidee didn't regret speaking her mind to her father.

"Ken-dee," a little voice said. Kenidee felt tugging on her shirt and looked down to see Brynn looking up at her.

"Yes, sweetie."

"Where's Daddy?"

Cam was staying late at work that night. Some of his clients were in town, and he needed to take them to dinner. He promised Kenidee that if they had cheesecake he would bring a piece home for her.

"He's still at work. So I get to tuck you into bed tonight. Would you like to read a story first?"

"Tory, yay, read me tory." She ran to her room and snatched up a favorite storybook and climbed up on her bed. Amanda finished putting on her pajamas and joined them on Brynn's bed.

Kenidee read them the fairy tale of the princess who lost a special golden locket and looked all over the kingdom to find it. The girls snuggled close to her as the princess went into the dark, scary forest and was approached by a mean witch. Of course, the handsome prince rescued her, and they all lived happily ever after.

"Yeah, like that ever happens," Kenidee said as she closed the book.

"What ever happens?" Amanda asked her.

"Oh, nothing," Kenidee told her. "Hey, it's time for bed, you two. Now how do you do your prayers?"

"We kneel down and pray together, then daddy listens to me," Amanda instructed, "and then he helps Brynn. She can't say her prayers all by herself yet."

"Okay," Kenidee said, kneeling next to Amanda's bed.

"Can we wait for Daddy?" Amanda asked.

"He said he's going to be very late, sweetie."

"Okay," she said with disappointment. "Will you tell him to still come in and kiss me good night, even though I'll be sleeping?"

"Me too!" Brynn added.

"I sure will," Kenidee told them, touched by their devotion to their daddy.

Amanda said her simple prayer first. Kenidee noticed that she remembered to bless her mommy, wherever she was. She then helped Brynn with a simple prayer. After the amens were spoken, the girls stood, and Kenidee gave them both a big hug. Then, glancing at the doorway, she saw Cam standing there with a gentle smile on his face.

"Girls, I have a little surprise for you," Kenidee said.

"A surprise," Brynn said breathlessly.

"What is it?" Amanda questioned.

Kenidee pointed casually to the doorway. When the girls saw who it was, they exploded with excitement and raced to their father's arms. He picked both of them up and plastered them with kisses. Then, as they giggled and wiggled, he plopped each of his daughters onto her own bed.

It took several minutes to get them settled down and tucked in, and they demanded more kisses from both Cam and Kenidee. But, finally, they were content to go to bed.

Pulling the door shut behind him, Cam followed Kenidee to the kitchen, where he poured himself a drink of cold juice.

"You look exhausted," she told him.

"Sorry to keep you so late. How was your day?"

"It was great."

"Amanda told me you're helping her with her letters and numbers."

"I hope you don't mind," Kenidee said with a start.

"Not at all. I want her to be ready when she starts school this fall," he said.

"Both of the girls seem really smart. But then, you got straight A's in school," she said, "even though you never studied."

"I studied," he feigned offense.

"Cam," she leveled her gaze and looked at him. "You're talking to me, remember. You used to brag about your ninety-nine percent grades on tests without studying."

"Did I really?"

"Yeah. You were pretty cocky."

"I guess I was. You probably thought I was a big jerk back then," he said.

"Not really. You were annoying," she joked, "but you weren't a jerk."

Cam chuckled. "Don't hold back your feelings."

"Sorry, it's true. You're not like that anymore, though."

"I'm glad!" he said with relief.

"Yeah, me too."

They looked at each other for a moment before Kenidee broke the silence.

"So, what did you think of me when we were younger?"

Cam smiled. "Well, I just thought of you as a little sister. But I always thought you were a cute little sister. I knew you'd grow up to be a knockout."

Kenidee laughed. "A knockout? Yeah, right."

"It's true. You always were cute, but now you're beautiful."

"Thanks," she said, feeling her cheeks and neck growing red.

"How are things at home? Are they getting any better?"

Kenidee shrugged. "I finally had a talk with my dad."

"How did that go?"

"It was emotional. We pretty much laid it out on the table. I told him exactly how I felt, and he finally answered my questions."

"Did it help?"

She nodded. "Yeah, a little. He told me something that helped me understand why he married Robin so quickly."

Cam leaned forward with interest.

"He told me that before my mom died, she told him she wanted him to remarry. She wanted him to have someone to share his sunsets with."

"His sunsets?"

Kenidee explained about the sunset her father had seen and how much he'd wanted to share it with her mother.

Cam didn't say anything. He just looked down at the empty glass in front of him.

"Cam? Is something wrong?"

"No," he answered. "Not really. I just know what he means, I guess."

"You do?"

"Sure. I have the girls, so it's not like I'm alone really. But so many times I wish I had someone to share things with, good and bad. I wish I had someone to come home to and talk about my day, or someone to go places with, do things together. Someday my girls won't be here, and I'll be alone, just like he was. That's not how I want to spend my life. There's nothing gratifying in loneliness. Success isn't as rewarding and happiness isn't as sweet without someone to share."

Kenidee knew what it felt like to not have anyone to spend time with, to not have anyone to call when she felt like talking. Except Cam. He'd become a friend, and she was very grateful for him.

"I don't really have anyone to hang out with or call," he told her. "My parents are there for me, but it's not really the same."

"You can call me, Cam," she said. "I've really appreciated your friendship since I've been home. All my friends have either married or moved away. To be honest, you're the only one around here I've been able to talk to."

Cam smiled. "I'm glad, Ken. And thank you for being there for me to talk to."

It was getting late. She got up from the table. "I'd better get going. I'm going to the temple early in the morning."

"That's a good idea. I need to find a day this month and go."

"Just let me know. I'll watch the girls so you can."

"Ken, that would be great," he said with an appreciative smile.

Their good-byes were short. Then Kenidee found her car keys and left the house with a great deal of satisfaction and peace. She didn't know why, but she didn't take the calm she felt inside for granted. Most likely it wouldn't stay.

# CHAPTER 10

Kenidee's early morning temple session the next day had been peaceful and refreshing. She felt as if there was a little more order and meaning to her life. Afterwards, she spent a few hours organizing her room and doing her laundry. Then, as a reward, she went for a long, refreshing run. She'd just finished getting showered and dressed when Robin and her kids returned from the grocery store.

"Look at what I found at Costco," Robin announced as she burst through the door from the garage, her arms filled with boxes of food. She plopped the boxes onto the counter and dug through one of them, pulling out a smaller box that she lifted as if she were presenting a gift to a king.

"Chocolate-covered fruit," she said breathlessly. "Now that's how I like to eat my fruit . . . covered in chocolate!"

The dried fruit had been dipped in luscious milk chocolate.

"I couldn't resist," Robin said. "Want one?"

Even though she'd just worked out, she couldn't refuse. Kenidee lifted one of the treats from the box and took a bite. The creamy chocolate melted in her mouth, the dried fruit adding its own tart sweetness to the flavor. "That's amazing," she said.

Robin had also taken a bite, and her mouth was full, so she just nodded and rolled her eyes in ecstasy.

The kids tumbled through the door also carrying items in from the van. "Hey, we want one," Mikey complained.

"After lunch," Robin told him.

"That's not fair!" David argued.

"You're right, it's not. But I don't care if my lunch is ruined if I eat this. But you're growing children, and you need to eat the right foods. Now go wash up," Robin told all of them.

The children left, and Kenidee and Robin finished their treat.

"Wish I could dip broccoli in chocolate. Maybe they'd eat it that way," Robin joked.

Kenidee laughed. She could relate. As a kid, she'd hated broccoli with a passion.

"I also bought one of those rotisserie chickens for dinner. And I found garlic mashed potatoes. I found some really great stuff. I'm supposed to be on a diet, but I just couldn't resist."

The phone rang. Kenidee licked the chocolate from her fingers and answered it.

"This is Brother Dennis, the executive secretary. Is Kenidee available?"

"This is she," Kenidee said, wondering why Brother Dennis was calling.

"Bishop Monson is going to be in his office at the church this evening and has some time at eight-thirty. He wondered if you could come in for an interview."

"Uh, yeah, sure."

"I'll let the bishop know. We'll see you then."

Not sure what the bishop could want, Kenidee thought about the possibilities for a moment. It couldn't be a calling, because he knew she was leaving. She'd just spoken in church, so that wasn't it. Finally, she resigned herself to the fact that she'd have to wait until she got there to find out.

\* \* \*

"Kenidee, come in," Bishop Monson said, offering her a seat.

As they both sat down, Kenidee searched his expression. *What am I doing here?*

"Why don't we start with prayer. Would you mind saying it?" he asked.

Kenidee shook her head, then folded her arms. It was difficult to pray when she didn't exactly know what to pray for. So she just asked for the Spirit to be with them. She certainly needed it.

"Thank you, Kenidee. I'm sure you're wondering why I've called you here."

She nodded.

"The other night when we ran into you at the park, I sensed that you were having some challenges in your life."

She nodded again.

"I thought I'd offer a listening ear, if it's something you'd like to talk about."

Even though talking couldn't really change the situation with her family, she appreciated the bishop offering her the opportunity to vent. She respected him and his opinion and would like to know what he would advise her to do.

She explained about the strain at home between her and Robin and her kids, which in turn caused a strain between her and her father.

"In some respects I feel like I've had to go through mourning all over again," she explained. "It wouldn't be so hard if I was back in my old house and it was just me and Dad. But I'm in a strange house, with a strange woman kissing my father. Not to mention three annoying kids. I'm just trying to hang in there until I can move to Salt Lake. Whenever that is. In the meantime, I'm looking for work."

"I see. And you think it's best that you just leave, without working things out?"

"Things are never going to work out. This woman isn't my mother. She never will be. I know it doesn't make sense, but I have this feeling of disloyalty to Mom because Dad's already replaced her in his life. But no one will ever replace—" a sudden sob caught in her throat. She swallowed, then cleared her throat, blinking quickly to clear unwanted tears. "I'm sorry."

The bishop reached over and patted her hand.

"It's just easier to leave," she said softly. "I just wish I could leave soon."

"This move to Salt Lake. Have you made it a matter of prayer?" he asked.

She opened her mouth to say, "Yes." Then she realized that would be a lie. She hadn't actually prayed for a confirmation, but she had just reasoned it out in her mind. It seemed like the perfectly sensible thing to do.

"No."

"Have you asked the Lord to help you accept Robin and her children?"

She looked down at her hands in her lap.

"No," she said sheepishly.

"Why is that?"

She knew why. She wasn't ready to ask because she didn't want to accept Robin or her kids.

"Sister Ashford." Bishop Monson spoke her name with authority, causing her to look at him. "I know, without a doubt, that the Lord will take this burden from you. He wants to take away your pain, but you have to humble yourself and go to Him in prayer. You have to hand it over to Him."

Kenidee nodded. She'd taught about the Savior her entire mission. She'd borne testimony of these facts to hundreds of people. So why did it seem so different to apply it to her own life? What was wrong?

Two thoughts came to mind. And neither of them was easy to accept.

First, she needed to exercise more faith. She needed to follow the instructions in the Book of Alma and have the desire to exercise faith that she could accept her new family situation. And second, she needed to pray and ask for the Lord to help her accept it.

"I know," she told him. "It's just so hard. I don't think I want to accept her. I can't do that to Mom."

"Have I ever told you about the last time I saw your mother, before she passed away?"

Kenidee looked up. "No." She craved hearing anything and everything she could about her mother's last days on the earth.

"Of course you know how physically hard the cancer was on her."

Kenidee nodded. She'd seen a few pictures of her mother toward the end, the pain apparent in her gaunt, thin face. Her father had told her of the agony her mother had experienced. For that one reason, death had been welcome, just to know her mom was no longer suffering.

"One night your father called and told me that the end was near, so I went to visit her one last time. I'd always known what a stalwart, faithful woman your mother was. So strong and determined, someone who never wavered, even in the midst of her suffering. She was a great example to all of us in life and in death."

Swallowing hard, Kenidee listened, grateful to have him share her mother's last moments with her.

"She took my hand in hers," he said, his own voice growing gravelly, "and she squeezed it with everything she had. Then she made me promise that I wouldn't let William spend the rest of his life alone. Her greatest fear was that he would be lonely, and she couldn't bear the thought of it. She knew you would be with him for a time, but that you would eventually marry and move away. I think your mother is at peace with your father's decision. There was a very special spirit at their wedding. I believe that those who'd passed on attended the ceremony."

Kenidee dabbed at the tears on her cheeks and thought about the bishop's words. Had her mother actually been there the day her father got married? Was her mother okay with his choice to marry Robin and help raise her children? Did her mother want *her* to feel good about this arrangement?

"Kenidee, I don't want you to think for one minute that I don't understand how hard this is for you. Coming home from your mission with a completely different family situation and to a different home is an immense load to deal with. May I share a scripture that might help?"

"Of course."

The bishop opened his scriptures and read from the book of Mosiah in the Book of Mormon.

*And I will also ease the burdens which are put upon your shoulders, that even you cannot feel them upon your backs, even while you are in bondage; and this will I do that ye may stand as witnesses for me hereafter, and that ye may know of a surety that I, the Lord God, do visit my people in their afflictions.*

"Of course, they are talking about physical burdens, but the Lord will ease emotional burdens as well. I know you have the power within yourself to do this. Like you taught on your mission, you just have to exercise faith in your Father in Heaven."

The bishop was right. Kenidee knew he was right. But it was so hard to do what was right when she just didn't have the desire. Still, having the bishop confirm the things her father had told her and knowing that her mother had "approved" somewhat of her father's new wife did make a difference.

"By the way, how's your missionary doing?" the bishop asked.

Kenidee smiled broadly. "He's doing great."

The bishop nodded. "Glad to hear it. Let me know if every-thing works out with you two."

She nodded and reached to shake his hand in parting, then paused. He'd used the word *if,* and she was tempted to correct him with the word *when.* She decided not to make a big deal of it. Brendan would be home soon enough, and there would be no more ifs.

Thoughts of the conversation ran through her mind as she left the bishop's office, knowing his advice was solid. She knew what she needed to do, but her heart still lacked the capacity to grow and accept these new people. It just wasn't there.

Maybe instead of praying for help in accepting Robin and her kids, she needed to start by praying to have the desire to accept them. Perhaps it wasn't the ultimate solution, but it was a step in the right direction.

\* \* \*

"No job yet," she told Lindsay on the phone. "Nobody wants to hire me if I'm not going to be around for a year or longer."

"How do you know you won't be around that long?" Lindsay asked. "It sounds like your friend Dolly isn't sure of her plans, and even if you move to Utah when Brendan gets home, he can't start school until January. I say quit telling people you're leaving and just get a job. Worry about how soon you're moving when it happens."

"I guess you're right. But part of me just can't accept that I'm going to be stuck here longer. It's so frustrating."

"Things will work out the way they're supposed to," Lindsay assured her. "You just need to exercise a little faith."

Kenidee groaned inwardly. That was part of the problem, and she knew it. She lacked faith.

"Anyway, I'll keep my eyes open. There's got to be a good job around here somewhere. It's probably right under our noses."

"Thanks, Linz. How are you feeling anyway?"

"Great! I can't bend over to tie my shoes anymore, but, hey, the weather's warm so I just wear flip-flops."

"Let's get together and go shopping or to lunch soon," Kenidee suggested.

"Sounds good. I'd love to go into the city. I'll check my calendar and let you know which day is good for me."

They said good-bye, and Kenidee tossed her phone on the bed. She was grateful to have Lindsay in her life. But even Lindsay was busy taking care of Matt and getting ready for the baby.

\* \* \*

Saturday morning, Kenidee's stomach growled as she went into the kitchen for a bowl of cereal. The two boys were in the family room arguing over which cartoons to watch, and Rachel was nowhere to be seen. A loud whirring and pounding could be heard over the sound of the television.

Wondering what it was, Kenidee left the kitchen and followed the noise to the basement. Here she found Rachel playing with Barbies in the corner of the playroom. The door to the "workout" room was slighty ajar and, since that was the location of the noise, she took a quick peek to see who was toiling away on the treadmill.

"Oh!" Robin exclaimed when she saw Kenidee. "You . . . startled . . . me," she said breathlessly.

"Sorry. I just wondered who was working out."

Robin mopped at her dripping forehead with a towel as she stepped off the machine.

"That was the longest twenty minutes of my life," she said, unscrewing the lid to her water bottle.

"It will get easier," Kenidee told her.

"It certainly can't get harder. The problem is, I only have six weeks to get in shape."

"Oh? What's going on in six weeks?" Kenidee asked.

"Didn't your father tell you? Since we never got a honeymoon after we were married, he's taking me to Hawaii. Isn't that exciting?" Robin was too busy blotting her face and neck to see the stunned expression on Kenidee's face.

Had she said anyplace but Hawaii, she wouldn't have cared . . . much. But of all places to take Robin, why did he have to choose Hawaii? Her mother had wanted to go there for years. Kenidee and Matt had always begged their dad to take them. But it had never happened.

And now he was taking Robin.

She got up to leave.

"Anyway, I'm going to be doing a lot more healthy meals: grilled chicken, salads, steamed veggies. Your dad and I are having a contest to lose weight. We started today."

Kenidee faked a smile and headed for the door. "I have some errands to run. I'll be back later."

"Okay. I'm going to try and get in another ten minutes. I have to teach Rachel how to call 9-1-1 first, just in case I have a heart attack," she joked.

Kenidee left without comment. She felt betrayed and angry. Without even showering or making her bed, she grabbed her purse and stormed out of the house.

Her father was mowing the lawn and waved at her as she rushed to her car, but she didn't wave back. Pushing the power button on her stereo, she turned on some soothing music to calm her down.

Thoughts raced through her head. If she couldn't move to Salt Lake, then at least she could move out on her own somewhere near here. She wished Matt and Lindsay had room for her. She'd be willing to sleep on a cot in the laundry room at their house, just to get away.

Driving aimlessly, she found herself in Cam's neighborhood, near the park where she took the girls. As if pulled by some invisible magnetic force, she drove to Cam's house and parked in front. She regarded him as a dear friend, someone she could talk to, someone who would listen. More than ever right now, she needed a friend. Although she needed someone to talk to, the last thing she wanted to do was burden him on his day off. Besides, he probably had something fun planned with the girls and wasn't even home.

"This is stupid," she said out loud and started the engine. Just as she put the car in gear to leave, the front door opened and out ran Brynn and Amanda. Her heart soared at their excitement in seeing her. Unable to resist at least saying hello, she got out and caught them up in a giant double hug.

"How are my girls today?"

"We're helping Daddy clean," Amanda said.

"The vacuum broke," Brynn told her.

"It did?"

"Daddy's sock got sucked."

Kenidee burst out laughing. "Uh oh, that wasn't good."

"Daddy can fix it," Amanda said. "He can do anything."

Kenidee smiled at the two girls, their father's biggest fans, and said, "Let's go see if he needs some help."

They walked into the house, where Kenidee heard Cam threatening to "bust this crazy thing if I have to."

"Daddy?" Amanda said to her father, who was still bent over examining the offending appliance.

"Girls, I told you to go play while I fix the vacuum."

"But Ken-dee here," Brynn told him.

Cam stopped immediately and looked up. He had smears of dirt on his cheek and forehead. "Hey," he wiped his hands on his jeans and stood up. "What are you doing here?"

"I was in the neighborhood and heard some colorful language coming from your house. Thought I'd rescue the girls."

"I wasn't swearing," Cam said. "I wanted to, but I didn't."

"Need some help?" she offered.

"You know how to fix vacuums?"

"No, but how hard can it be to get a sock out?" she teased.

"Hey, it's not that easy. I broke a screwdriver trying to pry it out."

Kenidee pushed up the sleeves of her shirt and knelt down beside the vacuum. She noticed that the sock was stretched and tightly wound around the beater bar. "Give me a pair of pliers," she said.

Cam handed her the tool and told the girls to watch the *expert*. Kenidee pushed the bar around until she found the toe of the sock. Latching on with the pliers she pulled as she rolled the bar, unwinding the shredded sock, until it finally came free.

The two little girls clapped their hands. Cam nodded, clearly impressed with her ingenuity. "I shoulda thought of that."

"Men like to make things more complicated than they really are."

"Oh, do they?" Cam replied, tossing the sock into the garbage.

"Daddy, we're hungry," Amanda said.

"You just ate breakfast," he reminded them. Then he looked at the clock. "It's that late? I guess it is time for lunch."

"I want a corn dog," Brynn said.

"Me too," Amanda added.

Cam looked at Kenidee. "Any idea where they picked up an addiction to corn dogs?"

Kenidee looked at him innocently. "Don't look at me. You know how healthy I eat."

"Ha!" Cam scoffed. "The girl who lived on french fries and chocolate shakes her entire three years in high school."

"I think all that dust from the vacuum clogged your memory."

"Daddy!" Amanda cried.

"Okay, okay. Corn dogs it is. I don't even know where they have corn dogs." While he looked at Kenidee for an answer, Brynn answered succinctly.

"The store," Brynn told him, taking her dad's hand in his. "I show you, Daddy." She tugged him toward the front door.

"Let me wash up first," Cam said.

"Come on girls," Kenidee said. "Let's do something with your hair while Daddy gets cleaned up and changes out of that old Michael Jordan T-shirt."

"Hey, this is my favorite shirt!" he protested. "There's nothing wrong with it."

"Cam, you wore that when you were a sophomore in high school."

"So."

"The neck is ripped and there's a hole in it."

"That's what makes it comfy." He looked at the three faces staring at him and said, "Oh, all right. I'll change. Sure stinks being the only guy around here."

The girls went straight to the bathroom where Kenidee styled their long hair into pony tails, complete with pink ribbons she'd bought for them. Rosy-cheeked and bouncing with energy, the girls waited by the front door, anxious for their outing to the store.

Cam walked out of his bedroom with a bold red polo shirt on and clean jeans. For a moment, he looked just like the old Cam from high school. It was nice to see a smile on his face.

"Corn dogs, huh?"

"Yes, Daddy," Brynn confirmed, grabbing her dad's hand again. Amanda grabbed the other one, and they dragged him to the door.

"You're coming, right," Cam said.

"Is that a question or a command?"

"It's your fault they're hooked on these things."

"Come with us, Ken-dee," Brynn cried, letting go of her dad's hand and grabbing Kenidee's.

"I guess so. I didn't mean to horn in on your day, though."

"It's a welcome break. The girls were getting bored."

They began walking, Brynn holding Kenidee's hand, Amanda holding Cam's.

"So, what brought you to my neighborhood?" Cam asked. "Everything okay?"

"I've made a decision," she answered.

"What's that?"

"I'm putting myself up for adoption."

He nodded, a smile growing on his face. "Which family do you want to adopt you?"

"I haven't decided yet. Maybe the British Royal Family. I always wanted to be a princess."

"You'd look good in a tiara." He looked at her with his head tilted, his forehead scrunched up, as if trying to picture her with a crown on her head.

"I think so."

"Did something happen at home?" he asked.

They crossed the street and turned the corner to the grocery store.

She told him about her father taking Robin to Hawaii, trying to explain the significance of going to the very place her mother had always wanted to go, a place their family had always wanted to go.

"It's like he's saving all the good stuff for now. Trips, going to all her kids' activities . . ." her voice drifted off for a moment. "I just have to get away from it."

"You know your dad isn't doing it on purpose. He's probably not thinking about how much you guys wanted to go to Hawaii. He wouldn't do that. He's not like that."

"It sure seems that way."

Once they arrived at the store, the girls ran straight to the deli counter.

"I take it you've done this a few times," Cam questioned.

"A few," she told him.

He ordered four corn dogs and drinks. Within minutes they all had their food and walked back out of the store.

"We can sit on the grass right there," Kenidee suggested, pointing to a shady area of lawn about half a block from the store.

The sun was warm and cheerful, and a soft breeze ruffled the leaves and flowers.

"Do you like corn dog with your mustard?" Cam asked, noticing her corn dog floating in a pool of yellow.

"I love mustard," she told him. "Try it."

"It's good, Daddy," Amanda told him.

Dipping his corn dog into the sauce, Cam took a big bite, his eyebrows rising as he chewed. "Mmm, this *is* good."

"Help yourself," Kenidee told him.

They all dipped and chewed while they discovered cloud shapes in the sky.

"How did you get through life without eating corn dogs?" Kenidee asked him.

"In high school, I was into really healthy eating and a lot of protein and stuff, you know, to build muscle, get big."

"I remember. It was annoying. You got Matt eating like that too."

"Hey, we ate some junk food occasionally."

She rolled her eyes, remembering how much scrambled egg whites and tuna fish her brother and Cam had eaten.

"Can we go to the park?" Amanda asked.

That was the only word Brynn needed to hear. She was on her feet and ready to go before Cam could answer.

"Ken-dee come, too!" Brynn said.

"Do you have time, Ken-dog?" Cam asked.

"Hey!" Kenidee said, giving him a playful sock in the arm.

"Daddy, why did you call her 'corn dog?'" Amanda asked.

"I called her *Ken-dog.* It's a nickname."

"She's not a doggie, Daddy," Brynn said with a giggle. "Ken-dee is a lady."

"That's true. A very pretty lady, too. I forgot I wasn't supposed to call her that. I'm sorry," he said to Kenidee, looking at her with a repentant expression.

Kenidee smiled, showing her forgiveness.

"Daddy," Amanda tugged on his shirt sleeve, "can we go to the park?"

"Sure." He glanced at Kenidee as he asked, "Can you go?" He offered her a hand to help her up.

"Sure," she told him as he pulled her onto her feet. Their gazes locked for a brief moment. Kenidee hadn't noticed how much gold was in Cam's brown eyes.

"Hurry, Kenidee!" Amanda called.

Kenidee shook off the strange feeling that had just washed over her. How silly of her to get caught up in Cam's deep brown eyes. It was Cam, for heaven's sake. She brushed away the incident knowing she could never have *those* kind of feelings for him. She glanced down at the ring on her finger. Her heart belonged to Brendan.

# CHAPTER 11

It felt good to sit in the sun and watch the girls play at the park. There was a happy, relaxed feeling.

Cam and Ken talked about recent sightings of old friends from high school and Cam's plans to take the girls to Disneyland at the end of the summer.

They reminisced about the time her brother had been allowed to invite Cam to go with their family to Disneyland. Kenidee hadn't been excited to have Cam along. In fact, she had felt it was unfair that her brother had been able to bring along a friend when she couldn't. But when her brother came down with the stomach flu while they were there and had to spend two of the three days in the hotel room, she was glad Cam was with them. They'd gone on all the rides together and had a lot of fun. She wouldn't have enjoyed going all by herself.

"I also remember that you had a thing about princesses?"

"I didn't have a *thing*. I just like the Disney princesses, okay? Every girl does."

"Yeah, I don't know how much I want to encourage my daughters to believe in all that fairy tale stuff. Reality is nothing like it."

"That's for sure. As a little girl, I dreamed of having a knight in shining armor ride up on a white horse and take me away to a castle where we would live happily ever after. Ha! Like that would ever happen."

"See, that's what I'm talking about. Why get their hopes up for something that doesn't exist?"

"Well, the happily ever after part exists. Right?"

"It does?" He faked complete shock at her comment.

"Sure it does." Then she thought about it for a moment. Cam certainly didn't have a happy ending to his marriage. Her parents didn't exactly have a happy ending, not in this life anyway. "At least I think it does."

They both looked at each other.

"Is Brendan your knight in shining armor?" Cam asked.

"Yeah, I think so. He's everything I could ever want in a guy. That's a pretty good place to start, isn't it?"

Cam nodded. "It sure is. I had the odds against me when I got married. Now I know why the Church frowns on gambling. That's what I did when I got married. Look where it got me."

All of a sudden Cam jumped to his feet. "Brynn, hang on!" He ran to the jungle gym to rescue his little daughter, who hung precariously by one arm from the top.

He gave her a stern talking to about climbing so high and not being careful, and then he let her go back to playing.

"That child's going to give me a heart attack," he said as he joined Kenidee on the bench.

"That's what my father used to say about me. I was always getting hurt. I'd been to the emergency room more times before I was five than Matt has been his entire life."

Kenidee's cell phone rang. She excused herself to answer it.

"Good afternoon, Kenidee," the woman's voice said. "This is Lucinda Erickson. I'm calling from the San Francisco Dance Studio."

Kenidee's heartbeat quickened. The San Francisco Dance Studio was one of the most renowned in the Bay Area. Many of the dancers who graduated from its program became professional dancers.

"I understand you are looking for a job teaching dance?"

"Yes, I am," Kenidee replied with surprise.

"Could you tell me where you received your training?"

"I studied classical ballet at the Peter Julian School of Dance under Margaret Woolf. During the summer between my junior and senior years in high school, I went to New York to study at the School of American Ballet, on scholarship. Then after my senior year, I studied in Chicago at the Joffrey School of Ballet, also on scholarship."

"Did you dance professionally?"

"I was in the San Francisco Ballet production of the *Nutcracker* my last two years of high school, and I did some local productions." Kenidee hoped her voice sounded professional.

"I would like to meet with you on Tuesday at eleven AM, if that works with your schedule."

"Eleven would be fine," she answered.

"Good. On Monday, I'd appreciate it if you could drop by a current résumé, as well as a video of one of your performances."

After going over necessary details and ending the call, Kenidee stared at the phone in her hand for a minute, still waiting for the conversation to sink in. She'd been hoping something like this would happen, and voilà, out of the blue, she gets a call for a job to teach. What were the chances?

"Hey," Cam's voice broke her thoughts. "Is everything okay?"

With a shake of her head, Kenidee looked at him and smiled. "I just got a job offer to teach ballet at the most prestigious school in the Bay Area. Well, at least I have an interview."

"Really? Wow! How'd that happen?"

"I don't know. I can't imagine who would have given them my name. Maybe someone at my old studio said something. They knew how badly I was trying to find a teaching job."

"I'm really glad for you," Cam said.

It dawned on her that he might be concerned she wouldn't be able to help him any longer. "Cam, I should be able to work my schedule around tending the girls. They don't teach any pointe classes until after school. In fact, most are usually in the evenings."

"Oh, don't worry about the girls. I've been needing to get another sitter lined up anyway. I just got lazy because you've been so good to help out."

"But I still want to help. I doubt I could teach enough classes to really save any money anyway. I'd like to continue tending for as long as I'm here."

"Why don't you see what classes they have to offer and then we can figure it out. I'm sure the girls would be sad to have you leave. I've never seen them so happy with a sitter. They really love you."

Kenidee smiled. "I love them, too. I'm sure it will work out."

\* \* \*

Kenidee burst through the door in search of that day's mail, hoping there would be a letter from Brendan. He was nearing the end of his mission, each day bringing him that much closer to her, and Kenidee wanted to know how things were going. She also wanted to know what he was thinking. His recent letters were strangely devoid of information regarding his plans after he returned home. She didn't want to distract him by asking, but now with this job opportunity presenting itself, she wanted to make sure she could commit to more than just the summer.

"There it is!" Kenidee shrieked as she spied the stack of mail sitting next to the telephone.

Rifling through bills and junk mail, she searched anxiously for a letter or postcard from her missionary, but there was nothing. She remembered how busy those last months on her mission had been and how anxious she'd felt to get as much work done as possible before going home.

"Kenidee?" a small voice said.

Kenidee hadn't even noticed Rachel come into the kitchen.

"Hi, Rachel," Kenidee said.

"Can you please get me a drink of water? Mommy said I can't bother her right now."

Kenidee got a glass out of the cupboard. "What's your mommy doing?"

"Something secret. She won't tell me."

"Secret?"

Rachel nodded and took a long drink of water. Then she tossed her glass into the sink of dirty dishes.

Without another word, she skipped out of the room.

*A secret?* Kenidee couldn't help but wonder what Robin was doing.

Remembering she had a batch of clean laundry to fold, Kenidee took her armload of clothes from the dryer and went to her room to fold them.

A few minutes later, her dad poked his head inside her door. "You hungry?"

"Hi, Dad."

"What's up, sweetie?" he asked as he walked in and sat down on the edge of her bed.

She didn't even want to get into the Hawaii trip with him, but she did feel like talking about Brendan.

"I was just hoping I'd hear from Brendan today." She matched two socks and rolled them together.

"Honey, I know it's hard when you don't get letters. But just remind yourself that he's serving the Lord. You wouldn't want him to put you over that, would you?"

"No, of course not."

"He probably doesn't have time to do much of anything except his work."

"You're right. I know our APs were very busy. I remember seeing one of them fall asleep in a meeting and tumble right off his chair. The president just said to let him stay there, he needed his sleep. It was funny, but I felt bad for him."

"Well, you should feel proud of Brendan, honey. He's a wonderful young man. I really like him."

"Yeah, me too. Oh, by the way, Dad, I got a phone call today from the San Francisco Dance Studio. They want me to come in for an interview so I can teach."

"That's great, Kenidee. I know how much you've wanted to get back to ballet and start teaching."

"The call came out of the blue. It was the strangest thing," she said.

"Well, I'm glad it did. I'm so happy to see you excited about something." He leaned over and gave her a kiss on the forehead.

"Oh, by the way," she said, "What's for dinner?"

"Robin and I found the best restaurant the other night. We've both been craving it, so I stopped by and got some take out and brought it home. It's called the Island Grill. The food is Hawaiian."

* * *

Monday, Kenidee was back at Cam's, trying to keep up with his girls. By the end of the day, she was exhausted. "Okay, girls, it's time for bed," she said, picking up the last two stuffed animals from the floor.

"No, bed," Brynn said. "I not tired." Instead of climbing under the covers, she began jumping on the bed.

"Don't jump, sweetie," Kenidee told her, as she tossed the animals into the toy chest and shut the lid. "I don't want you to get—"

*Thud!*

Brynn landed on the floor with her arm twisted behind her back. "Waa!" she screamed in pain.

"Oh my gosh, Brynn," Kenidee cried, trying to remain composed but feeling hysteria lurking just beneath the surface. She rushed over to the girl and told her not to move. Big tears rolled down Brynn's pale face.

Amanda started to cry, too.

"It's okay," Kenidee assured them both, certain that Brynn's arm was broken. "Don't cry, sweetie. It's okay."

"I want my daddy!" Brynn sobbed.

"I know," Kenidee said. "I want your daddy too."

She helped Brynn carefully sit up, while supporting the injured limb.

Brynn wailed at the slightest movement of her arm. Kenidee wracked her memory, trying to dredge up her first aid training. Her memory bank was locked, and she too felt like moaning.

"Amanda," she finally said, "can you get the phone for me? We'll call and see where your dad is."

Amanda shot from the room and returned with the phone almost before Kenidee knew she had left.

She dialed Cam's cell phone and prayed he answered.

"Hello."

"Cam, this is . . ." a choking sob stopped her from continuing. How had this happened? She was right there, practically next to Brynn, and she hadn't been able to stop it.

"Kenidee, is that you?"

"Yes." Kenidee struggled to get her words out without falling victim to the panic she was experiencing. She felt horrible that Brynn had been hurt, especially when she was supposed to be watching her.

"Is everything okay?" he asked anxiously.

Fighting for control so she wouldn't alarm the girls or their father, she quickly pulled herself together. "Brynn fell off the bed and hurt her arm."

"How bad is it?"

"It's hard to say." She chose her words carefully, not wanting to alarm the girls.

Cam understood what she was doing. "Do you think it's broken?"

"That would be my guess."

"Can you get her to the emergency room? It would be quicker if I could meet you there."

"I can do that," she told him.

"Are you okay?" he asked.

"Yeah," she lied. She felt responsible for the injury. She had failed Cam and the girls by allowing this accident to happen.

"I'll see you in about twenty minutes then."

Kenidee mumbled an answer before hanging up the phone.

Brynn's cries had turned into a whimper.

"It's okay, sweetie. Your daddy wants us to go to the doctor so they can look at your arm. He'll meet us there."

"Can I take my Ellie?" Brynn asked.

"Sure," Kenidee answered, grabbing Brynn's stuffed elephant.

The little one hugged the animal to her chest while Kenidee scooped her up in her arms. She noticed Brynn's swollen and misshapen forearm and had to stifle her reaction. "Okay, my brave girls," she said with forced enthusiasm. "Here we go."

* * *

Amanda explored Brynn's examining room while they waited for the doctor to join them with the results from the X-ray. The nurse had given each of the girls a water-filled latex glove along with some tongue depressors and oversized Q-tips. They had so much fun playing with their "hospital toys" that, except for the swelling in Brynn's arm, it would have been hard to tell why they were even in the emergency room.

The curtain parted, and, instead of the doctor, Cam stepped inside.

"Daddy!" Brynn cried, sitting up quickly, which painfully reminded her why they were there, causing fresh tears to erupt.

Kenidee jumped up, feeling her heart wrench inside of her chest at the sight of Brynn in pain.

Cam rushed over to his daughter and gave her a reassuring hug. After a moment, she calmed down and began showing him her hospital toys.

Both of the girls were too excited about their squishy gloves to be distracted for long. They soon resumed playing.

Cam told the girls to not squish the gloves so hard they popped, then turned to Kenidee.

"So," he said, "how are you doing?"

Her eyes immediately filled with tears. "Cam, I am so sorry. I was standing right next to her, and I couldn't stop—"

"Hey," he said as he pulled her into a hug, "it's okay."

Tears fell as Kenidee buried her head in his strong shoulder and allowed him to comfort her.

The curtains parted again, and this time the doctor stepped inside with an X-ray film that he slid onto a lit screen. Cam held

Kenidee's hand in his as they stepped closer. The doctor pointed out the buckle fracture caused by the impact when Brynn fell off the bed. He assured them her arm would heal just fine and that they would put on a cast, which she would wear for four weeks.

Brynn bravely allowed the doctor and his assistants to apply the necessary wraps to create a lovely purple cast for her arm. Once the procedure was finished and they were free to go, Brynn showed off her cast to the nurses and the other patients in the waiting room on their way out the door.

It was late, and they were all tired from the two-hour hospital visit. Cam's house was on her way home, so Kenidee followed them in her car to help get the girls to bed and make sure everything was okay.

Cam carried Amanda into the house, and Kenidee carried Brynn and her stuffed animal. They tucked the two girls into bed and then collapsed in the living room to recover from the stress of the evening.

"Kenidee, I don't want you feeling guilty about what happened to Brynn tonight," Cam told her. "It could have happened to anyone."

"I'd just barely told her to be careful. I was five feet away from her. I should have made her stop jumping on the bed. I should have caught her when she fell."

"But that's not how it works. God's right there by us, but sometimes we have to fall to learn an important lesson. Maybe she'll be a little more cautious from now on. I hope she remembers what happened so she won't have to go through it again. But, she might not remember. Isn't that what life is all about? Making mistakes and learning from them?"

"I guess. But it was so hard to see her get hurt. I wanted to take her pain away. I wanted to feel the pain for her."

Cam smiled. "You're starting to sound like a parent."

Kenidee chuckled. "I guess I am. Wow, I can't imagine how much more intense it must feel when it's your own child."

"You want to protect them from everything bad, but it's not possible. If you put them in a bubble, they'll never survive in the world."

Kenidee looked at him with admiration. He'd come a long way since those days when he'd hung out at their house and annoyed her and eaten all the good cereal.

"What?" he asked.

"Nothing. I was just thinking about what a good dad you are."

"You think?"

She nodded. "You're doing a great job with your girls. They're lucky to have you."

"I'm lucky to have them. Even though my marriage to Desiree was a disaster, I can't imagine not having Amanda and Brynn."

The love he had for his daughters was written on his face. She knew how challenging it was for him to be a single parent, but he was doing a remarkable job.

"Well," Kenidee said, feeling exhaustion kick in, "I guess I'd better get going. Are you sure you have everything covered for tomorrow? I can come help after my interview."

"Everything's taken care of. I'm hoping the girl who's tending tomorrow will want the job full time after you leave."

An unexpected clench in Kenidee's heart told her she didn't like the thought of someone else taking care of the girls. But she knew the situation was temporary when she started. With a weary groan, Kenidee got up from the couch and headed for the entry. Cam walked her to the door.

"Thanks for your help today," he said.

"Yeah, I helped Brynn right into a cast."

"Hey," Cam said firmly, "I don't want to hear another word about it. It was an accident."

"I know," Kenidee replied, still not convincing herself. "I'll call her tomorrow to see how she's doing."

"She'd like that."

"Thanks for being so understanding."

"You're welcome." He stretched his arms toward her and gave her a hug. She appreciated the gesture and the strength of his arms around her. "Let me know how the interview goes."

"I will." She stepped back and looked up into his golden brown eyes and smiled. "Good night."

\* \* \*

"Kenidee, Lucinda will see you now."

The receptionist showed Kenidee to the director's office.

Lucinda greeted Kenidee with a warm handshake and asked her to have a seat.

She was a classically beautifully woman, with a swanlike neck, a willowy frame, and thickly lashed eyes. As a former principal dancer for the San Francisco Ballet Company, Lucinda had danced the lead in nearly every ballet and still looked as if she could outdance and outperform any dancer on stage. Kenidee remembered when she'd attended ballets in the past and watched spellbound as Lucinda transformed the stage into an elegant, magical place. Perhaps were it not for a car accident that damaged her spine, she would still be dancing. Instead, she was now the director of the renowned San Francisco Dance Studio, which had placed dancers in companies all over the United States and in Europe.

"So, Kenidee, tell me about yourself and how ballet fits into your life."

Kenidee smiled and felt herself relax. She loved talking about ballet. "As long as I can remember, I have loved to dance. I enjoy all forms of dance, but the discipline and beauty of ballet is what I like the most. I'm too old to think about performing anymore, but dancing is still in my blood. I miss the physical challenge of dancing, the sound of the piano and pointe shoes, the music and movement. I have always wanted to teach, and I plan to get a degree in teaching and choreography from the University of Utah."

Lucinda smiled at her, then said, "Learning to dance and loving to dance are two completely different things. Anyone can learn moves to music, but a dancer feels the movement, feels the music. That is called passion. The only teachers I hire are teachers with passion. For then, and only then, can you truly impart what you have inside. You cannot teach passion to a student, but a student can feel your passion."

Kenidee nodded with complete understanding.

"I have spoken to your former teachers this morning. They are women for whom I have the utmost respect, and they have recommended you highly. I also watched footage of your Nutcracker performance and feel confident in your talents. I am looking for a teacher for my intermediate pointe classes on Tuesday and Thursday evenings and on Saturday mornings. As you probably know, this is the level that usually determines whether a student is cut out for the rigors of dancing on a higher, more demanding level. These students discover what they are made of and whether they have what it takes to go on to more difficult levels of training. I need someone who will push them, almost to the point of breaking, but will help them discover the exhilaration and pure joy of seeing themselves execute moves they never dreamed were possible. Can you do this, Kenidee?"

"Yes," Kenidee answered resolutely, inspired by Lucinda's fervency.

"I believe you can too," Lucinda said with confidence. "I would love to have you join my staff."

"Thank you," Kenidee said, trying to rein in her excitement. "I would love to teach for you."

"Then welcome, my dear. It is a pleasure to have you."

"Thank you," Kenidee said. "Thank you so much."

They made arrangements for Kenidee to attend one of Lucinda's classes where she would be oriented on basic class structure and techniques being taught to that level. Kenidee was confident in her abilities and excited to have a reason to put on her dance clothes and pull her hair into a bun. Miss Lucinda had a strict dress code for students and teachers. That was one of the things Kenidee liked about her.

Even though the future wasn't clear-cut, the path not yet defined, she began to feel that she was heading on the right course and that the Lord was guiding her.

# CHAPTER 12

"You teach ballet?" Amanda asked, as Kenidee pulled her hair into a ponytail.

"Yes. Do you think you would ever want to be a ballerina?" Kenidee asked her.

"Oh, yes! I want to dance on my toes. Do you do that?"

"Not anymore, but I used to. You and Brynn would be beautiful little dancers. And you'd look cute in a tutu."

Amanda giggled. "What's a tutu?"

"Toot-toot," Brynn echoed. She was busy dumping all the hair accessories onto the floor and slipping scrunchies onto her wrist like bracelets, one of her new favorite things to do.

"No," Amanda corrected her sister, "tutu."

"It's a fluffy skirt. Like the one your Barbie doll wears. That's called a tutu."

"I want to do ballet," Amanda said, tiptoeing from the bathroom with her arms overhead. Brynn followed behind copying her sister, which wasn't easy with one arm in a cast.

"Here. Let me show you." Kenidee had the two girls stand by the kitchen table and hold onto the arms of the chairs while she taught them how to put their feet in first position and how to do a plié.

Just as she was showing them second position, the doorbell rang. Kenidee dreaded answering it because she knew who was standing behind the door.

"Mommy!" the girls cried as they ran for the door.

Kenidee wondered where Cam was. He was supposed to be there while Desiree picked up the girls to take them for the afternoon.

They threw open the front door, and Kenidee gaped in disbelief. She hadn't seen Desiree since before her mission. Cam had told her that Desiree's appearance had changed. But she wasn't prepared for the bleached blonde creature standing in front of her.

Desiree stooped down to give each of the girls a hug and a kiss. Kenidee was concerned that she was going to skewer one of them with her long, glittering, acrylic nails.

"Look, Mommy." Brynn held up her arm for her mother to see.

"Daddy told me you had a little accident. I like the purple cast."

Brynn smiled proudly. Kenidee was fascinated that Desiree seemed to have no desire to know more about Brynn's accident or about how she was feeling.

Each of the girls took one of their mother's hands and pulled her into the house.

Desiree looked at Kenidee, and her eyes opened almost as wide as Kenidee's mouth.

"Kenidee, is that you?" she said.

Kenidee nodded, forcing her mouth into a semblance of a smile but too speechless to answer.

"I didn't know you were home. Cam didn't mention it."

"Mommy, Kenidee is teaching us ballet," Amanda said.

Desiree patted Amanda on the head. "That's nice, sweetie. So," she looked at Kenidee and slid one of the spaghetti straps of her lacy camisole top back onto her shoulder, "how are you?"

Kenidee wanted to ask, *"What* are you?" but managed to refrain. "I'm great, thanks. Cam should be here any minute. Do you want to sit down?"

Desiree glanced at her watch. "I hope he hurries. He always does this to me."

"Look Mommy," Brynn said. "Ken-dee helped us pack." The toddler pointed to a Disney Princesses rolling tote bag.

Without a reply, Desiree smiled patronizingly, walked to a nearby chair, and sat down, crossing her darkly tanned legs and tugging on the short skirt that barely covered her behind.

Brynn ran over to her mom and tried to climb up on her lap, but Desiree helped her sit next to her on the chair instead. "Mommy, are we going to the zoo?"

"We'll have to see. I have to talk to your dad first."

Kenidee realized she was staring in disbelief at Desiree and had to force herself to look away. The woman's transformation, with the help of strategic plastic surgery and an abundance of silicone, was so shocking, in an embarrassing, freakish sort of way, that Kenidee was afraid if she kept staring she'd either start laughing or turn into stone, like looking at the Medusa in Greek mythology.

The front door burst open, and Cam rushed inside.

"Daddy!" The girls erupted with joy at the sight of their father.

"Hey girls!" He took a moment to give them each a hug and a kiss. He then looked at Desiree and managed a noncommittal "Hi."

Desiree uncrossed her legs and stood, which was an amazing feat in Kenidee's opinion since her four-inch platform shoes looked like something that would defy gravity. The gap between her shirt and the waistband of her skirt revealed a pierced belly button, something Kenidee could have happily lived her entire life without seeing.

Because of an important business meeting, Cam had on a black suit and crisp white shirt, accented by a deep maroon tie. He looked very striking, very handsome. His appearance didn't go unnoticed by Desiree. She sauntered over to her ex-husband and stood alluringly close to him.

Kenidee watched her display with confusion and nausea.

"I was hoping you'd get home soon." She dipped her chin and batted her eyes at him. "I need to talk to you. Privately." Desiree turned and gave Kenidee an icy look.

"I just need to know what time you'll have the girls home," he said.

"That's what I need to talk to you about." Desiree reached out and stroked her long nails on the sleeve of his jacket. "I'm not sure I'm going to be able to take them."

Amanda looked at her mother with disbelief. Cam told Kenidee that nine out of ten times Desiree had some excuse why she couldn't take the girls. Of course, Cam didn't mind. He didn't want the girls around her anyway, but the girls still wanted to be with their mother.

Brynn's bottom lip curled out.

"Hey, girls," Kenidee quickly said, "why don't we check your room and make sure we didn't forget anything."

Casting her a grateful smile, Cam waited to pursue the conversation until Kenidee had the girls out of earshot.

Although she closed the door, she was tempted to listen to the conversation that ensued as soon as she and the girls left the room.

"Kenidee" Amanda said sadly, "why doesn't our mommy want to be with us?"

Kenidee's heart ached at the girl's question.

Brynn's bottom lip was still curled, and her big eyes were a few blinks away from tears.

"Oh, sweetie," Kenidee said, pulling both of the girls to her, "she does want to be with you. It's just that . . ." She groaned inwardly. Why did she have to make excuses for their mother who resembled an alien from the planet Weird?

"Com'ere, you two." Kenidee sat on the bed and pulled each of them onto her lap, wrapping her arms around them.

"Sometimes grown-ups get so busy doing things that they forget what's important. Your mommy loves you very much," she said, "but she has a lot of stuff going on right now. And even though that stuff isn't more important than you two, it keeps her so busy she sometimes forgets."

She didn't know if the girls understood, but it was the best she could come up with.

"Mommy doesn't smell good like you," Brynn told her.

Kenidee had noticed the strong odor of cigarette smoke when Desiree had come into the house.

"And she doesn't play with us like you do," Amanda added.

Not knowing what to say, Kenidee just hugged the girls. Noticing one of their storybooks on the nightstand, she decided it was probably best just to distract them from what was going on. The girls were soon drawn into the colorful pages of Alice in Wonderland. They were almost through with the story, when the bedroom door opened. Kenidee stopped reading and looked up.

"Guess what girls?" Cam said, coming into the room and kneeling by the bed where they sat. "Daddy's taking the rest of the day off work so we can play. How would you like to go to Paramount's Great America?"

Brynn and Amanda bounced on the bed and screamed with excitement. Cam smiled with relief. Judging by their exuberance, his backup plan worked.

"Daddy, can Kenidee come with us?" Amanda asked.

"Ken-dee come, too?" Brynn echoed.

Cam looked at Kenidee. "Of course, if she wants to."

"Please," Amanda begged, grabbing Kenidee's arm and hugging it tightly. Brynn grabbed the other one. "Please."

Luckily she had nothing planned and was grateful to have a reason not to go home. Robin was on a major health food and workout kick, all reminders of the trip she and Kenidee's dad were taking to Hawaii.

"Sure, I'll go."

More eruptions of excitement from the little girls.

"Great. I'll go change, and we can get out of here."

\* \* \*

While Brynn and Amanda rode the SpongeBob SquarePants ride for the fourth time, Cam and Kenidee sat on a bench and waved each time they went by.

"You're probably wondering why Desiree backed out today," he said.

"I figured it was none of my business," she answered. But yes, she was very curious to know what the girls' mom had that was more important than time with her daughters.

"Her boyfriend, Flash, and his band Mass Havoc, are going on the road, and Flash wants her to go with him."

"Wait a minute. I thought she was involved with the guy at the gym."

"That's over. She's now reached an all-time low."

"A rock star?" Kenidee shook her head trying to process it all. "That explains her appearance."

"I really hate the girls being around her influence. I know she's their mother, but I don't like them seeing how she dresses and how she acts. I've had to ask her a dozen times to not swear and take the Lord's name in vain in front of the girls."

"She doesn't even seem like the same person," Kenidee observed.

"She isn't. She wasn't like this when we were first together. I really believed we'd go through the temple and live happily ever after. Otherwise, I never would have married her. She had so many wonderful qualities."

"It's kind of scary how people can change, isn't it?"

"Tell me about it. Are you a little worried that your missionary is going to be different after two years?"

"No. Because I think we've grown in the same ways since we both served missions at the same time and we've shared similar experiences. I wish he would write more often than every three or four weeks, but I know he's doing what he's supposed to be doing."

Cam nodded approvingly. "He's a lucky guy."

"Thanks. You might have to remind him about that when he gets home."

The ride ended, and the girls ran with excitement to the next one.

"I think they've gotten over not going to the zoo with Desiree," Kenidee remarked.

Cam laughed. They watched the girls climb in the pretend cars that lifted high in the air and circled around.

"I'm sure they're having much more fun here than they would have had with her. She usually just gets them a Happy Meal at McDonald's, then turns on videos for them at her apartment." He sighed. "I know Desiree loves them in her own way, but her lifestyle isn't really conducive to children. I don't really know what to think about her."

"Speaking of being confused, I was a little bewildered by the way she was flirting with you today. Does she ever talk about getting back together?" Kenidee asked.

"No. She just flirts because she thinks she's so irresistible now. She's not interested in me anymore. And I'm certainly not interested in her. Now," he clapped his hands together and changed the subject, "enough about her. I'm starving. Are you hungry?"

"Yeah," Kenidee said. "I'm in the mood for a greasy burger and fries."

"Me too. Let's see if the girls will stop riding long enough to let us get some food."

It took some convincing, but Amanda and Brynn finally agreed to take a short break from their rides as long as their dad bought them each a churro. Carrying their trays of food to a table, Kenidee heard someone calling her name.

She turned to see Joey waving at her from another table. And with him was none other than . . . Lisa. They got up from their table and walked to where Kenidee, Cam, and the girls were sitting.

"Hi, Kenidee," Joey said, greeting her in true missionary style with a handshake.

Lisa smiled but didn't say anything.

"You two having fun?" Kenidee asked.

"We were until Lisa got a little nauseous on one of the rides."

Lisa finally spoke. "That doesn't usually happen to me. I'll be okay. I just needed something to eat."

"Hey!" Joey exclaimed. "Are you going to President and Sister Larsen's homecoming?"

"Yes, and Dolly is coming out for it too."

"Dolly?" Joey asked.

"I mean, Sister DeWitt."

"DeWitt's coming? That's great! We had a lot of fun when we were in the same district. I'd love to see her again."

"I'll call you when I know her schedule."

"Okay." He turned to Lisa. "You want to try some more rides?"

"Sure," she said brightly, even though she still looked pale and queasy.

The two walked off, and Kenidee turned to her food. The girls were already done with their churros and anxious to ride Dora the Explorer. They busied themselves climbing on the railing around the eating terrace while Ken and Cam finished their meals. Kenidee was amazed that Brynn's cast didn't slow her down at all.

"How's Lindsay feeling?" Cam asked as he dunked a fry in ketchup.

"She's doing great. They are getting so excited."

"Desiree never really enjoyed her pregnancies. She was kind of excited with Amanda, but not with Brynn. She hated getting fat."

"Lindsay's done really well with her weight. But she's stayed really active and eats healthy. She's even helped Matt clean up his eating habits. You know how addicted to fast food he got after high school."

"I've never known anyone more addicted to fast food and junk food than your brother."

"My mom tried so hard to make us healthy meals at home, then he'd go blow it on . . ." she looked down at her plate, "stuff like we're eating."

They both laughed.

"Lindsay takes good care of Matt," Cam said. "They have such a great marriage."

A tone of sadness lingered after his words.

"Hey," Kenidee said, "you'll have a marriage like theirs someday."

"You think?"

She nodded and smiled with assurance. "Yeah, I do."

\* \* \*

Thursday night Robin invited Matt and Lindsay over for a barbecue and some of their dad's famous homemade raspberry ice cream. As they sat on the porch enjoying the creamy dessert and watching the lengthening shadows, the conversation jumped from one topic to another—Lindsay's growing belly and Matt's job, to Robin's efforts to lose weight for the Hawaii trip, to Kenidee's new job teaching ballet and tending for Cam.

"How is Cam doing?" Matt asked. "We don't get to hang out much anymore."

"He's great," Kenidee answered. She told them about Desiree bailing on her turn to have the kids and how she and Cam had taken the girls to the amusement park to make them feel better. She went on and on about what a great father he was and how much she appreciated his friendship.

"He used to drive me insane when we were kids and he'd come and hang out at the house all the time," Kenidee said. "But now I don't know what I'd do without him. He's been such a good friend to me."

Matt looked at her with a strange expression on his face.

"What?" Kenidee asked.

"To hear you talk, you'd think you had a thing for Cam," he said.

Kenidee burst out laughing. "What? It's Cam. I don't have a *thing* for him. Sheesh, Matt!" She looked at her father, whose expression was also a little odd.

"Dad?"

"I didn't say anything. I believe you," her dad answered. "You do seem to have some special feelings for him, though."

Kenidee's mouth dropped open. Then she clamped it shut and looked to Lindsay for help. "Are you listening to this?"

Lindsay shrugged and said, "I don't really know Cam, so I can't say anything."

"Don't get all huffy, Ken," Matt said. "You just sounded kind of smitten. That's all."

"Smitten?" Kenidee held up her right hand and showed them Brendan's ring. "Hello. Did you think I'd forgotten about this?"

"Okay, okay," Matt said, holding up his hands in defense. "I was just asking. Besides, it would be weird to see you two together."

"Well you don't have to worry about it," Kenidee said.

Her father looked relieved.

"Dad, you weren't worried that I've been developing feelings for Cam, were you?"

"Oh, no. Not really. I'm glad to hear you're not, though. You have spent a lot of time over there."

"But Cam's not there when I am," she stated. "It's just me and the girls."

Her father nodded with understanding. Kenidee wasn't sure why they were even having this conversation. There was nothing developing between her and Cam.

Suddenly a high-pitched scream from Rachel pierced the air. She'd tried to climb up one of the trees with her brothers and couldn't get down. Everyone rushed from the patio to help Rachel, except Kenidee, who was grateful to escape to her room. Boy, was she going to be glad when Brendan got home and life could be simple and normal again.

\* \* \*

After the class completed the warm-up at the barre, Kenidee instructed the students to find a place in the center of the floor. The twelve dancers spread themselves out evenly across the floor of the studio and waited for her to continue instruction.

They did some simple tendu exercises, then combinations that included jumps, turns, and extensions. Movement and music filled the room, and as Kenidee demonstrated the pirouettes and fouettés, she felt the surge of excitement and joy that came from performing moves she'd spent years practicing and perfecting.

Class ended with leaps and pique turns across the floor that left the students sweating and breathless. The time had passed much too quickly. The students bowed to Kenidee and the pianist, then burst into applause. Kenidee's chest filled with joy.

After the girls exited the room, Kenidee changed from her ballet shoes to a pair of flip-flops with daisies on them. Even though she taught a pointe class, as the teacher she didn't wear pointe shoes, although several times during class she longed to wear the pink satin shoes that had been her passion for so many years.

"Well done, my dear," Lucinda said as she entered the room through the back door. "Several of the girls stopped me on their way out and said wonderful things about your class. I peeked in a few times and liked what I saw. You already have a good rapport with the students. That's the most important place to start."

Kenidee tingled with excitement at Lucinda's praise and reveled in the complimentary words throughout the drive home. She thought about her dreams and goals and knew that going back to school and getting her degree was very important to her. She hadn't spent all those years eating, drinking, and sleeping ballet, just to walk away. It was a part of her. She knew that now.

Receiving a college degree was something her parents had always wanted for her. Even as a young girl, her mother told her that she wanted her daughter to have an education. The thought of her mother's wish drove her decision to continue her education. As soon as Brendan got home and they were married, they would move to Utah and she would get back into school. Maybe even as soon as January.

The house was empty by the time she arrived home. She was starving and looked in the refrigerator for something to eat but found only half-filled containers of food from the Hawaiian restaurant. Instead, she grabbed a container of yogurt and a banana and sat down at the table to eat and think about her plans for the future.

Just as Kenidee took a large bite of banana, the telephone rang. Chewing and swallowing as quickly as she could, she grabbed the phone on the fourth ring before the answering machine picked up.

"Is Kenidee there?"

"This is she."

"Kenidee, this is Patricia Nielsen, Brendan's mother."

"Sister Nielsen, hi!" Kenidee had hoped to talk to Brendan's family sometime. They'd been out of the country when she'd gotten home. His father had business in South America.

"I'm sorry it's taken so long to call. We've been home about a week now, but it's taken a while to get back on track. I wanted to catch up and see how you are doing."

Kenidee told her about what was happening in her life and shared her excitement for her new teaching position at the ballet studio.

"Do you hear much from Brendan?"

Kenidee told her about the few letters Brendan wrote but kept her comments positive. She didn't want his mother to think she was a complainer, especially when her son was doing the Lord's work.

"I've noticed how much shorter his letters are," Sister Nielsen said. "I wish so much they could e-mail on a regular basis. The president lets him send an occasional e-mail, but it's still not enough. Has he told you about the family he baptized?"

"Yes, that's so wonderful. He really loves them."

"He's already asking if they can come over for a visit. I think he wants them to come a few weeks after he gets home."

"Really?" Kenidee wasn't sure she felt as excited as she probably should. But she couldn't help it. She'd waited almost two years to be with Brendan, and she didn't like having to share him with anyone other than his family.

"The plans are still a little unsure, but they seem to be determined to come."

"It will be wonderful to meet them," Kenidee offered, trying to convince herself.

"I'd love to get together with you sometime. Maybe we could meet for lunch and catch up."

"I'd like that."

"I'll call you soon then, dear."

Kenidee hung up with mixed feelings. She was glad to have finally touched base with Brendan's family, but she wasn't excited to learn that he had already mapped out plans for when he got home—and she didn't know where she fit into those plans.

Telling herself she was just being selfish, she pushed her feelings aside and went to take a shower. It would all work out the way it was supposed to, she told herself. She just had to have faith. Everything was going to be okay.

* * *

After an uneventful weekend, Kenidee went to Cam's on Monday morning to tend. Because Amanda and Brynn were content playing house, Kenidee decided to do some cleaning to help Cam out a little.

For a long time, she'd wanted to dust items above the cupboards in the kitchen, but there always seemed to be something more important to take care of. With most of the other house-cleaning done, she decided to tackle this project so she wouldn't have to look at the dust on the leaves of the silk plants one more day. It was a little obsessive of her, she knew, but her mother had always kept an immaculate house and had taught Kenidee how to work hard and clean thoroughly.

To get to the shelf, she needed either to climb a six-foot ladder or to stand on the counter. Since she couldn't find a ladder anywhere in the storage shed or garage, she opted for standing on the counter. With cleaning supplies placed at an easy reach, Kenidee began to work her way across the length of the cupboards, dusting and cleaning plants, baskets, and other decorative items that had probably not been cleaned since they'd been put there.

The dust caused her to sneeze and lose her balance. Quickly she grabbed the ledge and steadied herself, pulling in a few calming breaths to steady her racing heart. Determined to finish, she continued spraying and wiping and dusting, knowing that she'd be glad she'd gone to the trouble once she was finished.

The front door opened, and Cam came inside. "Girls, daddy's home."

Amanda and Brynn came running, nearly knocking him over with their hugs.

Within seconds, Cam noticed Kenidee doing her tightrope cleaning act.

"Do you need some help?" he asked, coming closer and looking up to examine exactly what she was doing.

"Almost done," she said." But would you take this?" she asked, reaching for a silk plant that needed a good hose spraying. The basket was far enough away that she had to reach on her tiptoes. Just as she grabbed hold of the wicker container, her foot slipped. With a scream, she felt herself falling.

"Got ya!" Cam said, catching her in his arms.

She kept her eyes shut for a moment while she took a few seconds to convince herself that she hadn't crashed to the ground and was safely in Cam's arms.

"Are you okay?" he asked, since she hadn't yet said anything.

"Yes," she answered, finally opening her eyes. "Thank you. That scared me so badly."

He looked into her eyes and smiled. "I'm glad I was here to catch you."

"Me too." She felt a quiver of something zip through her heart. Was it fear? Or something else?

Their gazes locked just for a moment before Amanda and Brynn's voices broke the connection.

"You almost fell like Brynn," Amanda said. "That was scary."

"Yeah, scary," Brynn added.

Cam lowered Kenidee's feet to the ground and held her gently until she was steady.

"You okay?"

"I'm fine," she answered, wondering exactly what that sensation was just then.

"Good. Next time, wait for me to come home before you do something like that. In fact, what were you doing?"

She swallowed and pulled her wits together. "Just cleaning. It was . . . dusty."

"Next time, leave the dust. I don't want you getting hurt."

"I will. Sorry," she said.

He noticed a note on the refrigerator telling him to call his brother.

"When did Trevor call?"

"About an hour ago." She gathered the cleaning supplies and stowed them under the sink. "How's he doing anyway?"

"Great. He works for his father-in-law's construction company. They can't keep up with the growth in the Salt Lake valley."

"Does he like living there?" She'd met Trevor only a few times but thought he was nice.

"Seems to. He's really close to his in-laws, and he and his wife, Brindy, love to snow ski, so I think it's worked out well. He's got a lot going on; that's why he called to talk to me."

"Oh?"

Cam was about to continue but the doorbell rang. It was his home teachers bearing a box of Krispy Kreme donuts. They invited her to stay for their message and a donut, but Kenidee had promised Lindsay that she would come by and see how the baby's nursery had turned out.

The girls each gave Kenidee a quick hug good-bye before hurrying off to see what the home teachers had brought. Cam walked her to the door to say good-bye.

"Thanks for your help today. And, keep your feet on the ground, will ya?" he teased with a big, dimpled smile. "I may not always be around to catch you when you fall."

She looked up at him to respond, but again their gazes locked momentarily.

A response was slow in coming because her brain was on pause. Finally, Amanda broke the spell when she came running to ask if she and Brynn could have a donut.

Kenidee snapped out of her trance and said, "Don't worry. Besides, you know me, I'm used to falling."

He chuckled, then stopped and looked at her, the teasing gone from his eyes. "But I couldn't bear to see you get hurt."

"Come on, Daddy!" Amanda tugged at his arm. "The donuts are waiting!"

He gave her one last look, then raised his hand in good-bye and shut the door.

# CHAPTER 13

"Thanks for coming over," Lindsay said as Kenidee came through the door.

"I'm sorry I haven't been over sooner," Kenidee told her.

"I know how busy you are, working two jobs and all. That's okay." Lindsay's eyes narrowed, "Hey, are you okay?"

It took a minute for the question to reach Kenidee's brain. "Sorry, what did you say?"

Lindsay looked at her closely. "Something's wrong. What's going on?"

"Uh, nothing," Kenidee answered, trying to push her confusion down deep so she could cover it up with fake enthusiasm. "Let's go see Emaree's room."

"Ken," Lindsay insisted, "your body is here, but your brain clearly isn't. What's up."

"Really, Linz, it's nothing. I'm just distracted, I guess."

Lindsay took Kenidee's hand and pulled her over to the sofa. "Come and talk to me for a minute. The baby's room isn't going anywhere." They sat down. "We never get to chat. Tell me how you're doing."

Kenidee talked to her about teaching and tending. Nothing in particular.

"How are things at home? Any better?" Lindsay shifted her position and stuffed a pillow behind her back to get comfortable.

"Yeah, I guess. Dad's trying a little harder to be involved in my life, but he's so busy with Robin and her kids. I know it's hard for him."

"How's Robin?"

"She's okay. I mean, I don't have anything against her. It just still seems somehow not right to see my dad with her. Sometimes I feel like I'm in some sort of twilight zone that won't end. But she's a nice person."

"How's Brendan?" Lindsay fished for more information.

"Great. He doesn't have much longer. He's really finishing strong. His letters are short and sweet. The few I get."

"How's Cam?"

"He's—" she stopped short. "What do you mean, how's Cam?"

"I just wondered. You two get to see each other a lot. I just wondered how he's doing," Lindsay clarified.

"He's fine. He's got something going on with his brother, but he hasn't really talked about it. Why do you ask?"

"You just came from Cam's house, and you seem really distracted, like you said. Is everything okay?" Lindsay's gentle tone and sincerity broke down Kenidee's defenses. Truth be told, Kenidee needed someone to talk to.

Kenidee put her hands over her face and groaned. Then she uncovered her face and looked at her sister-in-law. "I just had something odd happen, and I don't know what to make of it. Well, actually I do. I think I understand, but for a minute, it threw me for a loop. Confused me a little."

"What?"

Kenidee explained how Cam had caught her when she'd almost fallen off the counter and how her heart had reacted to it.

"I think it's just that I haven't had any contact with a guy for so long that it caught me off guard when Cam held me in his arms like that. I just need Brendan to get home, don't you think?"

Lindsay nodded. "That makes sense. Two years is a long time to be apart from your sweetheart. I guess it could be the reason for you to react the way you did. Or . . ."

"Or?"

"I guess it's possible you could be developing feelings for Cam."

Kenidee clapped her hand onto her forehead and groaned again. "I'm not developing feelings for Cam. I could never think of him that way. He's Cam. He's my brother's annoying best friend."

"Correction," Lindsay said. "He *was* your brother's annoying best friend. You're not kids anymore."

Kenidee shook her head. "That's true, but, really, I'm not developing feelings. I think I'm just vulnerable because I'm so ready for Brendan to come home. Brendan is everything I've ever wanted in a guy. I love him as much now as I did when he left. I wouldn't want to do anything to jeopardize our relationship."

Lindsay nodded with understanding. "So, you're okay?"

"I'm fine," Kenidee said, feeling her sense of commitment to Brendan strengthened. "I'm glad we talked. It helped me sort it out in my head."

"Good. I'm glad I could help. You know you can call me anytime you want to talk."

"I know," Kenidee said. "I'm so glad to have you."

The two girls hugged, then Kenidee followed Lindsay to see the baby's bedroom.

Everything was fine now.

\* \* \*

The month of June slid quickly into July. Kenidee put every penny she made into her savings and focused her efforts on Brendan's return. She didn't allow her thoughts and heart to wander anymore. As soon as he returned home in August, everything would be wonderful. Her wait was almost over.

In the meantime, Kenidee looked forward to traveling to Sacramento to see President and Sister Larsen return home and speak in church about their mission.

The timing was perfect because the dance studio took the first two weeks of July off to do cleaning and repairs, so she didn't have to teach. Cam had taken the girls to Salt Lake City to spend a week at his brother's house, their first time in an airplane, so

Kenidee didn't have to tend. She had plenty of time to get ready for her upcoming big weekend.

The biggest excitement was that Dolly was coming to stay with her and together they would travel to Sacramento to see the Larsens. They could also finalize plans for her to move, once and for all. Finally, things were falling into place.

Kenidee dressed quickly so she could do something she rarely did . . . join the family for breakfast. She entered the kitchen to find the three kids devouring French toast in pools of syrup. Robin was busy stuffing envelopes with a flyer announcing an upcoming Relief Society project. She was in charge of the big event and had spent countless hours preparing for it. Kenidee had never seen a person go to such lengths for a Relief Society Enrichment night. And if she wasn't doing something for her church calling, she was spending time on the computer. Kenidee never asked, but she wondered how Robin could spend so much time on the computer. Especially when the house needed so much attention.

Her dad was busy packing up his briefcase, but he stopped to greet her and give her a kiss on the cheek.

"Where are you off to, Dad?" Kenidee asked.

"Fresno. I've got a training seminar through the weekend. I'll be back late Sunday." He closed the lid of his briefcase. "Isn't this the weekend your friend comes to town and you go to Sacramento?"

"Yes. I pick up Dolly in the morning. We'll spend Friday together, then drive up to Sacramento on Saturday. The Larsens have a big open house that evening. Then we'll come back Sunday after their meeting. Her flight to Salt Lake leaves that evening around eight o' clock."

"Sounds like a fun weekend. Where are you staying up there?"

"We found an inexpensive hotel on-line. It's not too far from where the Larsens live."

"Well," he checked his wallet for cash and clipped his cell phone to his belt, "you two be careful driving. We'll see you Sunday night."

Kenidee sat down at the table and put a couple of pieces of french toast on her plate. She opted for fresh strawberries and blueberries instead of maple syrup. Robin had been making a huge effort to keep fresh fruits and vegetables around the house and Kenidee could tell both Robin and her father had lost a few pounds as a result of their efforts to eat healthier.

"I'll call you when I get there," Kenidee's father said to his wife as he pulled her into a hug and gave her a long kiss.

Kenidee tried to ignore them and busied herself with her breakfast.

The three kids finished eating, gave their stepdad a quick hug, and ran to brush their teeth and get ready for swimming lessons.

Kenidee finished her breakfast and cleared off the table, wishing Robin would teach her kids to at least carry their own plates to the sink.

"I can get that when I get home," Robin told her. "I'm just going to run these invitations around while the kids are at swimming. Then I'll be back. What have you got going on today?"

"I've got a hair appointment at ten."

"Oh? What are you having done?"

"I need a haircut really badly, and I want to have some caramel highlights put in."

"That will be pretty," Robin said, scooping up bags of invitations. "I guess I'll see you later then."

Kenidee watched her stepmother leave, sighing after the door shut. She felt like they'd arrived at a level of hesitant acceptance, but they still weren't comfortable with each other. It would probably always be a little awkward, but once she and Brendan got married and moved away, they would never really be home much anyway.

Noticing the lateness of the hour, Kenidee resisted the urge to load the dishwasher and scour the kitchen. Blocking out the mess around her, she went to her room to finish putting on her makeup. She was excited to finally get her hair done. Maybe she'd even go shopping for clothes after her appointment.

* * *

Fighting back tears until she got in her car, Kenidee managed to shut the door before she broke into uncontrollable sobs. She looked like a—she didn't have words to describe herself. All she'd asked for was a shoulder-length blunt cut with a few long layers in it, plus a subtle weave of caramel-colored highlights. She felt like a punk rocker for Halloween minus the black, skintight jeans and leather neck and wrist bands with metal studs in them.

And she'd paid money to look like this! "What am I going to do?"

She pulled at her over-teased hair that was shorter and more layered than she wanted it and wondered how long it would take to grow back. The color was closer to orange than caramel and was in big chunks, not subtle streaks.

She wasn't sure what to do. She couldn't be seen in public like this, yet she had a big weekend planned.

Putting on dark glasses and sliding down in her seat so no one would see her, she inserted the keys into the ignition and planned to drive straight home, crawl under the covers, and not come out until her hair grew three inches and the color magically faded away.

That was odd. When she turned the key, nothing happened. She tried it again and still the car didn't respond. Her heartbeat began to accelerate, and her breath grew shallow. Telling herself to stay calm and not panic, she removed the key, checked to make sure it was the right one, and tried it again. Nothing.

"This can't be happening," she said, gripping the steering wheel with both hands and resting her forehead on her knuckles. "Please, not now. Not today."

After a few minutes of breathing and trying to calm herself down, Kenidee optimistically turned the key one more time. Nothing.

Luckily she had Gilbert's number programmed into her phone in case of an emergency like this one. She immediately pushed "send" and waited for him to answer.

"Hello?"

"Gilbert, this is Kenidee."

"Kenidee, how nice to hear from you. I was hoping you'd call sometime."

She rolled her eyes. He probably wouldn't say that if he could see her.

"Listen, Gilbert, I'm having a bit of a problem. My car won't start."

"Oh dear. Is it the battery?"

"I don't think so, but I guess I could find someone to give it a jump. If that doesn't work, I just wondered if you guys could help me out. I probably need to get it towed somewhere so it can get—"

"I don't work at that dealership anymore."

Her heart sank.

"I got the job as a data analyst I was telling you about. You'll just have to call a tow truck and have the car towed to your mechanic."

"I don't have a mechanic," she said icily.

"Oh, that's too bad. It's a good idea to find a trusted mechanic."

"Yeah, I'll put that on my 'to do' list. In the meantime, I'm stuck at the beauty shop." *Should be called "ugly shop,"* she thought, catching a glimpse of herself in the rearview mirror.

"I'm sorry," Gilbert said. "If you give me a few minutes, I could probably slip away from my office and come and get you."

"No, that's okay. But thanks."

"Okay, well, if you need anything else, give me a call."

She hung up the phone and felt heat crawling up her face. Letting out a growl of frustration, she smacked the steering wheel and felt hot tears sting her eyes.

Once she settled down again, she tried Lindsay and her brother. Then she remembered that Lindsay had a doctor's appointment, and Matt had gone with her.

Finally, she did the only thing she could think of . . .

"Hi, Robin?"

"Kenidee? Is everything okay?"

"Actually . . ." A sob caught in her throat preventing her from saying another word.

"What's wrong?"

"My car . . . my hair . . ." she managed to say.

"Have you been in an accident?"

"No."

"Do you need me to come and help you?" Robin's voice was full of concern.

"Yes."

"Are you still at the beauty shop in the Valley View strip mall?"

"Yes."

"I'll be right there."

Kenidee hung up the phone and cried.

* * *

Kenidee climbed inside the minivan and sat in the passenger's seat. Robin went around to the other side and got behind the wheel.

"I could try a few more mechanics to see if they can get to your car quicker," Robin offered.

"We've already tried five. This guy at least promised to look at it today. I still won't get it until next week."

Robin didn't respond as she maneuvered the car onto the busy street and merged into traffic.

"Actually, the way I look right now, I don't feel like going anywhere anyway."

"Maybe you just need to go home and wash it and style it yourself. Not so spiky like the hairdresser did it," Robin consoled Kenidee.

"I wish I could just go back to bed and start this day all over again. I can't believe how horrible I look."

As they waited for a turning light, Robin offered a suggestion. "I don't know how you feel about this, but Eduardo, the guy who does my hair, is amazing at fixing mistakes. In fact, that's how I found him. I had a bad perm and thought I was just going to have to shave my head and start over, but he managed to save my hair and my sanity."

"You think he could help me?"

"I know he could."

"Do you think I could get in today?" she asked with desperation.

"I can call if you want me to."

"Sure, why not. It can't look any worse."

Robin placed the call on her cell phone and talked to Eduardo.

"You're a lifesaver," she told him just before she hung up the phone.

"What did he say?" Kenidee asked.

"He said he would try to squeeze you in."

Kenidee breathed a sigh of relief. Finally, something good.

"Thanks, Robin," she said.

"No problem. I know how you feel. Glad I can help."

* * *

"Are you ready?" Eduardo asked before he turned Kenidee around to look in the mirror.

Her eyes darted to Robin, who nodded and smiled.

Daring to hope that she no longer resembled an alien, Kenidee nodded. With her eyes shut, she waited anxiously while Eduardo turned her chair around and took off her cape.

"Okay," Eduardo said. "Open your eyes."

Kenidee slowly opened one eye and then the other. A surprised grin began spreading across her face until her mouth had to open to accommodate her thoroughly delighted smile.

"I love it!" she exclaimed, turning her head from side to side.

Instead of the neon highlights and spiky layers of her earlier hairdo, she had warm caramel streaks and soft, flippy layers that not only looked stylish but also flattered her cheekbones and round eyes.

Robin clapped her hand together. "It's so cute on you, Kenidee. I love it too." Then she turned to the miracle worker. "Eduardo, I knew you would know just what to do."

Eduardo bowed and accepted their applause.

"Am I going to be able to do this at home?" Kenidee asked, running her fingers through the soft layers at her neck.

He showed her how to put a foaming mousse product on her hair then round brush her hair until it was dry. With a little styling gel, she could arrange the wispy layers any way she wanted them.

She was so excited to have fun with the new cut, and she was thrilled beyond words with the color.

"I don't know how to thank you," Kenidee told her stepmom when they left the salon.

"I'm so glad it worked out well." Robin looked at her. "It is such a cute style on you. I really love it. It's tempting to grow mine out a little longer so I can do that flippy thing. It's so fun."

"You should. You'd look really cute with your hair this way," Kenidee told her with sincerity. Robin had a pretty face with petite features that would be framed perfectly with a similar hairdo.

"Is there anything else you needed while we are out?"

"I was thinking of going shopping, but that can wait," she didn't want to push her luck any further. "We can go home now. I feel bad I've taken up so much of your day."

"To be honest, it's nice to have a break. I've been working on that Relief Society Enrichment activity so much I'm kind of sick of it. In fact, I'm starving. How about you?"

"Yeah, I could eat."

"I know the best Mexican place that has wonderful salads," Robin suggested.

"Sure, if you have time."

"I've been doing good on my diet. I can splurge this once."

They ended up eating at the Mexican restaurant and talking about Robin's Enrichment night activity, which offered classes in compiling a Family Home Evening activity book, complete with handouts, and assembling 72-hour kits for each member of the family.

Since they were right next to the mall, Robin suggested they pop in so Kenidee could look for a new pair of pants. She found several pair of pants she liked, plus a new pair of shoes, and three fun T-shirts that were modestly cut.

Kenidee felt bad she'd taken up all of Robin's day. She couldn't deny that Robin had been an enormous help to her. In fact, she didn't know how she would've gotten through the whole ordeal without her help. She did know one thing she could do to help out.

"Robin, why don't you leave the boys home with me while you take Rachel to gymnastics?"

Robin looked at her with surprise. "Are you sure?"

"Sure. I'm not going anywhere, and I need to organize some things in my room. I'd be happy to keep an eye on them."

"I'm sure they'd rather stay home than go to Rachel's gymnastics studio and sit. Thanks, Kenidee."

"It's the least I can do for all you did for me today."

Robin brushed her comment away with her hand. "I was glad to help. I had fun."

"Me too."

\* \* \*

"Mommy, I'm ready," Rachel announced. She was dressed in a cute little leotard and shorts and had a pink Barbie gym bag slung over one shoulder.

"Okay, sweetie. Let me just tell the boys we're leaving."

As soon as they were gone, Kenidee sprang into action. She first started a load of laundry, then got to work on the kitchen. The dishes were gross and she hated scraping pots and baking pans clean, but she was on a quest to straighten up the house so Robin wouldn't have to worry about that on top of her Relief Society activity and taking care of her kids.

Since Kenidee's dad was out of town, the yard wouldn't get mowed. Knowing Robin, she would feel like she needed to mow the lawn, so Kenidee changed into some capris and tennis shoes and went outside and fired up the lawn mower.

The boys were easy to watch because all they did was play video games and eat popsicles. Kenidee stopped occasionally to check on them and get a drink of water.

She enjoyed being outside in the fresh air and breathing in the smell of fresh cut grass. As a kid, Matt had the job of mowing the lawn. However, Kenidee had her turn at doing yard work and knew how her dad liked things. She dumped the clippings and swept the walks so everything looked neat and tidy when she was done.

She was parched and sweaty when she finally went inside. The boys had finished playing games and were actually in their rooms playing with their toys.

Just as she sat at the table with a tall glass of lemonade, the phone rang. Checking the caller ID to see if it was the garage where she'd taken her car, she was surprised to see Dolly's number come up.

"Hello, Dolly!" she sang.

"Hey, Kenidee," Dolly answered, unenthusiastically.

"What's up?" Kenidee asked with dread.

"It's my grandmother," Dolly said, "She . . ."

Kenidee knew immediately what her friend was going to say.

"She died." Dolly began to cry, and for several minutes, they both remained silent while Dolly released her pain through quiet tears.

"I'm so sorry," Kenidee finally said. "I know how hard this must be for you and your family."

"We knew she wasn't doing well, but we felt so strongly that she would get better. I just wasn't prepared for this."

"I don't know if we ever are," Kenidee told her.

Dolly told her about her grandmother's final days and how spiritual they had been.

"I'm so grateful for the gospel. I don't know how anyone could survive the death of a loved one without the knowledge that they'll see them again," Dolly said.

"I know what you're saying."

Robin and Rachel came through the garage door while Kenidee was on the phone. Robin's face registered shock and surprise as she looked at the immaculate kitchen.

"I wanted to call and tell you about Grandma," Dolly said. "I also wanted to tell you that I won't be able to come to California this weekend."

Kenidee's jaw dropped with disappointment. "You can't?"

"I'm sorry. I can't leave my mom. She's devastated. She needs my help to plan the funeral. Please tell the Larsens hi for me."

"I will," Kenidee said. "If I get to go."

"What do you mean, if you get to go?" Dolly asked.

"My car broke down. I was thinking of calling some of the elders to see about catching a ride with them." This option was her last resort, but she was out of choices.

"Good. That way you don't have to go alone."

"Yeah." Kenidee tried to hide her disappointment but was having a difficult time doing so.

"I'm sorry I can't come. I'll see if I can change my tickets for another time."

"That'd be fun," Kenidee answered. "I'll call you when I get home and tell you about it if I go."

"And give the Larsens my love when you see them."

Kenidee hung up the phone and stood there wondering how much worse the day could get.

"Is something wrong?" Robin asked.

Numbly Kenidee answered. "Dolly's grandma died. She's not going to be able to come."

"I'm so sorry to hear that. Is she having a hard time with her grandma's passing?"

"Yeah, they were very close."

"Are you still going to go to Sacramento?"

That question flipped Kenidee's emotional switch onto high.

"Probably not," she managed to answer. Then, before tears erupted, she abruptly left the room and went straight to bed. The quicker this day ended, the less time there was for anything else to go wrong!

# CHAPTER 14

It was close to ten on Friday morning when Kenidee heard her bedroom door squeak open. She'd had a horrible time falling asleep and finally drifted off about two in the morning. She felt like Wile E. Coyote after the Road Runner dropped an anvil on his head.

Prying her eyes open, she rolled over to see who had opened the door.

"I thought I'd better check on you," Robin said. "You don't usually sleep in this late. Are you okay?"

"I think so."

"I'll let you go back to sleep then. Holler if you need anything. Oh," Robin said before leaving the room, "the repair shop called about your car. They can fix it, but they have to order the part and it won't be done until next Tuesday."

"Okay. Thanks."

Robin opened her mouth to say something, then closed it.

Kenidee rolled over in bed and pulled a pillow over her head to shut out the light . . . and the world.

An hour later, Robin came back.

Kenidee was surprised she'd fallen asleep again.

"Hi," Robin said. "Are you sure you're okay?"

Trying not to get annoyed with her stepmom, but wishing the woman would just let her sleep, Kenidee slowly shook her head as a yawn took over.

"Listen, I just wanted to tell you that if you still want to go to Sacramento, I can take you."

Kenidee opened one eye and looked at her. "What?"

"I said I would take you. My sister lives there, and I'd love to have an excuse to go visit her. Your dad's gone all weekend. It would be fun."

"What about your Relief Society activity?"

Robin brushed the concern away with her hand. "You know what, it doesn't matter. I'm sick of working on it, and I can delegate the rest to my committee. What do you think?"

Kenidee had hoped that she could catch a ride with Joey, or one of the other elders, but their cars were already full.

When she didn't answer right away Robin said, "Well, let me know what you decide. I'm still going to make some calls to take care of the last minute details just in case you decide you want to go. We could leave this afternoon anytime."

"Okay."

Robin began to close the door.

"Robin," Kenidee said.

"Yeah?"

"Thanks."

Robin smiled and shut the door.

* * *

"There should be a national holiday named after the guy who invented car DVD players and headphones," Robin said.

Kenidee looked back at the contented faces of Robin's three kids as they watched, spellbound, the most recent Disney movie. Suddenly they all burst out laughing, making Kenidee laugh at their funny giggles.

"Since Rachel can't read a clock yet, she measures time by television shows and movies. I told her that we'd be at Aunt Shelley's house by the time the movie ended. It makes traveling so much easier."

Kenidee was grateful to have the DVD player in the car too. She had been worried about keeping the kids entertained while their mother was driving.

"I'm glad you decided to leave today," Robin said. "Shelley wasn't happy we were coming for only two nights. She already has a lot planned."

"I'm excited to go to the Jelly Belly factory. I've never been there before."

"You'll love it. They have chocolate, too. It's like going to Willy Wonka's factory! You'll really like Shelley. She's a ton of fun."

"Is she younger or older than you?" Kenidee was curious about the woman in whose home she would be staying.

"Younger. Prettier. Taller. Thinner. Smarter. You name it. She got all the good genes in the family. I'd hate her if I didn't love her so much."

Kenidee chuckled.

"She was there for me when my first husband died. Gave up her job in Seattle and moved in with me to help me out. I don't know how I would've made it without her." There was a more serious note to Robin's voice.

"How did your husband die?"

"Car accident."

"What happened?" Kenidee asked, wondering how she'd never heard the story. "If you don't mind telling me."

"Oh, no, not at all," Robin said. "We were getting ready to go out for our anniversary, and he went to get the babysitter while I got the kids to bed. This was when Rachel was just a baby."

Kenidee glanced back at the little girl who had a Tootsie Pop in her mouth and her favorite stuffed animal in her arms.

"Anyway, I waited and waited, wondering if maybe he had to stop for gas or was talking with the sitter's parents—they were our good friends. But he never came and never came. The babysitter finally called to ask me when we were going to pick her up. Right then, I knew. I knew something bad had happened. Instead of panicking, I felt very calm. You've probably felt this before, but when a person receives communication from heaven, it's like you know volumes more than just the one fact of revelation you are receiving. Does that make sense?"

"Kinda."

"What I mean is that I knew Scott was gone. But I also knew that it was his time to go and that the Lord needed him and that he'd fulfilled his mission on earth. I also knew I would be okay and that the Lord was very aware of me and the kids and that things would work out. In maybe one second, I knew all this."

"Wow."

"That doesn't mean it was easy. Oh boy, it was anything but easy. I mean, I really loved Scott. He was the sweetest dad and the most loving husband, and I missed him so badly that even my bones ached. I understood the Lord needed him, but I needed him too. I had a lot of anger and frustration at times. I think I prayed continuously for two years straight. I'm sure the Lord got very tired of my constant dialogue with him."

Kenidee nodded, completely understanding Robin's emotions. In fact, it sounded a lot like herself after her mother died.

"Slowly, somehow, I was able to put my life back together and become functional again, but it took every ounce of strength and every grain of faith to keep putting one foot in front of the other. I did go into a bit of a depression—not wanting to get out of bed, not wanting to eat, stuff like that. Actually, that was the thinnest I've ever been in my life, but that was one heck of a way to lose weight. I'd rather be fat."

Robin glanced over at Kenidee, who smiled at her comment.

"I really thought I was going to be alone the rest of my life. I mean, who wanted a thirty-something mother of three who had cellulite, a mortgage, and little income or education? I wasn't the greatest catch in the pond."

"Robin, will you tell me about when you met my dad? He's kind of told me already, but I'd like to hear your version."

"You mean, the true version."

"Yeah," Kenidee said with a laugh. Her father had given so few details of their first meeting that he made it sound more like a business meeting than anything romantic.

"Neither of us was looking for a new spouse when we met. In fact, I had turned down every opportunity to be set up or go to single adult activities. I figured I didn't need a husband. I had Shelley, and that was enough. All I wanted was a companion, someone to go to a movie with occasionally or maybe travel with when the kids got older. I think your dad was lonely, especially with both you and your brother gone, so he might have been more open to the idea than I was. Anyway, I lived in Menlo Park, and a friend from my ward dragged me one night to see a movie. I wasn't particularly excited to go, but she'd been bugging me for months to go out with her, so I finally got a sitter and went. Well, I don't even remember the name of the movie, but it was about the dumbest thing I'd ever seen. Then, there was this love scene in it that made me very uncomfortable, so I got up and walked out. I bought some popcorn and sat in the lobby to eat it and wait until the show was over so my friend could take me home. It was about the same time that this gentleman also walked out of the movie. He bought a box of peanut M&Ms and sat down across from me. We both sat there and munched, occasionally catching each other's eye and smiling uncomfortably. I admired how handsome he was—he reminded me of George Clooney."

"Other people have told him that before."

"I can see why. I finally thought how ridiculous it was for us both to be sitting there and not say anything. So I asked him if he was enjoying the move, you know, jokingly of course. And he just started laughing. We both did. It wasn't even that funny but for some reason we cracked up. We started talking about how stupid the show was, and he told me that a colleague of his had dragged him to see it, kind of like me. We said that maybe we should set those two up on a date. I tell ya, Kenidee," Robin signaled to change lanes, "talking to your dad was as easy as talking to an old friend. It took a while to get him to open up, but once he did, we found out that we had a lot in common. He told me about losing your mother, and I told him about Scott. We were thrilled to find out that we were both LDS, too. In that forty-five minutes, we covered most of the highlights of each other's lives. But the most important thing we discovered was that we were both enjoying the company of someone of the opposite sex. Enough so, that we decided it would be fun to meet for lunch . . . the very next day."

Kenidee actually found herself caught up in the story, somehow forgetting that the man Robin was talking about was her father.

"I was sad to see the movie end because it had been such a long time since I had enjoyed a conversation with anyone as much as I enjoyed talking to your dad that night. Well, it blew my friend away when I told her that I'd met someone and had made a lunch date with him. She was really into the LDS single adult scene and had tried to get me involved. And wouldn't you know it, I got my own date." Robin laughed. "She was convinced I was taking a big risk by going out with a complete stranger, but I didn't feel that way. I felt like I was meeting a very dear friend for lunch.

"So I spent the next morning trying to look extra nice, which was really hard because in those six years I hadn't bought any new clothes and hadn't done anything with myself. I wanted to look so good for your dad. Well, I managed to find something—I think I wore black so I'd look thin—and I went to the restaurant. I was so excited I could hardly stand it. I went to the bathroom three times before he showed up because I was so nervous. And then he walked through those doors. He had on jeans, a white button-down shirt, open at the collar, and a deep brown, tweed sport coat. He looked so good I practically melted onto the floor.

"We sat down for lunch and two hours later we finally said good-bye. We had talked nonstop the entire time. I don't even remember if we ate because we were so busy talking. It was during that lunch that I fell in love with him."

Robin glanced over to Kenidee. "I'm sorry, that probably isn't easy for you to hear."

"No, that's okay." Kenidee actually liked hearing how much Robin loved her dad. She hadn't really thought that Robin married him just so she had someone to take care of her and her kids, but the thought must have been in the back of her mind because she changed her thinking after hearing Robin's story. "Please, go on."

"It was the way he talked about your mother and you and Matt that did it for me. He spoke with such reverence and gratitude and love. I saw it in his eyes; it showed on his face. He mourned deeply for the loss of your mother. I heard the pain in his voice when he told me about her. He was so proud about his daughter on a mission, and he told me how hard it was not to have you there when your mom passed away. I knew he was a very wonderful and special man, and I felt honored just to be there with him.

"We didn't make plans for another date after lunch, and I wondered if I'd ever see him again. I couldn't stop thinking about him. I missed him so much. When I was with him, I felt whole again. And I was happy. We laughed constantly when we were together, except when we cried together."

Kenidee didn't know what to say. But she began to see how important Robin was to her dad, and how important her dad was to Robin.

Robin went on, "That same night, about eleven o'clock, I was lying in bed, thinking about your dad. I'd just finished reading my scriptures and saying a prayer where I had thanked the Lord for letting me meet a wonderful man that proved to me that men, like your father and like Scott, still existed. It was then that the phone rang. It was your dad."

Kenidee smiled.

"We talked until two in the morning. Just like best friends. It wasn't a romantic thing, it was like talking to . . . a best friend, that's all I can say. He shared his grief with me. And because I knew exactly what he'd been through, I could completely understand. I really think it helped him to talk about it with someone he knew understood."

"I bet it did too," Kenidee said, knowing how much it helped her on her mission to have Joey talk to her.

"Our relationship didn't really become romantic until right before your dad asked me to marry him. I was content just to have him as a friend. We spent a lot of time together and the kids adored him. It was very easy, very natural. And I had told myself that if this was all that was meant to be, then I was grateful to have such a wonderful friend. I was completely blown away when he proposed, yet I knew it was right."

"Mom," David asked from the back, "are we almost there?"

"Not yet, sweetie. When the movie is over."

"Can I have a juice box?"

"Sure," Robin said, reaching back to feel for the bag containing treats for the kids.

"I can get that," Kenidee said and quickly found the item requested. Of course, once the others saw their brother get a drink, they wanted one too, and then came the peanut butter and jelly sandwiches their mother had made for them.

After the kids were settled again for the last part of the trip, Kenidee turned back around and found herself thinking of Robin's story. She began to readjust her thoughts and revise previous reasoning. Knowing how their relationship had unfolded changed the way she looked at her father and Robin's marriage. They'd been best friends first. They'd helped each other heal and move on.

"Kenidee, you want one of these?" Robin asked her, offering a plastic bag.

"What is it?"

"Chocolate covered cinnamon bears. Don't let the kids see. I brought fruit snacks for them."

"I've never tried one."

"They're to die for."

Kenidee liked regular cinnamon bears, so she picked one up and bit off its head. She chewed for a second before popping the rest of it in her mouth. "That is so good."

"Isn't it? I swear, there's nothing in the world that doesn't taste better dipped in chocolate."

Kenidee took a few more and handed back the bag. "Do they have these at the Jelly Belly store?"

"Are you kidding? Where do you think I got them? I keep a supply on hand at home. I'll show you where I hide them when we get back."

Kenidee smiled. Robin was seriously a chocoholic, but Kenidee decided, if that was her worst fault, she could live with it.

# CHAPTER 15

When they pulled up to the curb, Robin's sister Shelley raced out the front door, her arms waving wildly. She threw the van door open and grabbed Rachel from her seat, gave her a big hug, and twirled her around before setting her down on the ground and pouncing on the next child.

David giggled as Shelley tickled him and kissed him on the neck. "I missed you guys," she said moving to Mikey, who tried to escape from her but was unsuccessful. "Not so fast, mister. Not without my hug."

Mikey gave her a hug and let his aunt kiss him too, then quickly bolted from her clutches.

Robin rolled her eyes at Kenidee and said, "I warned you, she's very physical. And hyper."

During the drive to Sacramento, Robin had attempted to describe her sister to Kenidee. Consequently, Kenidee knew to expect the unexpected from Shelley.

Shelley yanked open her sister's door and devoured her in a hug. "Hey, Sis. This is so cool that you could come this weekend. We're going to have so much fun." Then Shelley noticed Kenidee in the passenger's seat. "Kenidee! Hi!"

Shelley released her hold on her sister and ran around the front of the van to the other side. Kenidee actually shrank back as Shelley tore open the door, but she didn't fight the woman's enthusiastic hug.

"Thanks for coming. It's so good to meet you. I hope you're hungry. I made dinner for you guys. Come in. We'll get your stuff later." Shelley's exuberant conversation left her listeners breathless.

She pulled Kenidee from the car and out onto the front lawn. Her home was a cute little rambler with a lawn and a few straggly bushes in front. She was much too busy living life to its fullest to do yard work, Robin had told her.

"Look kids," Shelley said when they came inside, "I have a surprise for each of you."

"Shelley, you don't have to buy them a toy every time we come."

"I know I don't have to, but I want to. Besides, who else do I get to buy toys for? Hurry up, you guys. Open them."

The kids ripped the wrapping paper from the gifts and squealed in excitement. Rachel received a princess Barbie that she'd been wanting, David got some sort of remote-control car, and Mikey had a new handheld video game. They were in heaven.

"I'm their favorite aunt," Shelley informed Kenidee.

"You're their only aunt on our side," Robin said.

"It doesn't matter. I don't get to see my kids often enough. I'm so glad you came to visit. Are you hungry? I made a magnificent salad and thought we could have some pasta."

"That sounds great, Sis," Robin said. "Let us help."

"Okay, sure," Shelley answered. "The kids can play while we talk." She reached an arm around Kenidee and gave her a hug, "I'm so glad you came. It's wonderful to meet you. I love your hair, by the way. Wait, don't tell me, Eduardo did it!"

Kenidee's mouth opened in surprise. "How did you know?"

"Are you kidding? He's the best! He's the only one I will let touch my hair."

Shelley's hair was long, thick, and coppery brown. Her only makeup was soft pink lip gloss. She was a little taller than Kenidee, probably five foot eight or nine, and she had the bluest eyes Kenidee had ever seen.

With a pot of pasta boiling on the stove, Shelley whipped up a light Alfredo sauce to go over it. Because she was vegetarian, she didn't add meat, but she had a vegetable salad with a raspberry vinaigrette dressing that set Kenidee's mouth to watering.

Robin spread garlic butter on french bread and broiled it in the oven until it was golden brown. The fragrance of everything mixed together was intoxicating. Calling the kids for dinner, they all sat down at the table and waited as Shelley placed the bowl of steaming pasta on the table before taking her own seat.

Following Shelley's lead, they all held hands around the table and bowed their heads while she thanked the great powers of the universe for the food and for their health. She prayed that they would have wisdom to make good choices and that mankind would realize that they were destroying the planet and would start taking care of it.

It was an unusual prayer but very heartfelt. Shelley was a naturalist, and while she didn't have a religious affiliation, she was very spiritual. She practiced yoga and was an environmental activist.

Robin said that they were close growing up until she joined the Church her senior year in high school. Then Shelley wouldn't have anything to do with her. Their parents had been hippies during the sixties and had raised their daughters without boundaries or rules and allowed them to follow their hearts and "find themselves." Robin found herself through the gospel. Shelley was convinced she was joining a polygamist cult.

It wasn't until Robin's husband died that the two put their differences behind them and Shelley came to help. They agreed to disagree about lifestyles and religion and to accept each other for who they were. After that, they were devoted sisters and best of friends.

Shelley's vegetarian meal was delicious, and Kenidee ate so much she thought she might have to be rolled away from the table like a giant beach ball.

The kids were dying to swim in Shelley's pool, so after waiting an excruciatingly long half hour, they were finally able to jump in.

Shelley, Robin, and Kenidee relaxed on lounge chairs in the warm summer evening and watched as the kids splashed and played in the water.

"So, Kenidee, tell me about yourself," Shelley asked.

"Not much to tell, really," Kenidee answered. She briefly explained about her mission, her studies before her mission, and her future plans with Brendan.

"Two years is a long time," Shelley observed. "How do you know things haven't changed between you?"

"I won't know for sure until he gets home. But we were busy doing the same thing at the same time, and I think that helped us grow even closer than we were before. He gave me this before he left." She showed Shelley her ring.

"Sweet. I guess you two are serious. Still, two years. A lot can change."

"Not me and Brendan. We're meant to be together." Kenidee spoke a little more smugly than she had intended.

"I still can't believe that kids willingly do these missions," Shelley remarked to them. "And that you pay your own way. That's amazing."

"I can't think of anything that has prepared me for life as well as my mission has," Kenidee told her. "Going away to school, living away from home, definitely is a similar experience, but on a mission, you can't call home when things get tough. You really find out what you're made of and how strong your faith is. It was hard. The hardest thing I've ever done, but I'm so grateful I did it."

Shelley smiled at Robin. "What a girl. I wish I'd known so much about myself when I was twenty-one."

"Or even thirty-one," Robin added.

"How about forty-one!"

They both laughed, their laughs sounding exactly the same. And Kenidee discovered that Robin's laugh wasn't as annoying as she'd once found it to be.

"Hey, after we get the kids to bed, let's play Uno," Shelley suggested.

"Great idea!" Robin exclaimed. "Do you like Uno?" she asked Kenidee.

"Sure. That sounds fun," Kenidee said.

Shelley clapped her hands together. "I'm so glad you guys came up this weekend. I was going to go hiking with a friend, but she pulled out on me at the last minute."

"The kids should be prunes by now," Robin said. "Let's get them out and to bed so we can have some fun."

\* \* \*

"You're such a cheater," Robin said accusingly to Shelley. "I'm sorry. I forgot to warn you about how much she cheats," she apologized to Kenidee.

"I don't cheat!" Shelley responded. "I'm just lucky."

"Ha!" Robin exclaimed.

They'd played cards for over an hour and had eaten nearly everything chocolaty or sweet within a five-mile radius. Apparently, both of the sisters were addicts.

"You hurt my feelings. I need more chocolate," Shelley said.

"It's not fair," Robin said to Kenidee as she watched her sister pop a bite-sized Snickers into her mouth. "Shelley can eat anyone under the table and not put on an ounce. I just look at food and my rear end grows wider."

"How do you stay so thin?" Shelley asked Kenidee.

"Doing ballet used to keep me toned and help me watch my weight, but now I mostly run. I'm starting to teach ballet again, so hopefully I can get back in shape."

"I love ballet," Shelley said. "I took dance lessons, but once I started on pointe shoes I stopped. Those things kill! How can you stand them?"

"Look at my feet," Kenidee told her and held out her mangled feet for display.

"Ahh!" Shelley shrieked. "Your feet are so ugly!"

"They look a lot better than when I was dancing six days a week."

"But, why would you do this to yourself? Look at your toes. They're all crooked."

Not only were her toes crooked, but she had bunions on the insides of her feet by her big toes, and her nails were discolored and misshapen.

"Gee, it's hard to believe that something so beautiful as a ballerina en pointe could look so hideous with her shoes off," Shelley remarked. "Is it worth it?"

"Ask me that when I'm sixty and can't walk," Kenidee answered. Then she said, "To me, it was worth it. That was the price I had to pay for the joy dancing brought to me. Just like a football player risks getting broken bones or concussions when he plays, it's something you do because you love it."

"That's how I am with chocolate," Robin said. "I love it so much I'm willing to be overweight for it."

Shelley gave her sister an appraising look.

"Okay, no I'm not. The one reason I hesitated coming here this weekend is because I knew I'd blow my diet. And I want to look really good in my swimming suit."

"That's what cover-ups are for. Just find yourself a couple of cute sarongs and you'll be fine," Shelley told her.

"I don't own a sarong. Actually, I haven't been swimsuit shopping either."

"Then that's what we'll do tomorrow. Trying on swimsuits will jump-start your diet."

"Or jump-start my heart!" Robin exclaimed. "I'll probably take one look at myself and have a heart attack."

The women giggled and talked about the horrors of swimsuit shopping and jeans shopping and bra shopping. They decided that men had no clue about what women went through to look good.

"Do men even have bad hair days? I mean, how hard is it to style a half inch of hair on your head. A bad haircut can change our lives for months!" Robin remarked.

"It's not fair," Shelley said.

They ended up talking and laughing until two in the morning. Kenidee hadn't had that much fun since sleepovers in high school.

* * *

Shelley's thirteen-year-old next-door neighbor, McKenzie, came over to babysit Robin's kids while the three women went shopping. The kids had known McKenzie for years and felt comfortable with her. McKenzie's mom would be home just in case they needed her for anything.

With three "kid-free" hours, they hit the outlet mall and began their search for the *perfect* bathing suit.

Shelley found the *perfect* pair of Birkenstocks and a couple of *perfect* pairs of walking shorts. Kenidee actually found a *perfect* three-tiered skirt with a little sparkle around the hem and an embellished T-shirt to match it. With strappy, low-heeled sandals it would be ideal to wear to the Larsens' open house that night. But no *perfect* bathing suit was to be found.

"I'm not going to Hawaii," Robin fretted as she looked at her reflection in the dressing room mirror. "I'll look like a beached whale. Especially in this black and white suit. Just call me Shamu."

"Sis, you look wonderful. Okay, maybe not in this particular suit, but you've got a cute shape. You've got great legs and after three kids you still have a nice chest. That's one thing I didn't get."

"I need one of those sarong things," Robin said. "A big one. A tent."

"I'll go look," Kenidee volunteered.

"And make it black. Black is slimming," Robin called after her.

Kenidee smiled and shook her head as she left the dressing room. She looked through all the options on the rack and found a simple black coverup that tied around the hips, and then she found a colorful Hawaiian print red sarong, with orange and pink plumeria flowers on it. As much as Robin liked color, she was bound to like it.

She was about to return to the dressing room when she spied a cute, solid-red bathing suit, halter style but not low cut. It had a built-in girdle that would slim the waistline, and the color matched the red sarong perfectly.

"Where is she?" Kenidee asked when she returned to the dressing room and Robin was nowhere in sight.

"Hiding like a chicken in the dressing rooms."

"I'm scaring away the other customers," Robin said through the curtain.

"I found you something I think will work. You just have to give it a chance."

"Is it made out of camouflage fabric?"

"No, but I think you're going to like it."

"Only if it's a magic bathing suit. Do you guys think liposuction really works?"

"You don't need liposuction," Shelley told her. "Just try on the suit and quit your whining."

"No more chocolate until I get on that plane," Robin told them. "I need you guys to help me, okay?"

Shelley rolled her eyes and circled her finger by the side of her head. Kenidee smiled.

They kept waiting for Robin to come out and model the suit, but her dressing room was silent.

"Hey," Shelley finally called. "Get out here."

"You guys aren't going to believe this."

"What already?" Shelley insisted.

"Shut your eyes," Robin said.

"Good grief!" Shelley complained.

"Just do it."

They both shut their eyes and heard Robin come out of the room.

"Okay, you can open them, but I want you to be honest."

Kenidee and Shelley opened their eyes and saw Robin standing before them, looking chic and trim in the red bathing suit and flower print sarong.

"Wow, sis."

"Yeah," Kenidee echoed. "Wow. You look great, Robin."

She did, too. The cut of the neckline and straps made Robin's torso look longer and thinner. The sarong covered up her trouble areas but showcased her shapely legs.

"You like it?" Robin asked.

"Are you kidding. You should get one in every color. That suit looks like it was made for you," Shelley told her.

Robin looked at Kenidee.

"You look hot!" The words were out before Kenidee realized she was describing her stepmother.

Robin giggled. "Right. I've never looked hot in my life."

"Well you do today," Shelley said. "Really. With a pair of low-heeled sandals, you'll fit right in over there."

Robin clapped her hands together like an excited child. "I'm glad you like it because I love it. Thank you, Kenidee. I never would have chosen it for myself."

She hurried over and gave Kenidee a hug.

Kenidee hugged her back and realized that she was happy Robin had finally found "the *perfect* suit."

She also realized that she was looking at Robin through different eyes. Robin would never replace her mother, no one in the world ever could. But Robin wasn't trying to. Robin just wanted to be her friend. And Kenidee was glad to have her as a friend.

\* \* \*

"So you'll just give us a call when your party is done?" Robin said, pulling over to the curb in front of the church.

"I can probably get a ride with one of the others, but I'll call if I need you."

"Okay. Well, have fun. You look really nice. I'm glad you found some shoes to go with your outfit. And you're definitely having a good hair night."

"Thanks for noticing. I wasn't sure I could fix it the way Eduardo did."

A group of missionaries pulled up behind them and piled out of the car. Kenidee recognized a couple of them and waved when they noticed her in the passenger's seat of Robin's van.

"Guess I'll see you later. Thanks, Robin."

Kenidee climbed out of the van and was greeted by several elders she vaguely remembered from a zone meeting. She was glad she remembered them since she'd only served in five different areas her entire mission and hadn't gotten to meet too many elders. However, the biggest problem she anticipated was that the guys looked a lot different not wearing their dark suits and white shirts.

She hoped they had name tags for everyone, or it was going to be a long night.

# CHAPTER 16

The foyer inside was jam-packed with missionaries. Most of them were elders, but several sisters were scattered throughout the crowd, sisters she didn't recognize.

Actually, maybe it was going to be a very short night. She would say hi to President and Sister Larsen, then call Robin to come and get her. She would have given anything to have Dolly there with her.

"Kenidee!" a male voice called.

Kenidee turned to see Joey pushing through the crowd. Just seeing familiar faces brought a sense of welcome relief to her.

"Hi you guys!" she said. "I'm so glad you're here." She lowered her voice, "I don't recognize anyone here."

"Sure you do. They just look different in their civvies," Joey said. He began pointing out missionaries she'd served with, and once she put the name with the face, Kenidee's recollection returned.

"Everyone will recognize you, though, even with your haircut," Joey said.

"Why do you say that?"

"I can say this now," he said to her, "but you were the best-looking sister in our mission. Oh, not that I was checking you out or anything," he reassured Kenidee.

"Uh, thanks."

"Hey, you know me, I always tell the truth. Where's Sister DeWitt?"

"She couldn't come. Her grandmother passed away."

"Ah, that's too bad," he said. "I was looking forward to seeing her."

Kenidee detected a note of interest along with his disappointment.

"She said she'd come and visit soon though. I'll let you know when she does, and maybe we can all get together," she suggested.

"I'll be in Utah soon. We can hook up there, too. Hey, why don't we go inside. President Larsen should be here any second."

Joey led the way into the gymnasium where several long banquet tables had been set up and some of the Larsens' family members were now busy covering them with refreshments for the evening.

Kenidee finally recognized one of the sisters helping and hurried over to her.

"Sister Andrews," Kenidee said as the girl placed a platter of cookies on the table.

As Sister Andrews looked up at Kenidee, a giant smile covered her face. "Sister Ashford!" she cried and rushed over to Kenidee. The two girls hugged, then reminded each other of their first names.

Someone on stage tapped on a microphone and said, "Testing, one, two, three." The elder warmly welcomed everyone and then introduced President and Sister Larsen.

President and Sister Larsen stepped through the curtains and the crowd burst into applause. Standing at the microphone, President and Sister Larsen waved at the crowd. Sister Larsen dabbed at her eyes, and President Larsen kept a loving arm around her waist.

They were a handsome couple, distinguished and refined. President Larsen was tall, with dark hair that had grown substantially more gray during his three years as mission president. Sister Larsen was petite and pretty, with rosy cheeks, a well-shaped nose, and blue eyes that sparkled.

Kenidee tingled with excitement as she looked at the couple who had come to mean so much to her. She loved them like surrogate parents. She never would have survived on her mission without them.

President Larsen finally held up his hand to quiet the cheering crowd. Then he leaned into the microphone. "Elders and sisters. What a blessing it is to be here with you tonight. Sister Larsen and I are overwhelmed with your support and attendance. We're so happy you could be here with us to celebrate the time we spent together serving the Lord. Each and every one of you mean the world to us. We feel as if you are our own sons and daughters, and we're grateful you would take time to be here with us tonight.

"We'll have an opening prayer and a blessing on the refreshments, then we'll spend roughly the next hour mingling and getting reacquainted. Some of you have asked for pictures, so we'll do that over here by the stage. When Elder Turner gives us the signal, we'll all meet in the chapel to watch a video presentation and sing a few hymns. Since Sister Larsen and I will be speaking in church, we'll dispense from sharing any comments tonight."

The elder who'd been assigned to offer the prayer hopped up on the stage and greeted President and Sister Larsen with a handshake. Then Sister Larsen hugged him, something she said she'd do to every elder as soon as they were all released since she wasn't allowed to hug them during the mission.

After the prayer and blessing on the food, the group separated, some going to the name tag table, others surrounding the food table, and still others crowding the stage. Kenidee was in the final group at the stage, and right next to her was Sister Andrews, whom she was now struggling to think of as Nikki.

"Don't you just love the Larsens? I hope someday I can marry someone just like President Larsen. Don't you?"

Kenidee had always wanted to marry someone like her father, but there were also many qualities about President Larsen she admired.

"I've made a list," Nikki told her.

"A list?"

"Of what I'm looking for in a husband. I wrote one when I was in Young Women, and I refined it while I was on my mission. Do you have a list?"

"I guess, kind of a mental one," Kenidee told her.

"You should write it down. In your journal. Then you'll know when you meet the right guy."

Kenidee didn't tell her that she'd already met the right guy.

"Sister Ashford!" Sister Larsen exclaimed when she saw Kenidee standing there.

Kenidee embraced Sister Larsen and felt tears sting her eyes. They'd become so close after Kenidee's mother had passed away.

"How are you, my dear?" Sister Larsen asked, holding onto both of Kenidee's hands as she spoke.

Kenidee blinked quickly, trying to clear her tears. "I'm doing great."

"And how are things at home? Is that going well?"

Kenidee automatically almost said something negative before she realized she had to correct herself. "Actually, Sister Larsen, things are going well."

"I'm so grateful to hear that. And how's your missionary?"

"He'll be home in a few weeks."

"Oh my goodness. I'll bet you're so excited!"

"A little nervous, but very excited."

"You'll have to let us know how everything turns out. One of my daughters waited for her missionary and was married soon after he got home. My other daughter waited for her missionary too, but when he got home, things just weren't the same. You just never know. But the Lord will guide your path, right?"

Kenidee nodded.

"It's so wonderful to see you. Let's talk more later." She then noticed Nikki and exclaimed, "Here's another one of my sister missionaries. I've missed you girls so much!"

Kenidee smiled at Sister Larsen, in some ways wishing that they were back on their missions at a mission conference. She stepped to the side to wait for President Larsen.

"Well, well," President Larsen said when he saw her. "If it isn't Sister Ashford. Finally, I get to hug my number one missionary."

With a laugh, Kenidee gave President Larsen a hug.

"How are you?"

"I'm doing well, thank you."

"How's your family?"

"Also doing well."

"I'm happy to hear it."

"I nearly called you a few times to see if you'd let me come back," she said. "But now everything's good."

"I certainly would have loved to have you back. You don't know how many times I wished I had you to help with training, especially the new sisters that came to the mission."

His generous words made her feel warm inside. She looked up into his kind eyes, saw the loving expression on his face, and was flooded with gratitude for the opportunity she'd had to serve with this outstanding man and his equally amazing wife.

"We were hoping you'd be here," President Larsen said. "And I'm glad to hear things are going well for you. It was hard to watch you go through such a difficult time on your mission, knowing how much you hurt."

"You and Sister Larsen were a great strength to me. You really picked me up when I was down."

"We were glad we could be there for you." He gave her a warm smile, his eyes reflecting kindness and fatherly love. They ended their conversation with another brief hug.

There was something familiar about their conversation. Maybe it was the way President Larsen could make someone feel like the most important person in the whole world to him. Or the warmth, wit, and sincerity that made him so endearing and such a great leader.

Then, she realized something very odd and wondered if she might have stumbled onto the reason the conversation felt so familiar. President Larsen reminded her of Camden.

\* \* \*

"So, how was it?" Robin asked when Kenidee came through the door. She'd waited up for Kenidee, who'd gotten a ride home with Elder Billings and his buddies.

"Sorry I'm so late. I stayed after talking to President and Sister Larsen. They are the neatest people."

"Your dad sure speaks highly of them," Robin said. "He told me how sweet they were when your mom passed away."

"Sister Larsen either visited me or called me every day for two months. I couldn't have made it through without them."

"I'm grateful they could be there for you."

"Me too. Maybe you can meet them sometime."

"I'd like that. And I know your father looks forward to meeting them," Robin told her. "How was the party?"

"A lot of fun. It was weird seeing all these missionaries I served with and feeling comfortable calling them by their first name. Some were just as cool as they were on the mission, others were a bit strange, and others had changed a lot."

"What do you mean?"

"They just seemed different than what they were like when I knew them on my mission."

"Better or worse?"

"Both."

"So, did you meet anyone interesting?"

"Not really. I mainly went to see President and Sister Larsen. After the program tonight when most of the people had left, we ended up having a good talk. They had a hard time coming home too."

"I can imagine," said Robin, " after devoting your life for three years to loving and serving like that. They sound like wonderful people."

"They are," Kenidee confirmed. Then she added, "I had this really unusual déjà vu experience while I was talking to President Larsen because I realized that he reminded me of someone."

"Really? Who?"

"He reminds me a lot of Cam. Or Cam reminds me of him, I don't know which. They just have certain qualities about them that I admire."

"You'll have to tell Cam," Robin said. "That's quite a compliment to him."

"If he knew President Larsen, I'm sure he'd think so."

They were quiet for a moment, then Robin said, "We've never really had a chance to talk about this, but . . ."

Kenidee sat down across from her on a padded wicker chair.

"I know how hard it was for you to have your mom pass away while you were gone. But then, to come home to your dad's new wife and three kids . . ." Robin swallowed hard. "I know how hard that's been for you. And I guess I just want to say that I'm . . ."

Watching Robin struggle with her emotions tugged at Kenidee's heart.

"I'm just so sorry it's been so hard on you."

Tears stung Kenidee's own eyes.

"Your mother is such an important part of this family, and I would never, ever try to take her place. But I would like to be your friend. Someone you know you can turn to and who will always be there for you and love you. I'd also like to get to know your mom somehow. I want to find out what she liked and didn't like, what she liked to do, things like that. I never want her to be forgotten because, without her, your father wouldn't be who he is today. He wouldn't be the wonderful, dear man I fell in love with. And you and Matt wouldn't be who you are. And I think you kids are very special. I'm so glad," she stopped and wiped tears from her cheeks, "I'm so glad my children have such wonderful examples to look up to."

Tears cascaded down both their cheeks, and Kenidee found herself going to Robin and giving her a hug.

"Thank you," Kenidee told her.

They both sniffed and cried and hugged until their emotions were finally exhausted. They sat down next to each other on the couch.

"I've been wanting to tell you that for a long time," Robin said, using the sleeve of her T-shirt to wipe her eyes. "I didn't mean to unload all of that on you, it just sort of came out."

"I'm so glad you said something. I know I've been difficult. That's not the kind of person I usually am."

"You haven't been difficult. I knew you needed time and your own space."

"It's just that I felt disloyal to Mom, I guess. But you're right; it's not about replacing her. No one can do that. But there is always room for a friend," Kenidee told her. "I'd really like that."

"Me too."

"I'm surprised Shelley's asleep. Isn't she usually the night owl?"

"The kids climbed into bed with her to watch a movie, and they all fell asleep."

"She's really great. I like her."

"She is great. She likes you too."

They both relaxed against the cushions as the lateness of the hour caught up with them.

"Mommy," a soft voice said.

Rachel walked into the room, rubbing her eyes. "I had a bad dream."

"Com'ere, sweetie," Robin said, gathering her little one into her arms.

Kenidee remembered being little and going to her mom when she had a bad dream, and how much better she felt with her mother's protective and loving arms around her. Warmth spread through her as she looked at Robin giving that same comfort to Rachel. She knew that she was blessed to have Robin as a stepmom.

# CHAPTER 17

Music from the piano flowed as beautifully as the dancers in the room. Kenidee's heart soared as she watched girls finally execute moves that had been so difficult for them weeks ago. This was what teaching was all about. She received great satisfaction seeing desire transform into performance.

One of the front desk girls appeared at the door and waited as they finished the pirouette exercises across the floor.

"Miss Ashford, you have an important telephone call."

Kenidee felt a surge of excitement.

"Genevieve," she said to her most advanced student, "could you please continue with fouettés."

"Yes, ma'am," the girl said and bowed her head.

Kenidee left the studio immediately and raced to the nearest phone.

"Hello, this is Kenidee."

"Ken-dog, it's Matt. We're at the hospital. Lindsay's having the baby."

"Matt, that's so exciting! Is everything going okay? Is she in pain? When is she going to have it? Which hospital?"

"Whoa, slow down, sis. She's doing great, and they've given her an epidural so she's in heaven. She's moving kind of slow right now, so it could be hours before she has the baby." He gave her a few more details including the name of the hospital.

"I'm almost finished with my class. Then I'll be right there."

She hung up the phone and hurried back to class, knowing the girls wouldn't mind if they ended a few minutes early.

Soon she was speeding down the freeway toward the hospital, filled with anticipation. She was going to be an aunt. Matt was going to be a dad. Her dad was going to be a grandfather!

Following the arrows to the labor and delivery area of the hospital, Kenidee was breathless when she finally found Lindsay's room. The door was partially shut and she tentatively peeked inside before entering.

"Kenidee!" Matt exclaimed when she walked inside.

"Is it okay to come in?" she asked.

"Of course," Lindsay called. "We're having a pre-birthday party."

She was greeted by a big hug from Matt, followed by Robin and her father.

Kenidee walked around the monitors and gave her sister-in-law a kiss on the cheek. "How are you?"

"I'm so good!" Lindsay answered. "The pains were getting pretty bad there for a while, so they gave me the epidural and now I feel like a new woman. They're just waiting for me to dilate to a ten. I'm at an eight right now, so it shouldn't be long. I'm glad you got here when you did. I want Matt and your dad to give me a blessing, and I wanted you here for it."

Kenidee gave Lindsay's hand a squeeze. "I'm glad you waited."

The men moved into position and placed their hands upon her head. Reverence filled the room as Matt gave her a blessing that bestowed peace and assurance upon her that all would go well with both her and the baby.

No one said a word when the blessing ended. It felt as if angels filled the room and they were in heaven at that very moment. No one wanted the feeling to go away.

But the world always had a way of intruding. A clamoring at the door broke the hallowed moment as several nurses came to check on their patient. Everyone but Matt was asked to leave while they attended to Lindsay.

Kenidee's dad gave her a long hug, confirming that they had shared the same feeling about Kenidee's mom just a moment ago.

Kenidee's dad and Robin decided to walk down to the cafeteria to get Matt a bite to eat. He'd been at the hospital several hours and hadn't eaten since lunch.

Finding an empty chair nearby, Kenidee sat down and tried to digest the sacred moment they'd all experienced. Not since her mission had she felt the presence of her mother as strongly as she had in that hospital room. It had been so powerful that she'd peeked out of one eye during the prayer, convinced her mother would be standing with the rest of the family.

Her cell phone vibrated, and she glanced to see who was calling. Camden.

"Hi there," she said.

"What's going on? I noticed you tried to call."

"We're at the hospital. Lindsay's having her baby."

"That's great. Is everything going okay?"

"It's amazing. Matt just gave her a blessing, and it felt as though—" her voice broke. "Um," she swallowed and took in a quick breath, "my mom was there with us."

"Oh, wow, Kenidee. I bet that was unbelievable."

"It was."

"That's really beautiful," Cam said.

"You should be here, Cam. Could you come to the hospital?"

"You don't think they'd mind?" he asked.

"They want you here."

"The girls are playing across the street with some friends from primary, so I'll call and see if they can stay while I come to the hospital."

"Okay. Hurry," she urged.

Robin and her dad came back with food for Matt and brought her a plastic bowl of fruit and a container of yogurt. Matt came out of the room and ate with Kenidee while Robin and their dad went in with Lindsay. They talked about the blessing and their mom, and both of them knew that they hadn't been alone in that room.

"I'm going to write down this experience when I get home, so I can tell Emaree about it when she gets older," Matt said.

"She'll be glad you did. You're going to be a wonderful father, Matt."

"Thanks, Ken. You're going to be a terrific aunt."

"You'd better believe it. I get to spoil her rotten."

The door to Lindsay's room opened quickly, and their dad rushed out. "Matt, I think you'd better come back inside. Things are really starting to get moving."

Matt looked at Kenidee and said, "Showtime!" He ran straight for the room and disappeared inside. Robin stepped out of the room as several nurses joined Matt a moment later.

Matt came back to the door and motioned for Kenidee to come to him. "We need you to come in with us."

"Me?"

"Yes. We want you to videotape the birth."

* * *

Tears blurred her vision as Kenidee witnessed a miracle take place before her very eyes. When Matt and Lindsay's baby let out her first cry, they all began to cry. It was the most sacred event Kenidee had witnessed in her life.

Kenidee kept the camera going while Matt cut his daughter's umbilical cord. Then she was gently placed in Lindsay's arms. After a moment, Emaree was taken to be weighed and measured, cleaned up, and wrapped in warm blankets.

Tears continued to streak down Kenidee's cheeks as she observed the moment of pure love and joy pass between Matt and Lindsay. A crowning moment for them, a moment they would never forget.

Kenidee recorded the activity surrounding the baby and chuckled at Emaree's cries of protest at being poked and prodded and diapered. She knew she would never forget this exquisite moment she'd been permitted to be part of.

A new person had joined their family and would make a difference—a blessed difference—in all of their lives.

Once the commotion died down, Matt told her she could quit videotaping. Feeling happiness she could no longer contain, Kenidee gave her big brother a hug and congratulated him on his beautiful new daughter, who had a full head of curls just like her mom. Kenidee hugged Lindsay and thanked her for letting her be there for the birth of the baby. Lindsay offered to let Kenidee hold the newborn. Kenidee was nervous but couldn't refuse. Matt helped place the baby into her arms, and Kenidee cradled the bundle and took a peek at the tiny face staring wide-eyed at the lights overhead.

"Hello, precious," she whispered. "I'm your Aunt Kenidee. We're going to have so much fun together."

Matt and Lindsay smiled.

"I love you, angel."

Carefully she handed the baby back to Matt, who had assumed the role of protective father without effort. She went outside to get her father and Robin, who were anxious to meet their grandchild. Next to them was Cam.

William and Robin rushed into the room to get their first glimpse of the baby, their oohs and aahs coming through the door as it closed behind them.

Kenidee looked into Cam's face and began to cry again, her emotions still at the highwater mark. Cam took her into a hug and held her as she released her tears of joy and awe.

"That was so miraculous," she said, her head resting on his shoulder.

"It sure is," he answered.

She lifted her head and looked into his face. "I can't believe you've done that twice already. It's just so incredible to watch a new baby come into the world."

"It's a miracle," he said.

"It is. That's exactly what it is. I'll never forget it. Ever."

"I know how you feel."

"The only way it could be any better would be when it's your own child."

"You're right."

They went to a pair of chairs and sat down together.

"You know, I'll admit, when Amanda was born, I wasn't a whole lot of help to Desiree during the birth. Of course, she didn't even want me to touch her or be around her, so I just stood back by the doctor and watched the whole process happen. I remember how overcome I was just after the delivery. And when I heard Amanda cry for the first time, wow, it was like angels singing."

"I know what you mean."

"It was the same with Brynn. I don't know if seeing a baby born could ever seem anything but a miracle," his voice broke as he spoke.

In his face, Kenidee saw sadness and pain. She reached for his hand and gave it a squeeze.

"Even then," he said, "I didn't feel close to Desiree. We shared the most intimate, spiritual experience a couple could share, and I still didn't feel close to her."

Kenidee reflected on her observation of Matt and Lindsay and the love they exchanged after the birth of the baby.

"I wanted it, I wanted to feel completed as a couple, but her heart just wasn't in it. The first thing she said after Brynn was born was that she wasn't going to breastfeed because she wanted me to be able to get up at night and help feed her because she wasn't going to be stuck doing it all herself like she had with Amanda."

Not knowing what to say, Kenidee just kept hold of Cam's hand and listened.

"Maybe that's why I'm so close to Brynn. I really didn't mind spending time alone with her at night, feeding her a bottle in the moonlight. I loved her warmth and cuddliness. Is that even a word?"

Kenidee shrugged. It didn't matter. She knew what he meant.

"Anyway, my girls are a blessing in my life. I wouldn't change anything at all because they are worth everything we've gone through just to have them."

"Oh, that reminds me, the doctor's office called to set up an appointment to have Brynn's cast removed."

"Okay, I'll call them and set one up."

"I can take her if you have a hard time getting away from work."

Cam smiled at her. "Thanks. I'm sure I can arrange it though. We'd love you to come with us. Brynn would want you there."

"You bet I'll come."

Cam gazed a moment longer into her eyes. "Kenidee?" he said.

"Yes?"

"I . . ."

She waited for him to continue.

"I . . ." he swallowed. "I'm glad I got to come today."

"Me too," she told him. "You want to go in and see the baby?" He nodded.

They stood up and walked into Lindsay's room together.

# CHAPTER 18

*Brendan comes home today.*

Kenidee paced the house like a caged lion. From the kitchen to the family room, to the living room, and then to her bedroom she paced. She stopped in the kitchen and looked in the fridge, picked up an apple, then changed her mind, put it back, and closed the door.

Glancing at the calendar, she noticed the big red circle around Thursday, August tenth, the day her waiting ended and her new life began with Brendan.

The last few weeks had passed by so slowly she wasn't sure how she'd survived. And now that it was here, she could barely stand the anticipation.

She walked into the family room where the kids were watching cartoons. She looked out the window and saw her dad mowing the lawn and Robin sweeping grass clippings off the sidewalk. Then she continued on to her bedroom where she checked her reflection in the mirror one more time, applied another coat of lip gloss, fluffed her hair, then sat down on the bed, only to get up again and start walking.

Her nerves were stretched so taut she was sure they would snap. Her stomach was one gigantic bunch of knots, the muscles so tight that she could barely stand up straight.

Brendan's plane landed in less than two hours.

She had debated and debated whether or not to go to the airport. He hadn't said one way or the other if he wanted her there. But his mother insisted. She was convinced Brendan would want her there with the family. Kenidee wasn't so convinced.

"What if he doesn't want me there," she murmured to herself as she paced.

Her cell phone buzzed, indicating an incoming call. She dropped the phone in her hurry to answer it and quickly snatched it up to make sure it wasn't broken.

"Hello?" she said, her voice strained and tight.

"Are you okay?" Lindsay asked.

"I'm going to throw up."

"Calm down. It's going to be okay. Can you believe he's finally coming home today?"

"No. I'm not ready."

"Yes, you are. The minute you see him, all the old feelings will come back and all the fears will go away. You'll see."

"I hope so." Kenidee heard the sound of her niece, Emaree, crying in the background.

"Well, I just wanted to check on you. The baby just woke up. She's starving as usual. She may be a girl, but she eats like a horse!"

Kenidee laughed.

"You call me as soon as you can."

"I will."

"Okay. Say a prayer and take a deep breath. Everything's going to be fine."

"I know. You're right. Thanks, Lindsay."

The sound of voices out front made her heart leap to her throat. Brendan's family was there to pick her up.

"I gotta go. They're here."

"Good luck."

Kenidee hung up the phone and said a one word prayer . . . help. Then she went to the door. This was it. After two long, life-changing years, the wait was over.

* * *

"Do you need to sit down?" Brendan's mother asked. "You're as white as a sheet."

Kenidee swallowed and nodded her head. She hadn't eaten a thing and felt very light-headed.

Patricia Nielsen helped Kenidee into a chair and told her to take some deep breaths. Kenidee was really uncomfortable being there. She appreciated Patricia being so supportive and encouraging, but what if Brendan wasn't expecting her? There was nothing she could do about it now. She was here, and his plane was landing. Soon it would be over, and she would know.

Her eyes scanned the terminal for the nearest ladies' room, just in case she needed a place to escape.

"I think this might be him!" his father announced as a fresh group of passengers headed for the baggage claim, most of them Oriental.

Brendan's family gathered, and his younger brother and sister held up their "Welcome Home" posters. Both sets of grandparents were also there, along with an aunt and uncle and their kids. It was quite a group, and Kenidee hoped to fade into the background so he could have time with his family first.

"There he is!" Patricia exclaimed. "There's Brendan!"

Kenidee tried to get a glimpse of him, but there were too many people standing in front of her. She broke out in a cold sweat and tears stung her eyes. Reminding herself to calm down and breathe, she kept looking for him through the crowd of passengers clogging the concourse.

Then she saw him.

He looked taller. He looked thinner. He looked balder. He looked . . . wonderful.

His mother was the first to hug him. She sobbed and clung to him, trying to squeeze two years of hugs into one giant-size hug. His father helped pry her away from her son, and then he hugged Brendan. His younger brother and sister hugged him at the same time.

Kenidee watched the homecoming with a lump in her throat. She completely related to what was going on behind the shocked look in his eyes. Her heart went out to him. It was overwhelming to say the least.

With plenty of time to get her emotions in check, Kenidee began to smile as his grandparents greeted him. Brendan was so tender and loving toward them, and they looked at him with such pride. His aunt, uncle, and cousins flocked to him while he exclaimed with surprise to see them and thanked them for coming.

Soon his family began firing questions at him, which he tried to answer, but he obviously struggled trying to find the English words.

Kenidee was charmed by his faltering language skills and the glow about him. He did look different, older and wiser, and very tired, but he was completely captivating.

His mom whispered something in his ear, and suddenly the talking stopped and all eyes turned to her. She swallowed and tried to smile.

Brendan stepped forward.

Her heartbeat stopped, along with her breathing. Their eyes connected.

And then he smiled and reached his hand toward her.

She took a step forward and reached toward him.

He took her hand in his and . . . shook it! She had to remind herself that he was still a missionary, after all.

"Welcome home," she managed to say.

"I wasn't sure you'd be here," he said.

"I wasn't sure you wanted me to be," she answered.

"It's good to see you."

"You too."

Patricia stepped up beside him. "Can we get some pictures?" she asked. She gave Kenidee a wink.

"Sure, Mom," Brendan said.

Kenidee stayed back while the family pulled together for pictures.

"Here, Kenidee, you need to be in these," Patricia said.

"Oh, no," Kenidee said. "Let me take them. That way the whole family can be in them."

She hurried to take the camera from Brother Nielsen and tried to steady her shaking hands so the picture wouldn't blur.

Several shots later she handed the camera back to Brendan's dad and watched from the periphery as pictures of various groupings were taken—Brendan with his grandparents, Brendan with his brother and sister, Brendan with his aunt and uncle and cousins, Brendan with his mom, then his mom and dad.

"I want one with Brendan and Kenidee," Patricia told her husband.

"Come on, Kenidee," Brother Nielsen said. "Your turn."

All eyes were on them as they stood close together but didn't touch. Kenidee knew that because Brendan hadn't been released as a missionary, he still lived the mission rules, which included no hugging. She respected him for that even though more than anything she wanted to grab him and hug the daylights out of him.

"One more, honey," Patricia told her husband.

They smiled for the camera and waited for the flash, then relaxed.

Before the crowd descended on him, Brendan leaned down and whispered, "Does it get easier?"

She looked up into his eyes and smiled, "Yeah. Not fast enough though."

"Come on, we're all going out to eat at Brendan's favorite restaurant," Patricia announced, looping her arm through her son's and leading the way.

Brendan looked back at Kenidee and grinned helplessly.

Kenidee smiled back. *Finally, he was home!*

\* \* \*

The awkwardness continued through the meal and on until the group finally parted ways and the commotion died down. Poor Brendan looked worn out and completely overwhelmed. Kenidee wished that she'd just driven her car to their house so they didn't have to drive her home, but there was nothing she could do about it.

"So," Patricia turned around and looked at her son, "what happened on your mission that you didn't tell me about?"

Brendan looked at his mother, then over at Kenidee, who sat in the captain's seat across from him. She just shrugged, and he cleared his throat. He'd actually told her about a hair-raising experience he'd had, one he'd decided not to share with his family until he got home.

"Well, Mom, there were a couple of things that happened that I didn't tell you about, but it was just because I didn't want you to worry."

"But I worried anyway, because I knew you weren't telling me everything," his mom responded. "So, what happened?"

Obviously, Brendan knew his mom wouldn't let up unless he told her everything. Finally, he said, "Well, we had a break-in one night, and the guy had a knife. Of course, I didn't know it at the time and tried to grab him. He took a swing at me with the knife."

"Did he stab you?" she asked, horrified.

"No, luckily it was just a cut about four inches long."

"Did you hear that, dear. Your son was nearly killed," she exclaimed as she grabbed her husband's hand.

"Honey," his father said calmly, "he's fine. Look at him. He's healthy and back home now."

"Did you need stitches?" his mother asked.

"About twenty."

"What happened to the guy, son?" his father asked.

"Oh, he took off running, and I was bleeding so badly I couldn't go after him. My companion stayed with me because he thought I was hurt pretty bad."

"What did the mission president have to say about it?" he asked.

"I was afraid he would close our area because of it, but thank goodness he didn't. We were teaching the Huang family, and I didn't want anything to mess that up. The Huangs were baptized shortly after that."

"Oh my goodness!" Patricia exclaimed. "Had I known I would have—well, I don't know what I would have done. Is there anything else?" she dared to ask.

"That's the worst. Everything else is just dumb stuff like getting mugged on the street. That's how I lost my CTR ring and my camera."

"Oh, so when you wrote and said you *lost* your camera, you meant it was stolen?"

"Yeah."

"Did things like this happen very often, son?" his father asked.

"It depended on which city I was serving in. Most of the rural towns were safe. It's generally the bigger cities."

Brother Nielsen turned onto Kenidee's street and pulled up in front of her house.

"So this is where you live now?" Brendan asked, peering through the van window.

"Yeah. Not the same as our old house, but I've gotten used to it."

"Is your family here? I'd like to meet your stepfamily."

"They drove to Santa Cruz for the day. They'll be home later." She put her hand on the door handle, ready to open it.

"Oh, here," he jumped out quickly. "Let me get that."

Brendan was still the consummate gentleman.

Patricia spoke quickly while he was going around the back of the van. "I'll have him give you a call later. The stake president is meeting us at the church to release him right now."

Kenidee didn't have time to respond before he opened her door. "Well," she said, looking up at him, "welcome home, again."

"Thanks. I'll call you later. I'll be glad to have someone to talk to who can relate to all of this."

"Believe me, I feel your pain."

He chuckled. "I know you do."

Instead of going back around to his side, he climbed back into the van. "Thanks for coming to the airport."

She smiled and nodded as he pulled the van door closed.

From the sidewalk, she watched as they drove down the street and out of sight. She hated to see him leave so quickly but knew he had to take care of important business and spend time with his family first. They would have time to talk later.

*He's home!* The thought thrilled her. He looked a little different. His sandy blond hair was much thinner, as was he, but his broad smile and blue eyes were still as incredible as ever. And, more importantly, they still connected. It was a lot all at once, but something was still there. She felt it, and she knew he felt it.

Feeling as though she were floating, Kenidee went inside to call Lindsay. She couldn't wait to tell someone how wonderful Brendan was.

# CHAPTER 19

"Okay, you guys," Robin warned her three kids, "best behavior tonight, I mean it. Or you'll be grounded to your rooms. Understand?"

"Yes, Mom," Mikey, David, and Rachel said in unison.

"Once we meet him, we'll get out of the way," Robin told Kenidee. "You two need time alone, to talk and catch up."

"If you kids are good, we'll go get pizza and ice cream," Kenidee's dad told the little ones.

The three erupted with jumps and cheers, the exact opposite of what they'd been asked to do. Quickly they remembered their promise and settled down.

"That's better," Robin said.

A knock came at the door, and everyone gasped.

"It's him," Rachel whispered, her eyes wide and scared looking.

Kenidee stood there, frozen to her spot.

"Honey," her dad said, "aren't you going to answer the door?"

"Oh, yes, of course," she said with a nervous laugh. With her hand on her middle to calm her stomach, this time from excitement, not nerves, she walked to the door and opened it.

"Hi," Brendan said with a warm smile.

"Hi," she replied, with an even bigger smile. "Come in."

As he came inside, her heart did backflips. He looked so good in a light blue polo shirt and jeans.

"There's something I didn't get to give you yesterday," he said to her.

"Oh?"

He surprised her by giving her a brief hug. It was so unexpected she didn't have time to enjoy it.

"Thanks. I'm glad you remembered," she told him. "Come on into the living room. There are some people who want to meet you."

He'd barely sat down on the couch when he stood up again as Robin and the kids and Kenidee's dad walked into the room.

Kenidee's dad walked over to Brendan and gave him a hearty handshake, then a one-armed hug with a series of manly back pats.

"Good to see you, Brendan," her dad said. "How is it being home?"

"A little strange, sir, but good to see my family. And I'll admit, I did enjoy a bowl of Cinnamon Toast Crunch for breakfast. Actually, two bowls."

Her dad chuckled. "Brendan, I'd like you to meet my wife Robin and her kids—Mikey, David, and this little princess is Rachel."

Brendan shook hands with the two boys and then, to Rachel's surprise, he kissed the top of her hand, causing her to giggle and look away.

"It's nice to meet you, Robin," he said, also shaking her hand.

"You too, Brendan. I've heard a great deal about you. All of it good and obviously true."

Brendan smiled. "I sure hope so."

"We're on our way to take the kids for pizza. Would you like us to bring you back anything?" her dad asked them.

Brendan's eyes lit up.

"If I remember right, Brendan likes Canadian bacon and pineapple," Kenidee said, looking at him to double check.

"Does that sound good to you?" her dad asked him.

"It sounds wonderful, if it's no trouble," Brendan said.

"None at all. We won't be long."

"Thanks, Dad," Kenidee said.

The kids began arguing about what kind of toppings they wanted on their pizza until they saw the look in their mother's eyes. Then they remembered their promise to be good and quickly stopped bickering. The garage door opened, and moments later the van pulled out of the driveway.

"Those are some cute kids, especially that little Rachel," Brendan said.

"She is cute," Kenidee answered. "It was pretty hard at first, but now I'm getting used to them."

"Robin seems really nice."

"She is. I like her a lot. That took some time too, though."

"I can't imagine how hard that must have been to come home to."

"It was really hard. I wasn't sure I would ever adjust, but we're all in a really good place." She appreciated him empathizing with her. "So, what are you thinking?"

"I'm thinking that I would give anything to go back to Taiwan, but that I'm grateful I can talk to someone who can relate to what I'm going through."

With a nod, Kenidee said, "It still doesn't feel the same as before I left. But how can it really? A mission changes a person in a lot of ways."

"It sure does. I guess it would be a shame if a person came home and wasn't different." He looked at her, their gazes locking. "So?"

"So?"

"I probably ought to apologize for not writing more at the end," he said.

"That's okay. I know you were busy."

"Time just sped up as the end got closer," he explained. "The harder I worked, the faster it went."

"I remember."

"So tell me, what are you doing now?" He looked so intently into her eyes she felt he could read her mind.

*Besides waiting for you to finally get home?* "I've been tending two little girls for Camden Parker, my brother's best friend. He's divorced."

"He's young to be divorced already."

"Yeah, it's sad. He's such a great guy. And he has two of the cutest little girls."

"That's great. So you tend during the day?"

"Yeah, while Cam's at work. Then in the evenings, I've been teaching classes at a ballet studio."

"I think you wrote and told me about it. How's that going?"

"I'd love more classes, but so far, it's going really well. That's about all. It keeps me pretty busy though."

"I'll bet. I haven't quite decided what I'm going to do yet. I was going to go back to BYU."

*Was?*

"But I'm thinking of staying here in the Bay Area and checking out some of the universities here. I love BYU, but I'm not ready to just take off and move there yet. Not when I just got home."

Kenidee thought about how badly she'd wanted to move to Utah. What if she had, especially if he was going to stay here now. Maybe that's why there had been so many roadblocks in her way to prevent her from moving.

Then she had another thought: but what about her education? If she stayed in the Bay Area, she wouldn't be able to study ballet at the U. But she wasn't going to worry about that now. She was sure there was a ballet program at one of the universities in the area. Right now she was just going to enjoy having Brendan home.

"I also decided to change my major. I want to study international law so I can use my language and keep close ties with the people in Taiwan."

"Wow, Brendan, that's great." So he had been thinking about his future.

"I know. What about you? Have you made any plans for college?"

She was stumped. She was basically going to go wherever he went, or at least in the vicinity.

"I'd like to get my MFA degree in teaching and choreography."

"That sounds great. Where are you going to go?"

"I haven't really decided yet."

"Oh," he said, "I'm sure you'll figure it out. I guess you don't plan on going to school fall semester then?"

"I hadn't planned on it. I thought I'd work and get some money saved."

"Same here. My uncle offered me a job helping him."

"Really? What is it?"

"You know, he installs those fire protection sprinkler systems for buildings and large homes. He said he can use my help on his next project. Since I worked for him before my mission, I'm already trained for the job."

"Right. Well that sounds great."

"It'll be fun. He's installing all the sprinklers in a new hotel that's being built."

"Really? Where is it?"

"Portland."

She blinked and tilted her head, wondering if she'd heard him right. "Did you say Portland? As in Oregon?"

"Yeah. We'll be gone almost two months. But he's going to pay me four thousand dollars to help him. I can't turn down that kind of money. We won't go there until next month. Which works out great because . . . did my mom tell you . . . the Huang family is coming over to visit?"

Kenidee forced herself to smile. "Yeah. She told me. I bet you're excited."

"I can't wait for you to meet them. You're going to love them. They actually have an uncle who moved here. They've wanted to come and visit him for some time, and now with me here, they felt like the time was right. It's something they've saved years for."

Kenidee kept the smile plastered on her face. She was beginning to wonder exactly how she fit into his plans.

"Anyway, I brought a photo album of pictures I thought you'd like to look at. I can show you the Huangs and all the other great people I met."

"Awesome," she said, her enthusiasm as fake as her smile. Not that she didn't want to see his pictures, but she was having trouble with his complete change of plans.

He ran out to the car to retrieve the album, and she gave herself a moment to digest everything that they'd talked about. She told herself to be patient and not jump to conclusions. It wasn't like he'd told her he wasn't still interested in her, although he didn't seem to be considering her in any of his plans.

"Here we go," he said as he burst through the door carrying a four-inch-thick binder. "Mom's been putting these in here for me while I was gone. I stayed up late looking at it last night. It brought back so many memories. All I can think about is what I've got to do to get back there. I'm sure you feel the same about your mission."

He didn't even look at her for a response, but instead opened to the first page and displayed a copy of his mission call. An hour later, they'd made it through one-third of the pictures. Kenidee's dad and the rest of the family came home bearing pizza and milkshakes.

Brendan was charming and darling and captivating as he told about experiences on his mission and asked the kids about themselves. They were enthralled by his P-day adventures and encounters with strange people. He barely drank half his milkshake and didn't even finish his second piece of pizza, but he exclaimed at how wonderful it tasted and said that his stomach had shrunk while he'd been in Taiwan.

Before she knew it, Kenidee was on the outside looking in as Brendan took the family through his photo album and entertained them with more stories and details of the culture and people so unknown to them. By the time he finished with the album, it was late, and he needed to be getting home. He wanted to work on his talk for church and call some of his friends who'd also returned from their missions.

Kenidee walked him out to his car.

"Thanks for coming over," she said, telling herself to give him time to adjust and settle back into being home.

"It was good to see your dad again and meet the new family. I like them."

"Me too."

"Are you working tomorrow?" he asked.

Her heart skipped a beat. "Yes, but only in the morning. There is a list of substitute teachers if I can't make it, though," she answered, making herself available.

"Sounds like the perfect job."

"It is."

"We're going to the city tomorrow to do some shopping and meet with a guy my dad knows who does international law. He said he'd be willing to meet us on a Saturday so we could have plenty of time to talk. He's willing to help me out any way he can."

"Terrific," she said, about at the end of her supply of enthusiasm.

"Maybe I'll call you when I get home tomorrow night."

"Okay. I'd like that."

He reached to shake her hand before he realized what he'd done. "Sorry, it's a habit." He gave her a quick hug and fished the car keys from his pocket. "I'll talk to you later then?"

She almost said "terrific" again, but caught herself. "Okay."

As Brendan drove away, Kenidee was left standing on the curb, wondering what to think. Telling herself not to think anything, she turned and went back in the house.

"So," her dad said when she got back inside, "how was it?"

"Just awesome," she said, a little too sarcastically.

"Kenidee, is something wrong?" he asked.

Robin stopped cleaning up the dishes and looked at her.

"No, I guess I was just hoping we'd talk a little about us, you know?"

"What did you talk about?" he questioned.

"His plans, my plans."

"Well that's good, isn't it?"

"I guess. But my plans pretty much were gonna be whatever his plans were. And now I see that his plans don't seem to include me."

"Ohhh, I'm sure he didn't mean it that way."

She looked at her dad and shrugged. "I'm not sure what to think."

"What did he say to you, Kenidee?" Robin asked, sitting down at the table.

Kenidee joined her and so did Kenidee's father.

"Well, before our missions, we talked about getting married and moving to Utah after we both got home. He'd go back to BYU and I'd go to the U of U. We were going to live somewhere in the middle, so we could both commute. It wasn't a perfect plan, and he even said he'd eventually move to the U to finish, but we had a plan. I was going to stick to it. That was part of the reason I was going to move to Utah."

"And now?" Robin asked.

"He's going to stay here to go to college, and he wants to study international law. *And* he's taking a job out of state for two months. But he doesn't leave until after the family he baptized in Taiwan comes to visit for two weeks."

Her father didn't answer.

Neither did Robin.

Then the phone rang.

Kenidee jumped, thinking maybe it was Brendan, calling to invite her to go with him tomorrow, or just to say that he'd forgotten that he hoped she would rearrange her plans and life to be with him.

It was Rylie from the ballet studio.

"Hi, Kenidee. Lucinda asked me to get you on the phone. Can you hold?"

"Sure," Kenidee answered, perturbed. She didn't expect Brendan to just drop down on one knee the second he saw her, but the least he could do was act like they had a future together.

"Kenidee, this is Lucinda. How are you?"

"Fine," Kenidee lied.

"Good. I hate to bother you, but I am in a horrible bind, but for a wonderful reason."

"Oh?"

"I've been asked to go to Europe for three weeks and do some private teaching. I wasn't sure it was going to happen but it looks like it did. The only problem is, I have to cover my classes at the studio, or I can't go."

"What can I do to help?"

"I've got all those afternoon classes that I need to take care of. Like I said, it's only for three weeks, starting next week. Could you help?"

"Let me make a call to my other job and see, then I'll call you back."

"Darling, I'll never forget this. Next time I go to Paris, I promise, I'll take you with me."

"Let's just see if I can make arrangements first." Kenidee hung up the phone. She knew it would be a trick for Cam to find someone for part of the day, but she really wanted to help Lucinda too. She at least needed to try. Besides, it was only for three weeks.

Saturday morning, she dialed Cam to talk to him about the chance of his getting some help so she could teach classes several afternoons during the week. He didn't answer. She decided to try him later, or talk to him when she went to babysit on Monday. Right now, she felt like putting on her workout clothes and running shoes and getting outside. It was the only way she could think of to clear her head.

\* \* \*

Monday morning, the girls were having fun running through the sprinklers and sucking on red popsicles. Kenidee watched them from beneath the shade of a tree as she too sucked on the frozen treat.

The phone rang, and she quickly swallowed a bite of cherry-flavored ice, which froze her throat as it slid down. "Hello?"

"Kenidee?" Cam asked.

She swallowed.

"Yes."

"It didn't sound like you for a minute."

"Sorry. I'm eating a popsicle. What's up?"

"I just had a break at work and thought I'd call and see what's going on."

"Not much. The girls are playing in the sprinklers. I'm about ready to join them it's so hot."

"We should be at the beach," Cam quipped.

"No kidding." She took a quick lick of her popsicle before it dripped onto her capris.

"So, everything's okay?"

"Yeah. Why wouldn't it be? Are you worried I'm going to break Brynn's other arm?"

Cam laughed. "Hardly. No, I was just wondering how you are. You didn't seem like yourself when I left today. Is everything going okay? You know, with Brendan?"

"Yeah, I guess so. I think I just had a different idea of what it would be like. So I'm just trying to be patient and give him time to adjust and figure out what he wants. But he's awesome. He looks great and had such a good mission. It's awesome that he's finally home." She decided right then that she was going to duct tape her mouth shut if she used the word *awesome* again.

"I see."

"So, yeah. That's about it. I just thought we'd talk about things so I could make plans for the future, since I've been kind of keeping it on hold until I knew what he was doing."

"Why don't you just ask him?"

"I can't do that!"

"Why? You shouldn't ever have to play games. You should be able to talk about anything with him. Especially if you're thinking of marrying this guy."

She knew he was right, but Brendan had been home only four days. She didn't want to send him into a stress-induced coma so soon after returning.

"By the way, did Fed Ex drop a package by?"

"Yeah, earlier. Looks like it's from your brother."

"That's the one."

"You need it?"

"No, it can wait until I get home."

"Okay."

"So, is there anything I can do?" he asked her.

"About Brendan? No, I just need to give him time and space. That's what I needed when I first got home. My plans will just have to continue on hold for a while until he figures out what he's doing. Oh, except I have to ask you one thing. You know how you were saying that the lady across the street offered to tend for you if you ever needed her to?"

"Yes."

"Well, Lucinda, the director of the ballet studio, is going to Europe for three weeks and needs me to cover her classes while she's gone. All the other teachers have all the classes they can handle because most of them have other jobs aside from the studio. I'm the only one with a boss nice enough to help me out."

"Ah, flattery. Very good tactic for persuasion."

"Thank you. I thought so."

"Did you say three weeks?"

"Yes. Just from two o'clock on."

"I'll give her a call and see if that will work. I don't see why it won't though. Besides, I have other sitters I can call."

"Okay. I just don't want to put you in a bind."

"No problem. I'll call you later after I figure things out. Plan on it though."

"Thanks, Cam," she said. She knew she could count on him to help her out.

# CHAPTER 20

Friday night after work, Kenidee was in a panic. She had a date with Brendan, and she didn't know what to wear.

"Robin," Kenidee called as she walked through the house carrying two shirts on hangers.

She finally got to Robin's bedroom and knocked.

The door opened, just a crack, showing one side of Robin's face.

"I need your opinion," Kenidee said, glancing above Robin's head to see what was on the computer monitor. She held up the shirts.

"Oh, sure," Robin said, opening the door wide enough so she could slip out, then pulling it shut quickly behind her.

"You have a date with Brendan tonight?" Robin asked as she walked into the kitchen.

"Yes, and I really want to look nice. Which one do you like?" Although Kenidee was tempted to ask her what she was doing on the computer, she knew it was none of her business.

Brendan had surprised her that morning by calling and asking her out on a date to dinner that night.

"I like the pink with your dark hair. You've got a little tan on your arms too so the pink looks really good."

"Okay, then, pink it is. Speaking of tans, how do you and dad like going to the tanning beds?"

"The first time I got in, I felt like I was climbing into a coffin, but now I quite like it. It's very relaxing. Your dad says he's going to have white feet because he's too long for the beds."

"It's still a good idea to get a little base tan before you get to Hawaii. You don't want to get fried over there."

"That would be a quick way to ruin our fun."

"So, Shelley will get the kids a week from tomorrow?"

"Around one, then we'll leave for the airport."

"It will be fun to see her again."

"That's what she said. She really liked you. She wants to stay a couple of days when she brings the kids back so we can all go shopping in the city or something. Would you like to join us?"

"I'd love to," Kenidee said. "I'll get someone to cover my classes that day so we can do that."

"I hate leaving you to go on this trip when things are in such a confused state with Brendan," Robin told her.

Kenidee was touched by her thoughtfulness. "I'll be okay. It's only for two weeks."

"I'll keep my cell phone on, just in case you need to talk."

"You may regret that. But thanks, Robin," Kenidee said.

"You're in my prayers, hon," Robin told her.

The next thing Kenidee knew she was hugging Robin. Right now the guidance and perspective of another woman was just what she needed, and she was grateful to have Robin's care and support.

"He'd be lucky to get someone as wonderful as you," Robin told her.

\* \* \*

"So, Brendan," Kenidee said, almost feeling that she should still call him Elder Nielsen since he was acting as if he were still a missionary, "what have you been doing?"

Brendan drove very cautiously, even under the speed limit. Cars were zooming around him and giving him dirty looks. But since he hadn't driven for two years, it took some getting used to.

"I've been organizing my room and going through old stuff from before my mission. You know, getting rid of clothes and shoes I won't wear again, CDs I won't listen to again, stuff like that."

"I did the same thing when I got home. Of course, all my stuff was still in boxes, so I basically had to unpack first, and then box the things I didn't want back up."

"How did you get adjusted back into normal life again?" he asked her. "I didn't think it was going to be this hard."

"It just takes time," she told him.

"I'm glad you can understand what I'm going through. My dad kind of gets it. He served a mission, but he didn't go foreign, and it's a little bit different. He doesn't understand that I don't just miss being on a mission, I miss being in Taiwan."

The light changed to yellow and Brendan slowed down, while the cars beside him sped up to get through the intersection before the light turned red.

"You remember how you felt homesick at the beginning of your mission?" he asked her.

"Sure. And when my mom passed away, I really wanted to be home."

"That's how I feel!" he exclaimed. "I'm homesick for Taiwan. All I can think about is what I have to do to get back over there. I'm so glad the Huang family is coming next week. It's the only thing keeping me sane. I don't even feel like I belong here."

Concern grew inside her. If she wanted Brendan, Kenidee realized, she'd better be prepared to embrace the new, "Taiwan-ized" version of him. With all the converting that had been going on during his mission, he'd converted to the people he'd taught and grown to love. He'd become one of them.

"That's why I'm going to study international law. I talked to my mission president about it. He said that if I really wanted to come back and work there, this would be a good profession to have. Isn't that great?"

"Awesome," she said, forgetting her vow to quit using that word.

He turned off the road into a parking lot where an Asian-styled building stood, surrounded by beautifully landscaped grounds with a lily pond and small bridge arching over a brook.

"The Beikou restaurant," he announced as he put the car in park. "Very authentic Taiwan cuisine. I'm so excited to bring you here."

Kenidee put on her "excited" face and waited for him to open her door.

The friendly hostess immediately fussed over Brendan when he spoke to her in her native language. Kenidee marveled at the beautiful decorations and furniture. And it smelled heavenly.

With a table next to a window, overlooking the gardens, Kenidee and Brendan admired the view, then turned their attention to the menu. Since she wasn't sure what to order, Brendan took over the job of choosing what they would eat. The waitress, also a native, arrived to take their order. Kenidee was taken by the exquisite beauty of the young woman. She was delicate and petite, with fine features and flawless skin.

The waitress was impressed by Brendan's language skills and laughed and talked with him for several minutes after taking their order. Kenidee marveled at how rapidly Brendan spoke and how similar he sounded to the natives. After the waitress left, Kenidee voiced her observations. "Are all the women over there beautiful?"

"They are a very beautiful people. Their children look like dolls, some of them so cute you can't take your eyes off them."

"And did everyone pick up the language like you?"

"Some," he said. "But I completely fell in love with it and studied the language constantly. In fact, when we had visiting authorities from the states, the president requested my help to translate for them. It was a gift, Kenidee. So many missionaries struggled, even after a year on their missions, but the Lord blessed me. Not only with a love of the language, but of the people."

"I can tell."

He smiled. "You can?"

"Very much," she answered. "They seem like very loving people."

"Oh, they are. They're amazing."

He went on to tell her about members in the ward and people he'd taught and about the Huang family. His animated expression and passionate voice testified of his strong feelings about the people he loved.

Soon their food arrived and covered the table.

"I ordered plenty so I could take some home for later."

He thanked the waitress, who bowed to him and then hurried away.

Steaming bowls of rice, dishes filled with different combinations of vegetables, meats, and noodles, tantalized her taste buds.

Brendan talked her through each dish, explaining the significance of each one and why he'd chosen it. Some he'd ordered because he'd loved them so much while he was in the country, others because people had made it for him and his companion and the food reminded him of these people, especially the Huang family.

"You'll be surprised when you meet them," he said, his chopsticks filled with rice.

"Who?" She'd resorted to a fork.

"The Huangs. They are very westernized. Both of the kids speak English. Their family owns a hotel so they talk a lot to tourists from America and Great Britain."

"That's nice. Then I'll be able to talk to them."

They enjoyed their meal, and Kenidee couldn't deny that the food was fantastic. By the meal's end, she knew she had eaten much more than she should have.

It was close to nine when Brendan took her back home.

"I had fun tonight," he told her.

"I'm glad," she said. "I had fun, too. The food was great."

"I knew you'd love it. Maybe we can go there again when the Huangs come."

"Maybe by then I'll be hungry again," she said.

Brendan laughed. This was the first time he'd laughed around her since he'd gotten home.

"Well, I'd better get you inside. It's late."

*No, it's not.* She wanted to spend more time with him. At this rate, they'd never get anywhere.

But he was out of the door and opening hers before she had a chance to blink twice.

"Before I forget, my mom invited you over for dinner after church on Sunday. Can you come around five?"

"Sure. That would be nice."

"Would you like me to come and pick you up?" he offered.

"I can drive. That's like an hour each way for you."

"If you're sure." He had a protective tone to his voice that Kenidee loved.

"Well, good night then. Thanks for coming with me."

"Thanks again for dinner."

She waited, hoping he would hug her, maybe even kiss her, but obviously he wasn't quite ready for that. Instead he waved good-bye, got back in the car, and drove off. She stood on the porch listening as the engine faded into the twilight shadows.

\* \* \*

"So, what's up with this Huang family?" Dolly asked her. "I mean, it's neat that they are so close and everything, but Brendan seems a little too close."

"I just think the timing just worked out for them to come now."

"When do you think you'll move to Salt Lake? We've almost got my grandma's house packed up, and then we're going back home."

"I don't know," Kenidee told her. "I wish I knew. I don't know whether to enroll for winter semester at the U or not."

"You'd better just talk to him. Tell him you need to know. You two are close enough you should be able to talk to him about anything."

"We should be able to, but he seems really . . . um . . . kind of . . . out of touch with reality a bit right now. I think I would really freak him out if I brought it up. To be honest, I can't really tell how he feels about me. It's not like it was before our missions, that's for sure."

"Hopefully he'll start coming around in a few weeks. Maybe once the Hu-nang family goes home."

"That's Huang," Kenidee corrected her. "Maybe you're right."

"What are you going to do all week, while the family is gone?"

"I'm not going to be home much myself. I'm covering ballet classes for our director and I'm still going to tend Cam's girls for a few days. I'd feel lost if I went a whole week not seeing them. They're sad enough that I'll see them only three mornings this week."

"It could be hard on them when you move."

"I know. I've thought about that. It's going to be hard on me too."

"Maybe you'll end up staying where you are if Brendan ends up going to school there."

"I feel like I'm supposed to be at the U though."

"Well, I don't know what's going to happen. Your life just gets more and more complicated with every passing day."

"It sure seems like it. That's why I need you to help me sort it out."

"You need a genie in a bottle to help you sort it out. I have no clue what you're supposed to do. You should've just come to St. George and stayed with me at my grandma's."

"But then I wouldn't have spent time with Robin. And we're in a really good place right now, the two of us."

"Yeah, I guess so. That's important. Guess you'll just have to be patient and let it all happen in the Lord's time. When the timing is right, it will all happen," Dolly told her. "Just remember to keep me posted."

"I will."

"Especially when the Ho-dongs get there."

"Huangs," Kenidee corrected.

"Whatever. Just call and tell me everything. Oh, by the way, guess who called me?"

"Who?" Kenidee asked.

"Joey. He's in Utah now and wants to get a bunch of missionaries together."

"That will be fun."

"I'll let you know if it really happens."

* * *

"So how's it going?" Cam asked her when she arrived Monday morning to stay with the girls until she left for the studio at noon.

"How's what going?" she replied, dropping her purse onto the hall tree in the entry.

"How's Brendan?"

"Um . . . he's good."

Cam's eyebrows narrowed. "You're not very convincing."

"No, really, he's good."

"Sorry, the repeater always is a giveaway."

"The what?"

"If you have to say it twice, the first time is to answer the question, and the second time is to convince yourself."

"Thank you, oh wise one."

"Hey, I'm not judging. I was just wondering."

"I know, sorry. By the way, where are the girls?"

"They're still asleep. I let them stay up late last night. So, tell me, what's really going on?"

She shrugged. "Nothing really. He's not himself right now. It's hard to say."

"You think he's just having trouble adjusting?"

"You could say that. Except, it's not that he's having trouble adjusting. He just plain doesn't even want to adjust. He just wants to go back to Taiwan. And he will, eventually. He has it all planned out. He's changed his whole focus on his education and life."

"That happens. A mission can really define a person."

"I think it's pretty much defined Brendan, or maybe a better word is, reinvented him. He's really different. He's got a family from Taiwan coming here to visit."

Cam's eyes opened wide. "Wow. That's cool."

"It's a family he baptized. I think it's his new family. He never stops talking about them."

"You know how attached you get to the people you teach and the ones who convert."

"Yeah, I do. I really do think it's neat."

"So, are you still moving to Utah?"

She rolled her eyes. She didn't even want to think about it, even though she knew she needed to figure out what she was doing.

"I don't know yet. We haven't talked about it. We haven't talked about anything but Taiwan and the Huangs."

"Sounds like an Oriental rock band," Cam said.

Kenidee laughed, then thought about it again and laughed harder.

"It wasn't that funny."

"I know," she said, gasping for air, "but if I don't laugh, I might cry. I wish I knew what to do."

"Just be patient, give it time. He's a good guy and was obviously a good missionary. And if he's smart, like you say, he will figure out what a lucky guy he is—"

"Daddeee!" Brynn's voice echoed through the house.

Cam didn't continue.

"Daddy, where are you?"

"I'd better go tell her good-bye before I leave."

"Wait," Kenidee said. "What were you going to say?"

Cam looked at her and said, "I was going to say," he paused for a moment, "if he's smart, he will figure out what a lucky guy he is to have someone like you in his life."

\* \* \*

With her dad and Robin in Hawaii and the kids gone with Shelley, the house seemed very quiet—and lonely. Kenidee spent as much time as possible at the studio, teaching and doing what she could to help out in Lucinda's absence. Staying busy helped keep her mind off Brendan, who called occasionally, and even invited her to go to the temple with him one day. Unfortunately, she had classes booked and couldn't join him.

They had another date scheduled for Friday night. This time they were going into the city to have dinner and to go shopping.

Brendan needed some new dress shoes, since his others had holes in the soles from his mission.

Kenidee didn't usually make a point of praying before dates, but she felt the need for some heavenly assistance with her that evening. Her goal wasn't to rush Brendan to the altar. In fact, it wasn't about getting married right away either, but she had decisions to make and she needed to understand Brendan's plans and goals better. She had based everything in her future on Brendan.

When Brendan picked her up that afternoon, he was looking more like his old self—T-shirt, jeans, and casual shoes. He also seemed more like his normal self, the Brendan she remembered.

"How's your week been?" he asked as they headed for San Francisco.

"Busy." She told him about everything she'd been doing at the studio and about tending for Cam. "How about you? What have you been doing?"

Since he was speaking in church, he'd been putting thoughts together for his talk. He'd also gone to the temple several times and gone on divisions with the missionaries in his area.

"I got to talk to President Miller and a couple of the office elders," he told her. "The mission is doing great."

"That's good." She almost said she was surprised it hadn't fallen apart after he'd left, but she managed to stop herself.

"What kind of food are you in the mood for?" he asked.

Kenidee almost said, "Anything but Chinese," then once again stopped herself. "How about Cheesecake Factory? I've been craving it since I got home." It had been a favorite place for them before their missions.

"Okay, that does sound good."

And it was good. Being somewhere that had significance to them together seemed to change the tone of the evening. Instead of talking about missions and Huangs, they reminisced about times they'd spent together, things they had in common. They talked about her mom and the impact her passing had on Kenidee's life. And, for the first time, Brendan reached over and held her hand.

"I tried very hard to keep my focus on missionary work and the Lord," Brendan told her. "I didn't want to let things at home and in Florida distract me," he said with a smile. "But when I found out your mom died, I prayed for you constantly. You were always in my thoughts."

"I'm sorry."

"No," he quickly said, looking straight into her eyes. "You don't need to apologize. It wasn't a distraction for me. If anything it brought me closer to the Lord and to the Spirit. I honestly felt like I had learned what it meant to draw upon the powers of heaven, to put my faith into action, to exercise it. I couldn't do anything to help you through that difficult time but pray for you."

"I felt your prayers," she told him softly.

His gaze deepened, and he held her hand a little tighter. They didn't speak. They had shared a monumental experience together, and nothing could change the bond they felt because of it. Kenidee felt that a turning point in their relationship had just occurred, and her heart filled with hope.

# CHAPTER 21

"How do you like these?" Brendan said, turning his feet side to side.

"Those look great. Traditional, but a little stylish."

"I agree." He looked at the price on the box. "I'm not used to spending money like this, but my mom gave me the money and I really need them."

"They'll last you a long time, Brendan. I think you'll be glad you got them."

He smiled at her. "You're right."

While he put the shoes back in the box, Kenidee looked around at the displays in the men's department. She saw some nice shirts on a rack and began looking through them.

"See anything?" Brendan asked her.

"I like this one. It would look great on you." She pulled the shirt off the rack and held it up for him. It was on sale, too.

"I could use some shirts. I don't have much left in my closet that I can wear."

She held it up to him. "This looks like you."

"You think?"

"Yeah, and it's not so different from stuff you've always worn, just a slimmer cut."

He took the shirt and examined it. She continued looking through the rack. A light yellow shirt with tiny colored stripes through it caught her eye. She immediately thought of Cam. It looked exactly like something he would wear.

"You like that one?" Brendan asked.

"No, I like the one you're holding better."

"Okay, I think I'll get it."

He took his purchases to the counter and paid for them. Kenidee was glad women's shoes didn't usually cost as much as men's. She could have two or even four pairs of shoes for the cost of one pair of men's.

Hand in hand, they strolled through the department store, remarking about new styles, things they were glad to see go out of style, and things they would miss.

"My mom says if you hold on to something long enough it will come back in style," Brendan told her.

"Yes, but the question is, do we really want them to come back in style. For instance, the eighties had some pretty crazy styles, you know? Girls had perms and wore their bangs out to here," she held her hand high above her forehead. "Guys had that swoopy 'flock of seagulls' hair thing going and those skinny-legged jeans."

"Ugh! I'm glad we were too young for all of that."

"Like your mom said, it will come back."

"To haunt us," he answered, and they both laughed.

On their way out of the store, they noticed a display for children's bathing suits on clearance.

"Oh, look," Kenidee said. "These are adorable. Brynn and Amanda would look so cute in these."

She combed through the rack trying to find two suits that matched in the girls' sizes. "Yes!" she said when she found what she needed. "I have to get these. The girls will be so thrilled."

"You seem really attached to those girls," he observed.

"I am. I love those two. I'll really miss them when I move—" she stopped.

Brendan looked at her, waiting for her to go on.

She didn't know how to finish the sentence.

"Are you thinking of moving?" he asked.

"Ah . . . well, sure, someday I will. Why?"

"I guess I was wondering. Before our missions, you said you wanted to go to the University of Utah and study ballet."

"I did—uh." She corrected herself. "I do."

"So, you're not going fall semester?"

"I hadn't planned on it."

"Oh, good," he said with a nod. "There's our trolley. Hey, do you want to stop at Chinatown? It might be fun to look around."

"Sure. That would be awesome." She couldn't help saying that word again. It was the only thing that came to mind when she needed to fabricate some enthusiasm.

\* \* \*

Kenidee wasn't sure how she felt about what she was going to do, but Brendan wanted her there with him at the airport. And that pretty much told the whole story.

"Are you excited?" she asked him.

"I can't believe they're actually coming here. You are going to love these guys."

"I'm anxious to meet them."

He squeezed her hand tightly and strained his neck to look over the crowd of passengers coming off the plane.

It seemed like yesterday that she had been here welcoming Brendan.

Brendan. It really was wonderful having him home. But things weren't quite the same as she'd thought they would be. Still, Kenidee remained hopeful that things would settle down and that she and Brendan could finally get their relationship figured out and back on track. There was no question that there was still something between them, but . . . things were different. She couldn't put her finger on what it was. She just knew it was there. Actually, it wasn't there, and that was the problem. Something was missing, she just didn't know what. But she aimed to get it back. And it appeared that he did too, since he called often and they were spending more and more time together.

They just needed to get these next two weeks out of the way first. Maybe once the Huang family left, they could bump their relationship up to the next level. Except when he went to Portland to work.

Argh! The whole thing got so frustrating when she thought about it.

Suddenly, Kenidee was pulled from her thoughts by a high-pitched squeal of excitement. The crowd before them parted and out shot a young woman who went straight into Brendan's arms.

Kenidee jumped back with alarm before realizing it had to be one of the Huangs because, a few seconds later, a young man joined in the hug, the girl still holding on. Several moments later, a middle-aged man and woman walked up, their toothy grins beaming like spotlights on a dark night.

Brendan hugged and bowed several times during the interchange of high-speed chatter between him and the family. The girl continued to hold firmly to Brendan's arm as the five people carried on a mind-boggling conversation that left Kenidee completely bewildered.

After a few minutes, Brendan seemed to remember she was there and turned to pull her into the group to meet the visitors.

"Kenidee, I want you to meet the best family I could have ever met on my mission." The family smiled, since they all understood English. "These guys are like my second family. This is Brother and Sister Huang, of course." The parents bowed to her and Kenidee bowed in return, like Brendan had shown her. "This is Ming, their son," he introduced. Ming smiled broadly and bowed. "And this is Lili," he added, "their daughter."

Lili looked at her for several seconds, then bowed.

"It's wonderful to meet you," Kenidee told them all. "Welcome to America."

"Thank you," Ming said. "We have waited a long time for this day." His accent was thick, but his English was understandable.

With the family sufficiently welcomed, they moved to the baggage claim area and waited for their suitcases to come around on the carousel.

Ming was full of questions and directed many of them at Kenidee. She enjoyed chatting with him and helping him understand the

American way of life. He seemed to drink in everything around him and had a clever sense of humor that Kenidee found delightful. She noticed that Lili dominated most of Brendan's attention, while the parents seemed a little more shell-shocked to be in a foreign country.

More than anything, Kenidee wanted to make them feel welcome and do her best to embrace the people Brendan had grown to love so deeply, and the culture they represented. She knew that if she and Brendan were going to be together, this would be a part of her life too. With that in mind, she eagerly answered Ming's questions and did her best to be friendly to Lili, even though the girl did a remarkable job of ignoring Kenidee.

Brendan had made reservations at the Beikou restaurant, where his parents would join them. He was excited to take the Huangs there, and they were interested in eating Americanized Taiwanese food.

As they rode the shuttle to the parking garages, Kenidee found herself squinting against the bright sunlight and pushing on her temples to help ease a headache that had crept up on her. She had a feeling it was going to be a long meal.

* * *

"I'm taking them to the city," Brendan said. "I'd love to have you come."

Kenidee appreciated being invited to all the places he took the Huangs, but she just wasn't up to spending an afternoon listening to Ming's unceasing questions and watching Lili cling to Brendan. Besides, she promised Brynn and Amanda she'd come and visit them. She hadn't been able to babysit Monday because she'd gone to the airport, or Wednesday when they'd spent the day shopping, and now it was Friday and the girls were missing her.

"I hope you don't mind, Brendan, but I've been having so much fun with you guys I've neglected some things I need to take care of."

"Oh, okay. Well, maybe later. We thought of watching movies here at the house. You want to come over for that?"

"Uh, sure. Sounds fun. I have to teach at six but I'm free after that." She wasn't sure she was convincing, but she tried to sound sincere, despite her lack of enthusiasm at the prospect of joining them. Not that she didn't like the family. She did. They were actually really neat people and she enjoyed them, but it gave her a headache to be around them too much. Between Ming's questions, Lili's incessant refrain of either "Oh, Blendan (the 'r' sound was hard for her to say), you so funny" or, "Oh, Blendan, you so smart," and the steady stream of Mandarin being spoken, she felt like her brain was being scrambled.

"Okay, well, get everything done so you can join us tonight," he said.

"I will. Thanks for asking."

Kenidee hung up the phone and breathed deeply and with relief. Glad to have a break from all the "fun," she jumped in her car and drove to Cam's house to see the girls. She even had a treat for each of them . . . chocolate.

* * *

"See this," Kenidee said to the girls. "When you crack open the chocolate ball, there's a toy inside."

Both of the girls' eyes opened wide with excitement.

With Cam's help, the chocolate balls were unwrapped and the chocolate was then smashed so the girls could find their prizes inside, a tiny duck for Brynn and a puppy for Amanda. In Kenidee's opinion, the toys weren't all that great, but the girls thought they were, which was all that mattered.

"So, what's going on?" Cam asked.

"What do you mean?"

"How are things with Brendan, your knight in shining armor?"

"Ha! Obviously he hasn't ridden up on his white horse and taken me away."

"I guess not. Maybe he hasn't located a white horse yet."

"I'm not sure he's even looking," she said under her breath.

"Sorry? I didn't hear you."

"Oh, nothing," she said. She took a piece of chocolate from Brynn's pile and popped it into her mouth.

"So, what's going on with the Hanger family?"

"The Huang family," she corrected. *Why couldn't anyone get these people's name right?*

"Sorry. How's that going?"

"Great. They are really neat people. They love America, and they are having a ball. Brendan has really gone out of his way to keep them busy and make sure they get the most out of their trip."

"That's good. And how are things with you two?"

"Great." Her tone of voice said, "Hey, just don't bother me about it right now."

Deciding to play along, Cam said, "Really. Well, that's good to hear." He raised his eyebrows only slightly.

She looked at him, trying to read his expression. "You don't believe me, do you."

"Of course, I do. If you say it's great, then it must be great."

"Why do you do that?"

"Do what? What did I do?"

"You think you know how I'm feeling, so you just patronize me."

"Kenidee, really, I'm not. I'm glad things are great." His forehead wrinkled. "It is, isn't it?"

"See, there you did it again!" she exclaimed.

"Did what?"

"What is it, Cam? Do you want me to tell you it's not good? That things are so strange between us that I don't even know Brendan anymore and that I think this Huang chick has got something for Brendan? Is that what you want me to tell you?"

Cam's eyes opened wide. "Kenidee. Just hold on. Really, I don't want you to tell me anything. I just wondered how everything was going, that's all. I promise. I'm concerned about you."

"Okay, then," she said, feeling a knot form in her throat. "Things are fine. They're just dandy." She looked away so he wouldn't see the hot tears that stung her eyes. And what in the world, she wondered, was she doing crying anyway! Things were fine, darn it, they were!

Cam sat silently, either afraid to say anything or uncertain what to say, Kenidee imagined. She realized it was a mistake to have come over. There was something about Cam that prevented her from dissembling. He knew her too well, or she knew him too well, she wasn't sure which. But they were too close to be anything but completely honest with each other.

She squeezed her eyes shut and allowed her tears to drop onto her hand in her lap. If things were so fine and dandy, then why in the world was she crying?

Wisely, Cam stayed silent. However, he did somehow sense her need for a hug, so without saying a word, he took her into his arms and held her while she cried. Her tears confused her, but she let them fall because it felt good to get them out of her system. And for now, she didn't need to know what they were about. Right now it felt good to release her emotions in the safety of Cam's arms.

* * *

Sunday, as Kenidee got ready for church, she found herself carrying on an inner dialogue with Heavenly Father, an extension of her morning prayer that carried on through her shower, blow-drying her hair, and putting on her makeup.

Now as she finished getting ready so she could attend Brendan's sacrament meeting to listen to him speak, she continued the conversation, wishing she could get stronger reception on the answers to her questions. Right now the conversation was a bit one-sided for her liking.

*Father, I just don't get it. Everything was perfect when Brendan left. We had everything planned out, or at least an idea of what we would do when we both got home. And now, things are totally amiss, like the puzzle pieces fit, but the picture isn't right. What is it? Help me.*

The phone rang, interrupting her prayer.

"Kenidee, honey? This is Dad. How are you?"

"Hi, Dad," she said. They hadn't been able to talk yet, since every time they called, she was gone, and every time she called them, they were gone. It was great to finally hear her father's voice live instead of recorded on an answering machine. "I'm fine. How are you guys? Are you having fun?"

"This place has been incredible. We're glad we got some color before we came. We got a little sunburnt the first day, but we're being more careful now and having a wonderful time."

"I'm glad, Dad."

"Have we missed anything?"

"No, not really."

"Honey, Robin wants to say hi."

Kenidee heard the phone exchange hands.

"Hi, Kenidee, are you doing okay?" Robin asked.

"Yeah."

"How's Brendan?"

"Okay. It's a little unsettling with these friends of his here, but it's okay." Kenidee wasn't telling a complete lie, but it certainly wasn't the whole truth either.

"Is the daughter still acting like Miss Gluestick?"

Kenidee had told her how attached Lili was to Brendan.

"Nothing's changed. I don't know what to think about her."

"Maybe you need to have a talk with Brendan and see what's going on with that."

"I need to talk to him about a lot of stuff," Kenidee told her.

"I'm sorry we're not there for you right now," Robin said.

"It's okay." She appreciated her thoughtfulness. "You'll be home soon."

"I'm bringing a suitcase full of chocolate-covered macadamia nuts home. They are to die for."

Kenidee laughed. Trust Robin to find something chocolate-covered in Hawaii.

Her father returned to the phone. "Honey, this island is amazing."

"I hope you've taken a lot of pictures," Kenidee said.

"We have. The Napali coastline is breathtaking. We took a helicopter ride over the whole island. I see why they call Kauai the garden island. It's like paradise. We have a video of it."

"I can't wait to see it."

They paused for a moment. "We'll be home soon. Hang in there, okay?"

"I will," Kenidee assured her dad.

She hung up the phone, grateful that her father and Robin were coming home soon. She missed them, and more than anything else, right now she needed help and advice. Not just her dad's either. She needed Robin's help, too.

* * *

Kenidee couldn't resist. She knew it was nosey, but she was curious to know exactly what Robin spent all her time doing on the computer. When she sat down at the computer table, she noticed nothing out of the ordinary on the desk, just a few bills and a letter Robin had received from a friend in Menlo Park.

She looked at the recently visited sites on the Internet and saw nothing alarming or strange there either, mostly web sites containing diet and exercise tips, or shopping sites.

Feeling guilty for even checking, Kenidee left the room just as she found it and went back to her room to get dressed for church. She was still puzzled though. Every time she caught Robin at the computer, Robin acted peculiar, almost as if she was hiding something. Kenidee knew Robin fretted about her weight, so maybe she was embarrassed about looking at diet web sites.

With no more time to worry about it, she hurriedly finished dressing and then said a quick prayer before leaving the house. Her prayerful thoughts continued as she drove to Brendan's church building and walked inside.

His mother spotted her almost immediately and motioned for her to join them. With a nervous smile, she walked up the aisle and was greeted by his mother and father.

"We saved you a spot." Brendan's mom pointed to a seat right next to Lili.

Lili smiled at her sweetly, looking ever so coquettish and demure.

Kenidee slid into the pew and took her seat, feeling like a super-sized person next to tiny, petite Lili.

Determined to keep up appearances, Kenidee leaned forward and greeted the other members of the Huang family, who responded warmly, especially Ming.

"You look very nice today," Ming told her.

"Thank you," she responded.

Lili tilted her head and examined her.

Kenidee felt uncomfortable under her gaze.

"You look different from picture," Lili said.

"Oh, which picture?"

"The picture Elder Nielsen show us on mission."

"He showed you a picture of me?"

"Yes. He tell us many things about you."

Kenidee glanced up at the seats where Brendan sat and caught his eyes. His gaze slipped from her to Lili and then back to her.

"Like what?"

"Many things. You are prettier in person."

"I am? Uh, thank you, I think," she said, wondering if that meant that Lili thought she was ugly in her picture.

The prelude music stopped as the bishop took a spot at the stand and welcomed the congregation to the meetings that day. He also welcomed all visitors and made a special effort to look directly at the Huang family, all of whom beamed with pride at being recognized. Kenidee half expected Ming to turn around and wave at everyone, but fortunately he didn't.

With sacrament meeting underway, Kenidee focused her thoughts on the meeting and the reverent feeling that came with shutting out the world and focusing on the Savior. During the sacrament, she turned to prayer to ask for help and understanding regarding Brendan and their future. She read and reread Doctrine and Covenants section nine, verses eight and nine:

*"But, behold, I say unto you, that you must study it out in your mind; then you must ask me if it be right, and if it is right I*

*will cause that your bosom shall burn within you; therefore,*
*you shall feel that it is right. But if it be not right you shall*
*have no such feelings, but you shall have a stupor of thought*
*that shall cause you to forget the thing which is wrong."*

All she'd been doing was studying it out in her mind. She'd analyzed the heck out of the situation and still didn't know what to think. Until she was able to understand exactly where Brendan stood on their relationship, she couldn't go to the Lord and ask for a confirmation. There was no decision yet that needed to be confirmed.

After the sacrament, a young boy gave a talk on the priesthood and what it meant to him to have just recently received the Aaronic priesthood. His talk was short, which meant that Brendan and the other speaker would split the remainder of the meeting.

The older man took his turn at the pulpit and gave a wonderful talk on the restoration of the Church and the priesthood. Kenidee had developed a deep respect for and testimony of the power of the priesthood. That power had helped her and strengthened her through her darkest hours. She'd turned to that power many times on her mission and was comforted to know that this power was available to her anytime she needed it.

As soon as the older man finished, Brendan stood. He looked handsome standing at the pulpit in his white shirt, tie, and dark suit. Kenidee's thoughts flashed back to the last time she'd sat in this building and watched him give a talk before leaving on his mission. That seemed like the very distant past, and she was grateful that was now behind them.

His wry humor and sincere love for the gospel made Brendan's talk captivating. He shared fascinating stories from his mission and bore powerful testimony that filled the chapel with an undeniably strong spirit. There was no doubt in Kenidee's mind that Brendan had been an amazing missionary. He had changed, that was true, but he was also an exceptional man.

She looked down at the ring on her finger and wondered if that ring would indeed become a sparkling wedding ring.

# CHAPTER 22

"Are you sad they're leaving tomorrow?" Kenidee asked Brendan over the phone. She was getting ready to go teach a class later that evening.

"Yeah, I have loved having them here. I think Ming and Lili would stay if their parents would let them. They love America," he said.

Maybe Ming loved America, but in Kenidee's opinion, Lili loved Brendan.

"They do seem to have adjusted quickly to being here. Just in the last two weeks I've even noticed how much their English has improved."

"Me too. This has been a good trip. But it's not too sad to have them leave because I know I'll see them soon."

"Oh?" Kenidee couldn't hide her surprise. "What do you mean?"

"Didn't I tell you? Some elders from my mission are going back to visit before school starts in January. They got a great deal on airfare because one elder's mother works for the airline. They invited me to go with them. My parents think it's kind of soon to be going back, but it's hard to turn down an opportunity like this. I talked to my uncle, and he was great about it. I know you understand how I feel though, don't you? You'd probably go back to your mission if you had a chance."

"Yeah," Kenidee said. She would, but going to Florida and going to Taiwan were completely different things.

"I'm so excited. Can you believe it?"

"It's really awesome," she said, using *that* word again. Kenidee suddenly realized that she now used that adjective only with Brendan and only when he talked about the Huangs. She agreed with his parents, it really was rather soon to be going back already.

"The main reason I called though is to see if you wanted to come over tonight for kind of a farewell party. Then I'd like you to go to the airport with me to take the Huangs tomorrow. They really like you and would love to tell you good-bye."

She wanted to support Brendan, and more than anything, she wanted to be as obsessed with all things Taiwanese as he was. But she wasn't. She tried desperately to embrace the Huang family, their culture, and the love Brendan had for all of it. But it wasn't that easy to develop the kind of devotion he had, especially when she hadn't been part of the experiences he'd had.

"I'm so sorry, but I have to teach tonight and I have four classes tomorrow, plus I have a ton of office work to do before Lucinda gets home."

"Are you sure? I really want you with me."

"I'll see what I can do," she told him, not wanting to disappoint him, "but I can't promise."

"Okay, please try. Either way, I'll see you after they leave. I want to talk to you."

"Oh? What about?"

She heard voices in the background, and Brendan responded in Mandarin. He came back on the phone, "Sorry. They are ready to go to the mall. We've had to buy more suitcases to get home all the stuff they've bought since they've been here. Anyway, I gotta run. Hope to see you tonight."

So, Brendan was on his way to Taiwan again in a few months. They certainly seemed to find an incredible number of obstacles in the way of their relationship, or maybe she just saw them as obstacles. Either way, she was glad he wanted to talk. It was time to get their feelings out on the table and find out where their relationship was going.

\* \* \*

"Kenidee?" her father's voice came through the cloud of confusion in her brain.

She looked up. "Huh?"

"Honey, that was the third time I've said your name. What's going on?"

She had just hung up the phone after talking to Genevieve at the studio. Apparently, the air conditioner had malfunctioned and the place was like a furnace. Classes were cancelled that evening until the repairman could fix the problem.

"Oh, nothing," she told him. "Just a problem at the studio. I think we've got it worked out though."

"You seem to have a lot on your mind lately."

"I guess," she said with a sigh. She sat down at the table where the family had been eating.

"So, you want to talk to us about what's going on?" her dad asked.

"Oh, the air conditioner went out at the studio. The guy is coming to fix it."

"That's not what I mean," her father said. "What's going on with Brendan?"

She needed to call him and tell him she could come over. She wasn't looking forward to spending an evening with the Huangs, but it was their last night. Part of her wondered if Brendan would be different after they left. She hoped so.

"There's not much to tell you," she answered. "Brendan's a great guy, but he's a lot different than he was before his mission. Right now there's a lot of stuff going on that is making everything—our relationship—so confusing. I don't even know why I call it a relationship. It doesn't seem like there is one."

"What can we do to help?" Robin asked.

"I don't know, nothing really. I just wish I had a clearer understanding of everything so I could sort out my feelings." Then a thought occurred to her. "Dad, would you mind giving me a blessing? I think it would help me get through this a little better."

"Of course, honey. I'd love to."

Kenidee asked Robin to come in with them. They went into her father's office and closed the door so the kids wouldn't disturb them. With only the quiet ticking of the clock on the bookshelf, Kenidee's father placed his hands on her head and began the blessing.

Immediately, Kenidee felt a sense of calm come over her. For the first time in weeks, she completely relaxed and cleared her mind so she could receive the message of the blessing and feel the Spirit of her Father in Heaven.

Her father spoke words of assurance to her, letting her know that the Lord was with her at this time and was aware of the challenges she faced and the confusion she felt. He also told her that in time these things would sort themselves out and she would know, without a doubt, the things she should do.

Blessing her with peace and strength to bear her burdens at this time, her father also told her that her mother served as a guardian angel to her and that her spirit would be with Kenidee. Tears trickled down Kenidee's face as she felt peace and warmth fill her soul. All was well and was in the Lord's hands—this she knew for sure.

After the blessing, her father, wiping away his own tears, took his daughter in his arms and gave her a tender hug.

"I love you, sweetie," he said. "Everything's going to work out."

She nodded, unable to speak for a moment.

He patted her back and held her as she gathered herself together and dried her eyes.

"Thanks, Dad. I love you too."

They parted, smiling and sniffing.

Then she turned to Robin and they hugged. "That was a beautiful blessing," Robin said.

Kenidee nodded.

They parted, holding hands for a moment.

"Thank you so much for being there for me," Kenidee told her.

"You're wel—" Robin's voice broke. She blinked her eyes quickly and cleared her throat. "You're welcome."

They embraced again, this time her dad joining them. Kenidee felt a sense of peace, a knowledge that things were just the way they were supposed to be.

"What do you think, Robin, wouldn't this be a good time to give it to her?" her father said.

Robin looked at Kenidee and smiled. "I think so."

"I'll be right back," her father said and left the room. He went to the bedroom, returning shortly with a DVD in his hand. "This is for you."

Kenidee looked first at the DVD in her hand and then at her father. "What is it?"

"Robin and I—well, mostly Robin—have been putting pictures onto this DVD with music."

"Oh? What kind of pictures?"

"Pictures of you and your mom and the family," he said.

She looked at both of them with pure shock. "What?"

Robin piped up excitedly. "We took all the family photos and scanned them into the computer, then put the pictures to music. It's taken forever, but we finally finished it. We made one for Matt, too. Now you have all the pictures on a disc for safekeeping."

So that's where the photo albums had been all this time, and that's what Robin, and her dad, had been secretly working on in their bedroom. Kenidee was ashamed of herself for jumping to wrong conclusions. Tears filled her eyes.

"Honey," her father said, "why are you crying?"

Kenidee sniffed and wiped the tears from her cheeks. "I just can't believe you did this. I wondered where the albums were and what you were doing in your room at the computer all the time."

Robin laughed. "It took me forever to learn the program. But once I finally got it, I got pretty good, didn't I, Will?"

"You really did," he answered, giving his wife a peck on the cheek. "She actually did most of the work."

"I have to watch it," Kenidee said.

"There are over six hours of pictures and music on there," Robin said proudly.

Kenidee shook her head. "This is so incredible. Thank you for doing this." Kenidee gave both of them a hug and felt an overwhelming sense of gratitude for her father and her stepmom.

* * *

Kenidee still couldn't get over the DVD she'd just watched. There were still five hours of pictures to see, but the first hour had been an emotional feast for her. She'd laughed and cried as she looked at pictures of herself with her mother and with Matt and her father. There were even pictures of Cam when they were all younger.

She was so happy she even became excited to go to Brendan's house and hang out with the Huangs. Although, she had to admit, she would be glad when they were gone so she could finally have him all to herself and they could focus on their relationship and future together.

On her way, she stopped to buy a banana cream pie for Brendan. Although it was his favorite, he still hadn't eaten any since he returned from his mission. She wanted to be the first to give him some.

Her phone rang as she exited the interstate. It was Cam.

"Funny you should call. I was just thinking about you," she said.

"You were?"

"Yeah. I was just looking at pictures of you when you were a lurpy thirteen-year-old," she said.

"Lurpy!" he exclaimed. "Who are you calling lurpy, brace-face?"

"Not fair, Cam. You had braces too."

"Okay," he relented. "But that lurpy comment really hurt."

"I'm sorry, but your arms were as long as your legs, and you were so skinny." She giggled at the image of his picture still in her head.

"You were the bean pole."

"I had a growth spurt," she countered.

"Yeah, well, me too."

"Why did you call me, anyway?" she asked.

"I'm beginning to wonder the same thing," he joked. "Actually I just wanted to tell you that Desiree came over. She wanted to talk to me about something serious."

"What?"

"I guess she's decided she isn't happy with the way her life has turned out after all. It's probably just because her boyfriend beat her and threw her out, but she's decided that she wants to make some serious changes in her life. She wondered if there was any chance we could salvage our relationship."

"You're kidding. What did you say?"

"I told her we don't have a relationship. But I can tell she's really trying. She's already gone to her bishop. I almost didn't recognize her when she showed up at the door. She had decent clothes on and she didn't smell like cigarettes."

"Wow, this is a surprise," Kenidee said.

"Tell me about it."

"What are you going to do?" she asked.

"Take it real slow. So much has happened, I'm not sure we could ever make it work again. But we do have the children to consider."

Kenidee didn't understand her reaction, but she felt possessive of Cam, protective even. She wasn't sure she trusted Desiree. Was the woman being sincere?

"Just be careful and prayerful, Cam," Kenidee told him.

"I will. Don't worry."

"Sometime I'll have to bring over the DVD that my dad and Robin made. You would love watching it."

"That'd be great."

They said good-bye, and Kenidee mulled over the idea of Desiree and Cam getting back together. And she didn't like it. Desiree didn't deserve Cam. He deserved a woman who would be loving and devoted, someone who would treasure him as a wonderful man and father, and who had the same goals and righteous desires as he did. She wasn't sure Desiree was capable of any of that.

As she rounded the corner to Brendan's street, she mentally shifted gears, and her thoughts changed to Brendan. She prayed that things would go well tonight. After the Huangs left, they could talk, and together they would plan their future. She was filled with hope and anticipation.

She was so busy making a mental list of all the things she wanted to talk to Brendan about that she drove right past his house before she realized it. Laughing at herself, she pulled over in front of a neighbor's house and checked her reflection in the mirror. Putting a quick coat of lip gloss on, she then took the pie out of the box so she could hand it to him when he answered the door.

The summer evening air was warm and relaxing. Her heartbeat quickened as she thought about seeing Brendan and taking their relationship to the next level. It was time, and she was ready to move things forward.

She heard giggling as she came around the corner of the neighbor's fence and stepped onto the lawn in front of Brendan's house. Scanning the yard quickly, she saw movement near a large a tree over in the corner. It was Brendan and Lili, wrapped in each other's arms.

And they were kissing!

Kenidee froze; her breath was trapped in her lungs. She blinked, hoping the image would be replaced by something else, but the picture remained the same. The ice that had frozen her limbs melted quickly as the heat of anger filled her chest.

They were still kissing. They didn't even know she was there! She wanted to scream, she wanted to rip the two apart and then slap them both, but she stood immobile.

Their kiss ended, and they slowly drifted apart. Then Brendan's gaze lifted.

"Kenidee!" he roughly pushed Lili away, knocking her to the ground. "I didn't see . . . you didn't call. I . . . I don't know what to say."

"Save it, Brendan," she said. "You don't have to say anything. Actions speak louder than words."

"But, it's not what you think," he protested.

Her mouth dropped open. "You're kidding me, right?"

"I . . . Lili . . . we . . ." he stammered.

Lili finally pulled herself up off the ground and cast a satisfied smirk in Kenidee's direction.

Kenidee walked closer to them.

"I guess I know where our relationship stands," she said. "I came over so we could talk about our future, and I think I found out what I need to know. So, I guess I'll leave so you two can get back to—"

"No, Kenidee. Don't leave. We need to talk."

"You take care of your precious little Lili, Brendan. We don't have anything to talk about."

Then she remembered the pie.

"Oh, one more thing," she said. "I forgot to give you this."

She lifted the pie and flung it in his face. Part of it sloshed ever so appropriately onto Lili, who then let out one of her inimitable squeals when it hit her.

As tears blurred her vision, Kenidee took off running for her car. In her hurry to escape, she didn't see the sprinkler head in the lawn and tripped over it, falling solidly to the ground.

"Kenidee!" Brendan exclaimed as he ran for her.

In the background, Kenidee heard Lili snickering with laughter.

"Are you all right?" Brendan asked, kneeling beside her. He reached to help her up as globs of whipped cream and pudding fell off his sleeve. Kenidee jerked her arm away from him. Her hands stung from scraping across the sidewalk and her knee felt like it had been bashed with a sledgehammer.

"I'm fine. Just let me go home."

"I don't want it to end like this," he said.

"There's no good way to end this, Brendan," she told him, pushing herself to her feet while trying to balance on her uninjured leg.

"I didn't mean for this to happen. I didn't mean to hurt you," he insisted.

"Well, guess what. You did," she shot back. "But, I'll get over it. I've survived worse."

"Can't we talk?"

"There's nothing to say. Go back to her, Brendan. If this is what you want, then go."

He looked at her with pain in his eyes. "I'm sorry."

"Yeah," she said. "Me too." *Sorry I waited around for you. Sorry I put my life on hold for you. Sorry I ever met you.*

"I gotta go," she said, taking a step. With no warning, her knee buckled. She caught herself before she went down again.

"Let me help—"

"NO!" she exclaimed. "I'm fine."

Trying desperately not to fall as she hobbled away, Kenidee fought for strength to walk away with a semblance of dignity, at least until she got in the car. Her face felt hot and tingly. Pain clawed at her heart and constricted her airway.

*Just get to the car,* she urged herself. *Then you can fall apart.*

After fumbling with the keys, she managed to push the button that released the lock, and she climbed inside. Her trembling fingers inserted the key into the ignition. Somehow she managed to start the car, buckle herself in, and turn on the lights. Slowly she pulled away from the curb and headed down the street, away from Brendan's house.

Just like that, after two long, devoted years, it was over.

\* \* \*

"You're leaving?" Cam asked.

Kenidee couldn't look at him, or at the girls. If she did, she wouldn't be able to hold in her emotions.

"Where's Kenidee going, Daddy?" Amanda asked.

Cam cleared his throat and gently answered his daughter. "She's going to visit a friend for a while."

"For how long?"

Cam looked at her, and Kenidee shifted her eyes. She was close to breaking down.

"Probably just a couple of weeks, right Kenidee?" he asked.

She nodded and pulled in slow, deep breaths.

The truth was, she didn't know how long she'd be gone. However long it took to recover from a broken heart. However long it took to want to get out of bed again. However long it took to erase the image of Brendan kissing Lili.

Brynn walked over to Kenidee, put her small hand on Kenidee's cheek, and stroked it. "Kenidee's sad," she said.

"That's because she's going to miss you two," Cam said, pulling Amanda onto his lap and hugging her close.

"Why is Amanda crying?" Brynn asked, her bottom lip poking out and starting to quiver.

Cam patted Amanda's head and tried to soothe her.

Suddenly, Brynn drew in a shaky breath and burst out crying.

Cam pulled his youngest daughter onto his other knee and tried to calm both of his girls.

Kenidee shut her eyes, unable to watch the sadness she had created. She didn't have a choice, though. She needed to leave. Even if for a little while, she just had to.

"It will be okay," Camden told them. "Kenidee will be back before you know it. You can draw her some pretty pictures while she's gone."

"I'd like that," Kenidee said, holding steady. "And I'll bring you back something really special."

Brynn lifted her head from her father's shoulder and looked at her with a tear-stained face. "A toy?" she asked.

Kenidee smiled. "Yes, I'll bring you a toy."

Those magic words dried up Amanda's tears too. Kenidee hated to bribe them, but she couldn't take any more tears. She'd wanted to say good-bye over the phone, but she knew that would be insensitive. Now she wasn't so sure. In person had turned out to be much, much harder.

"You girls want to give her a hug before she goes?" Cam asked his daughters.

They both flew to Kenidee's arms and hugged her tightly, taking with them part of her broken heart. She would miss these hugs.

After a moment, Kenidee stood to leave. She needed to get home and get packed.

"Sorry to put you in a bind like this," she told Cam.

"Don't worry, we'll manage. I have a lot of babysitters to choose from during the summer."

She nodded and took a step toward the door.

"Well," she paused, and took one last look at them. "I'll see you."

Cam's hand flinched, as if he were going to raise his arm and had then decided against it.

"Bye," she said with a half wave.

# CHAPTER 23

As the airplane wheels touched down, Kenidee released a sigh of relief. They'd arrived safely in Salt Lake. Considering her luck lately, she regarded the safe landing as slightly less than a miracle.

Dolly would be there, waiting to take Kenidee back to her house. And then Kenidee would try to piece her life back together. But she knew it would be like trying to do a jigsaw puzzle with missing pieces. There would be holes in the picture, holes that would never fill back up.

Numbly, she waited her turn to leave the airplane. This wasn't the type of trip to Salt Lake that she'd been looking forward to. This wasn't a vacation. It was therapy, prescribed by her father and Robin. Even Matt and Lindsay agreed. They all felt that she should get away.

A couple across the aisle gave her a look of sympathy as they stood and waited for their turn to leave. Kenidee looked away, embarrassed that they'd noticed her crying during the first half of the trip. The second half she'd been in an exhausted sleep. She couldn't help it. She just couldn't seem to shake the image of Brendan and Lili in each other's arms, the shattering of her dreams. Sure, things hadn't been perfect, but she'd been willing to give Brendan all the time he needed to adjust and get settled back into regular life. She'd even been willing to switch from going to college in Utah and to attend a school in the Bay Area where she could work on her degree.

But all that loyalty and commitment couldn't compete against the one thing he loved most—Lili.

Just the thought of them together brought a new stab of pain to her heart.

Finally it was her turn to exit the plane. She carried her bag down the aisle and walked through the long corridor to the gate and into the terminal where she would meet Dolly by the baggage claim.

While she was riding the escalator toward the baggage claim, Kenidee heard a high-pitched scream and immediately recognized Dolly's voice.

"Kenidee!"

Looking out over the crowd, she saw her tiny friend jumping up and down and waving her arms with excitement.

The warm welcome was appreciated. Kenidee was grateful Dolly had been willing to have her come and stay for a while. Dolly had been almost as astonished about the news of Brendan as Kenidee's family was. Her father had taken it pretty hard and had even called Brendan to see if he could find out exactly what had happened. And after he'd talked with Brendan, her father had literally slammed the phone down into the receiver so hard it broke off the antenna.

Dolly nearly knocked her over with a hug when Kenidee finally got off the escalator.

"You look great," Dolly said, "No worse for the wear."

Kenidee scoffed. "You never were a good liar," she said. "I was there when you tried grits for the first time, remember?"

Dolly's expression fell. "Oh, yeah."

"Go ahead and say it. I look awful. I'm a mess."

"You aren't a mess," Dolly assured her. "You just need some rest and something to get your mind off all of this."

Kenidee nodded. It was true. A distraction would be nice. Sleep was the only form of distraction she had, but she couldn't do that 24/7, although she had slept for seventeen hours one night, making her father and Robin extremely nervous.

"How was your flight?"

"Fine," Kenidee answered.

"You hungry?"

"No," Kenidee said.

"You look like you need some food. I'll take you home and feed you. Then we can catch up and make plans."

"I just want to sleep," Kenidee told her.

"Are you kidding? I've waited so long for you to come, I'm not about to let you sleep away our time together. Besides, getting involved, staying busy, and working hard is the cure-all for whatever is bothering you. Remember? You were the one who said that all the time."

"I lied," Kenidee told her.

"Then I guess we're even. Still, there's too much to do so I'll just drag you along with me if I have to." She looked around. "Let's get your bag and get going. My mom and dad can't wait to meet you."

After getting her luggage, they cruised along the freeway, racing from the airport across the valley to the foothills of Salt Lake City. Dolly chattered away, updating her on family issues and any mission news she'd heard since they last talked two days earlier.

"Joey said to call him when we get settled. He wants to come and see us," Dolly said.

Kenidee really didn't feel like explaining what had happened between her and Brendan, to Joey or anyone else for that matter. This was much different from when she'd lost her mother. The pain actually felt better when she talked to people about it, especially people who understood. But she'd just been rejected and humiliated. That was a whole different kind of pain.

"Okay, maybe in a few days, when you're feeling better," Dolly said.

Kenidee doubted that she'd be feeling better in a few days or even a few weeks. It wasn't like she had the flu and would bounce back by drinking lots of fluids and enjoying bed rest for two days.

Dolly's house, an older style home probably built in the seventies, was well taken care of and very large and spacious. Because all of Dolly's siblings were married and living on their own, there were numerous empty bedrooms.

Dolly's parents were warm and welcoming. Even though Kenidee was certain they knew the situation surrounding her visit, they were gracious enough not to ask her about it.

After eating a wonderful dinner of barbecued chicken and fresh corn on the cob on their back porch that overlooked the Salt Lake valley, Dolly and Kenidee went inside and watched TV for a while until Kenidee couldn't keep her eyes open any longer.

It was close to noon when she awoke the next day.

A note on the kitchen counter from Dolly told Kenidee to help herself to some food in the refrigerator and to expect Dolly back soon. Kenidee looked in the fridge and saw some hoagie sandwiches and a bowl of bite-size cantaloupe and watermelon pieces. She ate a few pieces of the melon, then put everything back in the fridge. She just didn't have an appetite.

Ten minutes later, she heard an engine roar up the driveway then heard Dolly's voice. Kenidee hoped Dolly wasn't bringing anyone home with her. She was still in her pajamas.

But it was just Dolly on her cell phone.

"I'll talk to her and call you later so we can plan it then." Dolly waved hello when she saw Kenidee at the table. "Sure, that sounds fun. Thanks for calling."

She hung up the phone. "Joey," she said, fastening her phone into the little clip on her belt. "He wondered what we were doing tonight."

Kenidee pulled a face.

"I told him we'd talk. He also wants to know if we want to go country dancing. It's tons of fun and—"

Kenidee shook her head.

"Or we could just stay here and watch videos or something," Dolly suggested.

"That would be fun."

Dolly filled up a plate of food for herself and joined Kenidee at the table.

"So. What else do you want to do today," Dolly asked.

"Uh, nothing really. I'd like to sit outside in the sunshine and read a book or something."

"Don't you want to go shopping and down to Temple Square, or to a movie, or—"

"Dolly, you can go if you want. I don't want you to stay home with me. I'm fine. Really."

"I don't want to leave you here," Dolly insisted.

"But I want you to. It's okay."

"We can just stay home and watch movies," Dolly said.

Kenidee brightened. "I'd like that."

\* \* \*

For the next few days, Kenidee followed a predictable routine. She slept in until mid-morning, she stayed in the same T-shirt and pajama pants, and she kept her hair in a ponytail. She didn't leave the house except to sit outside in the sunshine and read.

Every time Dolly tried to talk to her about what had happened with Brendan or what her future plans were, Kenidee shut her down. She didn't want to confront her feelings by talking about them. The best way to avoid confronting her feelings was to either sleep or suppress and deny them.

Every time her dad and Robin or Matt and Lindsay called, she shut them down, too. She assured them she was fine, but she had a feeling Dolly was keeping them apprised of her progress—which was basically no progress.

Kenidee didn't care that she hadn't showered in three days, or that she couldn't eat, or that all she did was sleep. Nothing mattered.

She knew she wasn't handling the breakup well, but she was handling it the only way she could—by not handling it at all. How was she supposed to deal with rejection of such epic proportion, when all of her coping skills had been used up trying to deal with her mother's death?

She couldn't. So she didn't.

* * *

The ringing of the telephone woke Kenidee. She rolled over and looked at the clock. It was after ten.

Warm rays of sunlight streaked through the window, bathing her bed in a golden glow. It was so annoying. Why couldn't it be rainy and dreary? Even the sun seemed to be trying to cheer her up.

A tap on her door jarred her from her thoughts.

"Come in."

"Hey there," Dolly said as she opened the door. "Joey just called. He wondered if we wanted to go downtown to lunch and to Temple Square."

Kenidee thought of the Herculean effort it would take to get up, get showered, do her hair, and get dressed.

"Maybe another day," she said. "Why don't you go ahead, though."

Dolly opened her mouth to say something, then closed it again. Kenidee didn't encourage her to say what was on her mind because she didn't want to know.

"I guess I'll see you later then. Mom bought some lunch meat if you want to make a sandwich," Dolly said.

Kenidee nodded.

"Maybe we could go for a walk later? Or drive up the canyon," Dolly suggested.

Kenidee thought for a moment. A drive would be nice. Walking took too much effort.

"I'd like that."

"I'd better go get ready. I'll see you later." Dolly looked at Kenidee, her face lined with worry. Again, she looked as if she wanted to say something. Instead she just sighed and closed the door.

Kenidee stayed in bed a few minutes longer, wishing she wanted to go with Dolly and Joey, wishing she wanted to do something—anything. But she didn't. Having fun just didn't appeal to her.

She finally dragged herself out of bed and padded to the living room, where she found Dolly waiting for Joey.

"You look nice," Kenidee told her. Dolly wore a white cotton skirt, with a turquoise shirt and turquoise sandals to match.

"Thanks. I found this great little shop at the mall. I'd love to take you there while you're here."

The slam of a car door outside caught their attention.

Kenidee sat up, ready to make herself scarce before Joey saw her. She might have been out of touch with reality but not enough not to know she was a frightful sight.

"Hey," Dolly said, looking out the window, "I wonder who that is."

"Who *who* is?"

"A very good-looking man with two little girls. And he's coming to the door."

Kenidee's heart stopped.

The doorbell rang.

She wanted to run out of the room but her legs wouldn't move. Then she wondered, *Would Cam actually come and see me?*

Her heart started beating again, triple time.

"Hello, could you tell me if I have the right address? I'm looking for 3032 Crystal View Drive. The Wattersons' home."

Kenidee's heart stopped again. It wasn't Cam.

"They live down at the end of the street in the red brick house with the circular driveway. I think their address is 3230."

The man chuckled. "Oops, I wrote it down wrong. Sorry to bother you."

"Isn't this Kelsey's house?" one of the little girls asked.

"Sorry, sweetie. But she's just down the street. We're almost there."

"Yay," the little girl cheered. The other little girl, probably her sister, chimed in. They chatted excitedly about seeing their friend as Dolly shut the door.

"Cute little girls. They looked like they were on their way to a birthday party."

Kenidee couldn't speak. She was unprepared for the emotion that had just been triggered.

"Oh, there's Joey," Dolly exclaimed. She turned to Kenidee. "Are you sure you don't mind that I go?"

Kenidee shook her head, remembering how wonderful it used to feel to get excited when Brendan picked her up for a date. She was happy for Dolly and Joey. She really was. She just couldn't help wondering if something would have happened between her and Joey had she not locked her heart for Brendan.

"I'll see you later then. Call me if you need anything."

Kenidee nodded.

Dolly left in a rush, the slamming of the door behind her echoing throughout the house and into Kenidee's empty, cold soul.

Tears leaked from her eyes, but she fought to keep them back, afraid that the small leak would set off a tidal wave of the emotions she'd kept bottled up inside.

And she was right. Once they started, they wouldn't stop. She began to cry. They started out as tears of self-pity. First she lost her mom and now Brendan. Why did everything have to happen to her? She'd invested over two years of her life in Brendan. They'd planned their lives together. And then, in a flash, it was over. Everything had changed.

Then tears of anger began. Two years she had stayed loyal and committed to him. Through missions and months of waiting, she remained true and faithful to him. For what? She pounded the couch cushions with her fists. So many people had tried to prepare her for the possibility that things might change. But she was dumb enough to believe they wouldn't, they couldn't change.

As the hot tears of anger changed to tears of sorrow, she felt the well of emotion finally begin to run dry. She had given him nearly two and a half years of her life. And now, she finally realized, she was still giving herself to him. She did it by not letting go, by not moving on, by wallowing around in self-pity, and by letting him rob her of her dreams and her future.

Exhausted, she rested her head against the back of the sofa and pulled in a few deep breaths. Her throat hurt from crying. Her face was tight from salty tears. She was embarrassed by her attitude and her appearance. But inside she felt like a new woman.

*Why in the world would I want to spend one more minute on that man? He isn't worth it. He took my devotion and threw it away like yesterday's newspaper. He isn't worth it.* Kenidee shook her head to clear the cobwebs of confusion that had stalled her thought processes for so long.

And besides that, when she really thought about it, he had changed. A lot.

If she married him, she would have been expected not only to embrace his changes but to change herself as well. And she didn't want to change. She shouldn't have to change. If he didn't love her for who she was, then she didn't want him.

She didn't want him!

A burst of energy ignited her. She sprang to her feet.

Brendan wasn't worth the brain cells she was wasting on him by being sad.

She hurried to her room and pulled open the blinds, letting glorious sunshine fill the room. Then, for the first time since she had arrived, she made the bed and tidied the room.

From the time he'd stepped off the plane, she'd noticed how much Brendan had changed. Although she tried to convince herself otherwise, she knew that they didn't have as much in common anymore. But she'd been willing to change, give up her dreams, conform to his plans.

"Duh!" she smacked the pillow on the bed. "What an idiot!" She addressed that to him and to herself. How could she have been so stupid? She'd seen it all along but had chosen to ignore it because she'd been so loyal to him and committed to their plan.

"He can have Lili and the Huang family. And the entire country of Taiwan!" she exclaimed as she gathered up dirty laundry and shoved it into a bag with a vengeance.

She felt free. Finally, she felt ready to move on.

Gathering what she needed from her suitcase so she could get showered and cleaned up, Kenidee accidentally knocked her purse onto the floor, spilling the contents. As she put all the junk back inside, she picked up her cell phone. She'd kept it turned off on purpose, but now she was curious.

She listened to the half dozen messages from her family, just calling to see how she was doing. Then she froze as another message played. The sound of the voice went through her like a volt of electricity.

*"Hey, Ken-dog. Oops, sorry, I didn't mean that. Hey, how are you? I've tried to call you a dozen times, but you aren't answering your phone. I can't quit thinking about you. We miss you. I've got some big news to tell you. Call me."*

Big news? What was his big news?

# CHAPTER 24

Cam didn't answer his phone, and his voice mailbox was full.

Kenidee was going crazy. What was his big news?

For the last five days, his had been the only face she hadn't been able to completely block from her mind. During the months after she had returned home, he had become her dearest friend. She had talked to him about everything in her life. And he had always listened—and cared. Never judging, but giving her honest advice. With Cam, she felt secure and safe, something she never felt with Brendan.

So where was he? She needed to talk to him.

Anxiety coursed through her veins.

Leaning forward, she carefully outlined her lips before filling them in with tinted lip gloss.

"Kenidee?" Dolly's voice called from the doorway of the bedroom.

"In here."

"Listen," Dolly said, standing just outside the bathroom. "I have been trying to be really patient with you and give you your space to work through all of this, but I have to tell you, it's time for you to snap out of this. I can't just sit around any longer and watch you just wither away. You were never this bad even when you lost your mom. I think you need to talk to someone about your problems."

Kenidee stepped out of the bathroom, her hair styled, her makeup on, her outfit clean and coordinated.

"I agree. You're absolutely right."

The shocked expression on Dolly's face made her laugh. Dolly looked at her, then around the room. "What's going on? You're showered and dressed. Your suitcase is packed."

"I'm going home. I have to talk to Cam."

"Be serious."

"I am. I've had an epiphany," Kenidee proclaimed. She walked to her suitcase and tucked her makeup bag inside.

"What are you talking about?" Dolly insisted.

"I've been an idiot, and I actually probably do need some therapy. But right now I only know two things, actually three. First, Brendan's a loser, and I'm an idiot for wasting a microsecond on being sad our relationship is over."

"Good." Dolly nodded her head once in agreement.

"Second, Cam's the greatest guy in the world, and I'm an idiot for not being able to see it. But I'm afraid his ex-wife is making the moves on him, and I think I'm in love with him and I have to go home and find him and tell him."

Dolly's eyes doubled in size. "Really?"

"Yes. I can't imagine not having Cam in my life. And I love his daughters like my own. It was right there in front of me all the time, and I let Brendan get in my way of seeing it."

"What's the third thing?"

"I'm famished. Can we stop at Wendy's on the way to the airport?"

"You're leaving now?"

"Yes. My plane leaves in three hours. That gives us time for food and travel."

"But . . ." Dolly stood speechless.

"I'm sorry I've been a mental case. I promise I'll look into therapy when I get home. But right now, please, Dolly, take me to the airport. I don't want to lose the best thing that's ever happened to me."

"Okay," Dolly answered, her mind and tongue still out of sync.

"By the way, how was your date with Joey?" Kenidee asked.

"Good," she answered. "He wants to go out again tonight."

"Yes!" Kenidee erupted and threw her arms around her friend. "You two would be perfect together. This is wonderful. Isn't life just slap-you-upside-the-head-and-punch-you-in-the-gut wonderful?"

* * *

Kenidee had arranged to have Robin pick her up at the airport. She didn't explain anything to her over the phone except that she was coming home and that she wanted Robin and no one else to know she was coming. She wanted Robin's help with this because she believed that out of everyone in the family, Robin was the one who could understand the best.

Which explained the look of concern and curiosity on Robin's face when they met at the San Jose airport.

"Are you okay?" Robin asked.

"I'm terrific!" Kenidee assured her.

Robin's eyebrows arched high on her forehead.

"I have so much to tell you."

They waited until they were in the car before Kenidee exploded with her story. By the time she finished, she was crying again, but this time with joy.

"I don't know how I missed it, but I'm in love with Cam. I don't know how he feels about me, but I have to tell him. I'm scared because he may not feel the same. He may even be getting back with Desiree, but I have to do this."

Robin remained thoughtful for a moment, then said, "Kenidee, do you remember when we were at Shelley's and you came back from your mission reunion?"

"Yes."

"Do you remember what you said about your mission president?"

"Not specifically."

"You said that Cam reminded you of him."

"I did?" She thought for a moment. "That's right, I did."

"I knew the minute you said that, that you had feelings for Cam, and that Cam must be a pretty amazing guy."

"He is," Kenidee said.

"Tell me what you like about Cam?" Robin asked.

Kenidee didn't even know where to begin. "He's a wonderful dad. He's kind and honest and hardworking. He's thoughtful and appreciative. He has a strong testimony. He's handsome. And he makes me laugh."

"You should see the light in your eyes when you talk about him. Actually your whole face lights up," Robin said.

"It does?" She put her hands on her cheeks. She didn't know what it was that Robin saw on her face, but she did know that inside she felt like she could fly.

"I wasn't sure how everything was going to work out for you, but I had a hunch these feelings for Cam would surface."

"My head was driving my feelings for Brendan, but it's my heart that drives my feelings for Camden."

"That's where feelings are supposed to be," Robin told her.

"I'm kind of afraid to talk to him. What if he doesn't feel the same? What if it's too late?"

"You have to know, either way."

Kenidee knew she was right.

"It will be okay," Robin assured her. She reached for Kenidee's hand and gave it a squeeze.

"I know." Kenidee looked at her stepmother and felt a warmth in her heart. She missed her mother dearly. There would never be a day that she didn't. But she was so very grateful to have Robin as a part of her life. "Thank you for listening and for helping."

This time Robin's eyes filled with tears, but she quickly blinked to clear her vision. "You're welcome," she managed to say.

Kenidee handed Robin a tissue, something her purse was full of.

Robin wiped the tears from her cheeks and began to chuckle.

"What?"

"I just realized that if you and Cam end up getting married, you'll be a stepmom too."

Kenidee had never allowed herself to think of marrying Cam, let alone being a stepmom to his children, but now that Robin mentioned it, she was right. Kenidee also started to laugh.

"You'll do a wonderful job too. You already love those girls."

"I do," Kenidee told her. "Very much."

"Then they'll be lucky to have you."

"Just like I'm lucky to have you," Kenidee said.

Robin's eyes filled with tears again. "You know, that's what Lucinda said before she left on her trip for Paris."

"When did you talk to Lucinda?"

"I've known Lucinda for years. We met in the hospital when I was having Rachel and she was having back surgery. We hit it off like old friends, and we've stayed in touch through the years."

"So that's how I got the job," Kenidee said.

"Actually, she didn't know we were family. I just told her I knew of a wonderful girl who would be a great teacher. She was as surprised to find out that you are my stepdaughter as you are to find out we're friends."

"Really?" Kenidee liked knowing that she proved herself on her own merit.

"Yes. And she is so grateful to have you on her staff. You really helped her out while she was in Paris."

Kenidee looked at Robin. Again she felt the warmth in her heart increase. This woman was such a blessing in all their lives. She was so glad she could finally see it.

For the first time in days, Kenidee felt peace and hope in her heart. Once she talked to Cam, she would know one way or the other what her future held.

# CHAPTER 25

Turning into Cam's neighborhood, Kenidee felt her stomach turn inside out. She was about to do either the dumbest thing in the world or the smartest. Following the bend in the road, Kenidee felt her pulse race in anticipation. His house was just around the corner.

She slowed the car and took several deep breaths as she turned the corner onto his street. And then she saw it. The "For Sale" sign boldly placed in front of his house. Gasping for breath, she managed to pull over to the curb and stop her car. Why was his house for sale? Why was he moving? Where was he going?

Making a conscious effort to get out of her car and make her legs move her toward the front door, Kenidee finally stood on the porch. She was numb. Her paralyzed hand would not ring the doorbell.

This was it. She was either going to complicate his life or give him something to laugh about. She still couldn't do it. She stepped off the porch and walked halfway across the driveway, stopping abruptly. A stack of empty boxes was piled on the side of the house. He was already packing? How long had he known he was leaving? Why hadn't he told her?

Robotlike, Kenidee turned around and walked back to the porch. She had to find out how Cam felt, once and for all. She pushed the doorbell and waited and listened for the girls to come running to the door, even though Cam had a rule that they couldn't open it without an adult with them.

But there was no pitter-patter of little feet. There wasn't any noise or sign of movement. Where were they?

Climbing back into her car, she sat in the silence, wondering what to do. Then she did the only thing she had been able to do throughout the entire ordeal . . . she shut her eyes and offered a prayer. Her prayer became fuzzier and fuzzier as her body relaxed and her mind finally stopped whirling, and slowly, very slowly, she drifted to sleep.

\* \* \*

A sharp knocking on the car window woke Kenidee up with a start.

She wiped drool off her chin and then looked out the window. Amanda and Brynn were staring in at her and laughing. Kenidee opened the door, and the girls crowded inside. She lifted Brynn onto her lap and put an arm around Amanda.

"Why are you sleeping in your car?" Amanda asked her.

"Why is your chin wet?" Brynn asked.

"I was waiting for you guys to come home," Kenidee told them. "Where have you been?"

"Daddy took us to McDonald's, then we went to hunt for boxes."

"I see. Where is your daddy?" She experienced a sinking feeling in her stomach.

"He took some boxes in the house," Amanda said. "I'm glad you came home."

"Me too!" Brynn piped up.

They both gave her kisses on the cheek and choking hugs. The two girls pulled her from her car and held her hands as they led her to the house. With each step she took, Kenidee's uncertainty grew. Maybe talking to him was a mistake.

The front door was wide open, and they found Cam reinforcing boxes with packing tape.

"Hey, there," he said, glancing up briefly before going back to his task. "Welcome back. What are you doing?"

"What are you doing?" she countered.

"I have some exciting news," he said, grabbing another box. "We're moving."

"I noticed."

"I tried to call you, but you wouldn't answer my calls."

"I know. I'm sorry. I was going through something I can hardly explain. I felt like I was in the Land of Desolation," she confessed.

"I guess I just wanted to make sure you were okay. You know, like friends do."

"I'm sorry, Cam. I had some kind of out-of-brain experience. But I finally figured things out. That's why I came home."

"Good. I'm happy for you." He continued taping boxes and stacking them. He took out a magic marker and wrote a name on the box. Desiree.

Kenidee stood there. Watching him. Feeling hopeless. He was moving. He was going to leave and take his girls with him. Was Desiree part of this?

The thought was almost more than she could bear, and she suddenly knew she had to get out of there or she would crumble right in front of him.

He remained focused on his task, ignoring her.

"Well, I can see you're busy," she said, fighting to keep her voice steady.

She turned to leave. Her face was flushed and hot. She was a volcano of emotions set to erupt.

That was it. He was leaving her. If something was meant to be between them, the chance was gone now.

Fumbling for her keys, Kenidee blindly made her way back to her car as tears blurred her vision. She yanked the door open, tumbled into the driver's seat, and pulled the door shut behind her. In the confines of her car, she allowed the dam to break. Now what did she do?

With both hands grasping the top of the steering wheel, she rested her head on her knuckles and let the tears fall. *I don't understand, Heavenly Father. Please help me. I thought this was the right path for me.*

Why did love work out like this? She'd been sure she and Cam had experienced magical moments together, moments when something had clicked. She'd seen it in his eyes. At least she thought she'd seen it. Maybe she'd wanted something to be there that wasn't there at all.

What a dope!

A loud rapping on the window brought her head up with a snap.

To her horror, it was Cam. She covered her tear-stained face with her hands. Why hadn't she at least driven around the corner before she had her breakdown?

He tried to open the passenger door, but it was still locked. He knocked on the window again, but she shook her head. She didn't want him to see her like this.

"Open it, Ken," he told her.

She shook her head.

"Please, I want to talk to you."

She didn't want him to tell her that she was a nice girl, but he just didn't have feelings like that for her. She couldn't bear more humiliation.

"Darn it, Ken, open the door!"

Good sense told her to start the car and drive away, but a minute fraction of hope still existed in that portion of her partially ruptured heart that made her want to listen to what he had to say. Reaching out, she pushed the unlock button.

He opened the door and got inside, his long legs barely fitting into the space in front of the seat.

He pulled the door shut, then turned to her. She was busy wiping her eyes and nose. "Are you okay?" he first asked.

She nodded.

"I'm sorry. I didn't mean to make you cry."

"Where are you going?" she asked.

"My brother has been after me for years to help him with his construction company. He just lost one of his key employees and really needs me. This is the perfect opportunity to move, before Amanda starts school. Trevor can barely keep up with the growth in the Salt Lake valley, he's so busy. It's the perfect situation for us.

He has kids the same ages as my girls, and there's a house on his street that he says is perfect for us."

"When are you moving?"

"In the next couple of weeks. I just need to get packed and get the house in order. I want to be there so Amanda can start school the end of August."

She nodded and dabbed at the last bit of moisture in her eyes.

"What about Desiree?"

"She's moving, too."

Kenidee shut her eyes, her brain and heart turning numb to the pain. She couldn't believe this was happening.

"Oh." She looked down at her lap.

"She's moving to Las Vegas. I guess her boyfriend called and begged her to come back to him. They found a job in Vegas for a year at a casino, so she thinks they'll be able to settle down together. It never would have worked between us, even if she had changed. We have nothing in common. She's not even the same person anymore."

Kenidee almost smiled, she was so relieved to know they weren't getting back together.

"Ken, I get the feeling there's more to your visit here this morning. Is everything okay?"

This time, she couldn't nod but only managed to dip her chin.

"You know you can talk to me about anything. What's up?"

She shut her eyes, feeling the ache in her heart go straight to her core. That was the problem, she could talk to him about anything. Aside from the fact that she'd fallen in love with him, he was her best friend.

"Hey," he said softly, reaching for her hand, which he managed to grab because she had her eyes shut. "Talk to me."

"I can't."

"Why?"

"Because I came to tell you something, but you're moving. My timing is all wrong."

"What did you come to tell me?"

He wasn't going to give up without an answer.

Right or wrong, she had to find out. "Okay." She took a deep breath and let it out slowly. "I came to tell you that I realized I'm glad things didn't work out with me and Brendan after all because I didn't really love him. I thought I did, but looking back, I realize that we didn't have anything in common anymore and that I was going to have to change everything about myself to be with him."

"It's good you figured that out," Cam said.

"I also realized that I was in love with someone else."

"Oh?"

She chewed her bottom lip, unable to continue. He still held her hand.

Then, she turned and looked up into Cam's eyes. Their gazes locked.

"Who are you in love with?" Cam asked softly.

Kenidee could barely breathe.

He tightened the grip on her hand.

She was going to do it. She was going to tell him. She was convinced she was going to have a heart attack if she didn't.

"I'm in love . . ." her breath was shallow, "with . . ." she swallowed. *Just say it,* she told herself.

He leaned in closer to her.

"You."

His eyes opened wide as she shut hers tightly. She waited for him to say something and prayed he wouldn't laugh. She felt his grip tighten.

"I love you too, Ken."

She turned to look at him.

Even though he was smiling, he had tears in his eyes.

"You do?" she asked, her own eyes filling up again.

"I knew it the day I came home when you were dusting the tops of my kitchen cabinets, and I caught you in my arms. I didn't want to let you go. I almost told you at the hospital, when Lindsay had her baby, but I knew it wasn't the right time. I knew you had your missionary."

She smiled at him, touched at his thoughtfulness and willingness to sacrifice his feelings for her. This was one of the many reasons she loved him.

"Say it again," she pleaded, leaning in closer to him.

He leaned closer to her until his nose almost touched hers. "I love you."

His words bathed her wounded heart with a healing balm. He let go of her hands and circled his arms around her. Then, finally, he kissed her.

Kenidee had had a few special kisses in her life, but none of them, even all combined together, equaled the thrill and meaning of that kiss. That was the kiss that sealed their love. That kiss changed everything. It was the kiss of a lifetime.

* * *

"The ballet was wonderful. Thank you," Kenidee said, leaning over to kiss Camden on the cheek as they waited for the stoplight to change to green. "Did you really enjoy it, or are you just saying that because you love me?"

"Does it matter?" he teased.

She rested her head on his shoulder and laced her fingers through his. "I know that you would do anything for me, but I would be happier if I knew you actually enjoyed it. Now, honestly, did you like it?"

The light turned green and he accelerated onto the freeway on-ramp. "I like the dancing. And I appreciate the athleticism of both the men and the women, but I just really have a hard time with men in tights," he said.

She laughed. "That's something you just get used to. Especially if you didn't grow up watching much ballet."

"I didn't know anything about it until you," he said. "I remember being at your house when you'd come home from ballet class—and you'd take your ballet shoes off in the same room where Matt and I were sitting."

"So."

"We'd have to leave the room. I thought locker rooms smelled bad, but pee-eww! The smell from your pointe shoes could knock out NFL linebackers."

She smacked him on the shoulder. "Thanks!"

"You don't still have stinky feet, do you?" he asked.

"I don't know. Why don't we see?" She leaned over to take off her shoes.

"No, don't. It's okay. I don't want to know. Besides, if I pass out from the odor, who will drive?"

"It isn't that bad."

"I'm just teasing you," he said, planting a kiss on top of her head.

She sighed contentedly.

"Happy?" he asked.

"Mmm. Very. Are you?"

He glanced away from the road to look at her. "I've never been this happy in my whole life."

She shut her eyes and savored his words, his presence, and the absoluteness of his love.

"You're spoiling me, you know," she told him.

"I don't see how."

"Dinner, movies, flowers, ballets, trips to the beach, romantic picnics. You even postponed moving to Salt Lake for me. I don't see how you could possibly ever top yourself."

"You don't know me very well then, do you."

She giggled. "You realize that since I got back from Salt Lake we have spent every possible moment together. I can't believe you're not sick of me."

"I could say the same. Especially since we have Amanda and Brynn with us most of the time. That's got to be a recipe for sickness."

"Cam, I love your girls. You know that."

"I know you do. Have you really thought about how much you're taking on when you get involved with me and my life?" he asked.

She sat back in her seat and angled herself so she could face him but still hold onto his hand.

"I have discussed this a lot with my dad and Robin. They have been really good to talk to me about the realities of a situation like this. And Robin did a fantastic job of preparing Dad for this possibility. I've spent hours in prayer and fasting and going to the temple trying to know for sure that this is right."

Cam nodded, gave her hand a squeeze, and took a deep breath before speaking. "I know it's a huge and difficult task, and I know it won't be easy and that I'll make mistakes, but I have felt an assurance that it is right and that the Lord will be with us and help us."

She leaned toward him. "I love you Cam. The only way I know to be happy is to have you and the girls in my life. Everything that has led me up to this point has been for a reason. I understand that now. Even the times when I thought I would never survive the pain. I'm glad these things happened because I've grown so much through it all. My mission, my mom, Dad's remarriage and new family, even that whole farce with Brendan—they've all shaped me and prepared me for this."

He lifted her hand to his lips and kissed her knuckles.

"I feel the same way," he said. "It's all been worth it, if in the end I get to have you."

# CHAPTER 26

Kenidee parked her car near the park and waited as Cam had told her. She wasn't sure what was going on, but her excitement mounted until she could hardly stand it.

The last month had been the most enchanting time of her life. Every possible moment she and Camden could be together, they were. And in that short time, their relationship had grown to a completely new level of commitment. Without barriers and concerns, they had been free to allow their love to blossom and grow. It was staggering and breathtaking all at the same time.

And together they looked toward the future with joy and hope.

She was enrolled for winter semester at the University of Utah, and it had turned out that her boss, and Robin's friend, Lucinda, was very close to the director of the ballet program at the U.

Kenidee didn't know how life could get any better.

The clip-clop of horses' hooves caught her attention. Suddenly, around the corner came a beautiful white horse and on top of it was a man wearing shining armor.

Kenidee felt her mouth drop open. She looked around and saw no one else in the area, so this had to be for her. She began to giggle. What had Cam done?

The rider approached slowly. Then, as he came closer, he lifted the visor of his helmet. Only his eyes were visible.

"Cam?"

"You were expecting someone else?"

"No, of course not," Kenidee stuttered.

"I'm here to take you away."

"Where are we going?"

"How about. . . paradise?"

"Oo, I like that."

"Then join me, m'lady."

"You mean, get on with you?"

"Of course."

"Do you really know how to ride this thing?" She looked at the horse with a critical eye. He didn't look the type to buck or bolt. But then, she didn't really know horses.

"That is for me to know and for you to find out. You're going to have to trust me."

"Okay. How do I get up?"

"That is for you to know and me to find out."

"Cam!"

"Okay, okay. Just put your foot in the stirrup and I'll help you get on."

It was tricky and awkward, and Kenidee wasn't sure how they managed, but she finally found herself on the horse, sitting behind Cam. His armor wasn't the stiff, tin-man type but a soft metal mesh.

"I like your suit," she told him.

"Thanks. It's the newest thing in Europe. All the knights in shining armor are wearing them."

"I'm sure it will catch on when people see you wearing it. You'll be a fashion leader."

"A fashion leader," he said with a laugh. "That's a first."

"By the way," she asked, "where are the seat belts?"

"Just hang on to me," he told her. Then he clicked his tongue and the horse began walking.

"Why are you doing this?" she asked.

"That's for me to know . . ."

"And me to find out."

"Right."

They traveled three-quarters of the way around the park when Kenidee spied a white stretch limo parked alongside the curb.

"Hey, look, Cam," she said, not daring to point for fear she'd slide off. "Someone famous, or rich, is in the neighborhood."

"Or," Cam said, "someone very lucky."

He stopped the horse near the limo, and the driver immediately stepped out. From the trunk of the car, he pulled out a step ladder and placed it next to the horse.

"Cam, what's going on?"

"This limo is your ride to paradise."

She allowed the limo driver to help her down off the horse. Then he opened the door for her and motioned her inside.

She turned. "Aren't you coming?"

"I'll join you shortly."

She was disappointed he wouldn't be there with her but knew he'd gone to great lengths to plan this thing, whatever it was. She did as he asked and got inside the limo.

After the driver closed the door, Kenidee looked out through the dark, tinted window to see Cam, sitting tall on the white horse, waving good-bye to her. Her heart leaped in her chest, and she knew she was the luckiest girl alive to have this wonderful knight in shining armor in her life.

On the seat across from her was a beautiful, long-stemmed red rose and a silver box tied with a red ribbon. And a card, with her name on it.

Giggling with excitement, she took a deep whiff of the rose, slid the ribbon off the box, and opened the lid. She pulled out a lovely tropical print dress with purple, red, and turquoise flowers on a white background. Also inside the box was a pair of sandals in tan leather. Inside the box was another note that said, *"Put this on."*

Just to make sure she had complete privacy, she checked the divider separating her from the driver. Then Kenidee quickly changed from her T-shirt and walking shorts into the silky softness of the dress. She slid the sandals onto her feet and found a tube of lip gloss in her purse, which she quickly applied.

Her stomach was filled with butterflies—she was certain they were not frogs this time—and her heart with anticipation. What was Cam up to anyway?

The car began to slow down and the driver turned on some island music that made Kenidee's pulse race. She glanced out the window but didn't recognize where they were. She could see nothing but trees and bushes on either side of the car. Then they emerged from the foliage into an enormous landscape of sprawling lawn, giant palm trees, and colorful flowers—in pots, beds, and hanging baskets.

Where were they?

The driver finally stopped the car. Kenidee waited anxiously, wondering what was going to happen next. The car door opened, and the driver reached in politely to help her step out of the car. She took his hand and stepped onto a red carpet. The driver slipped a purple orchid lei around her neck, then stepped out of the way, motioning for her to walk across the red carpet to the entrance of a magnificent Mediterranean-style mansion.

Again she wondered, *Where are we?*

The carpet ended when she stepped through onto the stone-tiled entry. An expansive entryway with a wide staircase welcomed her, and a path of sprinkled flower petals directed her. Taking the stairs, she marveled at the elegance of the mansion and the beautiful decor. It was breathtaking.

As she continued following the trail of petals, Kenidee walked through a pair of glass doors into a sitting room. Overstuffed chairs and a Venetian glass chandelier added to the room's charm. On the far side of the room was another pair of glass doors leading outside.

Catching her reflection in a mirror, she stopped and checked her appearance before going outside. The dress was slim-fitting, not loose like a muumuu. The fragrant lei matched the flowers in her dress. She finger-combed her hair into place, took a deep breath, then pushed open the doors and stepped outside.

Her breath caught in her throat. The terrace, where she stood, overlooked the grounds below, where a large pool with its own rock waterfall and fountain sparkled in the evening sun. Gorgeous potted palms and more flowers graced the terrace. Cam had said something about paradise, and she was certain this was it.

A movement out of the corner of her eye caught her attention.

She turned and there stood Cam, in white linen pants and a shirt made out of the same material as her dress. She gasped audibly. To her he was the most handsome man she'd ever met, and his smile was meant for no one but her.

They walked toward each other as if drawn by nature's supernal force. When they finally reached each other, they kissed.

"You look incredible," he whispered into her ear.

"So do you," she answered, keeping her eyes shut to prolong the magic of the moment. "What's going on, Cam? What is all of this?"

He kissed her neck. "This is all because I love you, Kenidee."

She held onto him tightly, never wanting to let go. But he had other plans.

"Come," he said, taking her by the hand and leading her around to the other side of the terrace where a round table had been set with candles, china, and fluted crystal goblets filled with sparkling white grape juice.

Cam picked up the glasses and handed one to her. "To us," he said, clinking his glass against hers. They sipped the sparkling sweet liquid and kissed again.

Cam picked up a small remote and pushed a button. The same soft, tropical music she'd heard in the limo began to play. Cam pulled her into his arms, and they began to sway to the music.

"Where are we?" she asked, still feeling as if she were living a dream.

"Paradise."

"But why?"

"I just wanted to show you how much I love you."

"You've done a wonderful job. But I already knew how much you love me."

"Good, then I must be doing something right." Cam gave her a satisfied grin.

"Tell me, whose house is this? What are we doing here?"

"My brother did some work on this place. He's a good friend with the owners, who so very conveniently happen to be in Europe for the next three months. They asked me to keep an eye on the place while they are gone and said they didn't mind if I did some entertaining while they were away."

"I can't imagine heaven being any more breathtaking than this."

"There's something else I need to show you."

They put their glasses on the table and walked to the balcony together, looking out onto the pool and lush garden, as the sun blazed golden red on the horizon.

They might have been transported in time and place. Nothing else seemed to exist but them, their love, and the beauty surrounding them.

"Look at how beautiful that sunset is," she said, snuggling close to Cam.

"It's better because we're watching it together, don't you think?"

She remembered what her dad had said and was touched Cam had remembered. "Yes, much better."

After drinking in the incredible sunset, Cam turned to Kenidee and took both of her hands in his.

"Kenidee, I'm not much of a knight in shining armor, but I can't imagine not having you in my life. I want to spend the rest of my life and eternity with you, watching sunsets together and making every day paradise. Because no matter where we are, with you every day is paradise."

A lump formed in her throat, and tears filled her eyes. Kenidee had to blink away the tears to see him.

"I love you, Kenidee," Cam said as he sank down on one knee. "Will you marry me?"

His question captured both her breath and her voice for a moment. She knew there was no one she would rather spend her life with than this amazing, wonderful man kneeling before her.

"Yes, Cam," she answered through her tears and laughter. "I love you too. I will marry you."

He stood and pulled her close. They kissed, hugged, and kissed again, their joy as radiant and warm as the setting sun.

But Cam was wrong about one thing. Because to Kenidee, Camden was every bit her knight in shining armor, the man of her dreams.

# EPILOGUE

"You want me to rub some more tanning lotion on your back?" Cam asked as he took a long drink of his fruit smoothie.

"Yes, please. I don't want to get burned."

He squirted some of the piña colada–scented lotion onto his hand and rubbed it onto her bronzed skin.

"I'm not ready to go home," he said. "This week has gone by so fast."

"I know," Kenidee said lazily, sad that their honeymoon was almost over. "Guess we'll just have to come back again. But next time, we're bringing the girls. They would love playing in this pool and in the ocean."

They'd spent the last week at the Coral Princess resort on the island of Cozumel— snorkeling, swimming, scuba diving, eating, exploring, and being together.

"They're having the time of their lives at your parents' house, though. Robin has really made it fun for them."

"She's pretty incredible, isn't she," Kenidee said.

"Yeah, she really is. I'm glad everything's worked out."

"Me too."

Cam finished putting lotion on her back, then smeared a little on his arms before he lay down next to her, their faces just a few inches apart.

"We need to take something special back to her for helping out with the girls."

"I agree. We owe her a lot. In a way, she's responsible for getting us together. She helped me understand what I was really feeling and who I loved. She encouraged me to open my eyes, and my heart, and my mouth—which was probably the scariest of all."

"Then we need to thank Brendan, too, even though he hurt you. How is he anyway?"

"Last I heard, he was back in Taiwan. His mom said he's spending a lot of time with Lili. She expects they'll get married as soon as Lili can go through the temple."

"I hope they're happy."

"Me too," Kenidee said, sincerely. "This really has been the most glorious week," she said. "Thank you again for bringing me here. If life with you is this good now, how can it possibly get better?"

"We have eternity to find out."

# ABOUT THE AUTHOR

In the fourth grade, Michele Ashman Bell was considered a daydreamer by her teacher and was told on her report card that, "She has a vivid imagination and would probably do well with creative writing." Her imagination, combined with a passion for reading, has enabled Michele to live up to her teacher's prediction. She loves writing books, especially those that inspire and edify while entertaining.

Michele grew up in St. George, Utah, where she met her husband at Dixie College before they both served missions—his to Pennsylvania, and hers to Frankfurt, Germany. Seven months after they returned they were married, and are now the proud parents of four children: Weston, Kendyl, Andrea, and Rachel.

A favorite pastime of Michele's is supporting her children in all of their activities, traveling both in and outside the United States with her husband and family, and doing research for her books. She also recently became scuba certified. Aside from being a busy wife and mother, Michele is an aerobics instructor at the Life Centre Athletic Club near her home, and she currently teaches in the Relief Society.

Michele is the best-selling author of several books and a Christmas booklet and has also written children's stories for the *Friend* magazine.

If you would like to be updated on Michele's newest releases or correspond with her, please send an e-mail to info@covenant-lds.com. You may also write to her in care of Covenant Communications, P.O. Box 416, American Fork, UT 84003-0416.